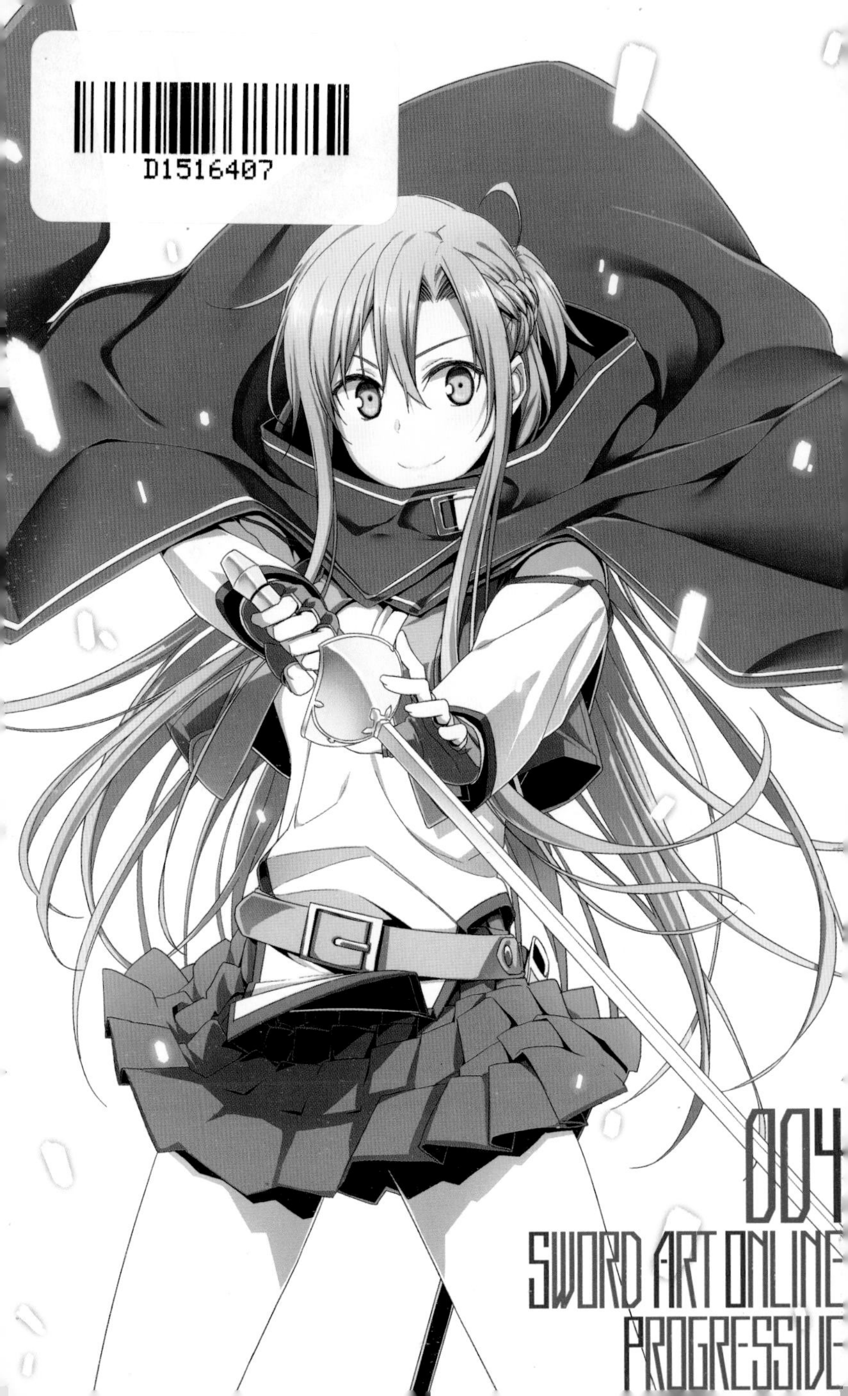
004
SWORD ART ONLINE
PROGRESSIVE

SWORD ART ONLINE PROGRESSIVE 004

CONTENTS

ART: KISEKI HIMURA
ORIGINAL STORY: REKI KAWAHARA
CHARACTER DESIGN: abec

#016: Strategy Meeting

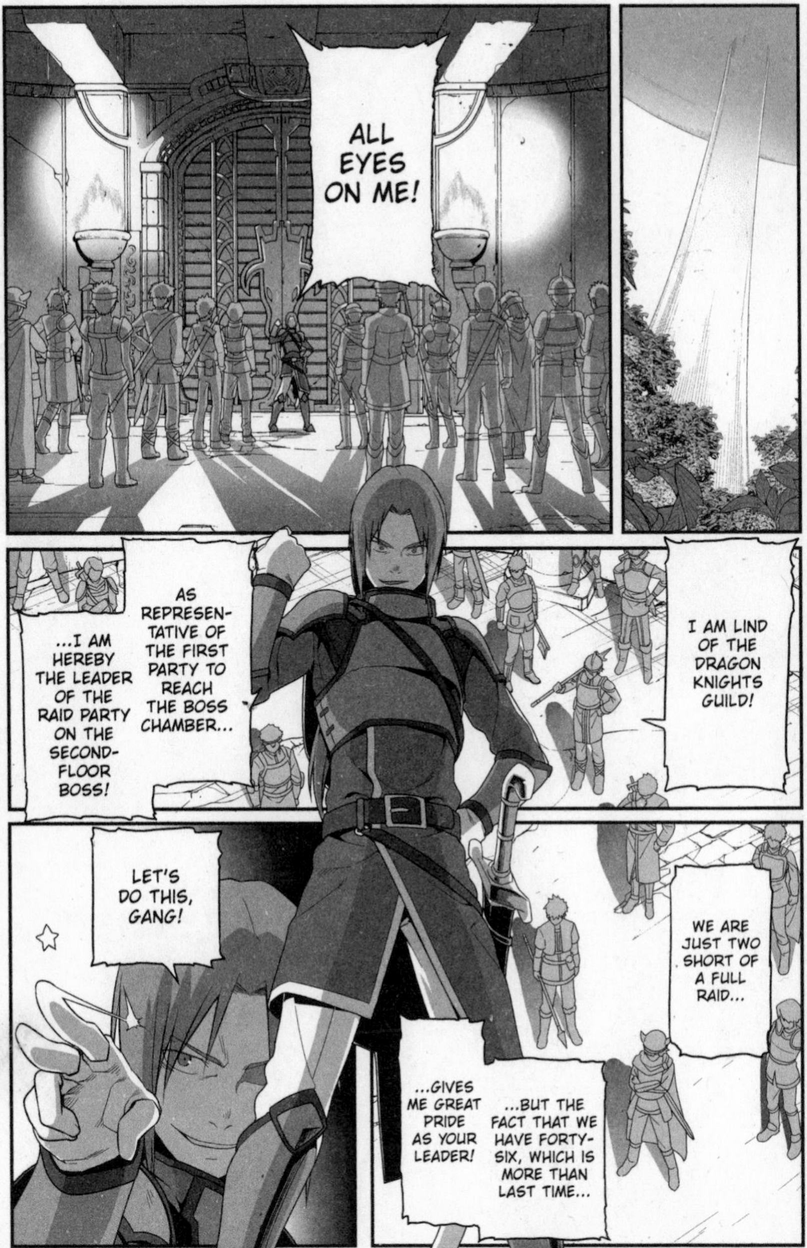
ALL EYES ON ME!
I AM LIND OF THE DRAGON KNIGHTS GUILD!
AS REPRESENTATIVE OF THE FIRST PARTY TO REACH THE BOSS CHAMBER...
...I AM HEREBY THE LEADER OF THE RAID PARTY ON THE SECOND-FLOOR BOSS!
WE ARE JUST TWO SHORT OF A FULL RAID...
...BUT THE FACT THAT WE HAVE FORTY-SIX, WHICH IS MORE THAN LAST TIME...
...GIVES ME GREAT PRIDE AS YOUR LEADER!
LET'S DO THIS, GANG!

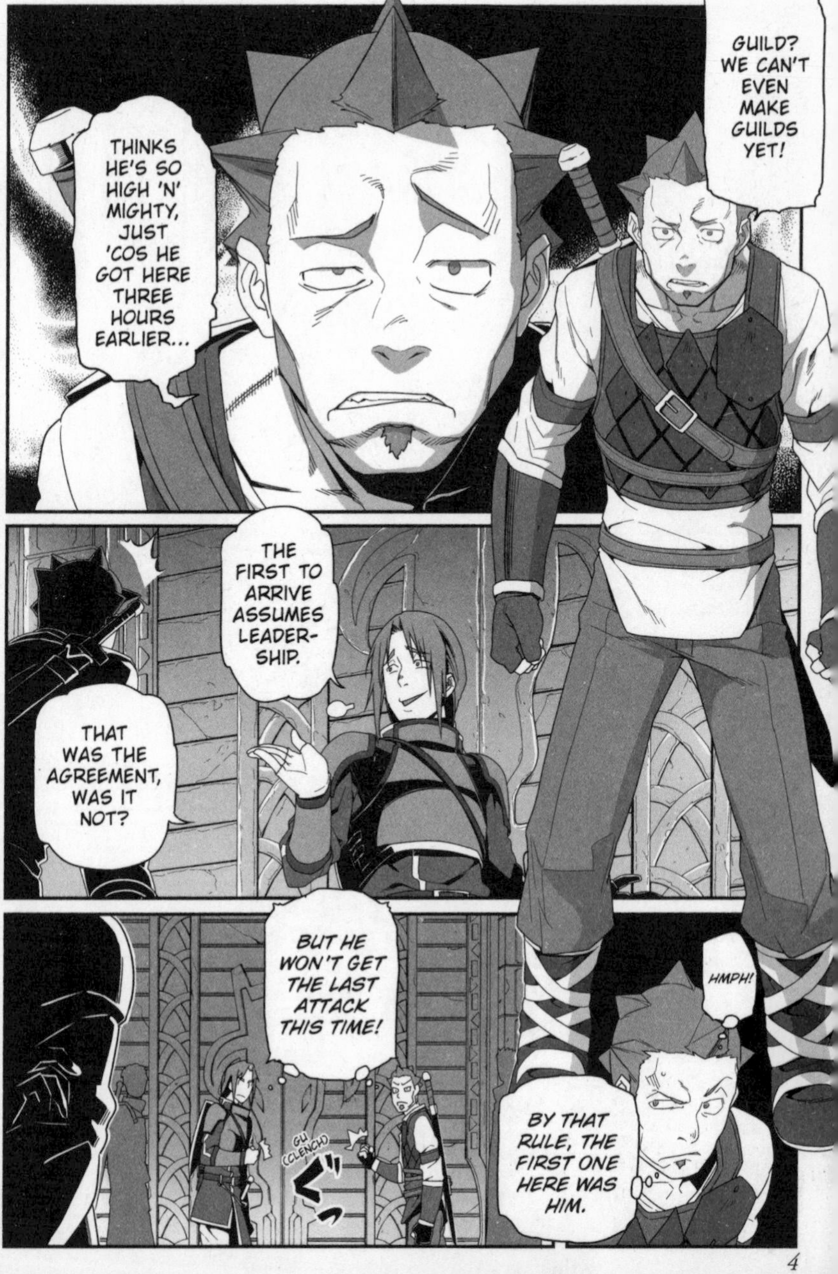
GUILD? WE CAN'T EVEN MAKE GUILDS YET!
THINKS HE'S SO HIGH 'N' MIGHTY, JUST 'COS HE GOT HERE THREE HOURS EARLIER...
THE FIRST TO ARRIVE ASSUMES LEADER-SHIP.
THAT WAS THE AGREEMENT, WAS IT NOT?
HMPH!
BY THAT RULE, THE FIRST ONE HERE WAS HIM.
BUT HE WON'T GET THE LAST ATTACK THIS TIME!
GU (CLENCH)

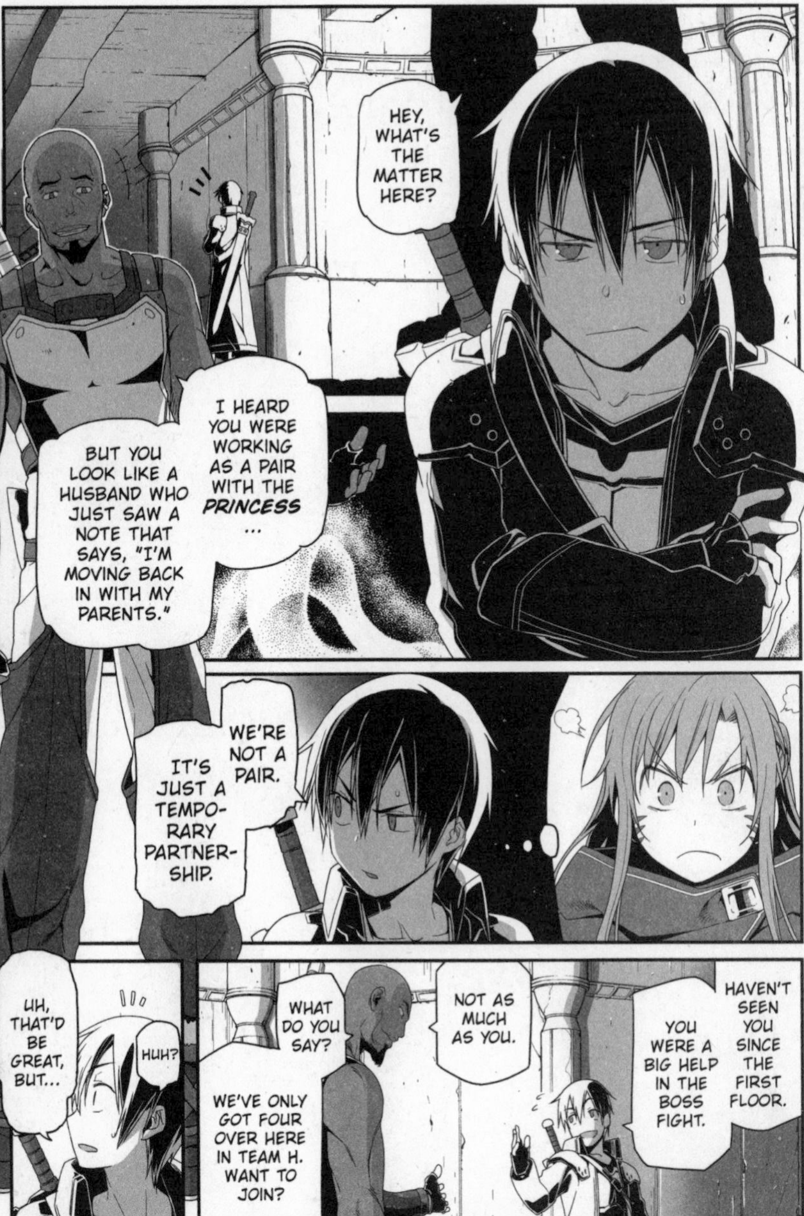
HEY, WHAT'S THE MATTER HERE?
I HEARD YOU WERE WORKING AS A PAIR WITH THE *PRINCESS* ...
BUT YOU LOOK LIKE A HUSBAND WHO JUST SAW A NOTE THAT SAYS, "I'M MOVING BACK IN WITH MY PARENTS."
WE'RE NOT A PAIR.
IT'S JUST A TEMPORARY PARTNERSHIP.
HAVEN'T SEEN YOU SINCE THE FIRST FLOOR.
YOU WERE A BIG HELP IN THE BOSS FIGHT.
NOT AS MUCH AS YOU.
WHAT DO YOU SAY?
WE'VE ONLY GOT FOUR OVER HERE IN TEAM H. WANT TO JOIN?
HUH?
UH, THAT'D BE GREAT, BUT...

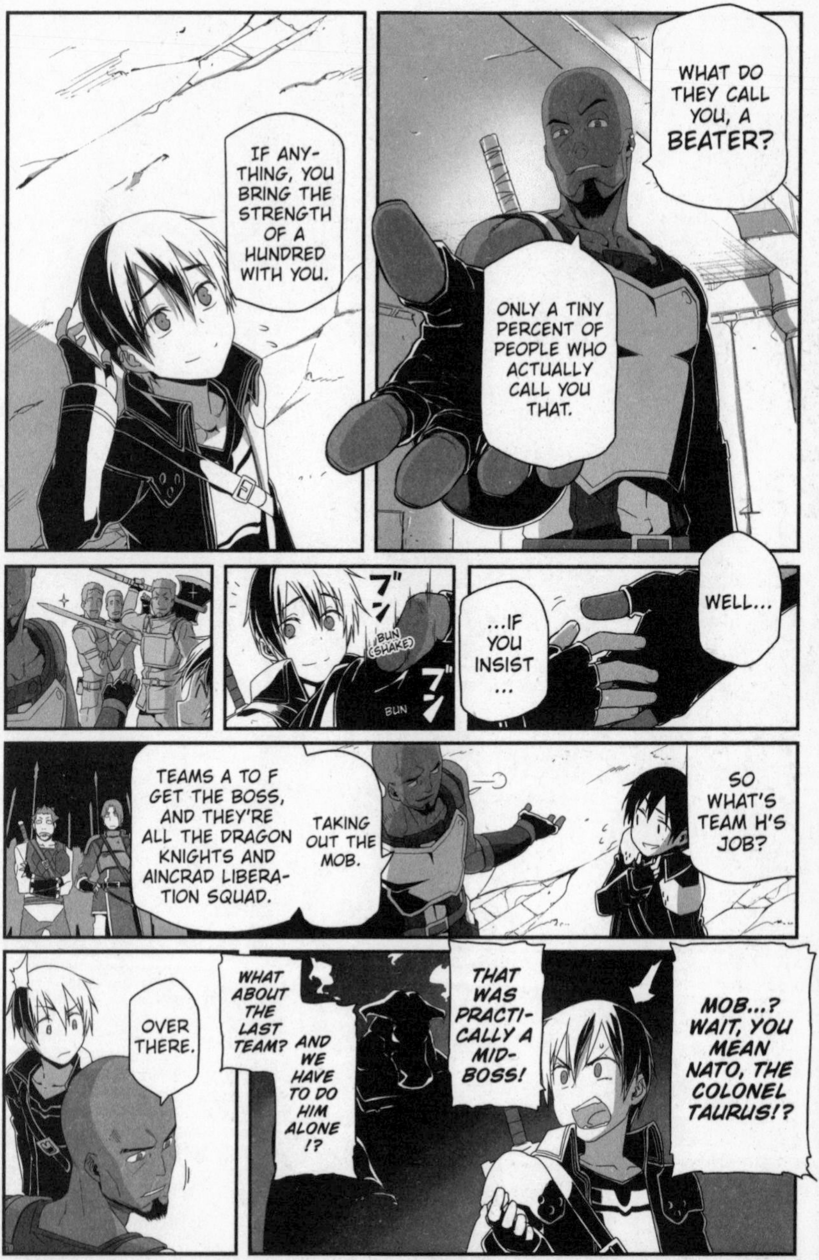
WHAT DO THEY CALL YOU, A BEATER?
ONLY A TINY PERCENT OF PEOPLE WHO ACTUALLY CALL YOU THAT.
IF ANY-THING, YOU BRING THE STRENGTH OF A HUNDRED WITH YOU.
WELL...
...IF YOU INSIST...
BUN (SHAKE)
BUN
SO WHAT'S TEAM H'S JOB?
TAKING OUT THE MOB.
TEAMS A TO F GET THE BOSS, AND THEY'RE ALL THE DRAGON KNIGHTS AND AINCRAD LIBERATION SQUAD.
MOB...? WAIT, YOU MEAN NATO, THE COLONEL TAURUS!?
THAT WAS PRACTICALLY A MID-BOSS!
AND WE HAVE TO DO HIM ALONE!?
WHAT ABOUT THE LAST TEAM?
OVER THERE.

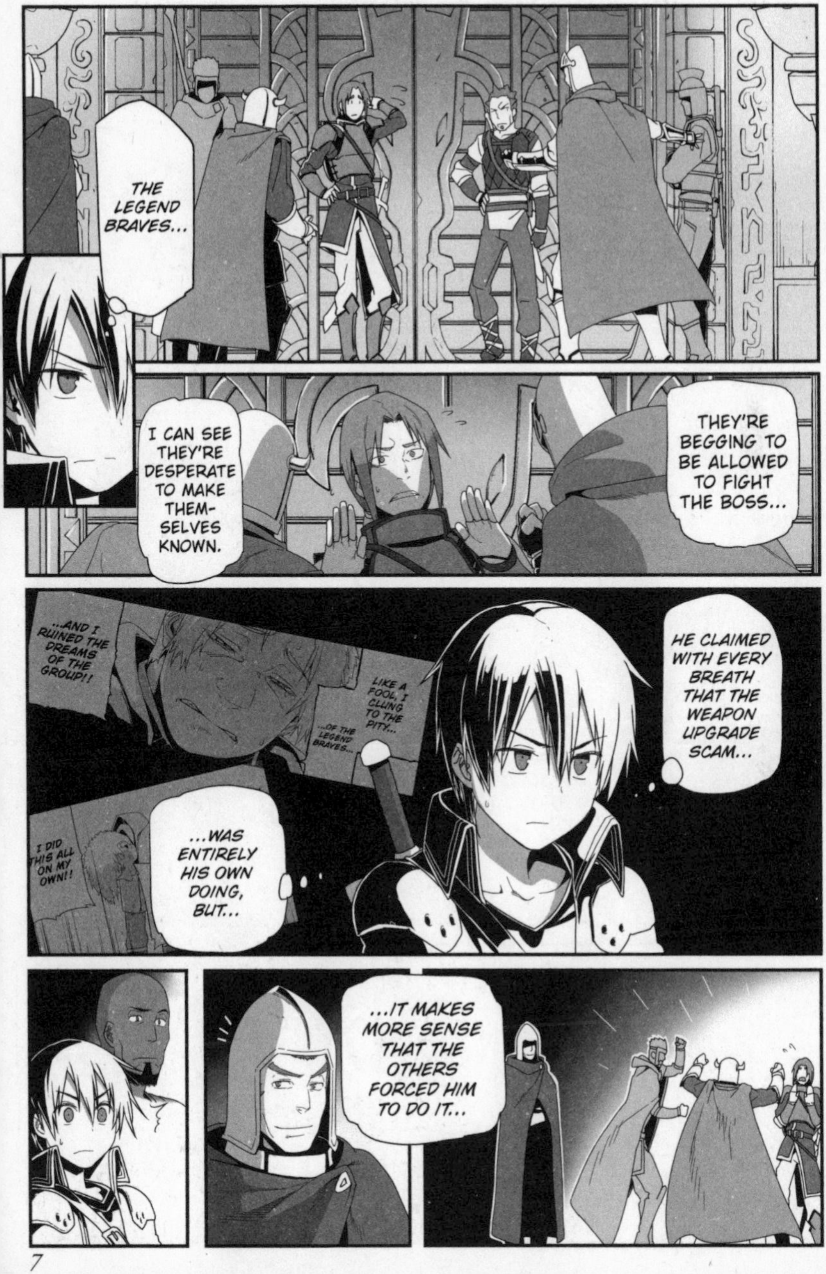
THE LEGEND BRAVES...
THEY'RE BEGGING TO BE ALLOWED TO FIGHT THE BOSS...
I CAN SEE THEY'RE DESPERATE TO MAKE THEM-SELVES KNOWN.
HE CLAIMED WITH EVERY BREATH THAT THE WEAPON UPGRADE SCAM...
LIKE A FOOL, I CLUNG TO THE PITY...
...OF THE LEGEND BRAVES...
...AND I RUINED THE DREAMS OF THE GROUP!!
...WAS ENTIRELY HIS OWN DOING, BUT...
I DID THIS ALL ON MY OWN!!
...IT MAKES MORE SENSE THAT THE OTHERS FORCED HIM TO DO IT...

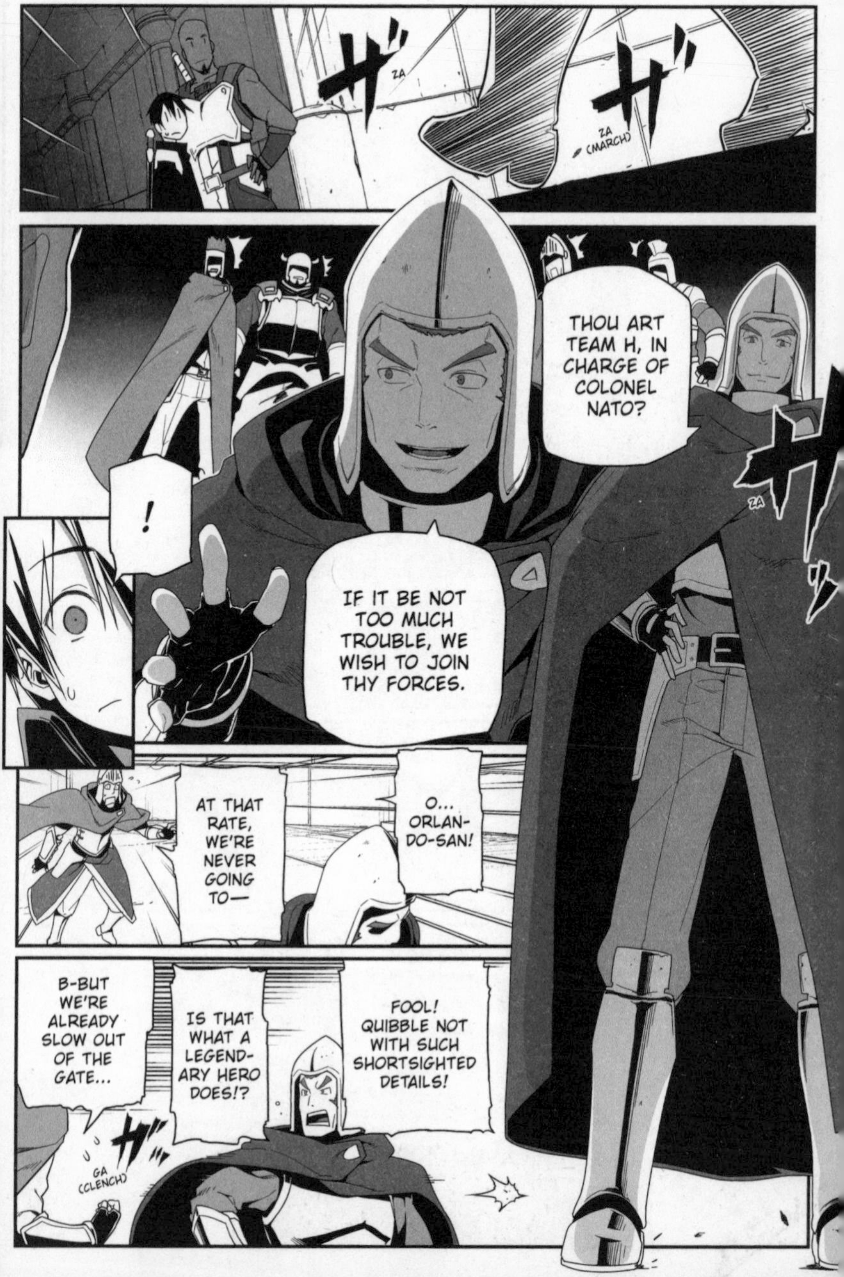
ZA (MARCH)
ZA
THOU ART TEAM H, IN CHARGE OF COLONEL NATO?
ZA
IF IT BE NOT TOO MUCH TROUBLE, WE WISH TO JOIN THY FORCES.
!
O... ORLAN-DO-SAN!
AT THAT RATE, WE'RE NEVER GOING TO—
FOOL! QUIBBLE NOT WITH SUCH SHORTSIGHTED DETAILS!
IS THAT WHAT A LEGEND-ARY HERO DOES!?
B-BUT WE'RE ALREADY SLOW OUT OF THE GATE...
GA (CLENCH)

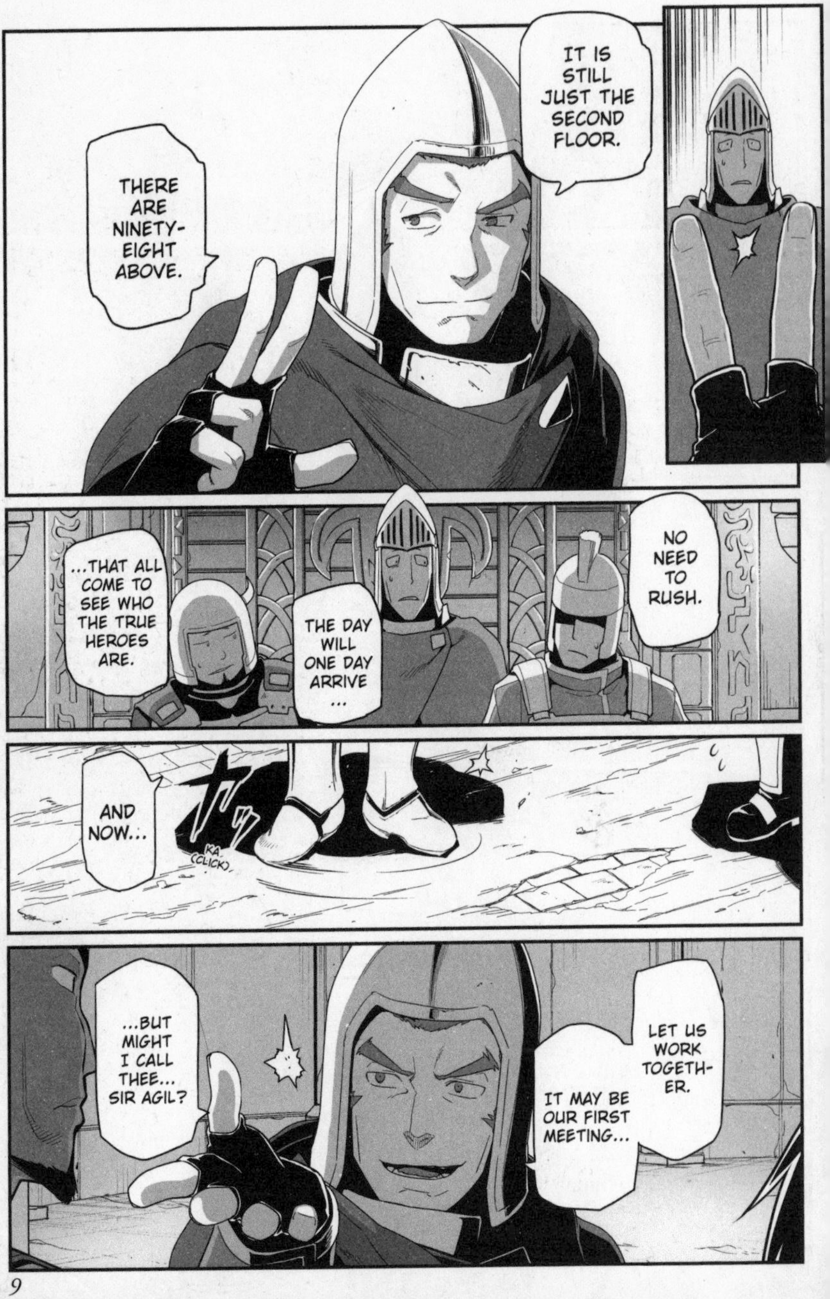
IT IS STILL JUST THE SECOND FLOOR.
THERE ARE NINETY-EIGHT ABOVE.
NO NEED TO RUSH.
THE DAY WILL ONE DAY ARRIVE ...
...THAT ALL COME TO SEE WHO THE TRUE HEROES ARE.
AND NOW...
KA (CLICK)
LET US WORK TOGETHER.
IT MAY BE OUR FIRST MEETING...
...BUT MIGHT I CALL THEE... SIR AGIL?

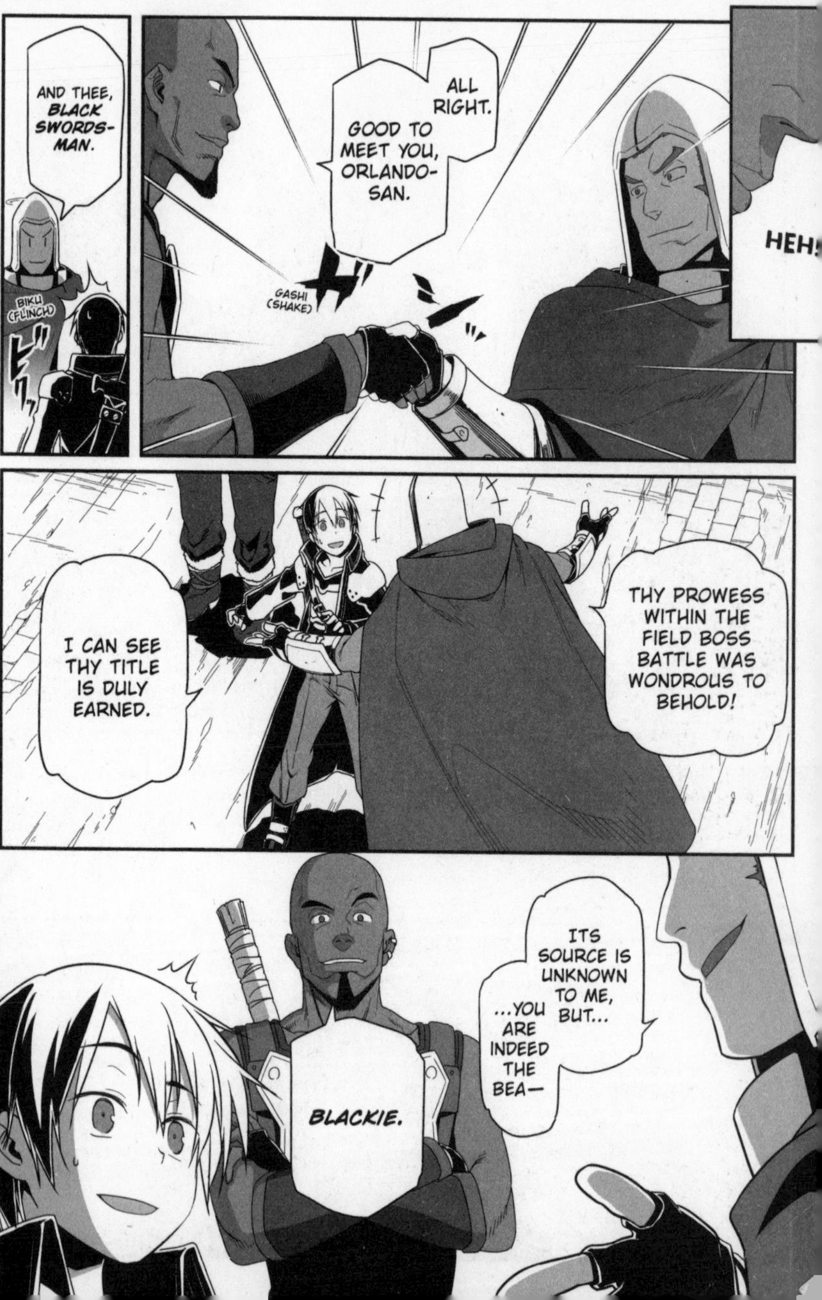
HEH!
ALL RIGHT.
GOOD TO MEET YOU, ORLANDO-SAN.
GASHI (SHAKE)
AND THEE, BLACK SWORDS-MAN.
BIKU (FLINCH)
THY PROWESS WITHIN THE FIELD BOSS BATTLE WAS WONDROUS TO BEHOLD!
I CAN SEE THY TITLE IS DULY EARNED.
ITS SOURCE IS UNKNOWN TO ME, BUT...
...YOU ARE INDEED THE BEA—
BLACKIE.

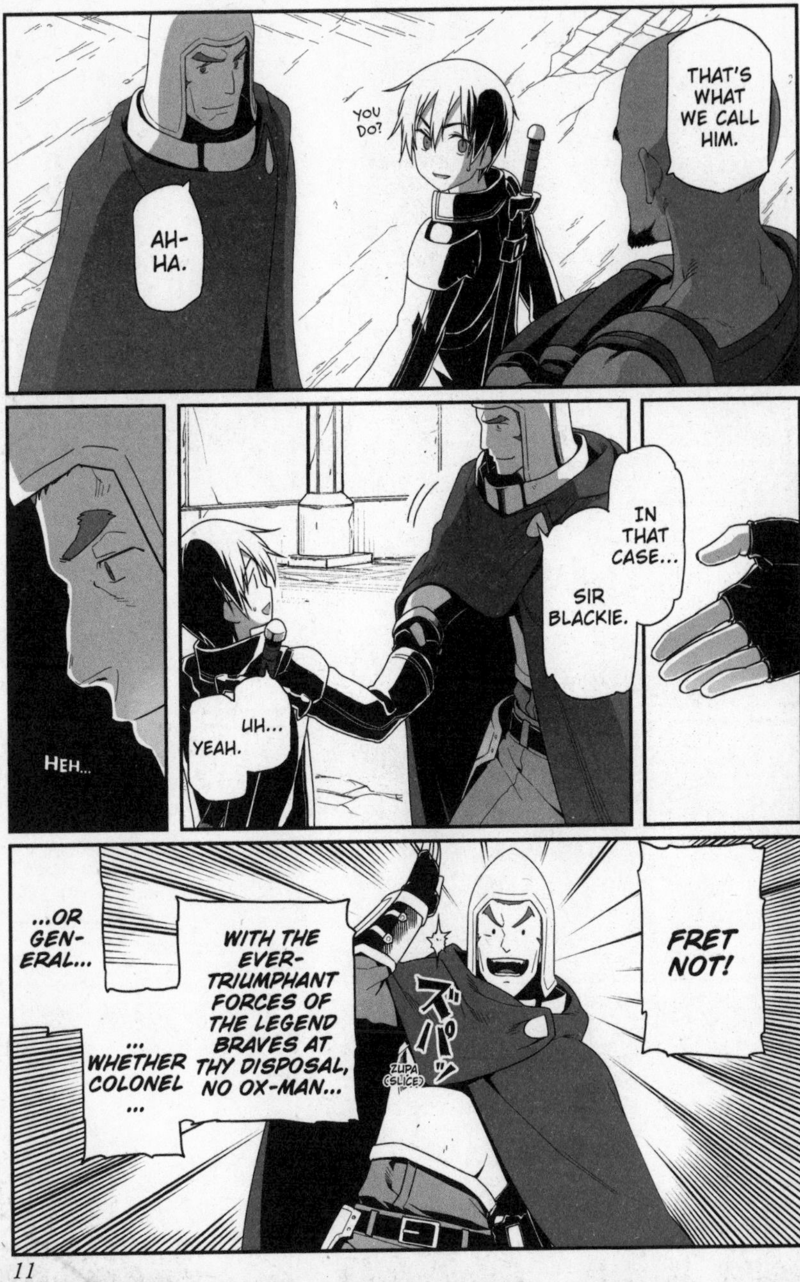
THAT'S WHAT WE CALL HIM.
YOU DO?
AH-HA.
IN THAT CASE...
SIR BLACKIE.
UH... YEAH.
HEH...
FRET NOT!
WITH THE EVER-TRIUMPHANT FORCES OF THE LEGEND BRAVES AT THY DISPOSAL, NO OX-MAN...
ZUPA (SLICE)
...WHETHER COLONEL...
...OR GENERAL...

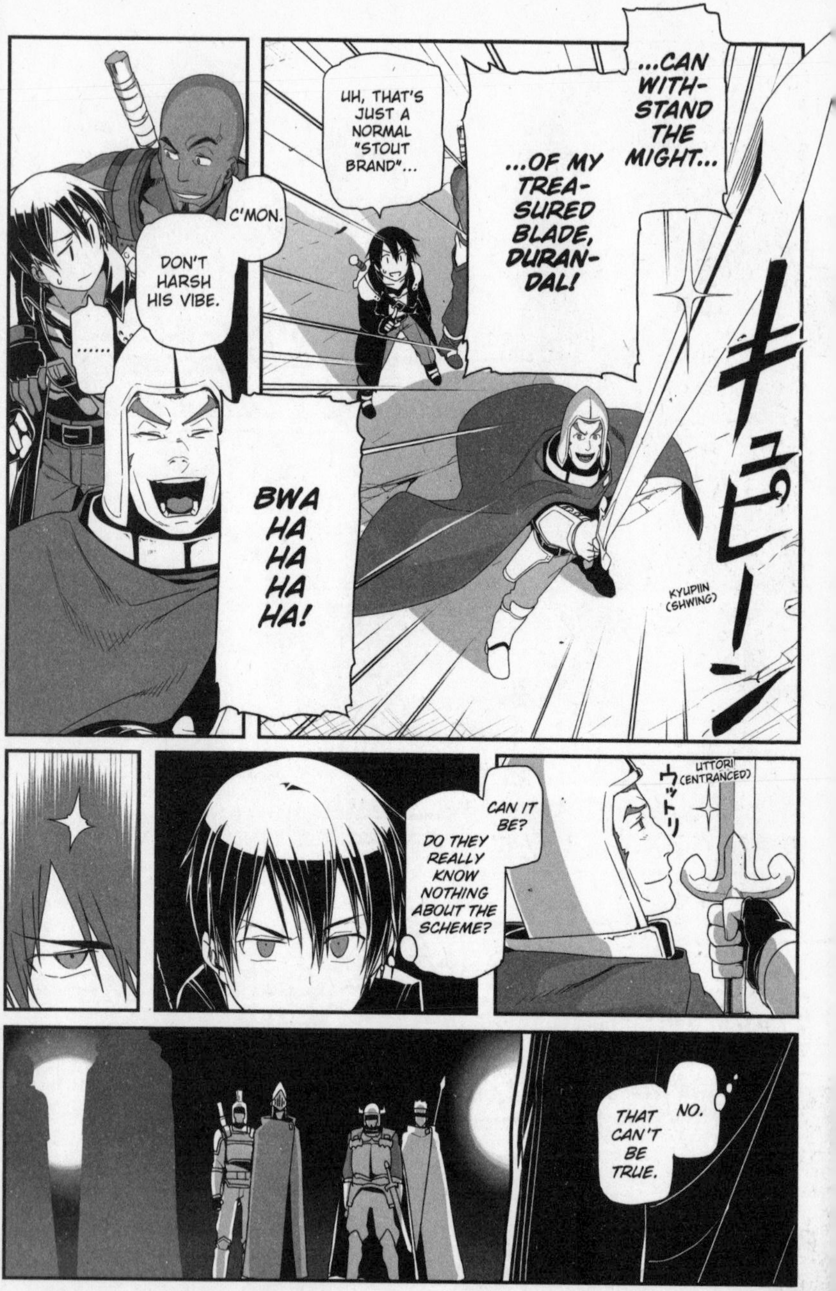
...CAN WITH-STAND THE MIGHT...
...OF MY TREA-SURED BLADE, DURAN-DAL!
UH, THAT'S JUST A NORMAL "STOUT BRAND"...
キュピーン
KYUPIIN (SHWING)
BWA HA HA HA HA!
C'MON.
DON'T HARSH HIS VIBE.
......
ウットリ
UTTORI (ENTRANCED)
CAN IT BE?
DO THEY REALLY KNOW NOTHING ABOUT THE SCHEME?
NO.
THAT CAN'T BE TRUE.

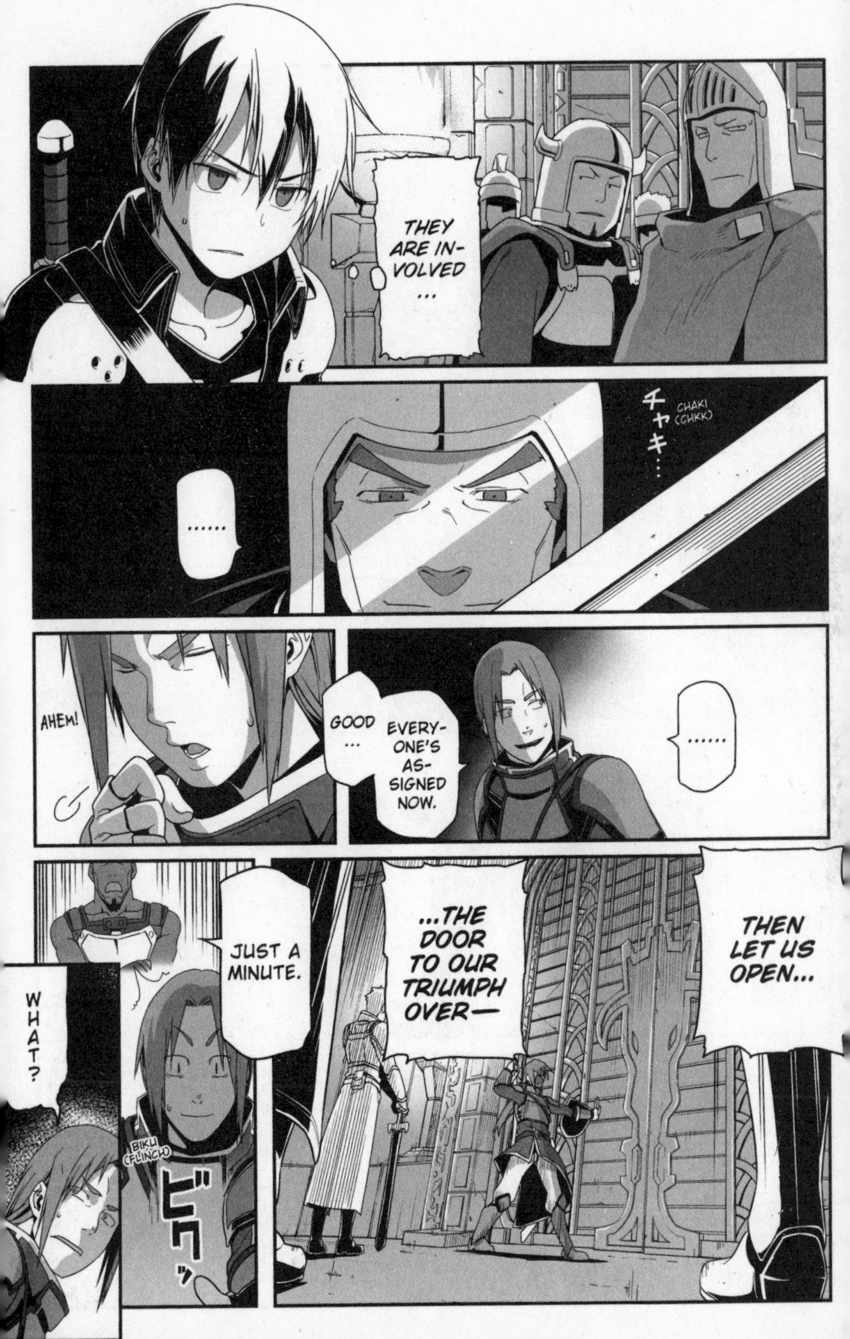
THEY ARE IN-VOLVED ...
チャキ… CHAKI (CHKK)
......
......
GOOD ... EVERY-ONE'S AS-SIGNED NOW.
AHEM!
THEN LET US OPEN...
...THE DOOR TO OUR TRIUMPH OVER—
JUST A MINUTE.
WHAT?
BIKU (FLINCH) ビクッ

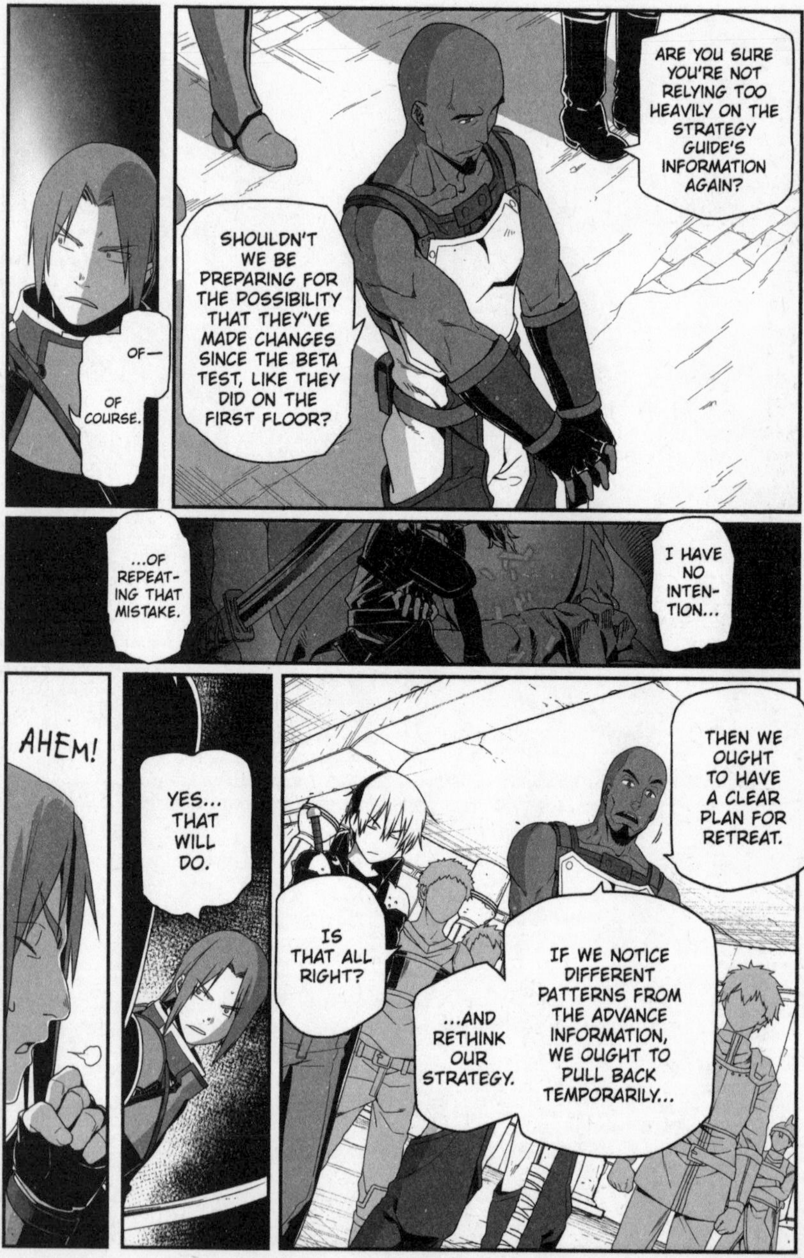
ARE YOU SURE YOU'RE NOT RELYING TOO HEAVILY ON THE STRATEGY GUIDE'S INFORMATION AGAIN?
SHOULDN'T WE BE PREPARING FOR THE POSSIBILITY THAT THEY'VE MADE CHANGES SINCE THE BETA TEST, LIKE THEY DID ON THE FIRST FLOOR?
OF—
OF COURSE.
I HAVE NO INTEN-TION...
...OF REPEAT-ING THAT MISTAKE.
THEN WE OUGHT TO HAVE A CLEAR PLAN FOR RETREAT.
IF WE NOTICE DIFFERENT PATTERNS FROM THE ADVANCE INFORMATION, WE OUGHT TO PULL BACK TEMPORARILY...
...AND RETHINK OUR STRATEGY.
IS THAT ALL RIGHT?
YES... THAT WILL DO.
AHEM!

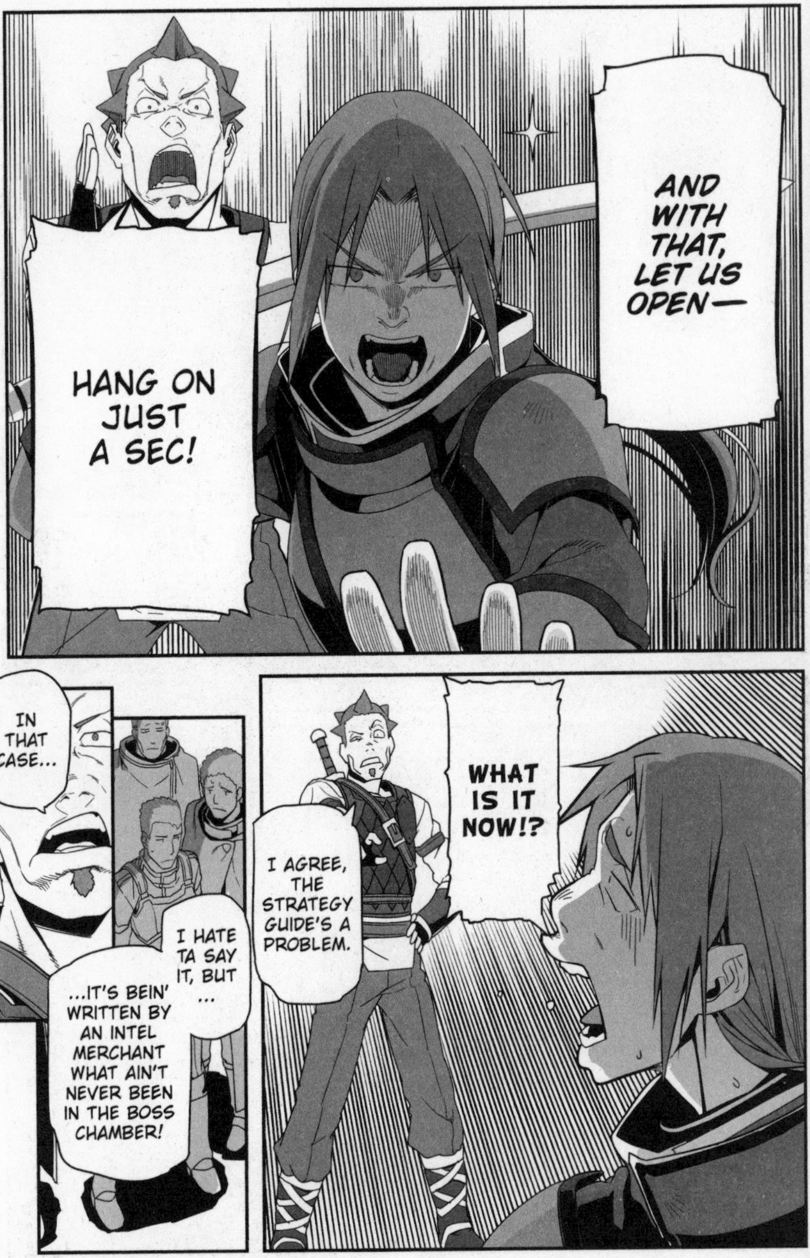
AND WITH THAT, LET US OPEN—
HANG ON JUST A SEC!
WHAT IS IT NOW!?
I AGREE, THE STRATEGY GUIDE'S A PROBLEM.
IN THAT CASE...
I HATE TA SAY IT, BUT ...
...IT'S BEIN' WRITTEN BY AN INTEL MERCHANT WHAT AIN'T NEVER BEEN IN THE BOSS CHAMBER!

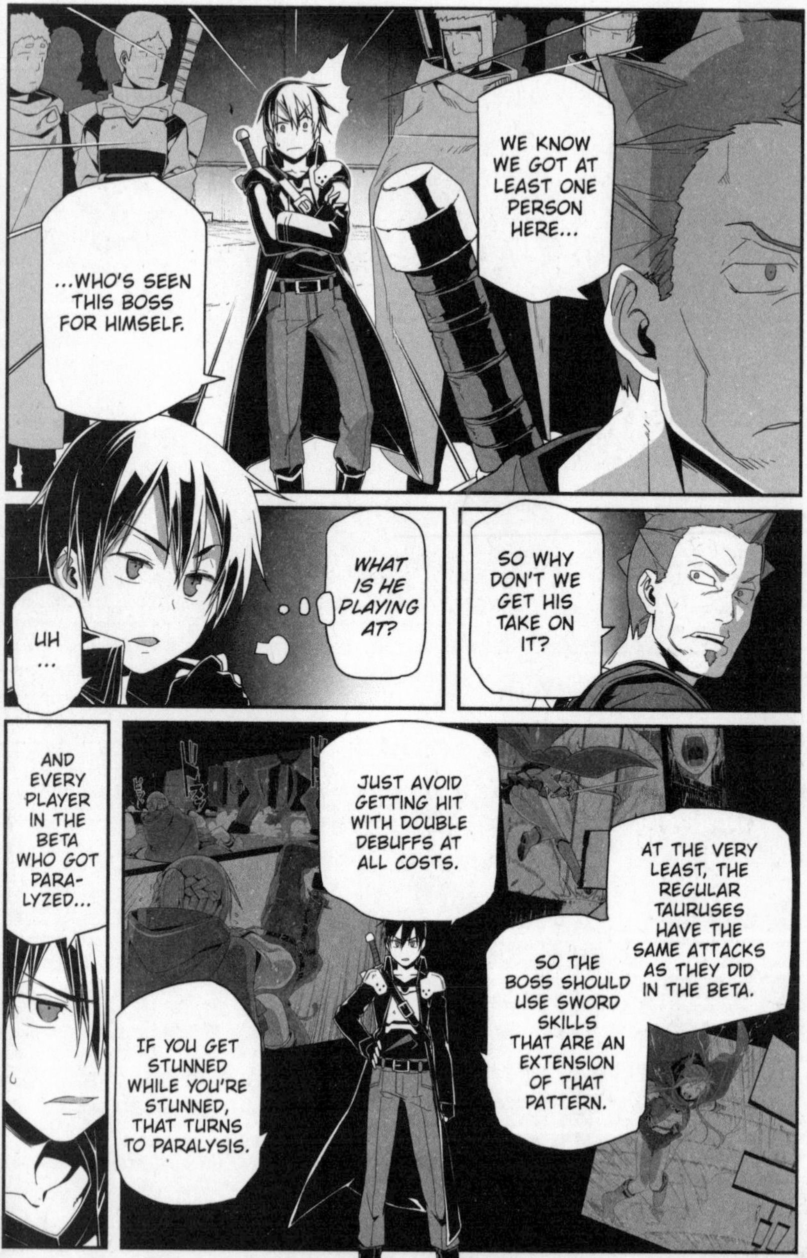
WE KNOW WE GOT AT LEAST ONE PERSON HERE...
...WHO'S SEEN THIS BOSS FOR HIMSELF.
SO WHY DON'T WE GET HIS TAKE ON IT?
WHAT IS HE PLAYING AT?
UH ...
AT THE VERY LEAST, THE REGULAR TAURUSES HAVE THE SAME ATTACKS AS THEY DID IN THE BETA.
SO THE BOSS SHOULD USE SWORD SKILLS THAT ARE AN EXTENSION OF THAT PATTERN.
JUST AVOID GETTING HIT WITH DOUBLE DEBUFFS AT ALL COSTS.
IF YOU GET STUNNED WHILE YOU'RE STUNNED, THAT TURNS TO PARALYSIS.
AND EVERY PLAYER IN THE BETA WHO GOT PARALYZED...

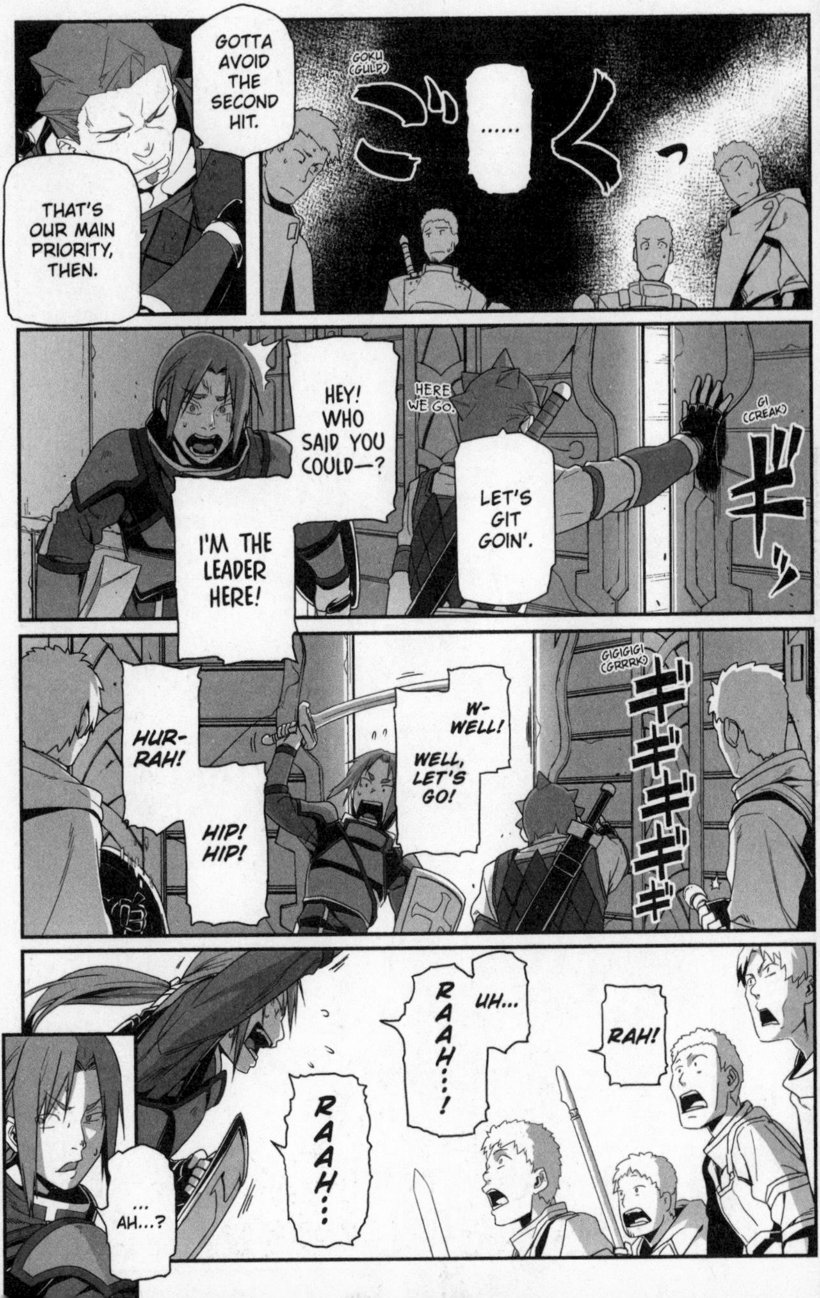
GOKU (GULP)
ごくっ
......
GOTTA AVOID THE SECOND HIT.
THAT'S OUR MAIN PRIORITY, THEN.
GI (CREAK)
ギッ
HERE WE GO.
LET'S GIT GOIN'.
HEY! WHO SAID YOU COULD—?
I'M THE LEADER HERE!
GIGIGIGI (GRRRK)
ギギギギギ
W-WELL!
WELL, LET'S GO!
HUR-RAH!
HIP! HIP!
RAH!
UH...
RAAAH...!
RAAAH...
...AH...?

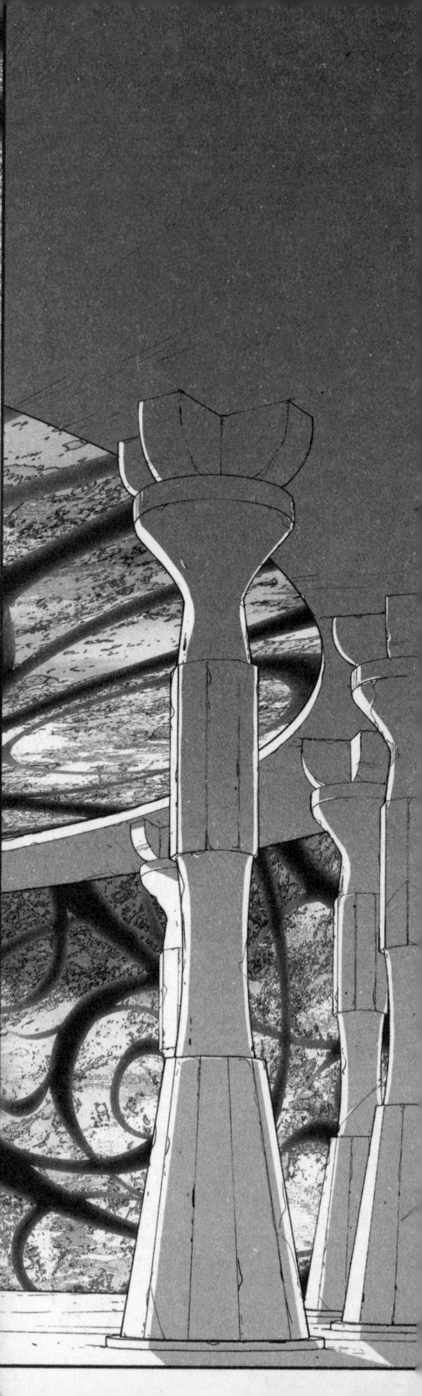

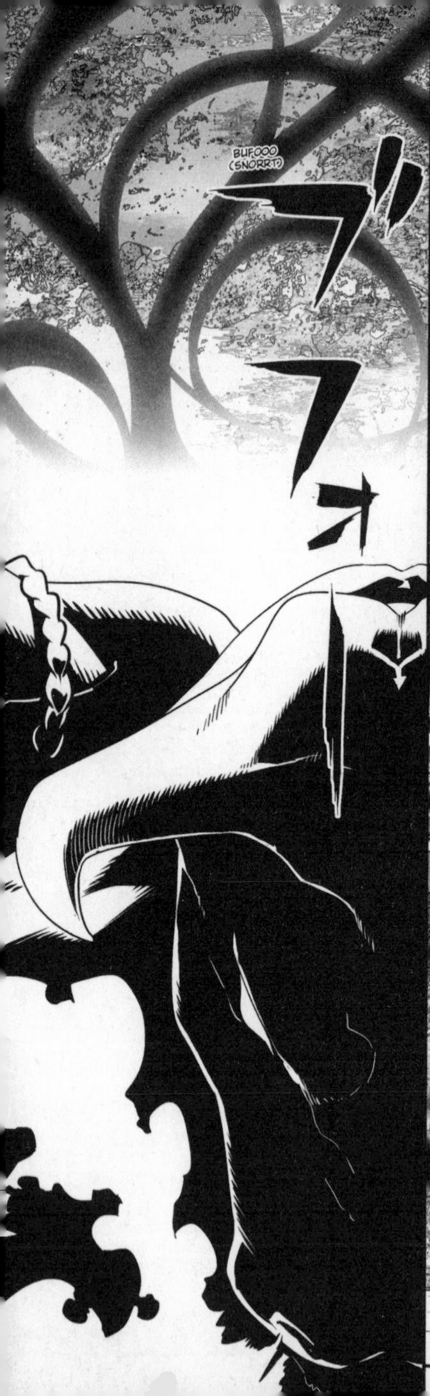

ブフォー
BUFOOO
(SNORRT)

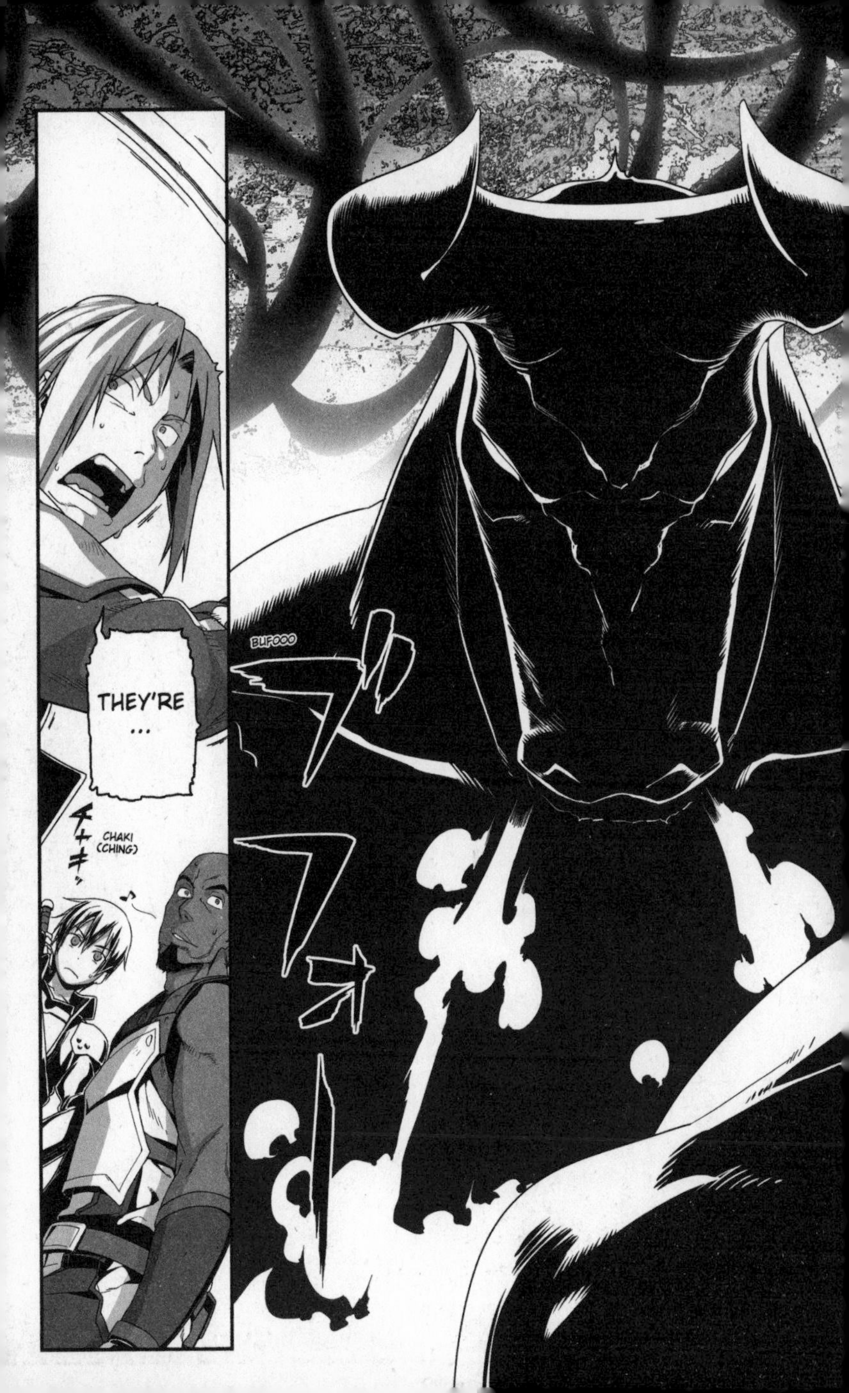
BUFOOO
ブフォオー
THEY'RE ...
チャキッ
CHAKI (CHING)

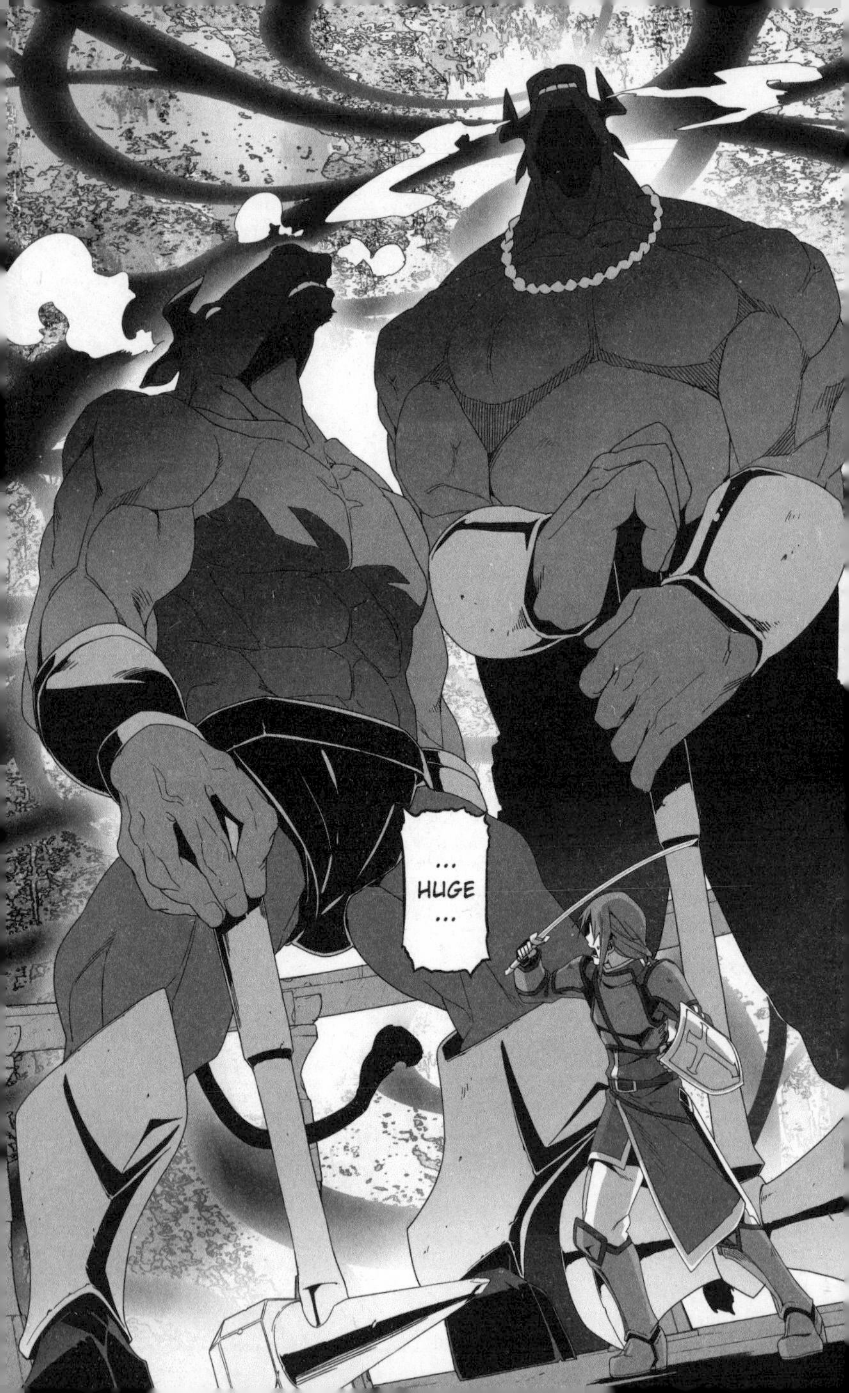
...HUGE...

#016.5: Battle

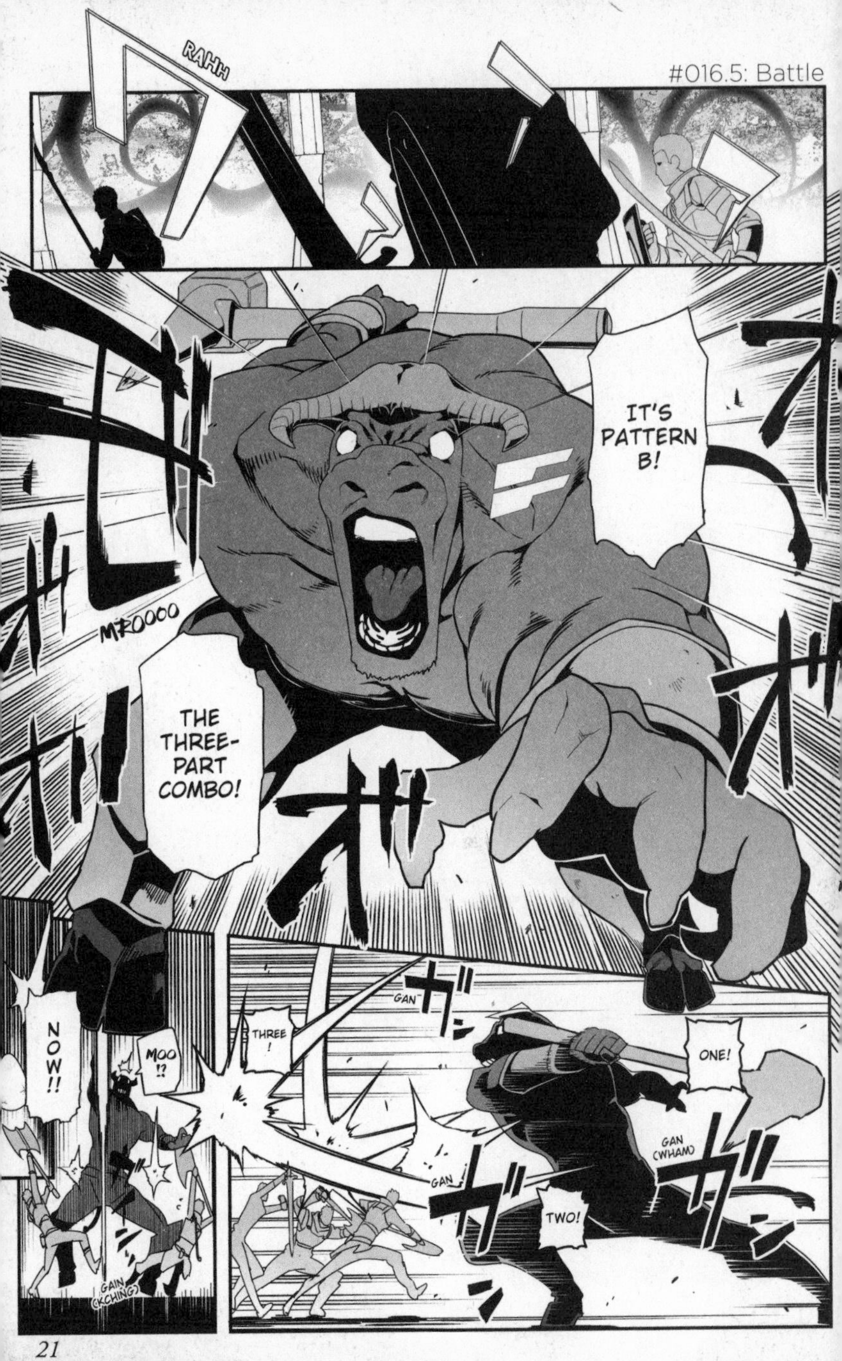
RAHH
IT'S PATTERN B!
MROOOO
THE THREE-PART COMBO!
ONE!
GAN (WHAM)
GAN
TWO!
GAN
THREE!
NOW!!
MOO!?
GAIN (KCHING)

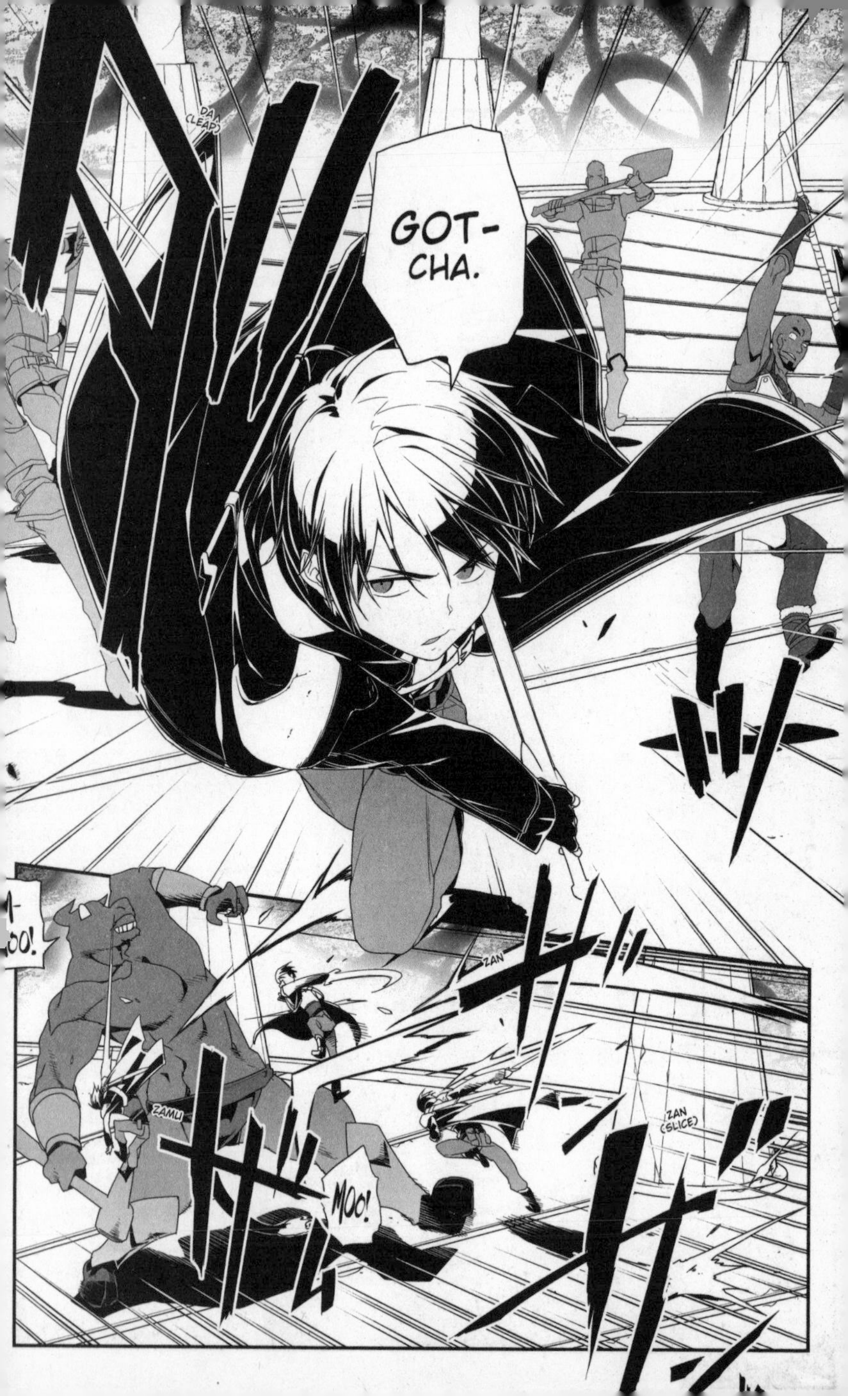
DA (LEAP)
GOT-CHA.
ZAN
ZAN (SLICE)
MOO!
ZAMU

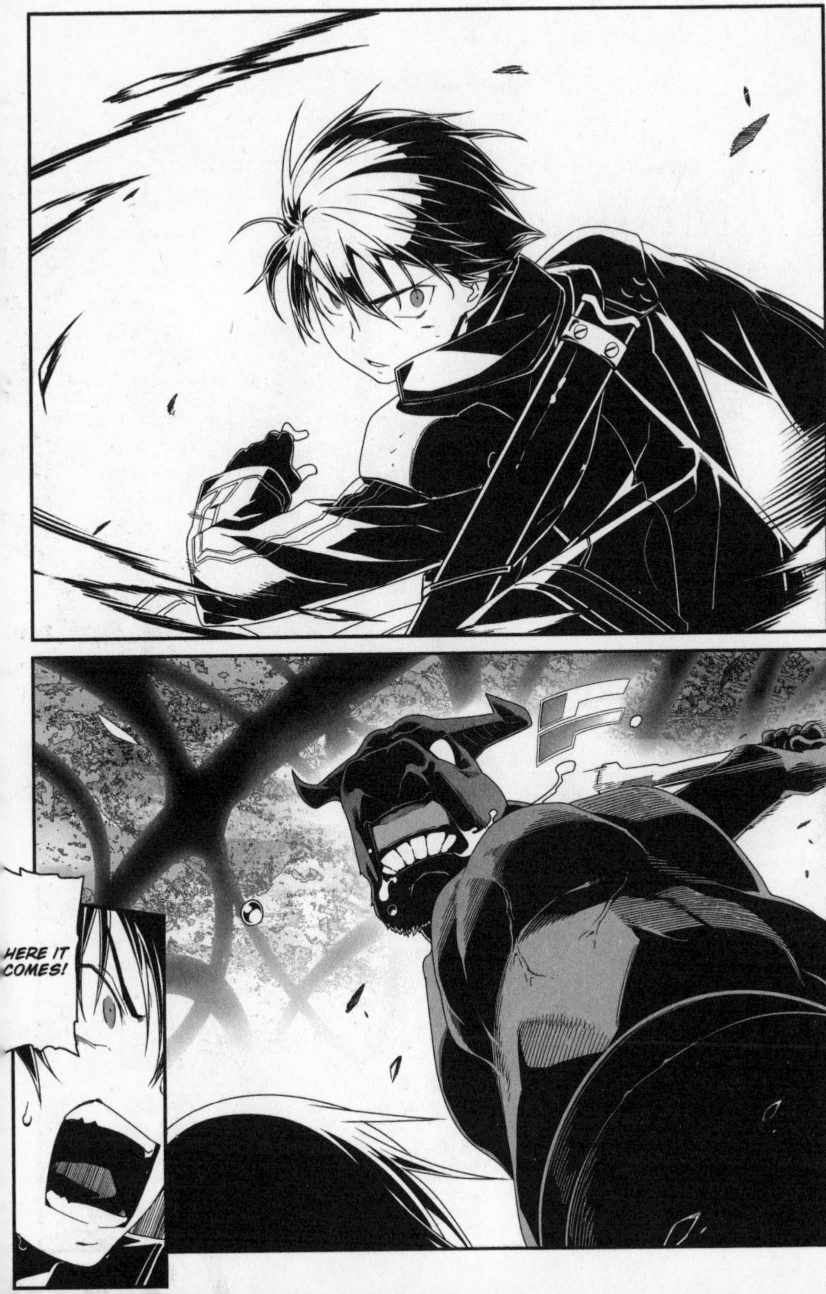
HERE IT COMES!

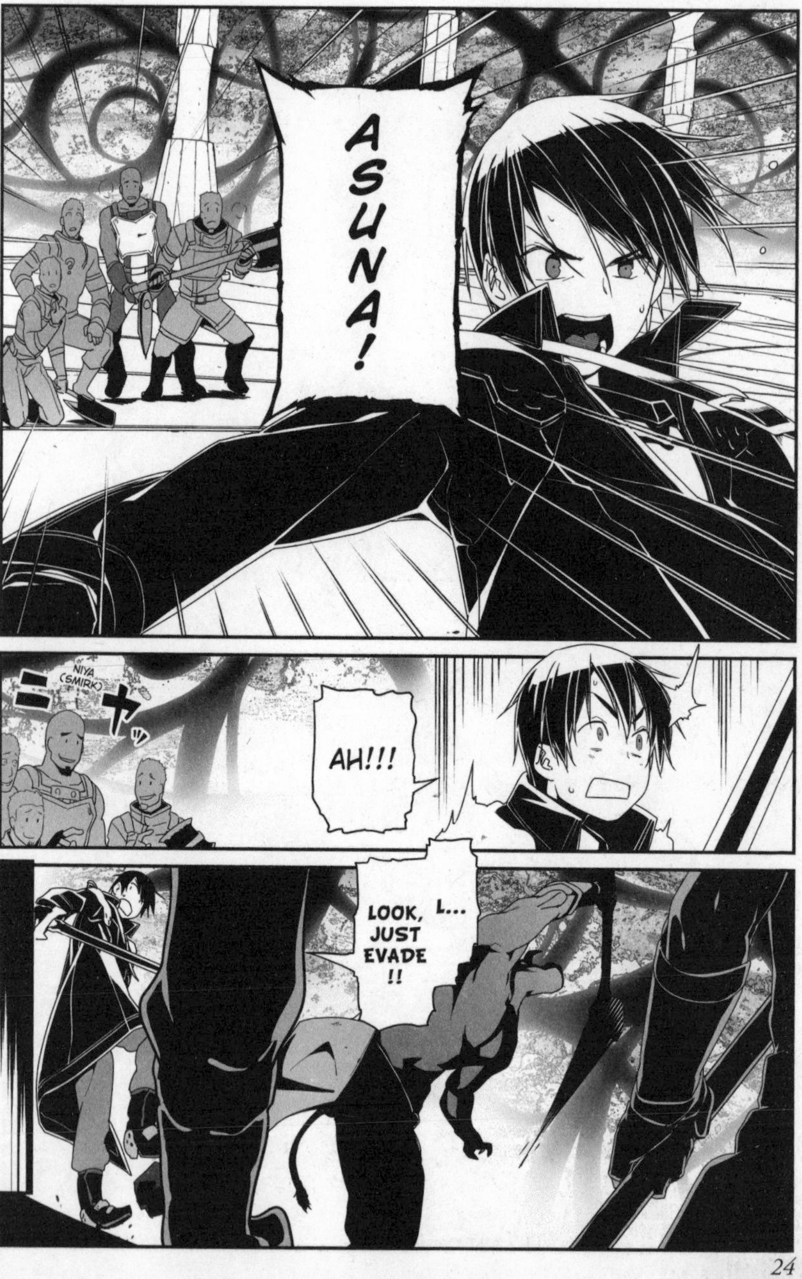
ASUNA!
AH!!!
NIYA (SMIRK)
L...
LOOK, JUST EVADE !!

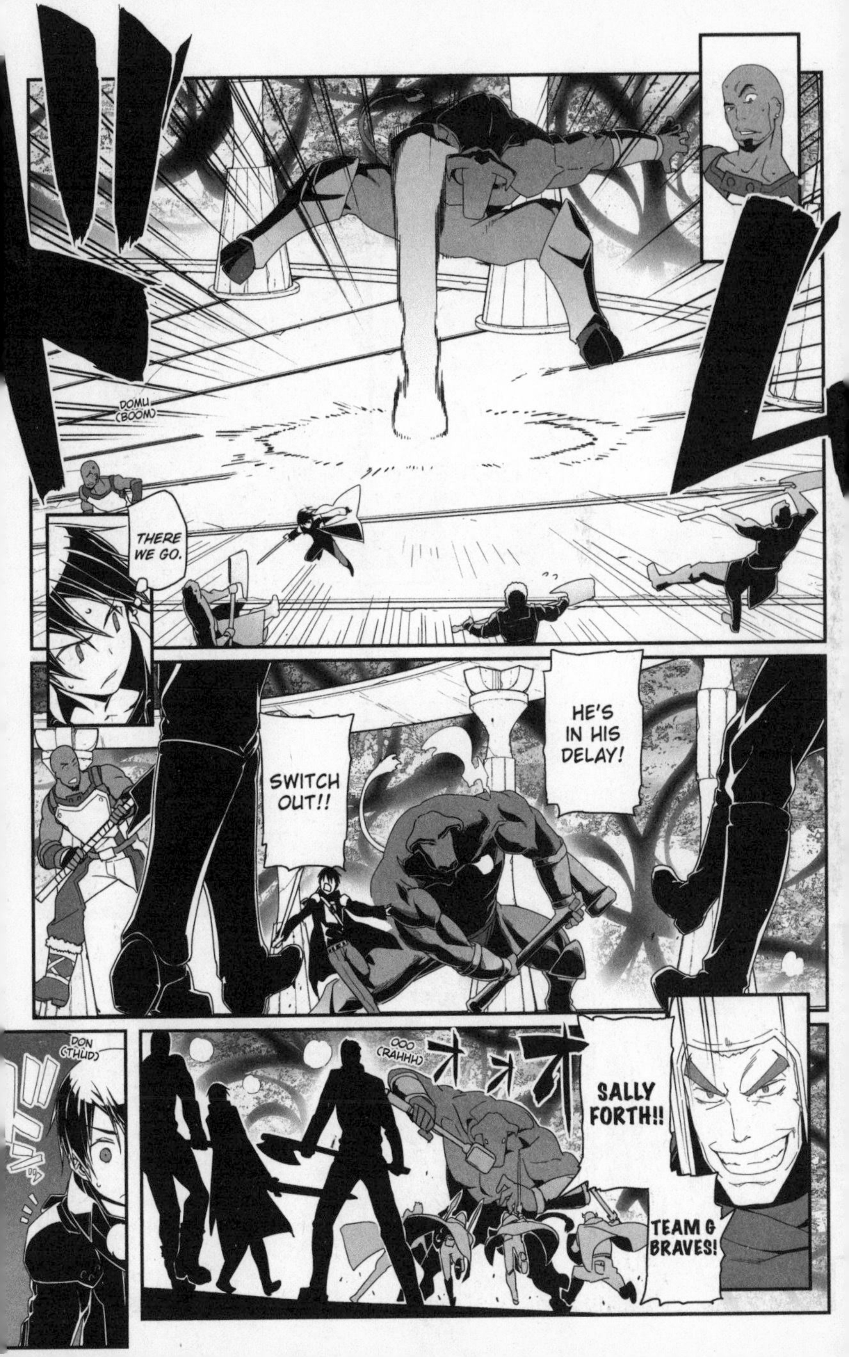
DOMU (BOOM)
THERE WE GO.
HE'S IN HIS DELAY!
SWITCH OUT!!
SALLY FORTH!!
TEAM G BRAVES!
OOO (RAHHH)
DON (THUD)

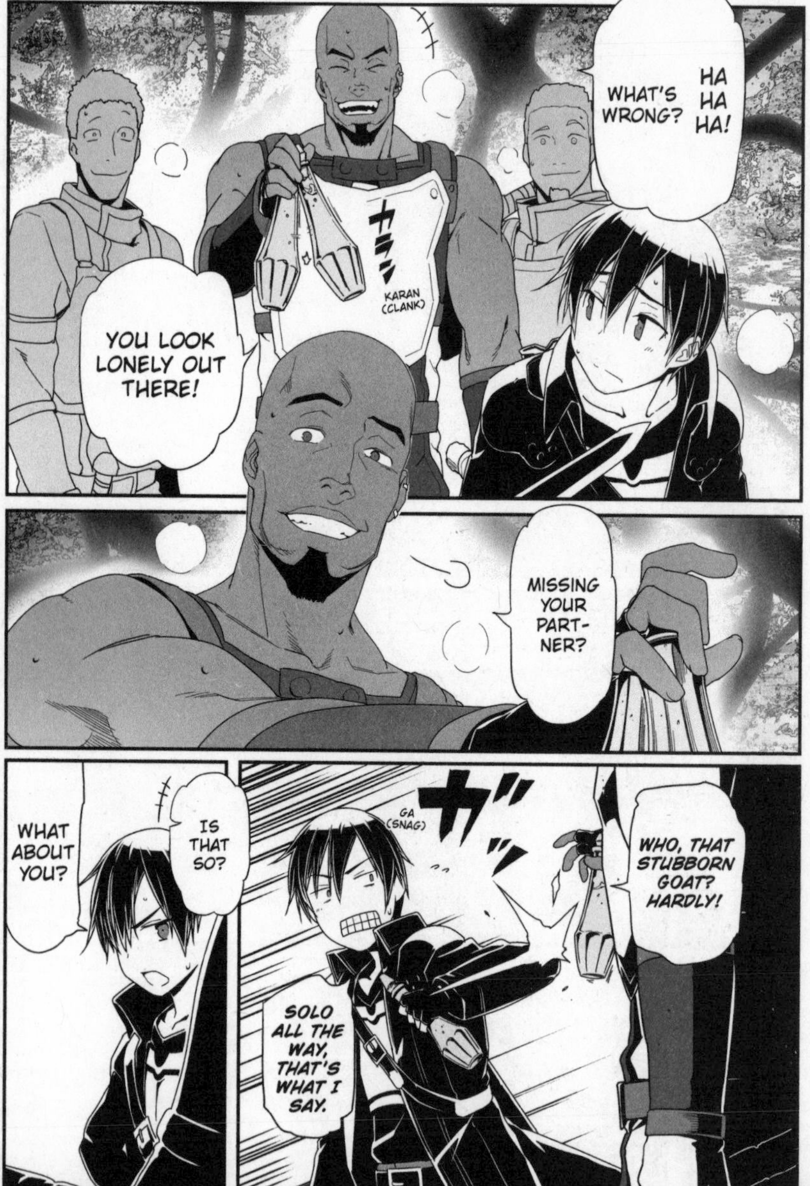
WHAT'S WRONG? HA HA HA!
カラン
KARAN (CLANK)
YOU LOOK LONELY OUT THERE!
MISSING YOUR PART-NER?
ガッ
GA (SNAG)
WHO, THAT STUBBORN GOAT? HARDLY!
SOLO ALL THE WAY, THAT'S WHAT I SAY.
IS THAT SO?
WHAT ABOUT YOU?

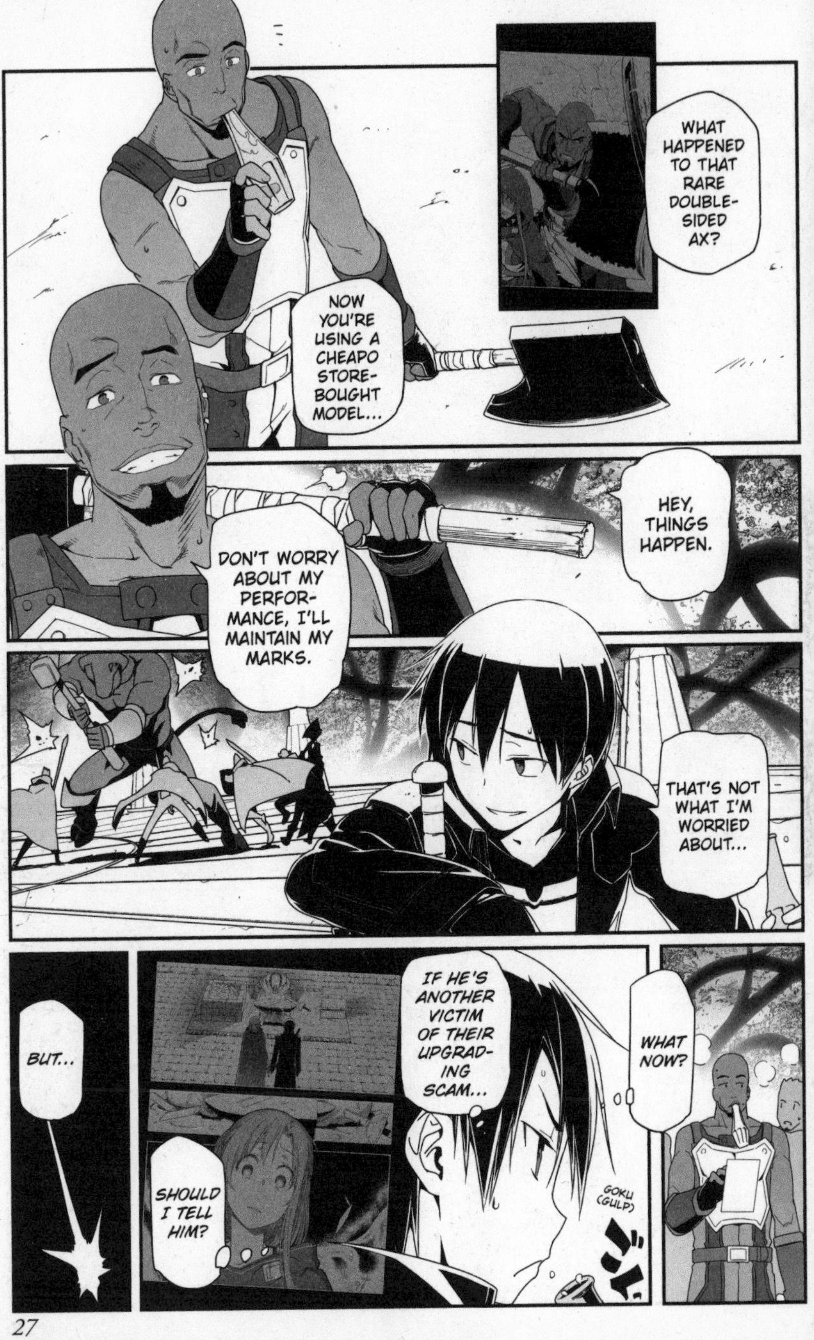

WHAT HAPPENED TO THAT RARE DOUBLE-SIDED AX?
NOW YOU'RE USING A CHEAPO STORE-BOUGHT MODEL...
HEY, THINGS HAPPEN.
DON'T WORRY ABOUT MY PERFOR-MANCE, I'LL MAINTAIN MY MARKS.
THAT'S NOT WHAT I'M WORRIED ABOUT...
WHAT NOW?
IF HE'S ANOTHER VICTIM OF THEIR UPGRAD-ING SCAM...
GOKU (GULP)
SHOULD I TELL HIM?
BUT...

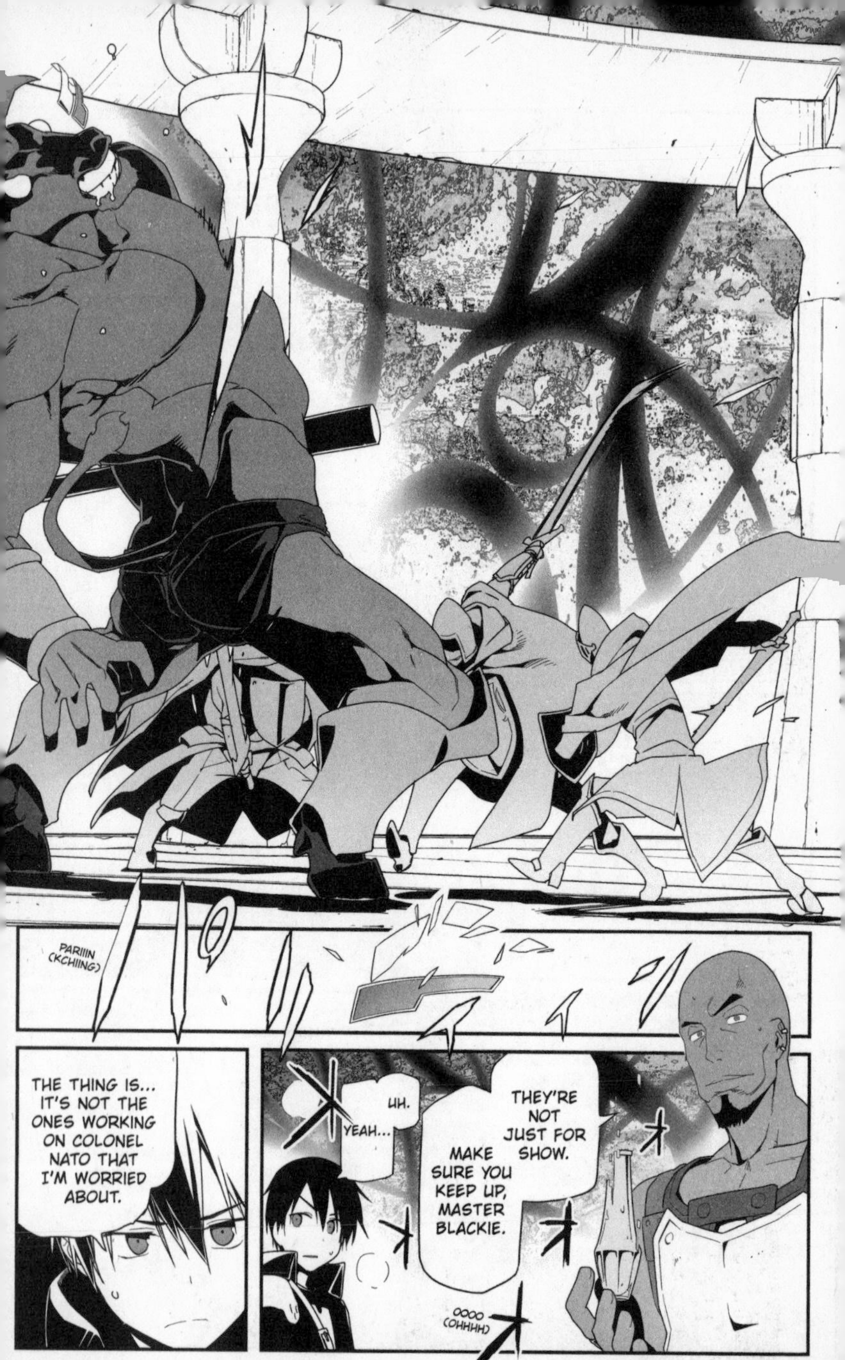
PARIIIN (KCHIING)
THEY'RE NOT JUST FOR SHOW.
MAKE SURE YOU KEEP UP, MASTER BLACKIE.
UH. YEAH...
OOOO (OHHHH)
THE THING IS... IT'S NOT THE ONES WORKING ON COLONEL NATO THAT I'M WORRIED ABOUT.

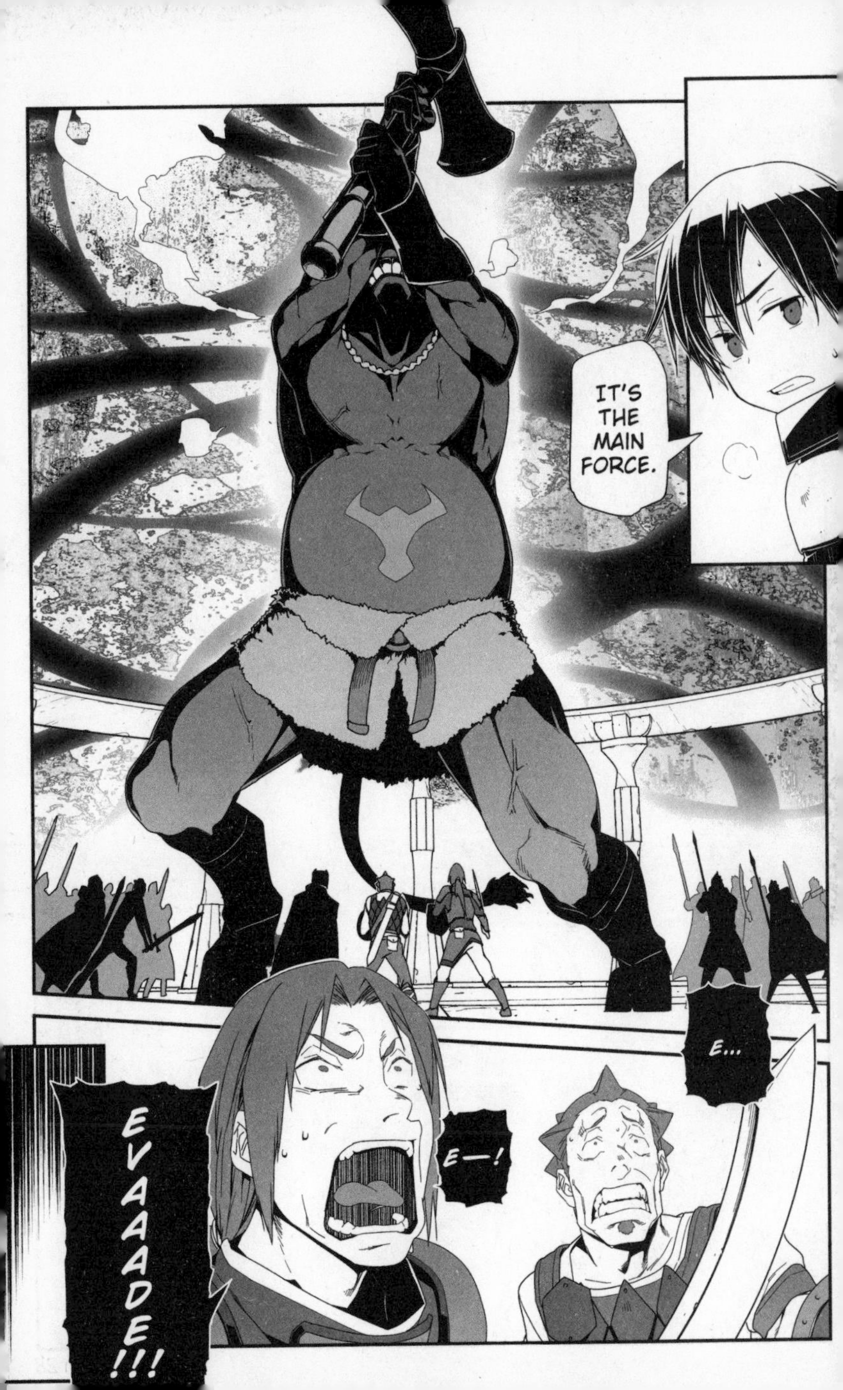
IT'S THE MAIN FORCE.
E...
E—!
EVAAADE!!!

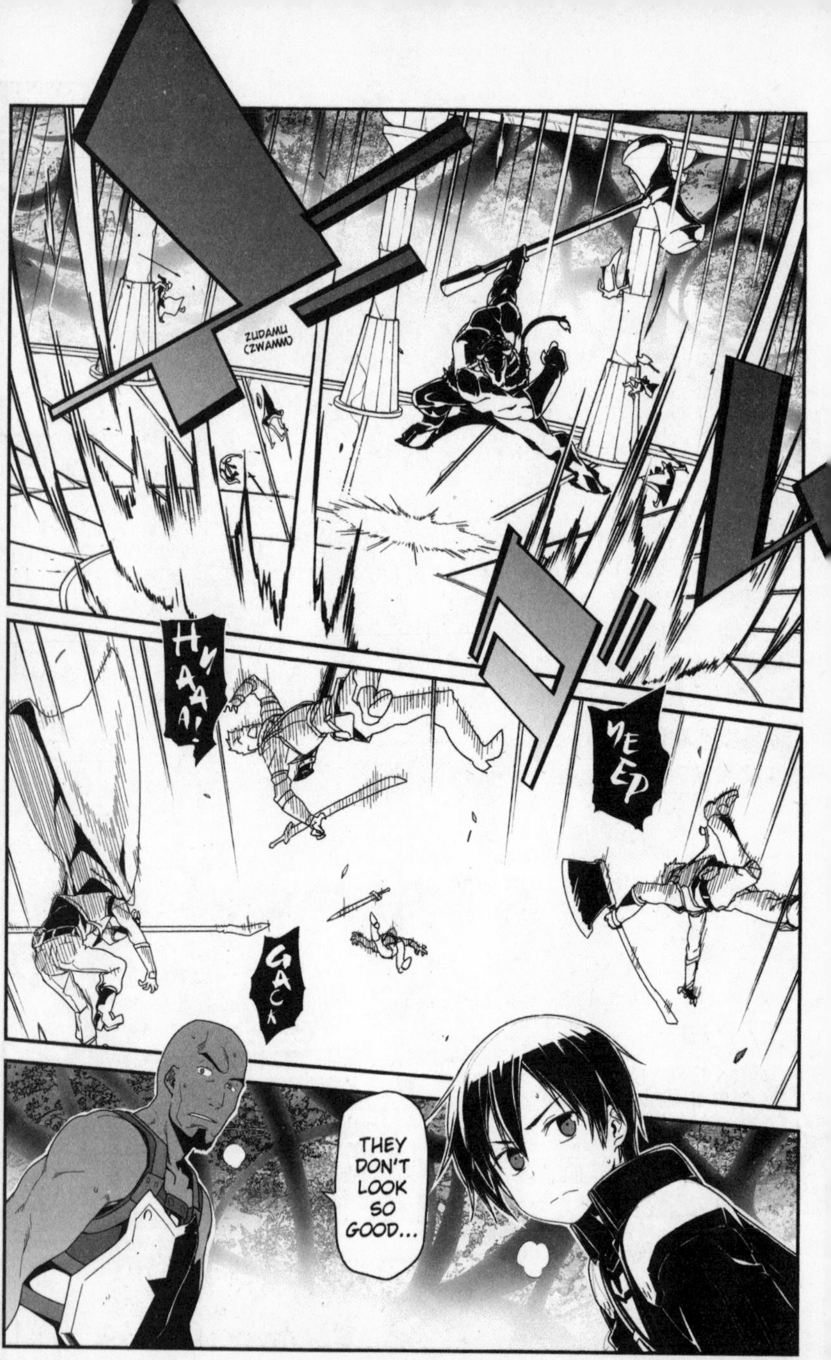
ZUDAMU (ZWAMM)
NEEP
HYAAA!
GACK
THEY DON'T LOOK SO GOOD...

#017: About-Face

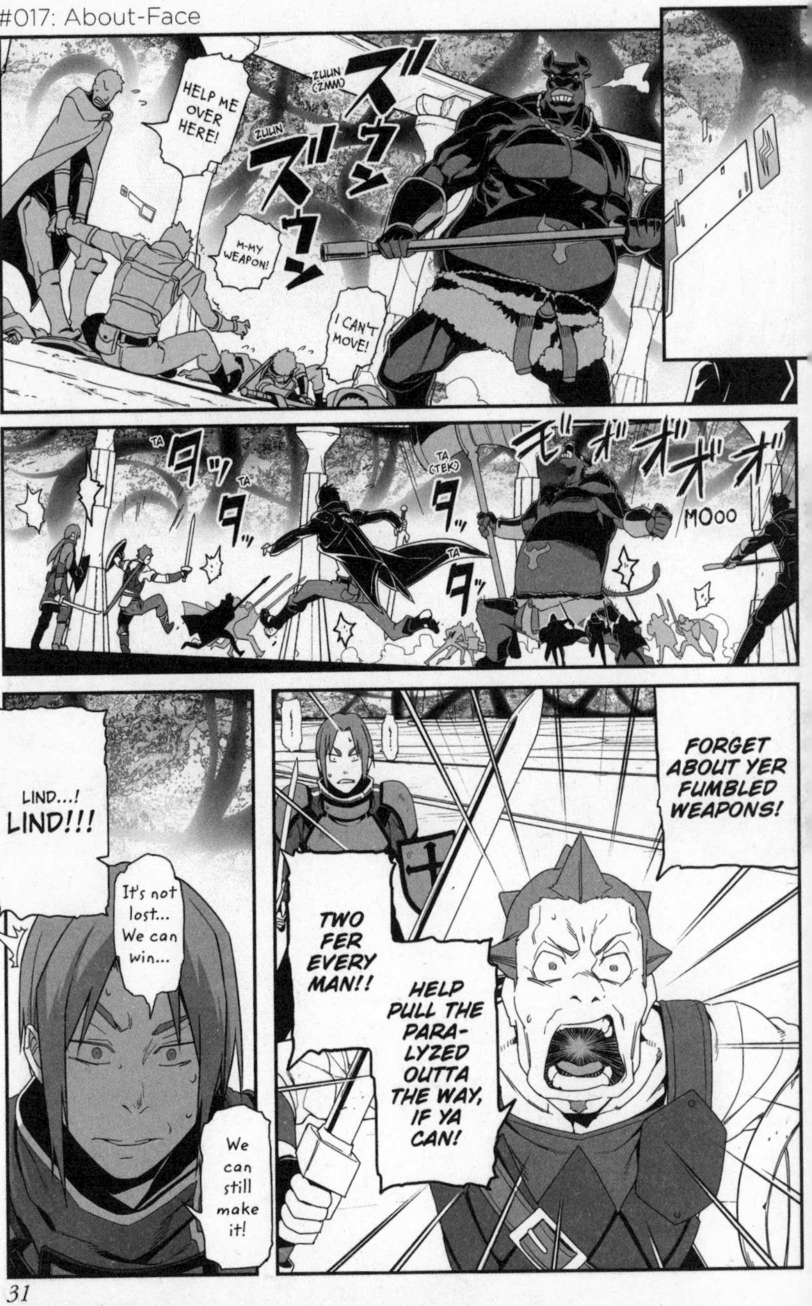
ZUUN (ZMM)
ZUUN
HELP ME OVER HERE!
M-MY WEAPON!
I CAN'T MOVE!
MOOO
TA (TEK)
TA
TA
TA
FORGET ABOUT YER FUMBLED WEAPONS!
HELP PULL THE PARA-LYZED OUTTA THE WAY, IF YA CAN!
TWO FER EVERY MAN!!
LIND...! LIND!!!
It's not lost... We can win...
We can still make it!

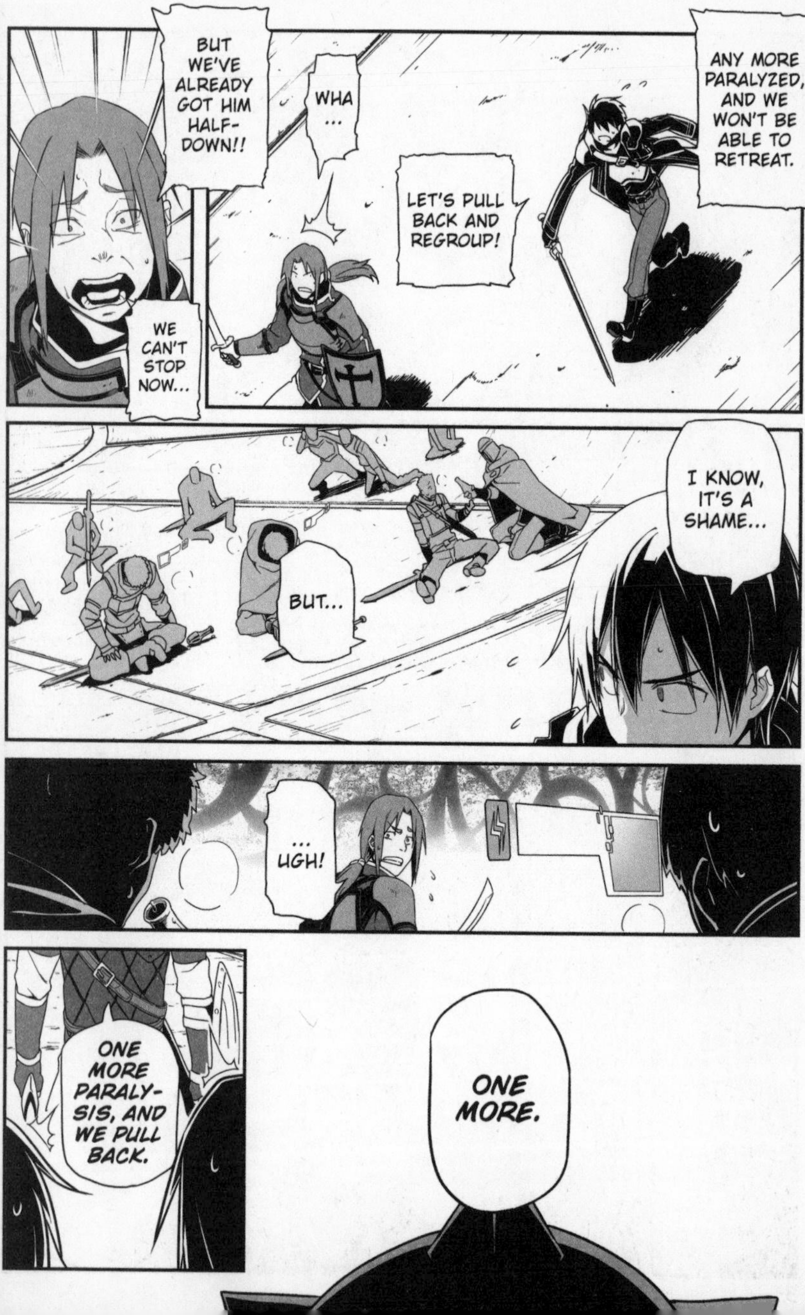
ANY MORE PARALYZED, AND WE WON'T BE ABLE TO RETREAT.
LET'S PULL BACK AND REGROUP!
WHA...
BUT WE'VE ALREADY GOT HIM HALF-DOWN!!
WE CAN'T STOP NOW...
I KNOW, IT'S A SHAME...
BUT...
... UGH!
ONE MORE.
ONE MORE PARALYSIS, AND WE PULL BACK.

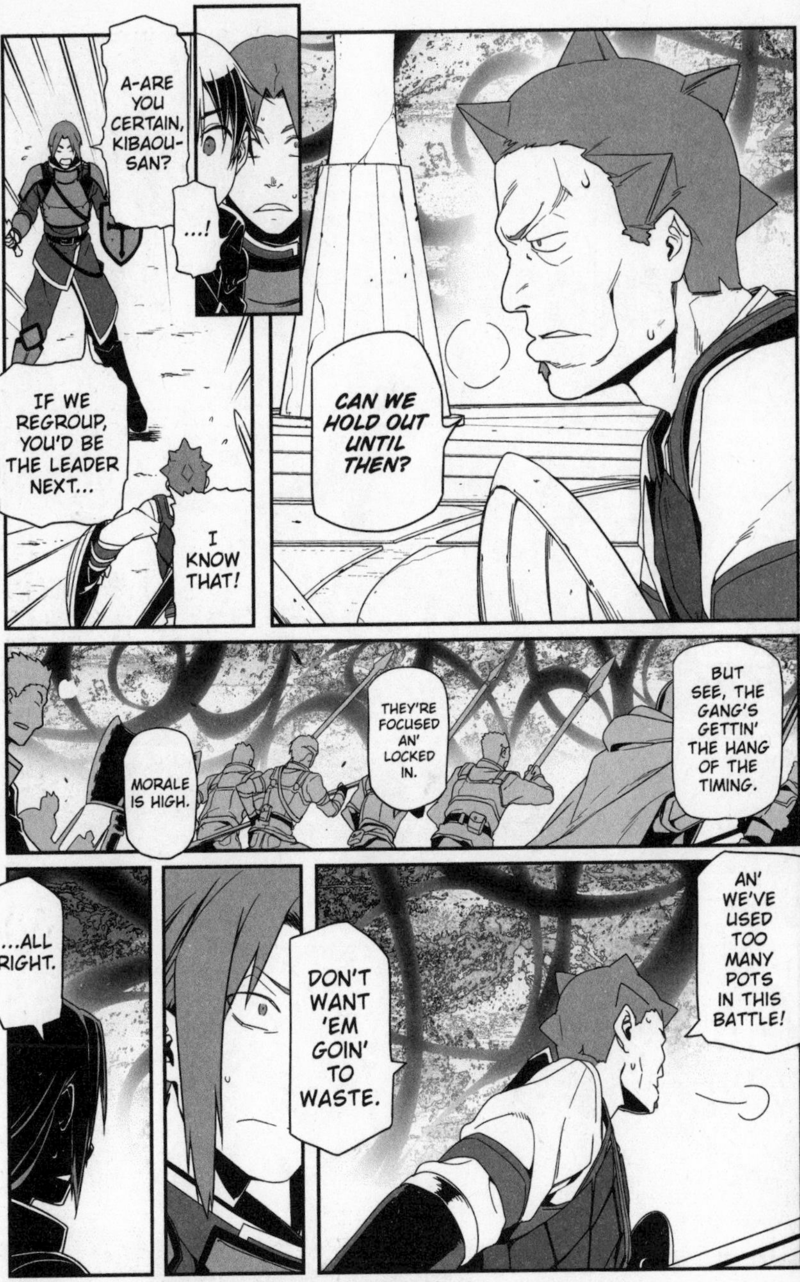

CAN WE HOLD OUT UNTIL THEN?
...!
A-ARE YOU CERTAIN, KIBAOU-SAN?
IF WE REGROUP, YOU'D BE THE LEADER NEXT...
I KNOW THAT!
BUT SEE, THE GANG'S GETTIN' THE HANG OF THE TIMING.
THEY'RE FOCUSED AN' LOCKED IN.
MORALE IS HIGH.
AN' WE'VE USED TOO MANY POTS IN THIS BATTLE!
DON'T WANT 'EM GOIN' TO WASTE.
...ALL RIGHT.

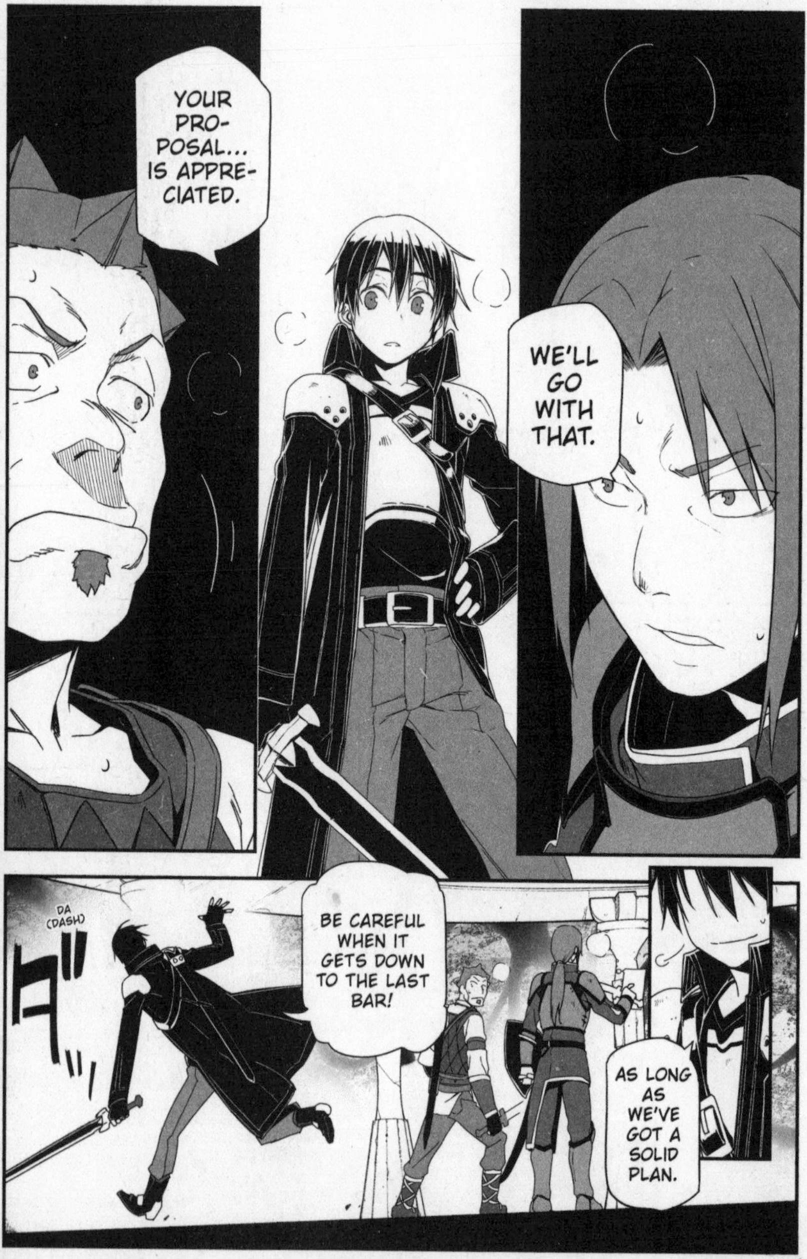
WE'LL GO WITH THAT.
YOUR PRO-POSAL... IS APPRE-CIATED.
AS LONG AS WE'VE GOT A SOLID PLAN.
BE CAREFUL WHEN IT GETS DOWN TO THE LAST BAR!
DA (DASH)
ダッ

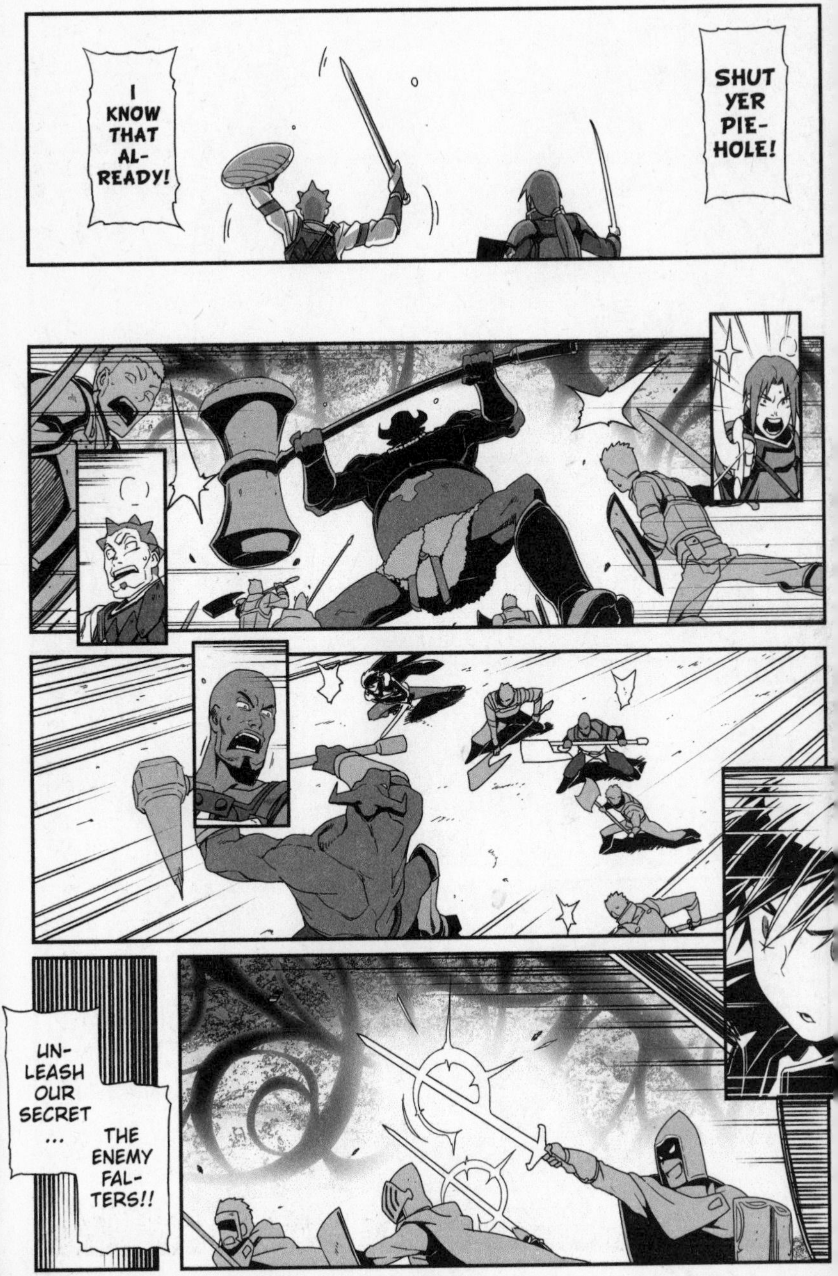
SHUT YER PIE-HOLE!
I KNOW THAT AL-READY!
UN-LEASH OUR SECRET ... THE ENEMY FAL-TERS!!

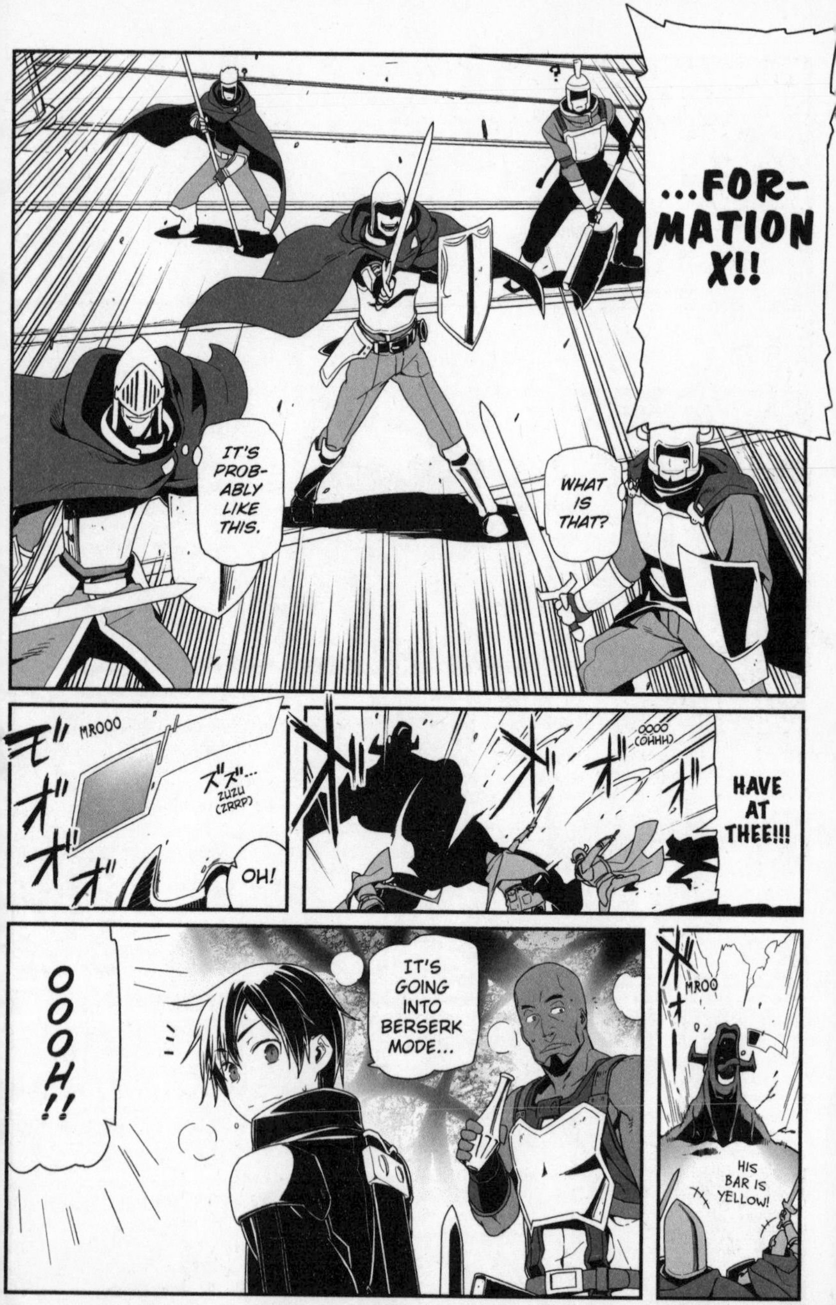

...FORMATION X!!
WHAT IS THAT?
IT'S PROBABLY LIKE THIS.
HAVE AT THEE!!!
OOOO (OHHH)
MROOO
ズズ... ZUZU (ZRRP)
OH!
MROO
HIS BAR IS YELLOW!
IT'S GOING INTO BERSERK MODE...
OOOOH!!

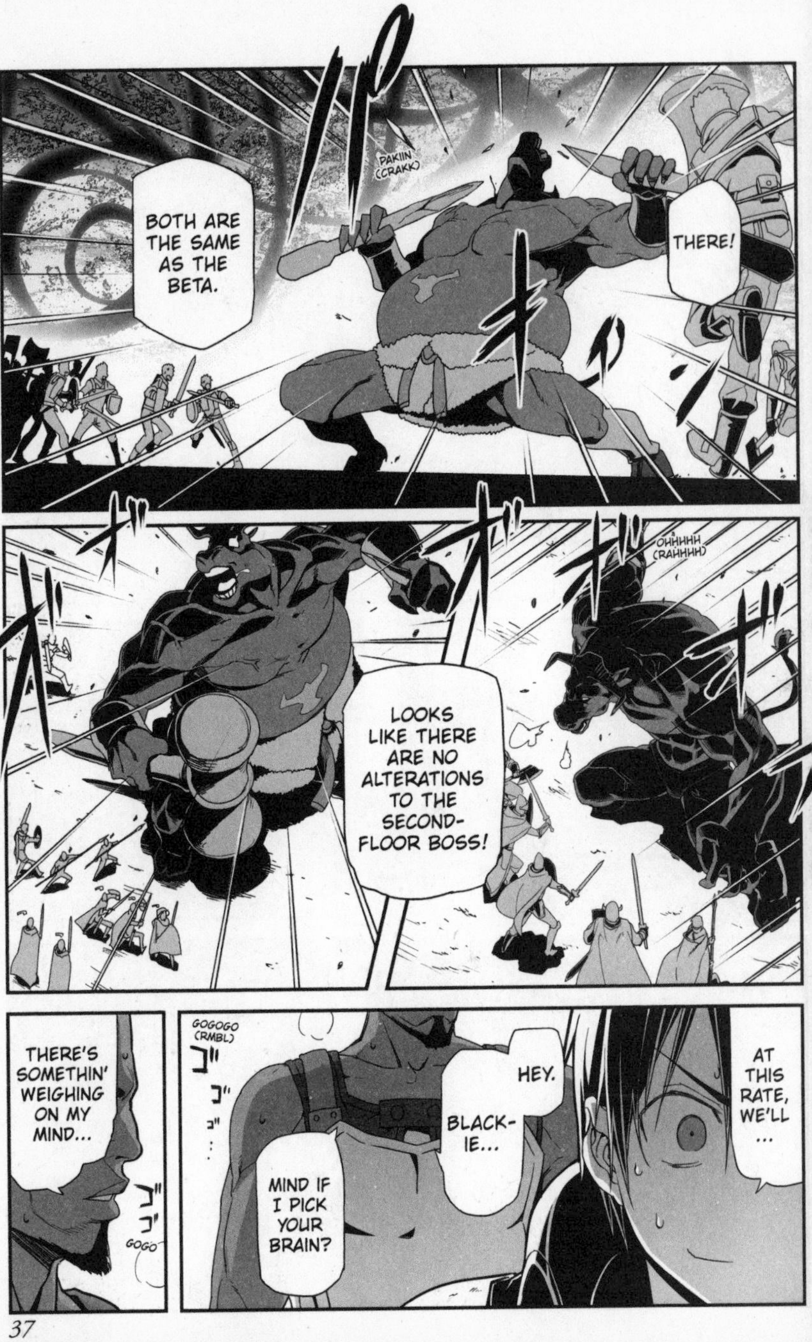
THERE!
PAKIIN (CRAKK)
BOTH ARE THE SAME AS THE BETA.
OHHHHH (RAHHHHH)
LOOKS LIKE THERE ARE NO ALTERATIONS TO THE SECOND-FLOOR BOSS!
AT THIS RATE, WE'LL ...
HEY.
BLACKIE...
GOGOGO (RMBL)
MIND IF I PICK YOUR BRAIN?
THERE'S SOMETHIN' WEIGHING ON MY MIND...
GOGO

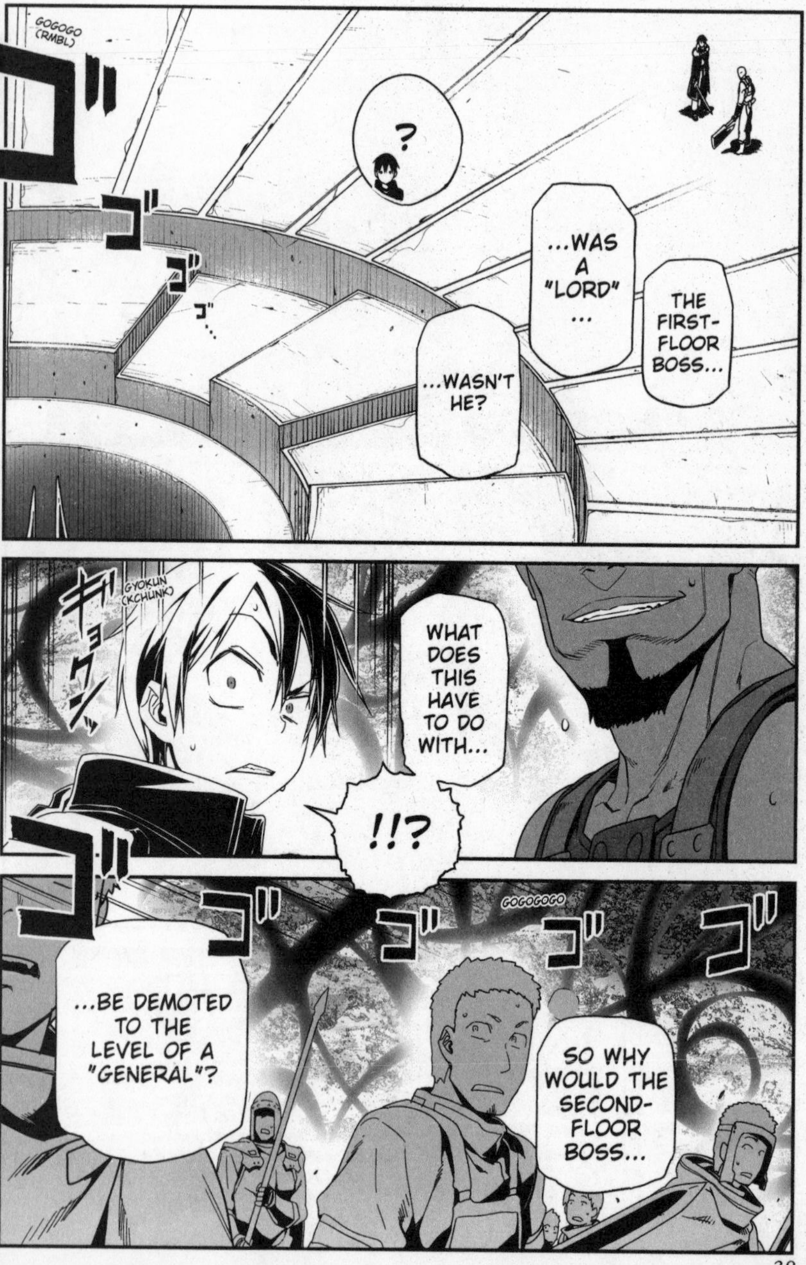
THE FIRST-FLOOR BOSS...
...WAS A "LORD" ...
...WASN'T HE?
?
GOGOGO (RMBL)
WHAT DOES THIS HAVE TO DO WITH...
!!?
GYOKUN (KCHUNK)
GOGOGOGO
SO WHY WOULD THE SECOND-FLOOR BOSS...
...BE DEMOTED TO THE LEVEL OF A "GENERAL"?

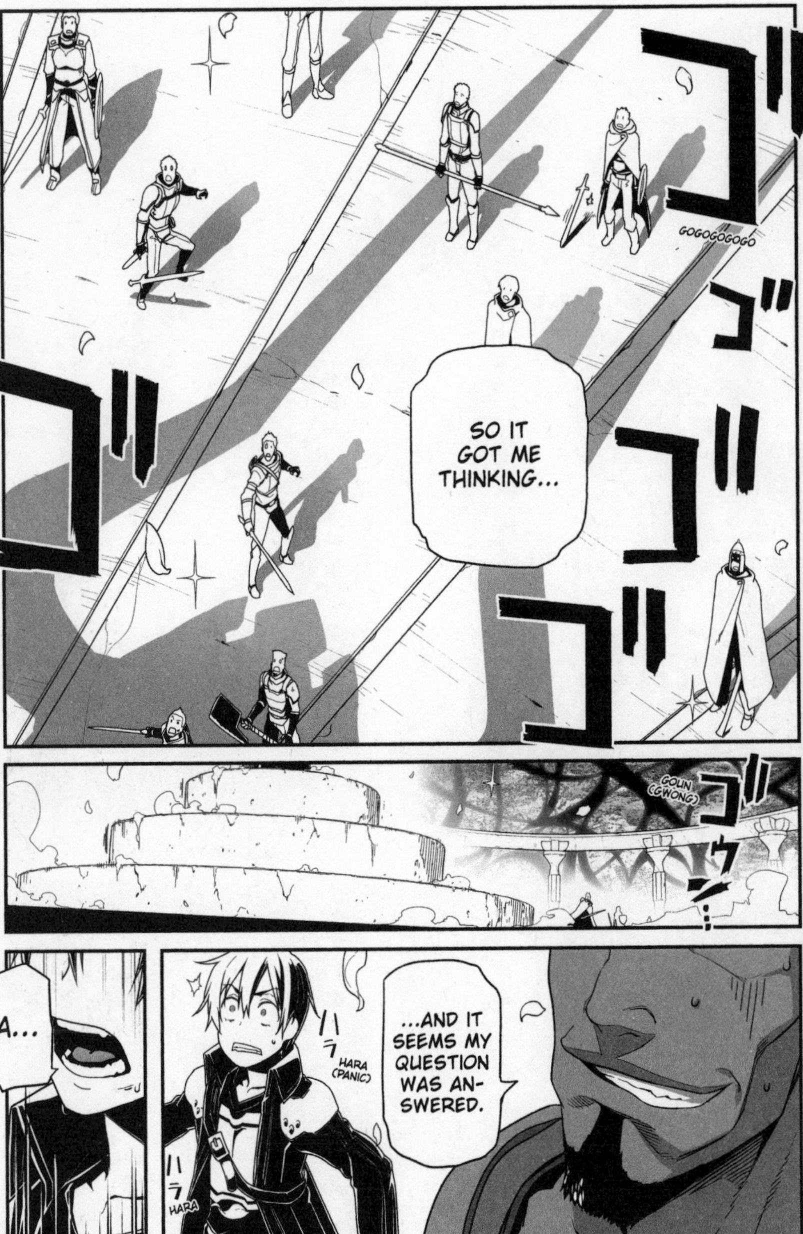
ゴゴゴゴ
GOGOGOGOGO
SO IT GOT ME THINKING...
ゴゥン
GOUN (GWONG)
...AND IT SEEMS MY QUESTION WAS AN- SWERED.
ハラ
HARA (PANIC)
ハラ
HARA
A...

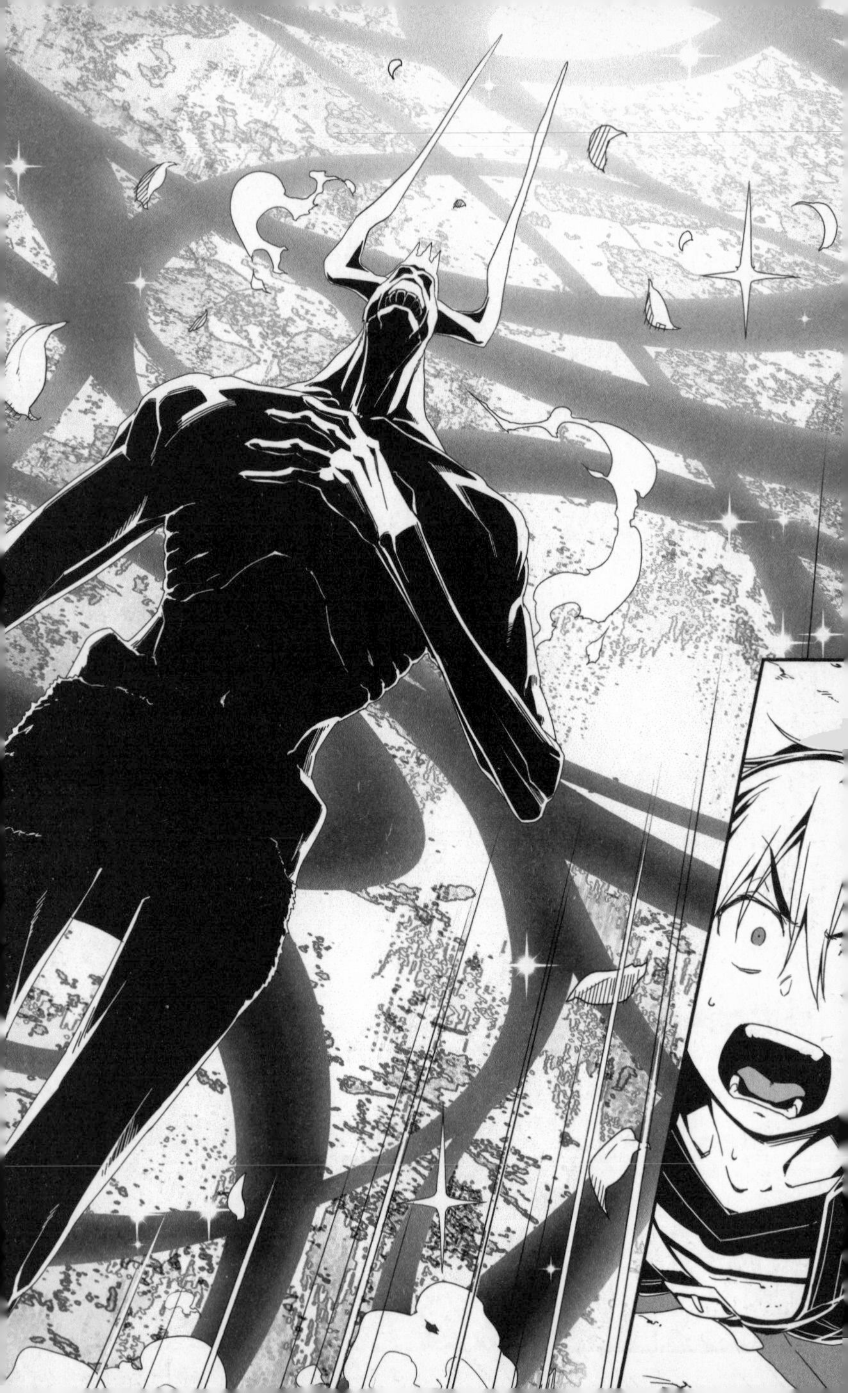

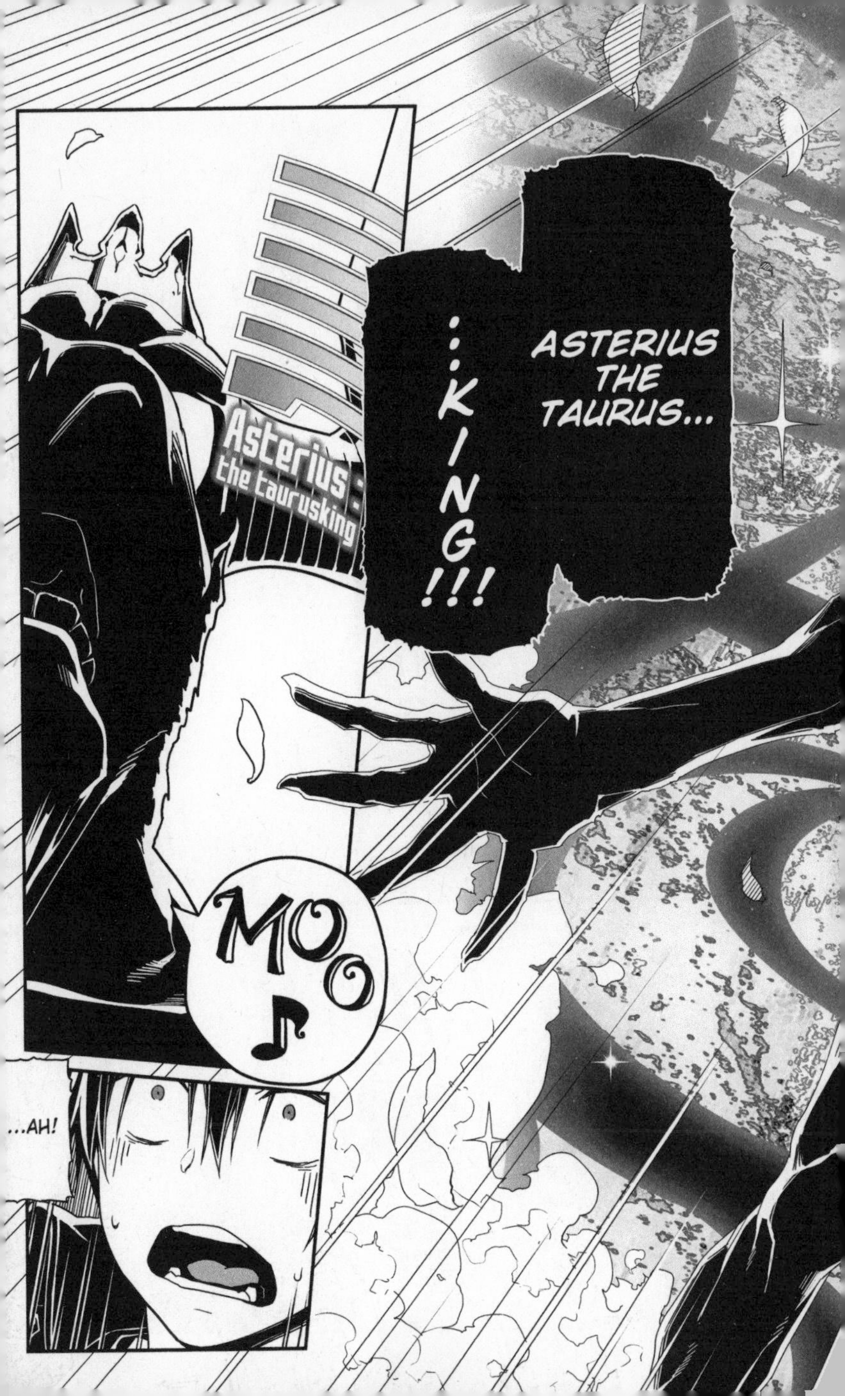
ASTERIUS THE TAURUS...
...KING!!!
Asterius - the taurusking
MOO♪
...AH!

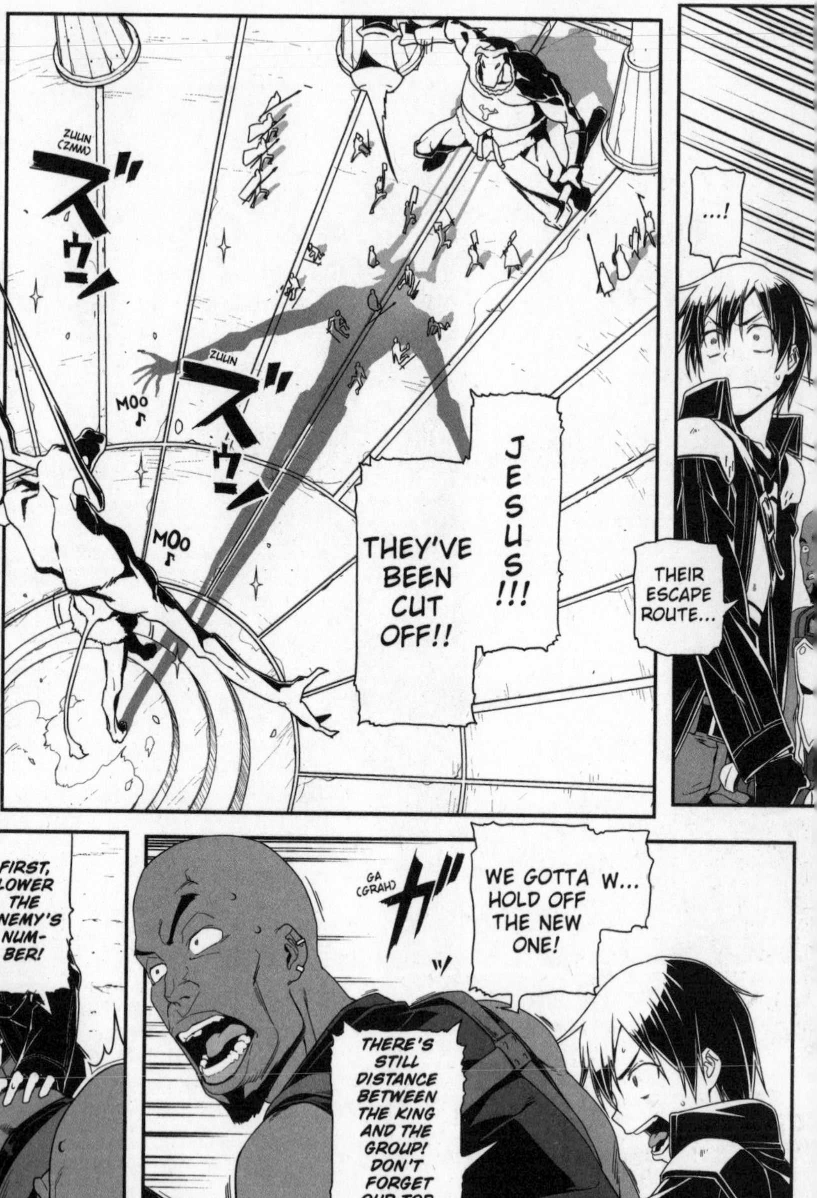
...!
THEIR ESCAPE ROUTE...
JESUS!!!
THEY'VE BEEN CUT OFF!!
ZUUN (ZMM)
ズゥン
ZUUN
ズゥン
MOO ♪
MOO ♪
WE GOTTA W... HOLD OFF THE NEW ONE!
GA (GRAH)
ガッ
THERE'S STILL DISTANCE BETWEEN THE KING AND THE GROUP! DON'T FORGET OUR TOP PRIORITY!
FIRST, LOWER THE ENEMY'S NUM-BER!

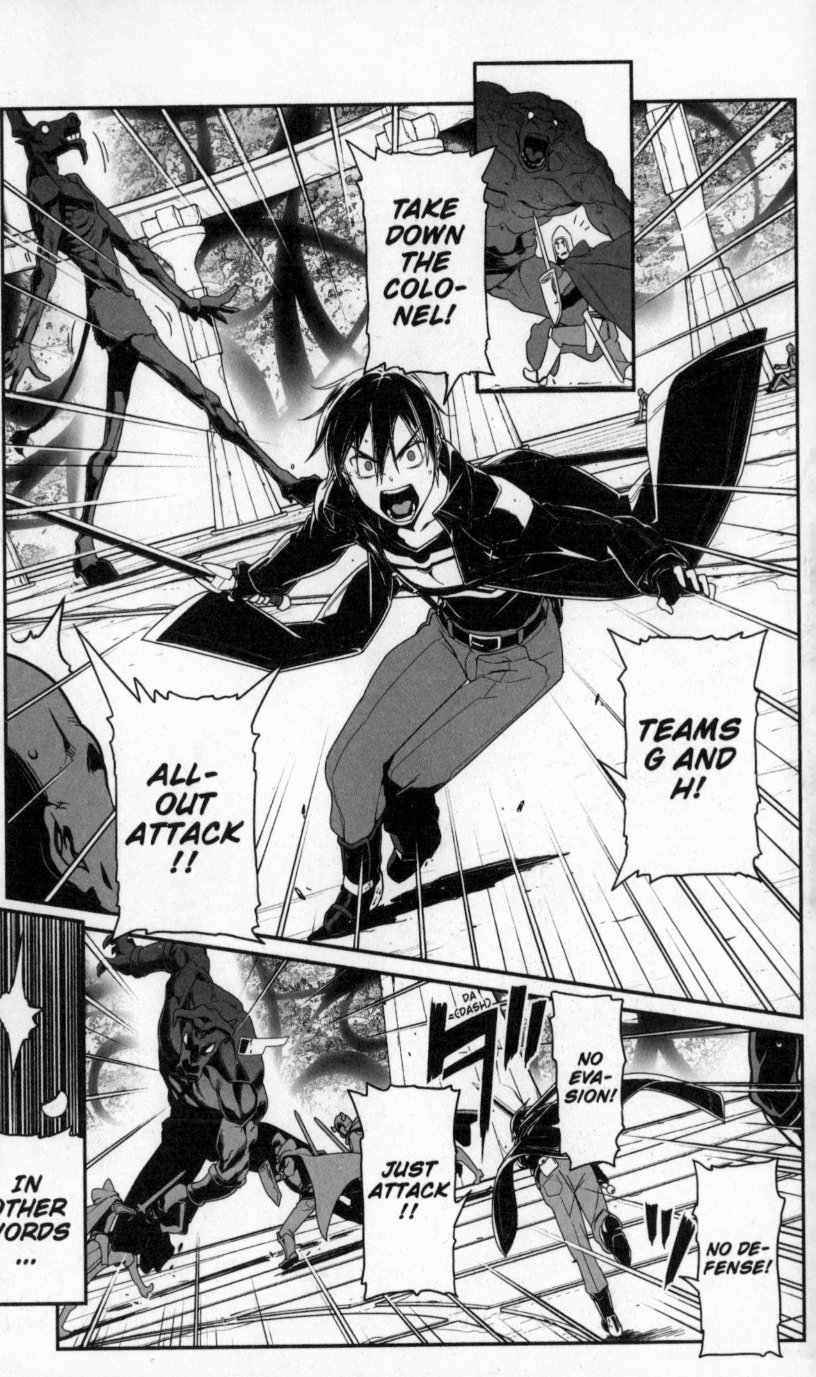
TAKE DOWN THE COLO-NEL!
TEAMS G AND H!
ALL-OUT ATTACK!!
DA =(DASH)
NO EVA-SION!
NO DE-FENSE!
JUST ATTACK!!
IN OTHER WORDS...

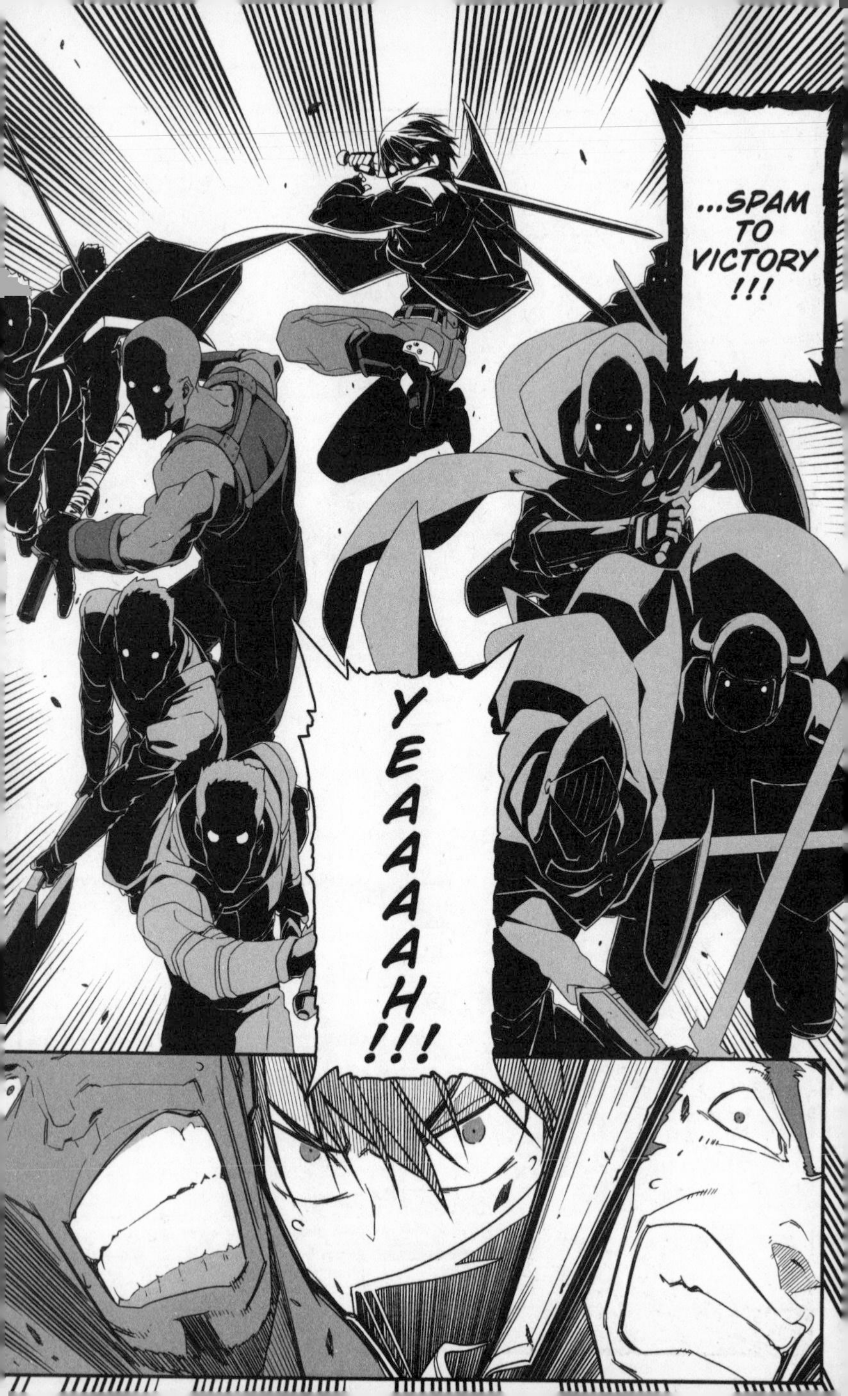
...SPAM TO VICTORY !!!
YEAAAAAH!!!

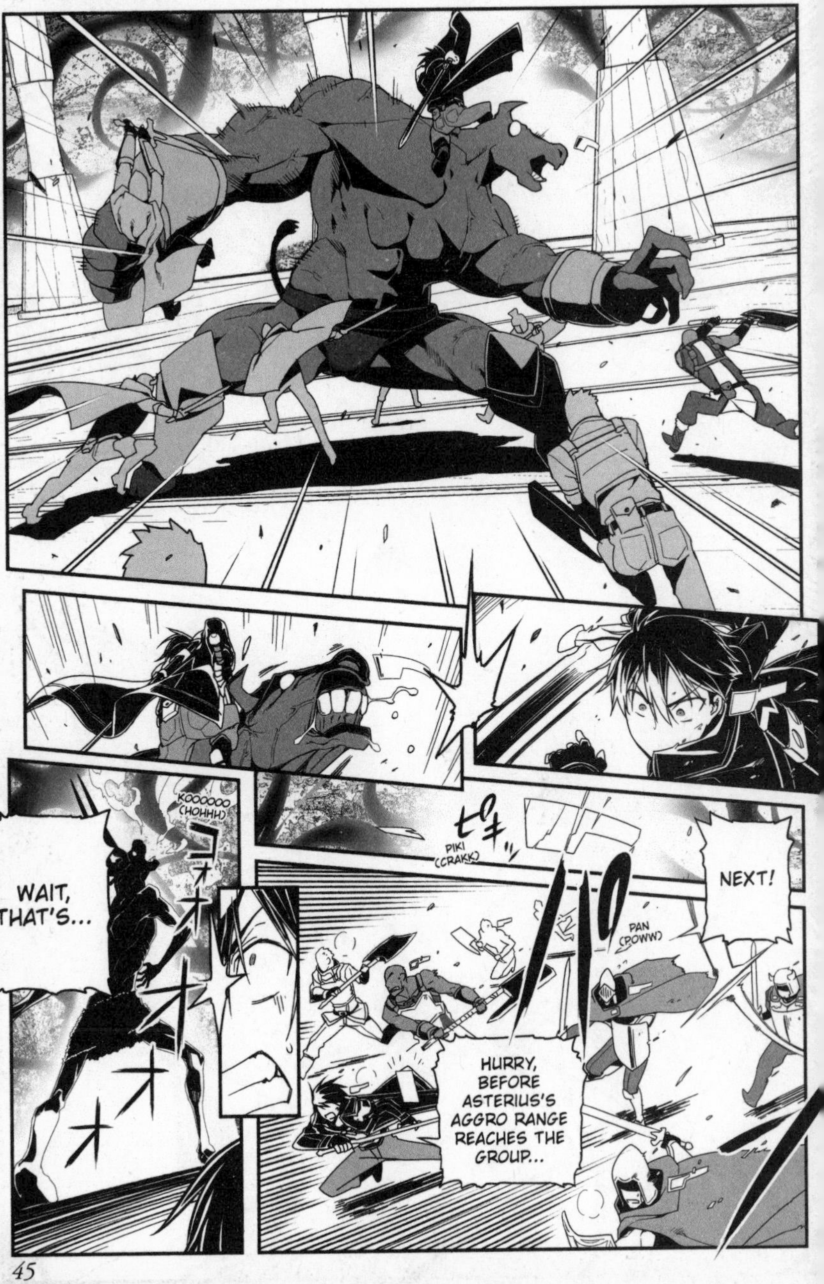
PIKI (CRAKK)
NEXT!
PAN (POWW)
HURRY, BEFORE ASTERIUS'S AGGRO RANGE REACHES THE GROUP...
KOOOOOO (HOHHH)
WAIT, THAT'S...

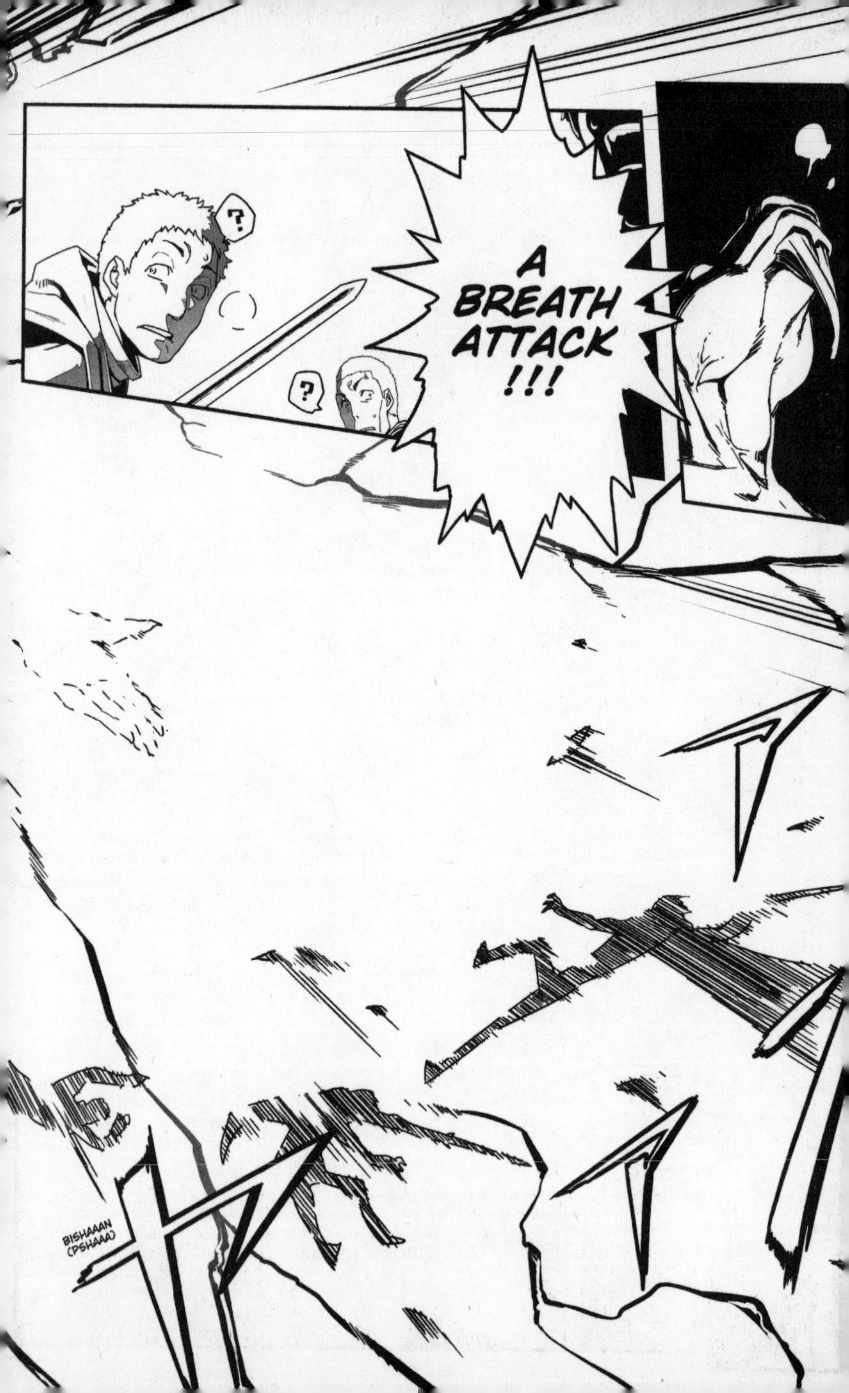
?
?
A BREATH ATTACK!!!
BISHAAAN (PSHAAA)

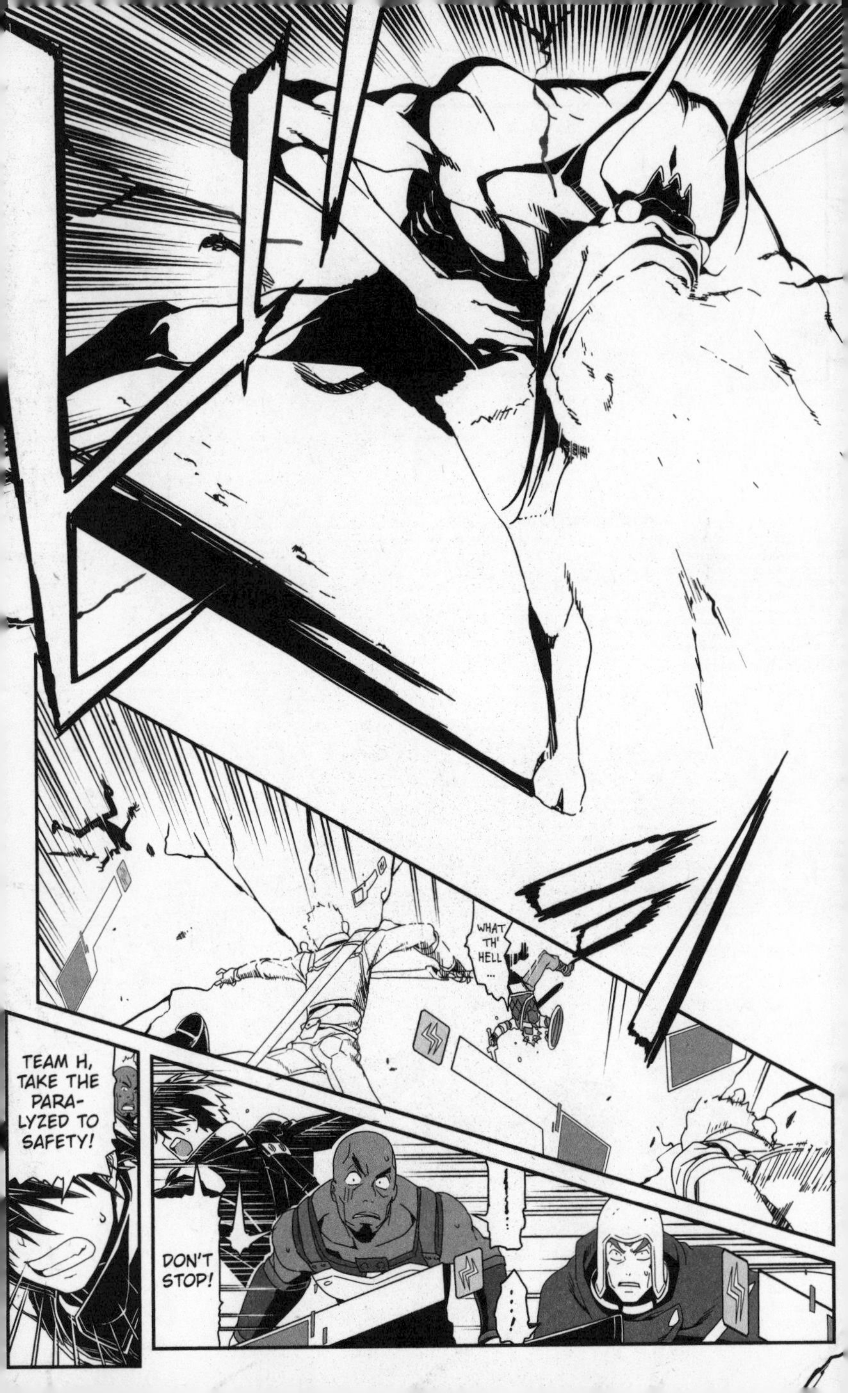
WHAT TH' HELL...
...!
TEAM H, TAKE THE PARA-LYZED TO SAFETY!
DON'T STOP!

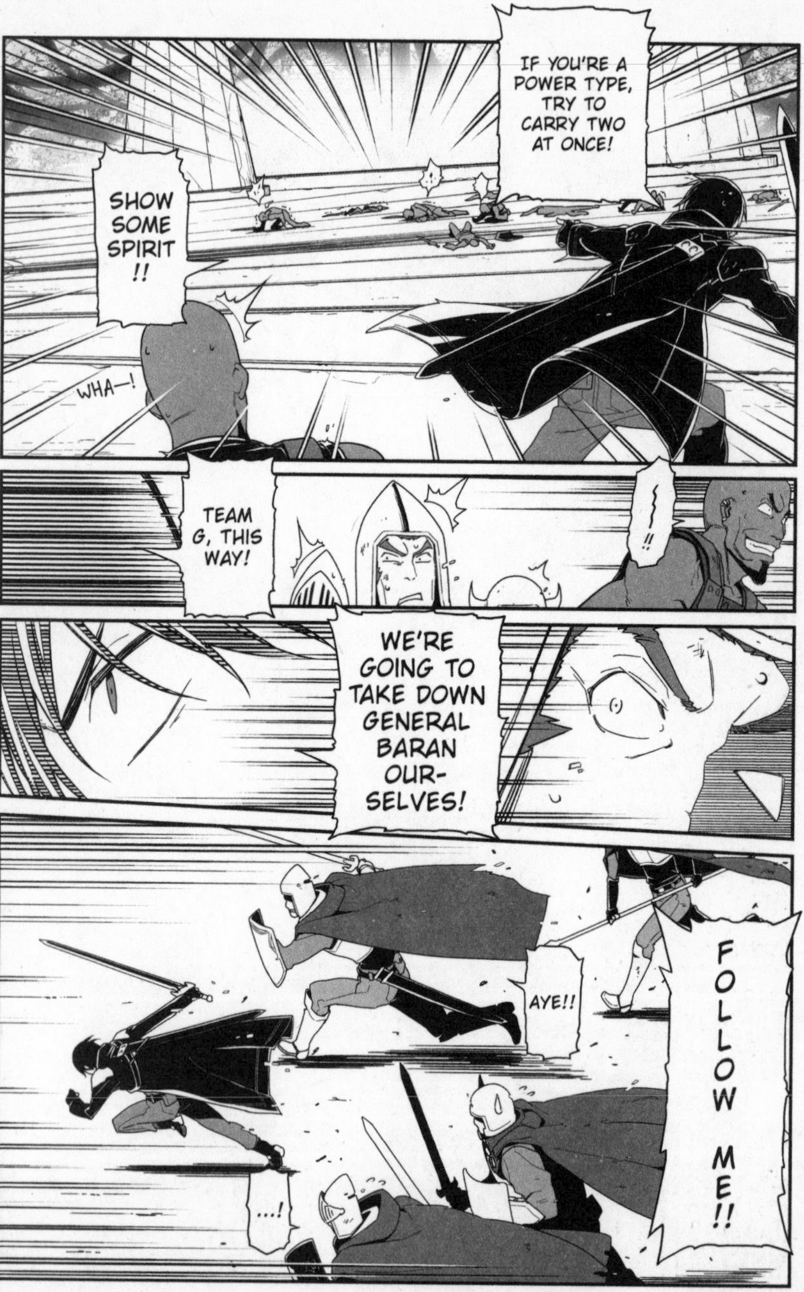
IF YOU'RE A POWER TYPE, TRY TO CARRY TWO AT ONCE!
SHOW SOME SPIRIT !!
WHA—!
—!!
TEAM G, THIS WAY!
WE'RE GOING TO TAKE DOWN GENERAL BARAN OUR-SELVES!
FOLLOW ME!!
AYE!!
...!

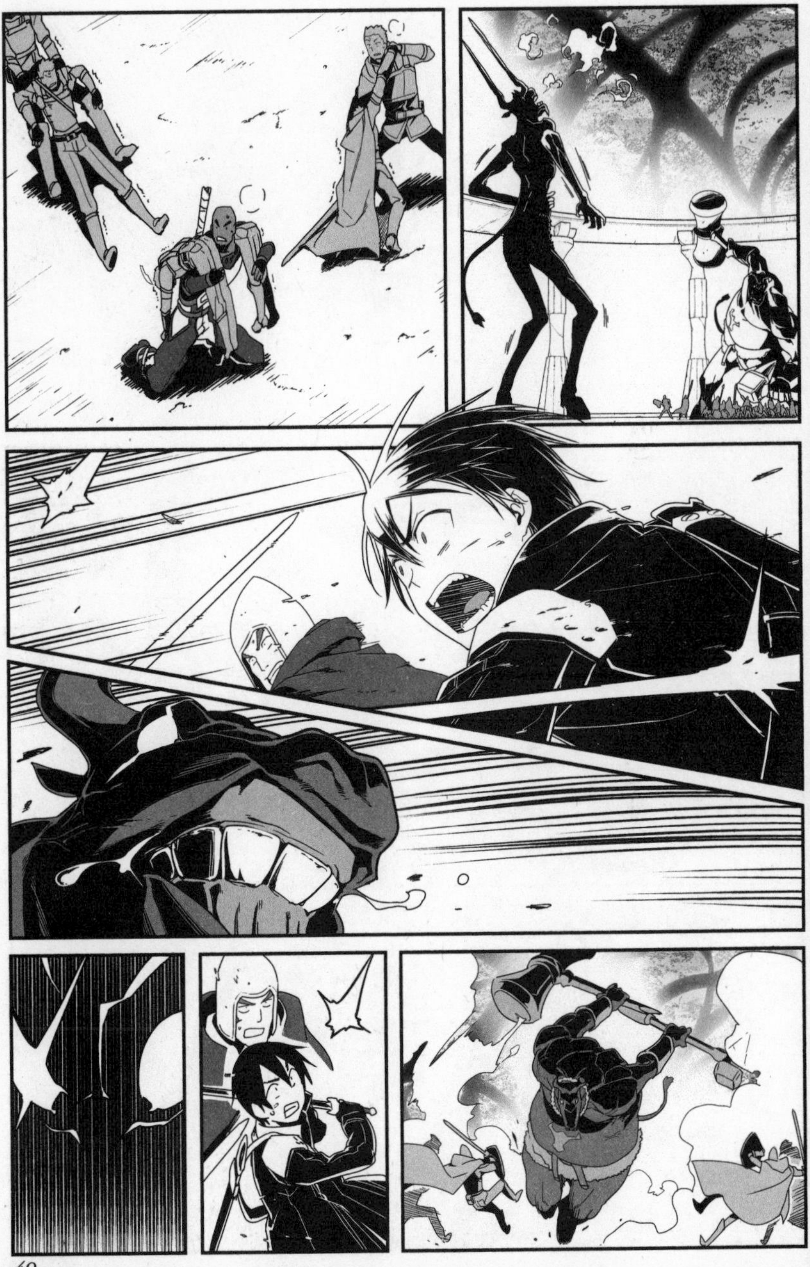

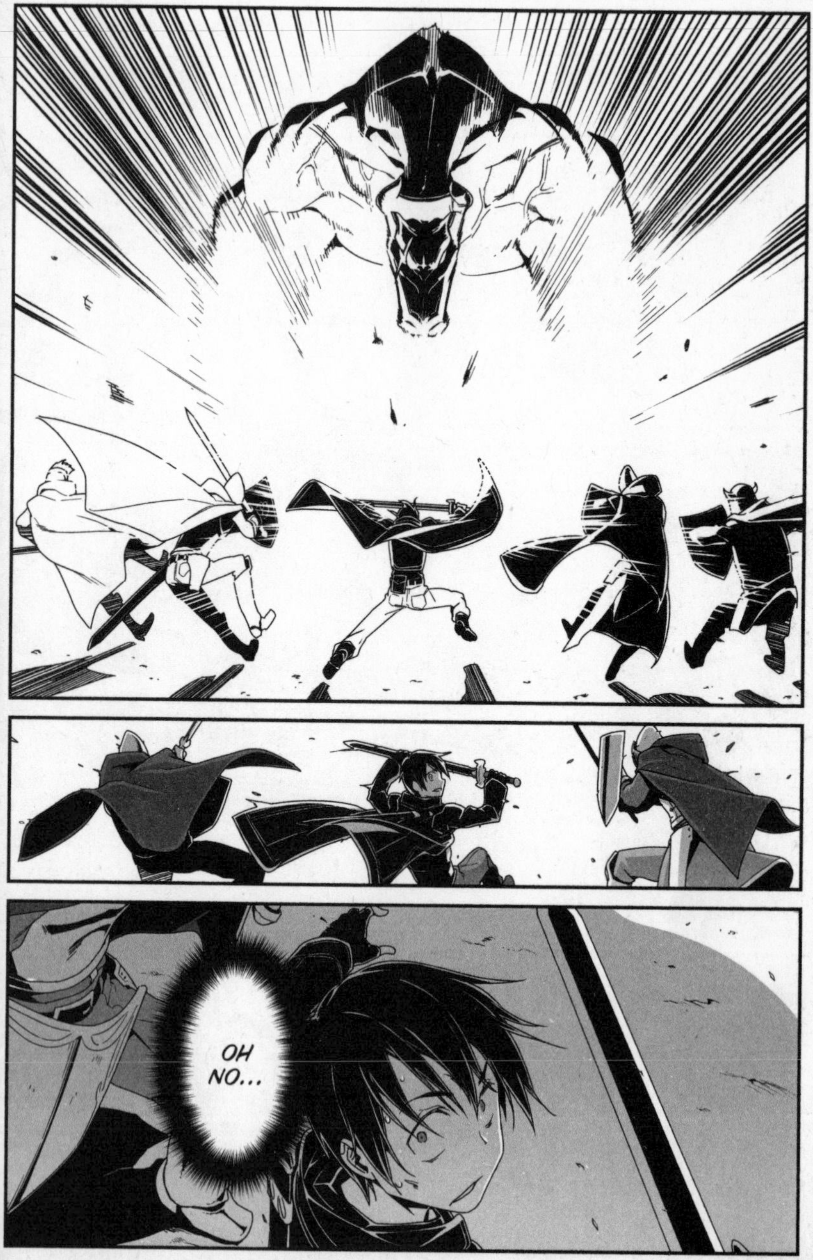
OH NO...

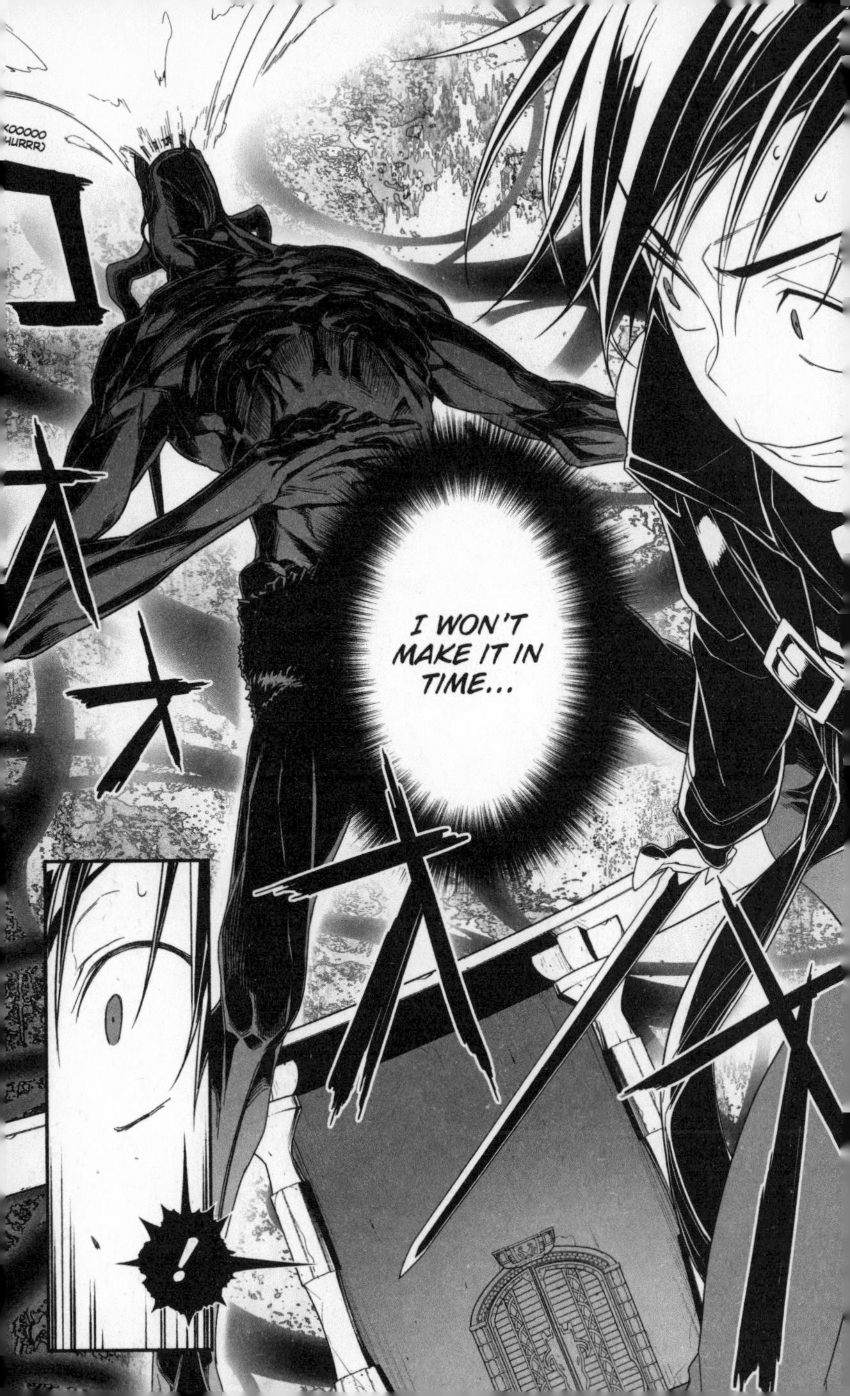

I WON'T MAKE IT IN TIME...
KOOOOO HURRR)
!

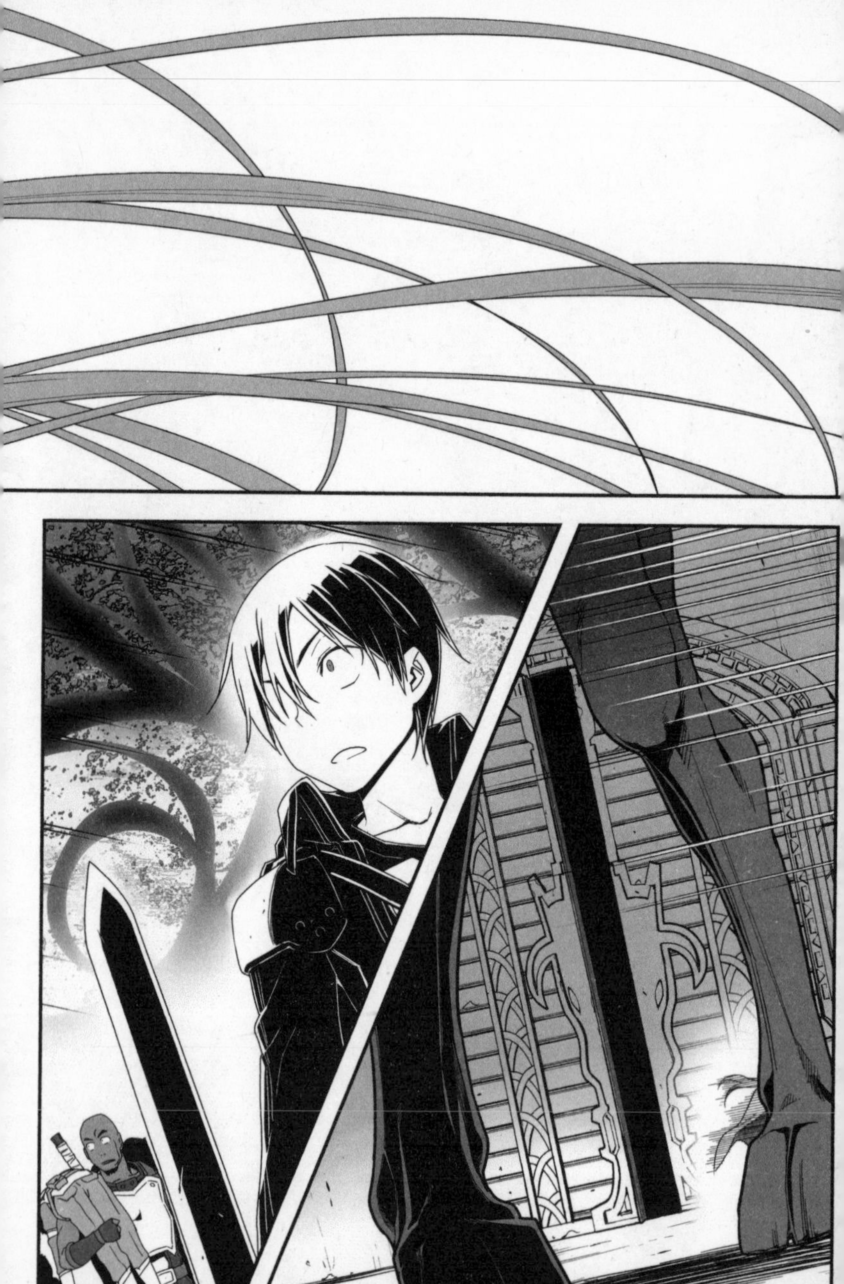

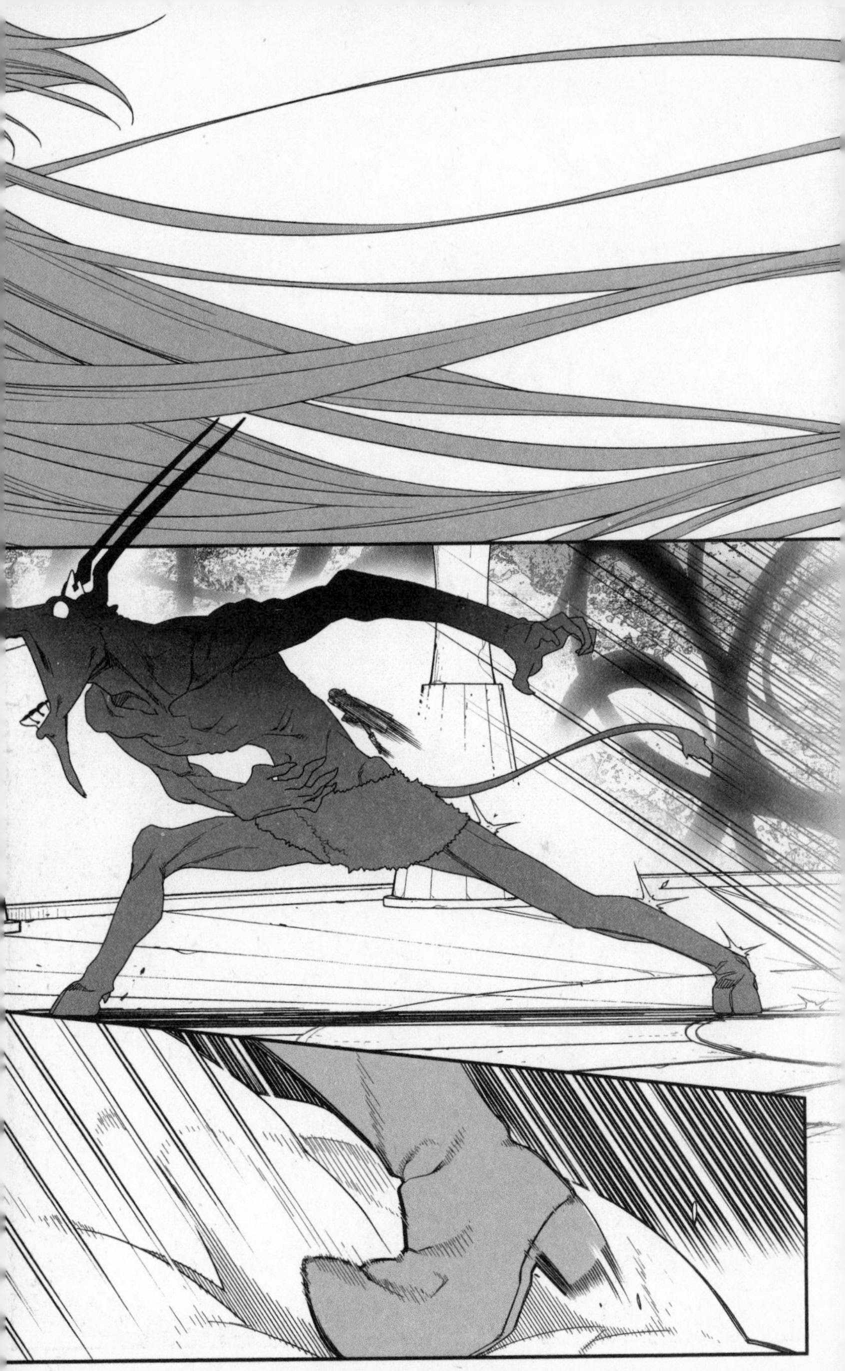

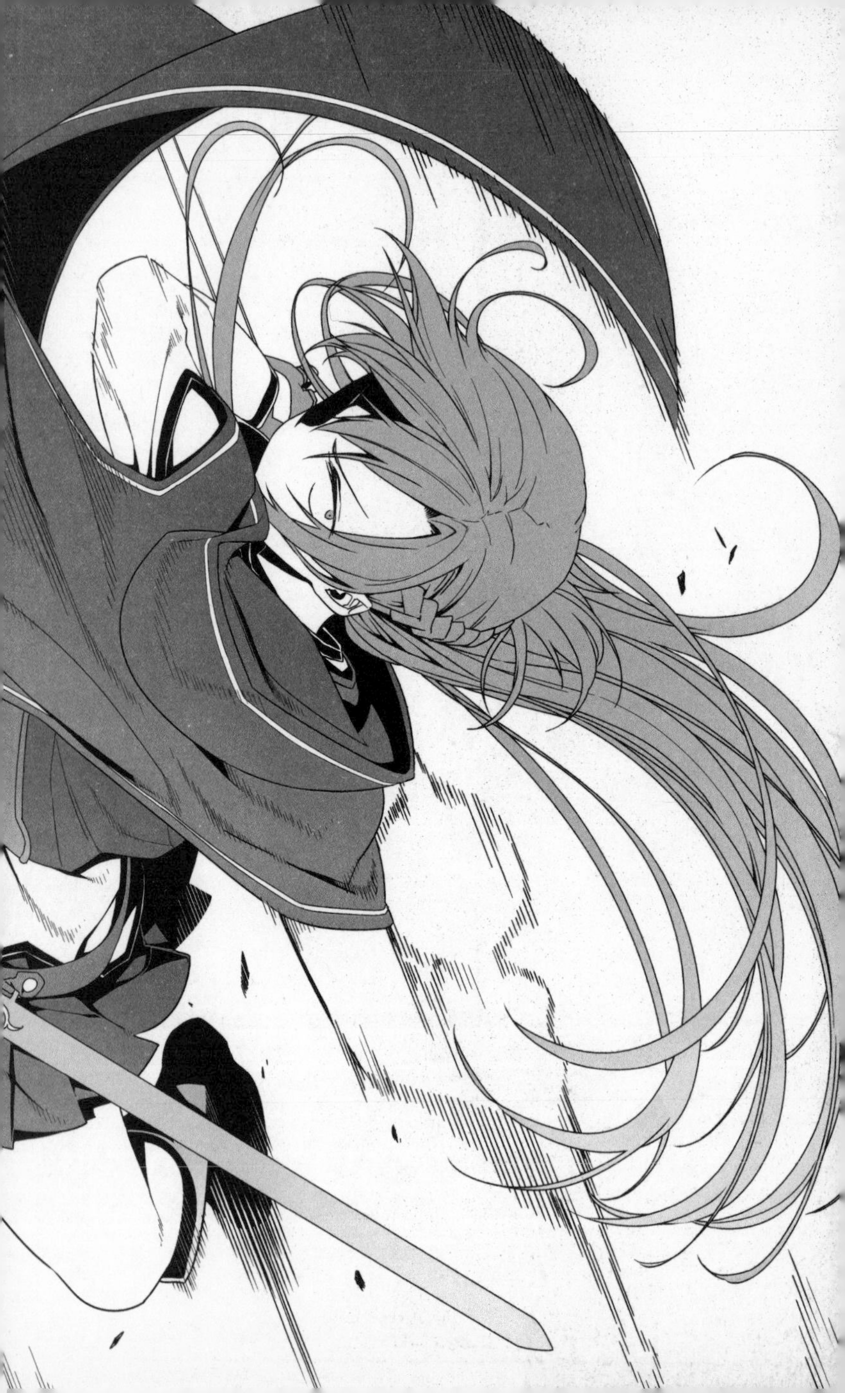

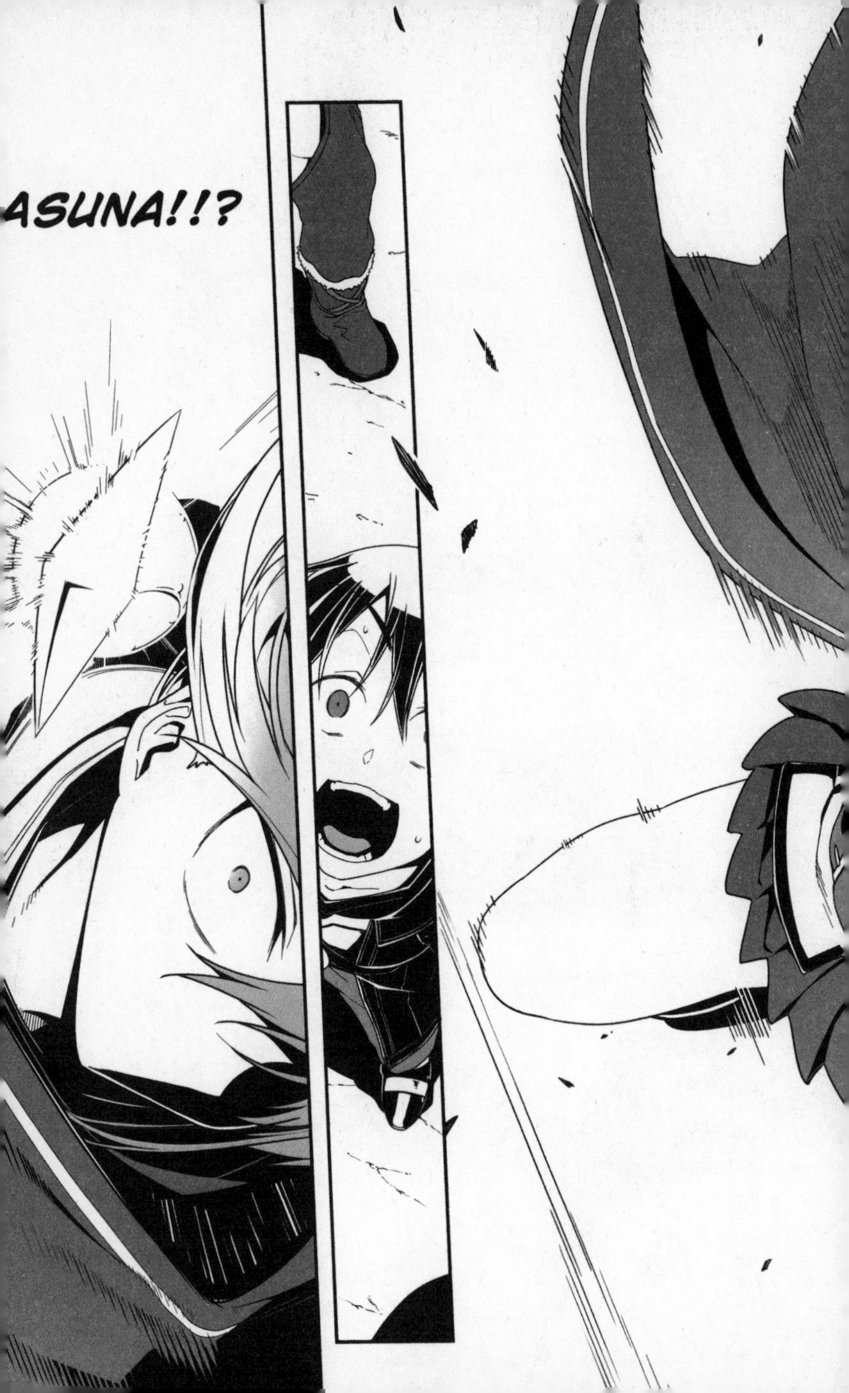
ASUNA!!?

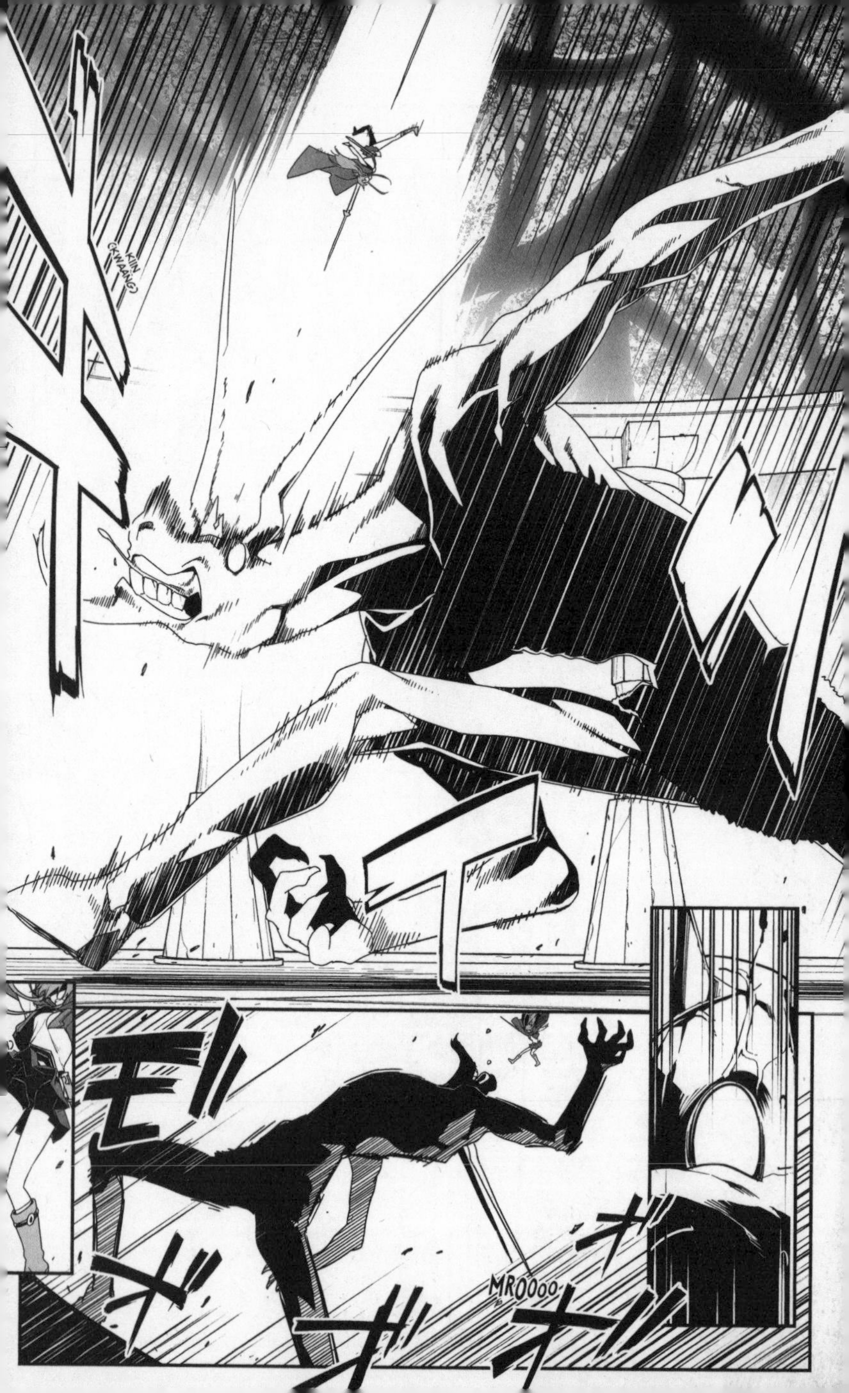
KIIN (KWAANG)
MROOOO

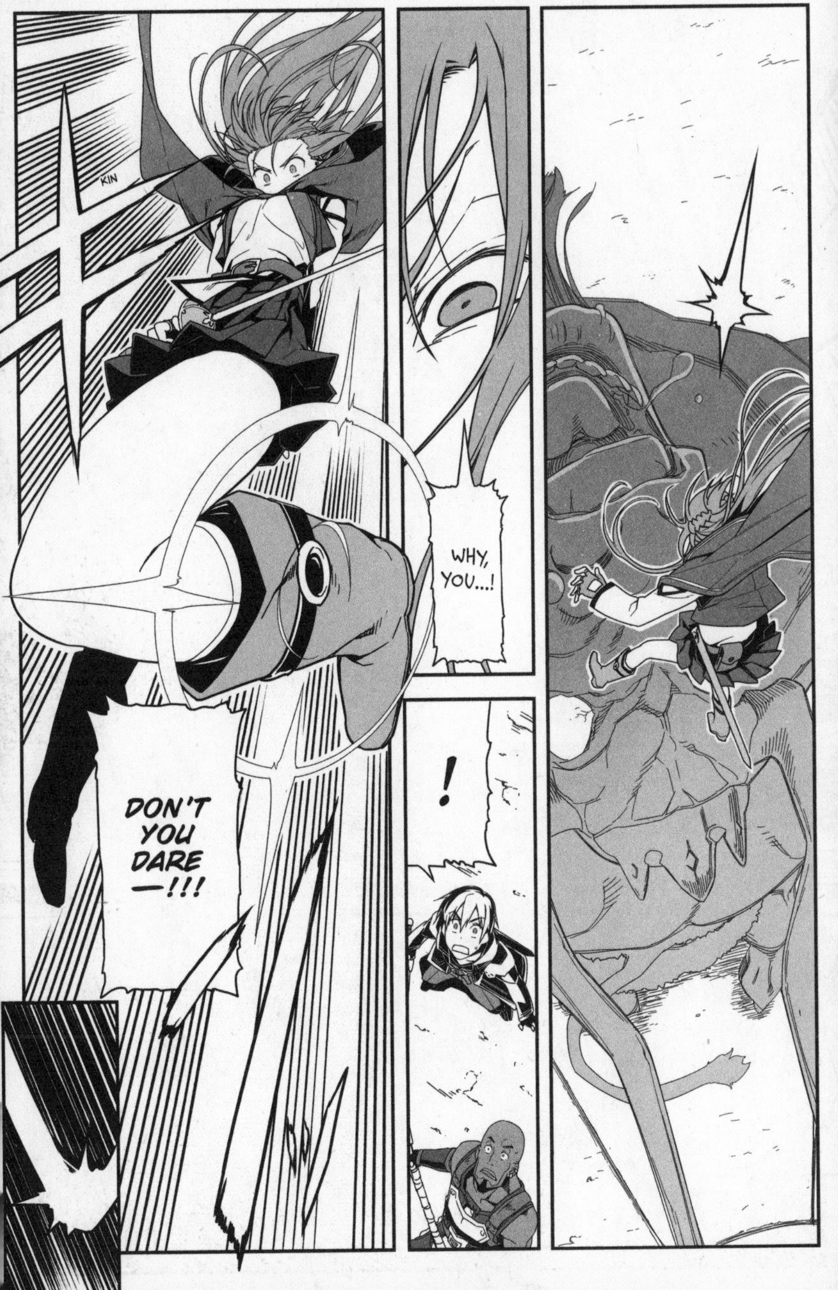
WHY, YOU...!
!
KIN
DON'T YOU DARE—!!!

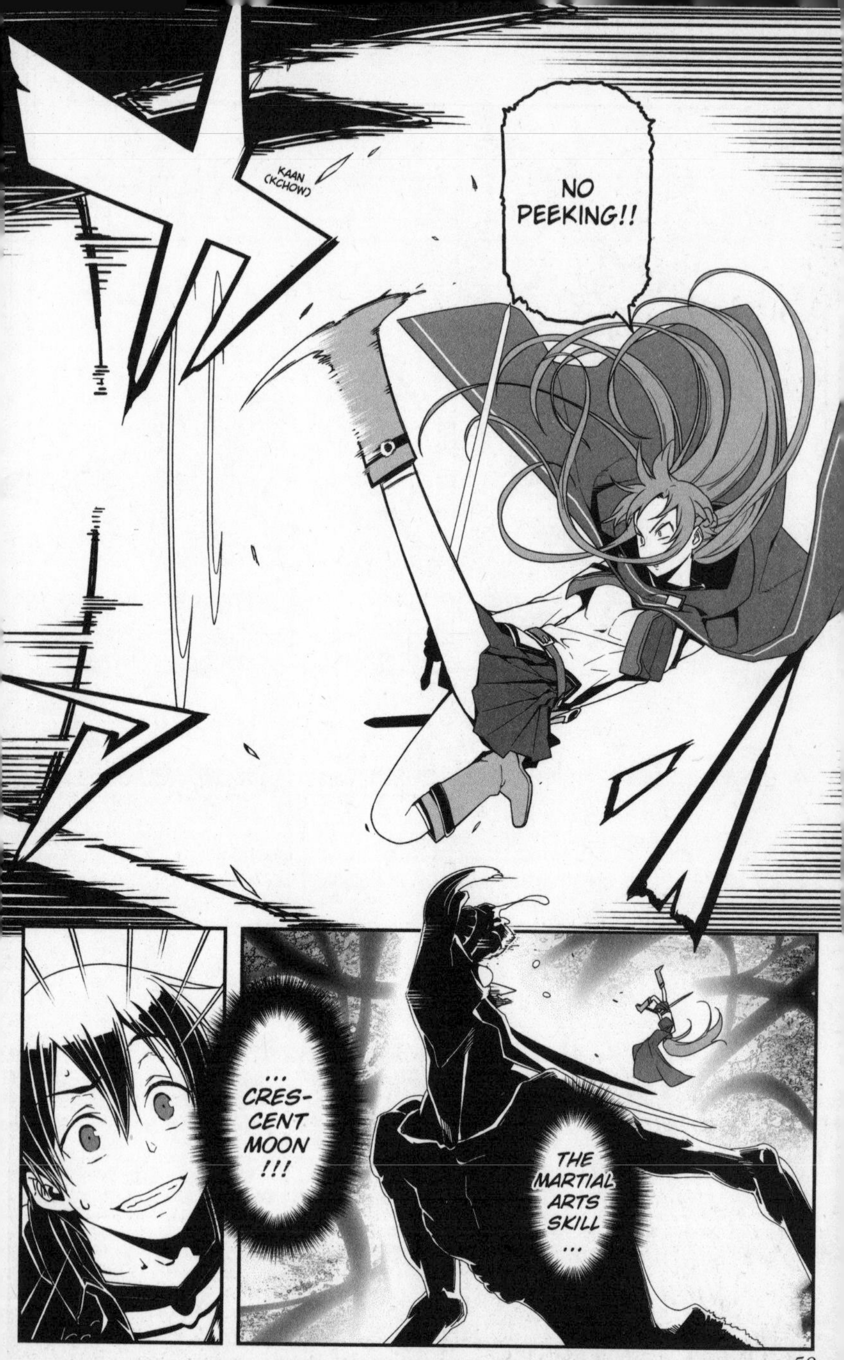
NO PEEKING!!
KAAN (KCHOW)
THE MARTIAL ARTS SKILL ...
... CRES-CENT MOON !!!

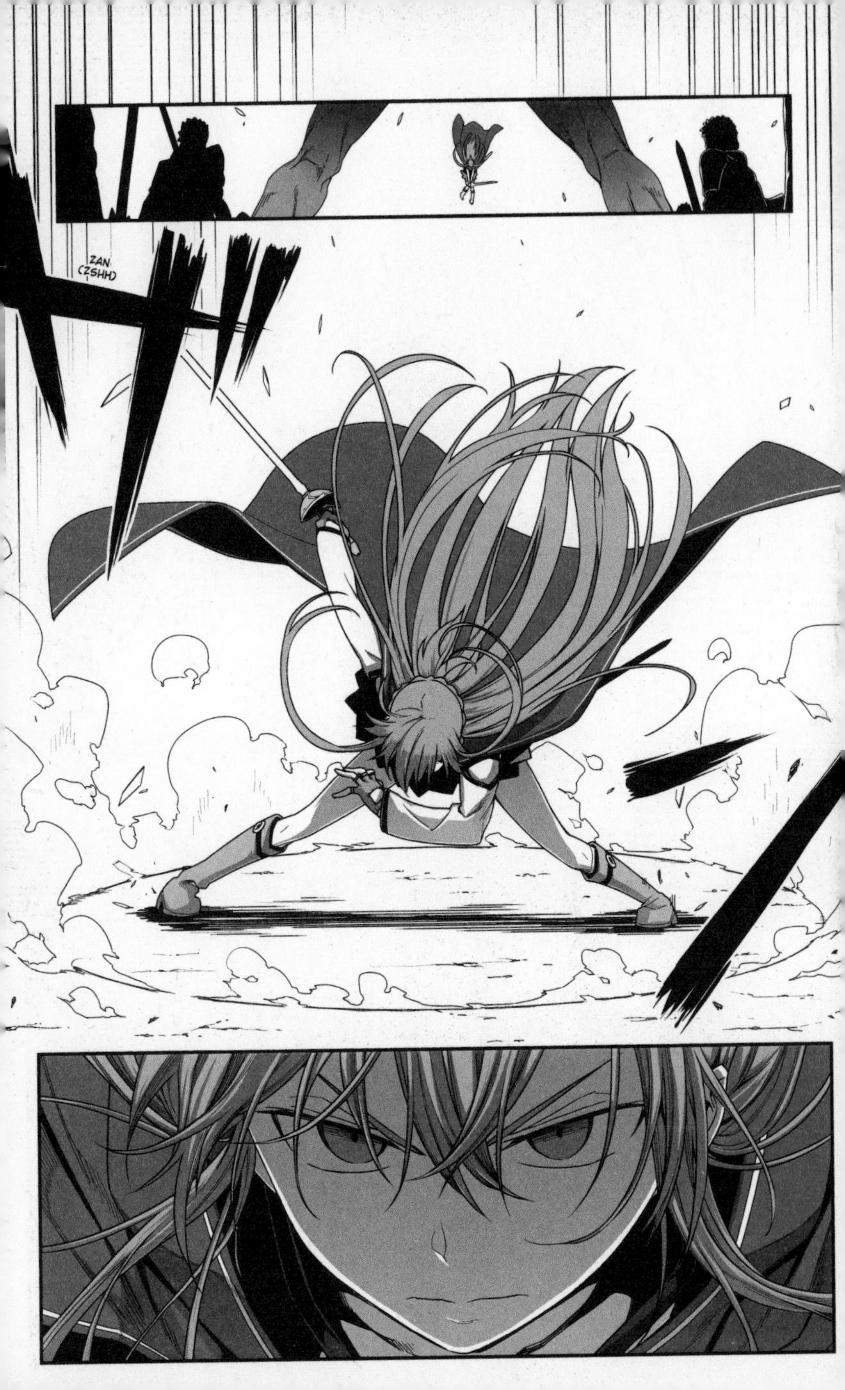
ZAN
(ZSHH)

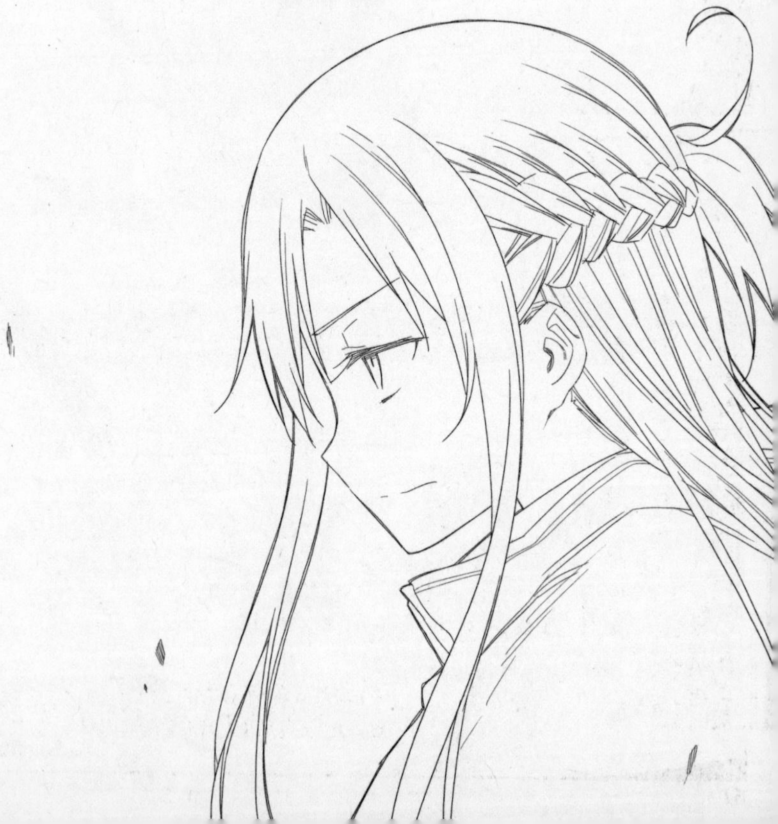

#018: Don't Know

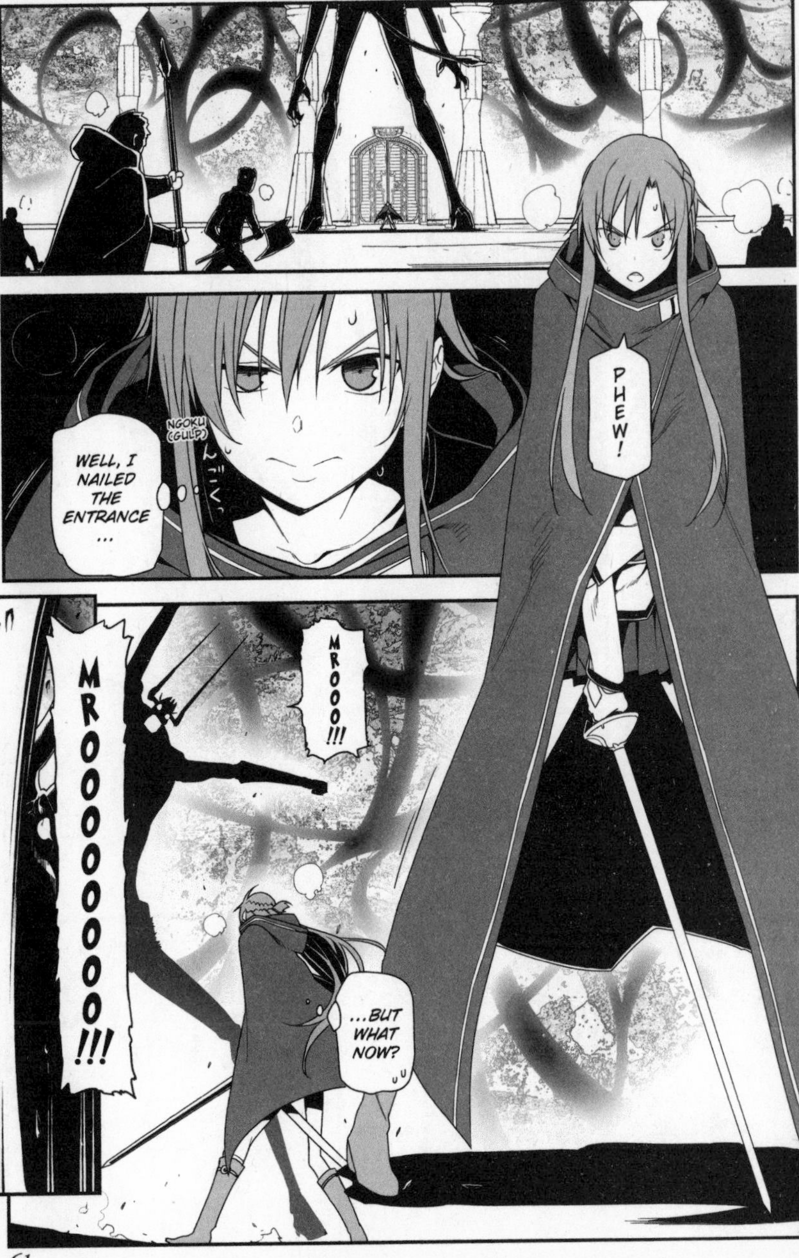
PHEW!
NGOKU (GULP)
WELL, I NAILED THE ENTRANCE...
MROOO!!!
MROOOOOOOOO!!!
...BUT WHAT NOW?

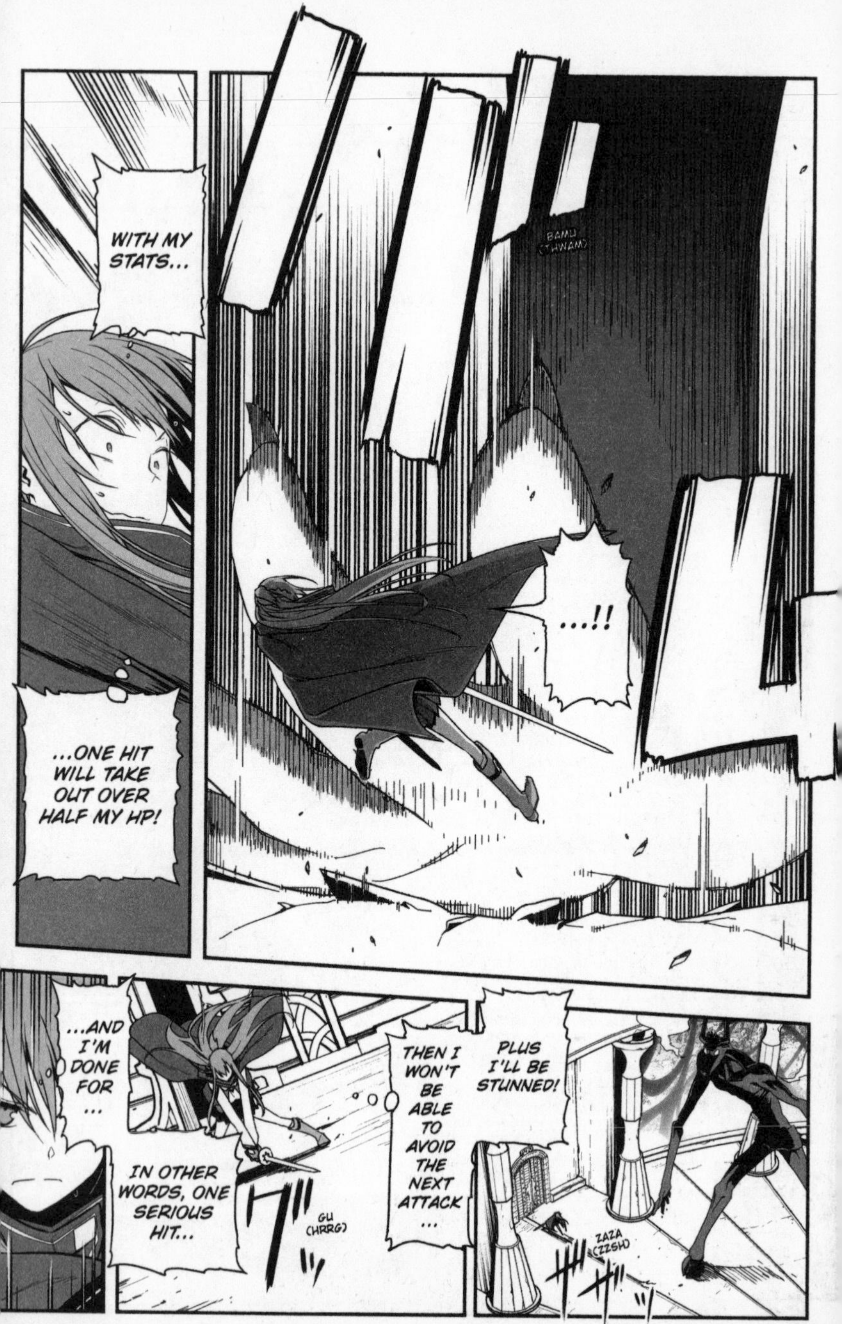
BAMU
(THWAM)
...!!
WITH MY STATS...
...ONE HIT WILL TAKE OUT OVER HALF MY HP!
PLUS I'LL BE STUNNED!
THEN I WON'T BE ABLE TO AVOID THE NEXT ATTACK...
ZAZA
(CZZSH)
IN OTHER WORDS, ONE SERIOUS HIT...
...AND I'M DONE FOR...
GU
(HRRG)

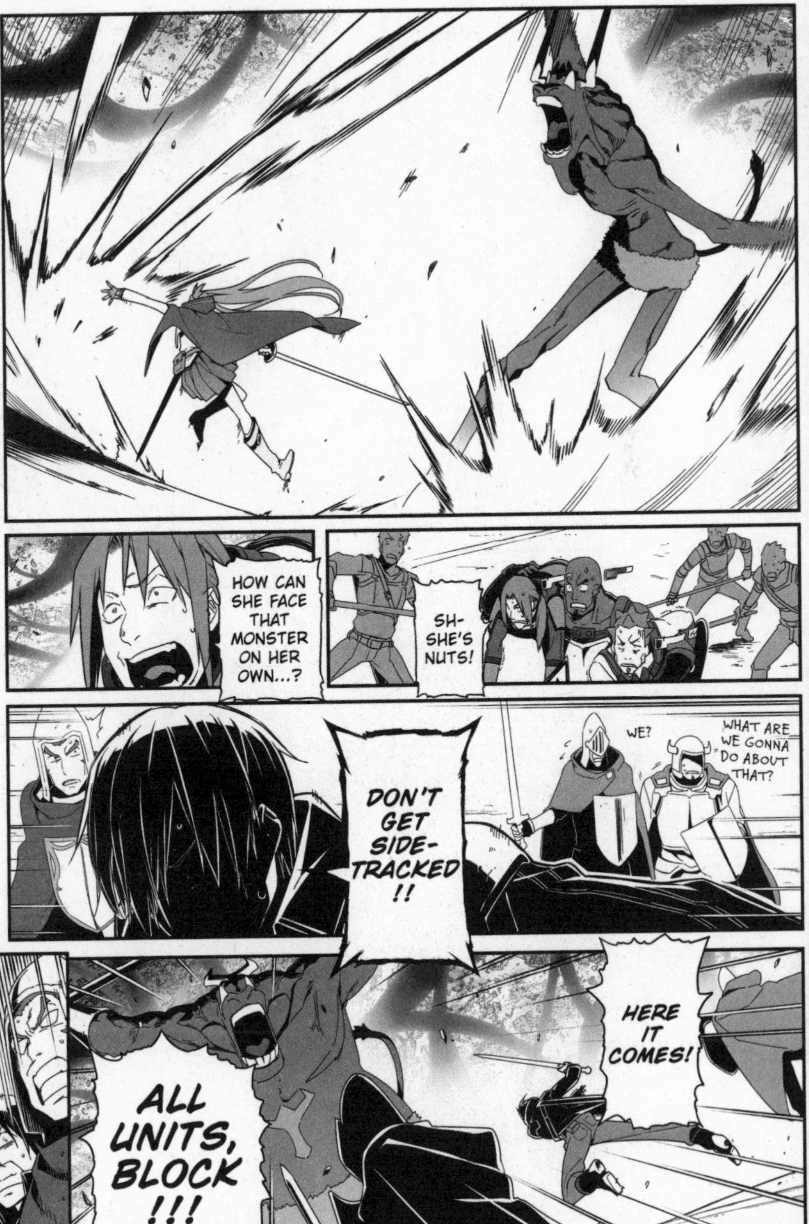
SH- SHE'S NUTS!
HOW CAN SHE FACE THAT MONSTER ON HER OWN...?
WHAT ARE WE GONNA DO ABOUT THAT?
WE?
DON'T GET SIDE-TRACKED!!
HERE IT COMES!
ALL UNITS, BLOCK!!!

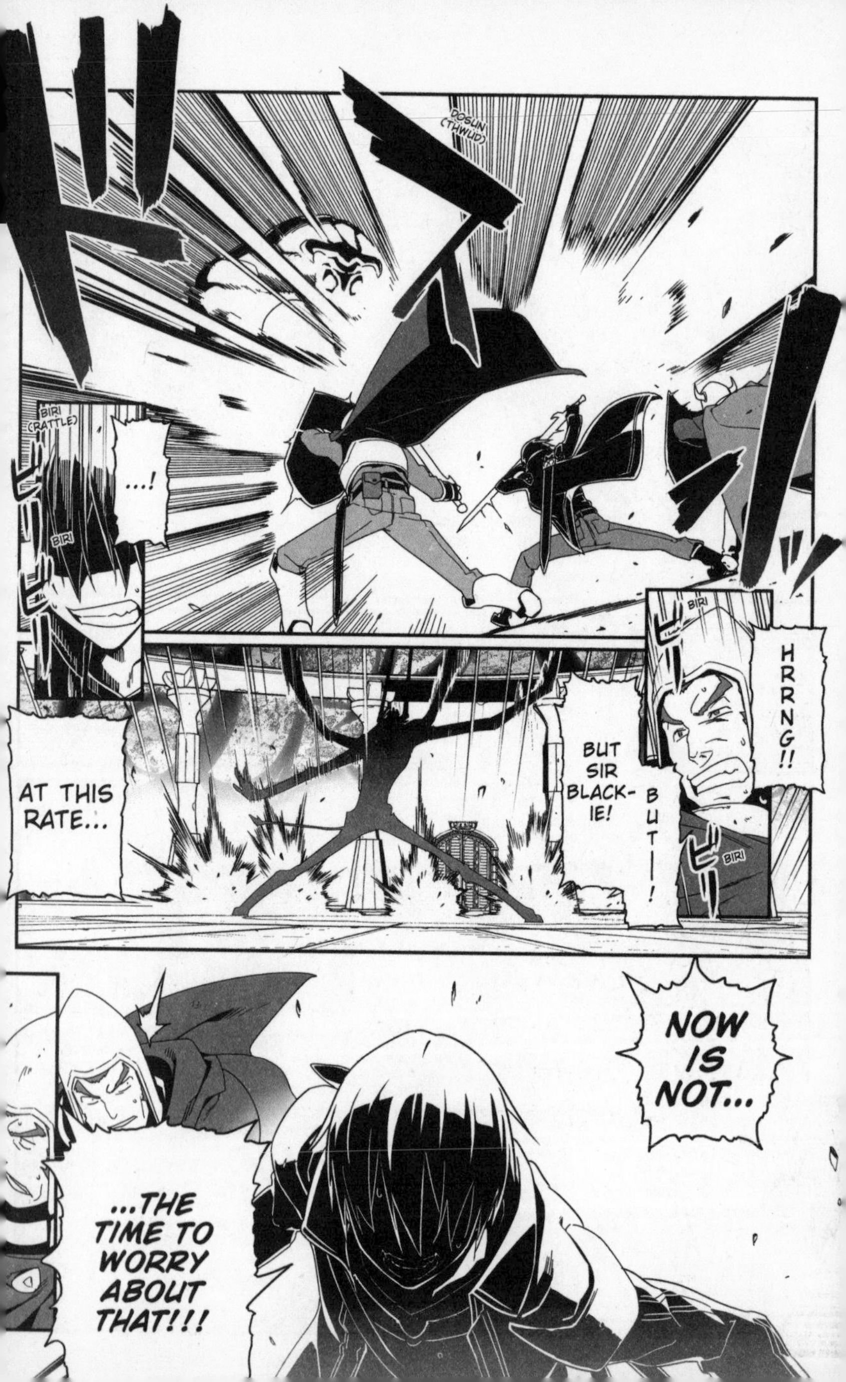
DOSUN (THWUD)
BIRI
HRRNG!!
BIRI
BUT SIR BLACKIE!
BUT——!
AT THIS RATE...
BIRI (RATTLE)
...!
BIRI
NOW IS NOT...
...THE TIME TO WORRY ABOUT THAT!!!

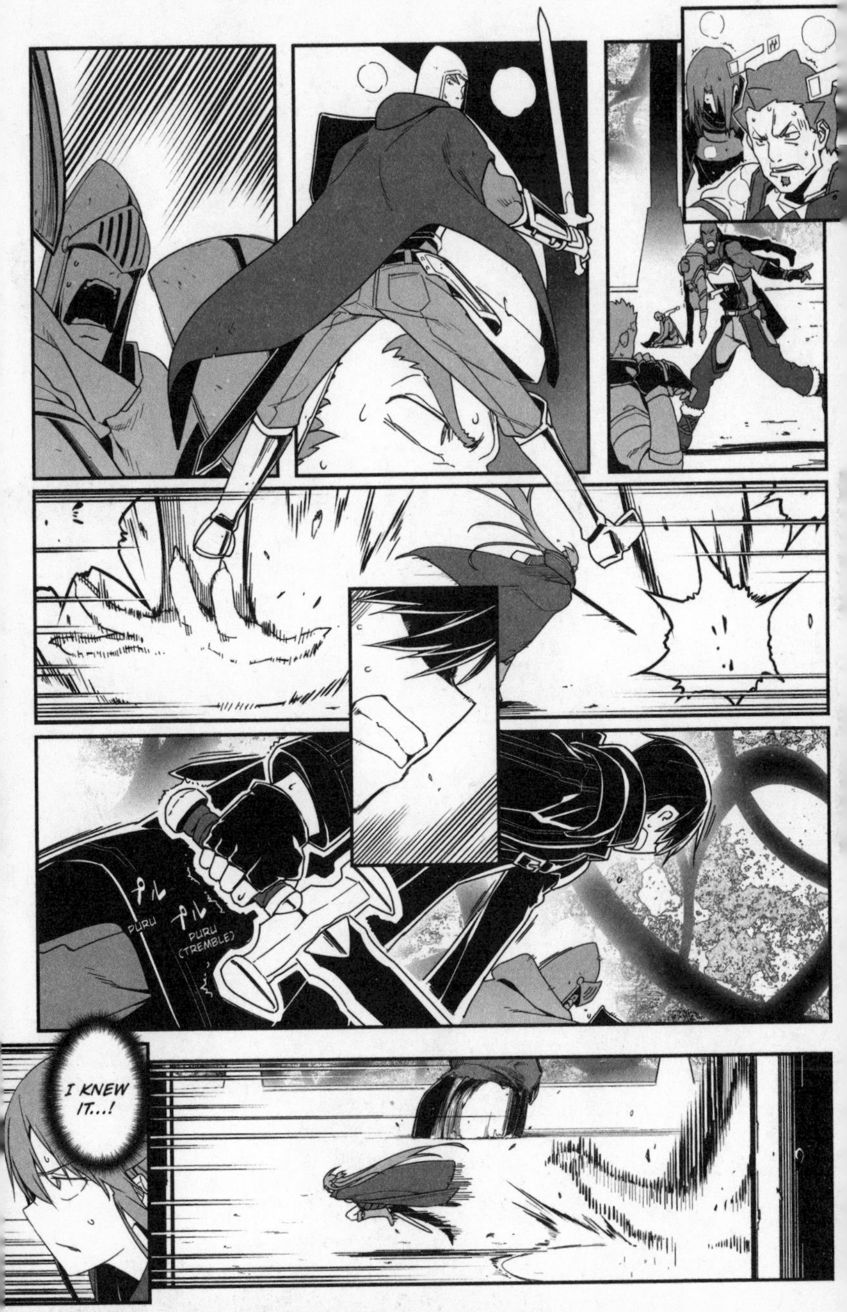
プル
PURU
プル
PURU
(TREMBLE)
I KNEW IT...!

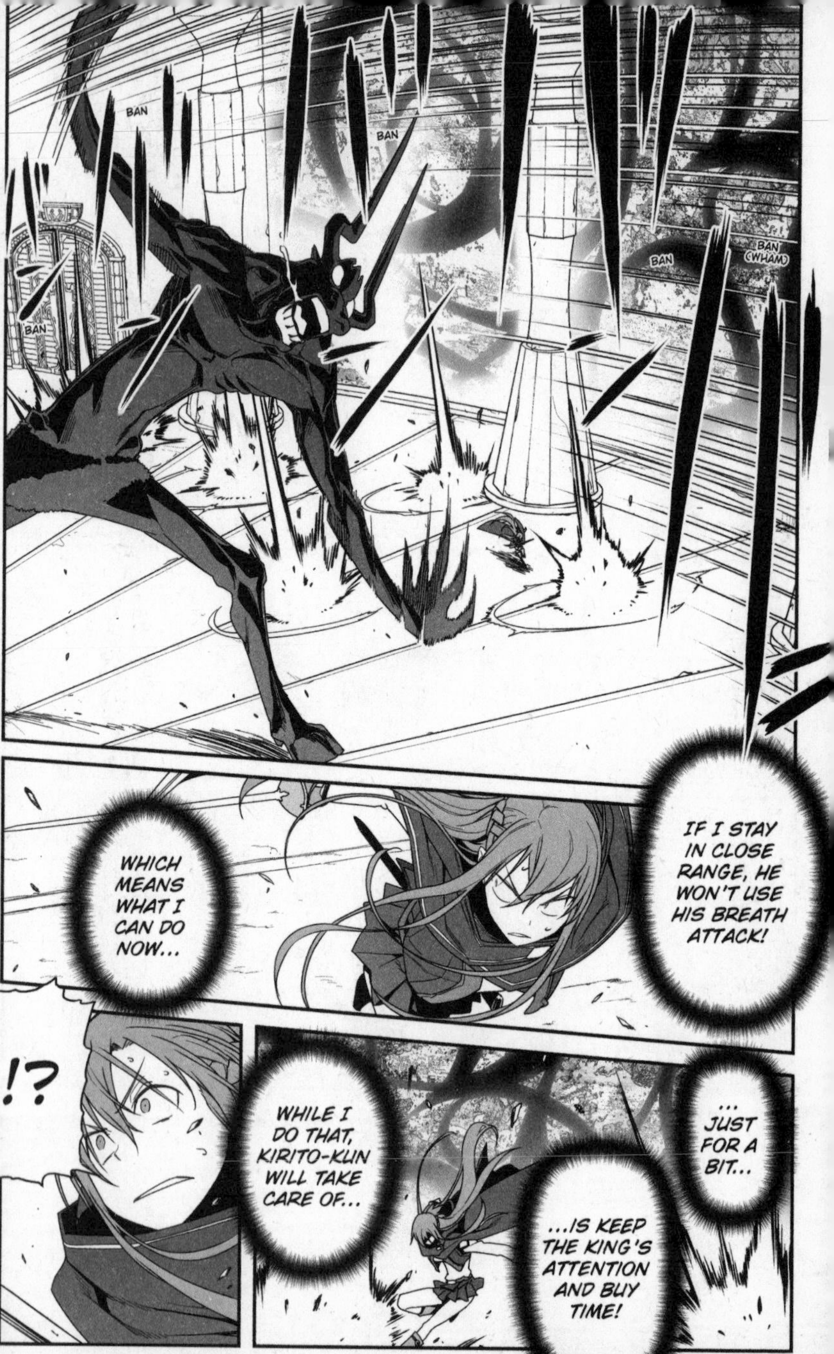
BAN
(WHAM)
BAN
BAN
BAN
BAN
IF I STAY IN CLOSE RANGE, HE WON'T USE HIS BREATH ATTACK!
WHICH MEANS WHAT I CAN DO NOW...
...IS KEEP THE KING'S ATTENTION AND BUY TIME!
...JUST FOR A BIT...
WHILE I DO THAT, KIRITO-KUN WILL TAKE CARE OF...
!?

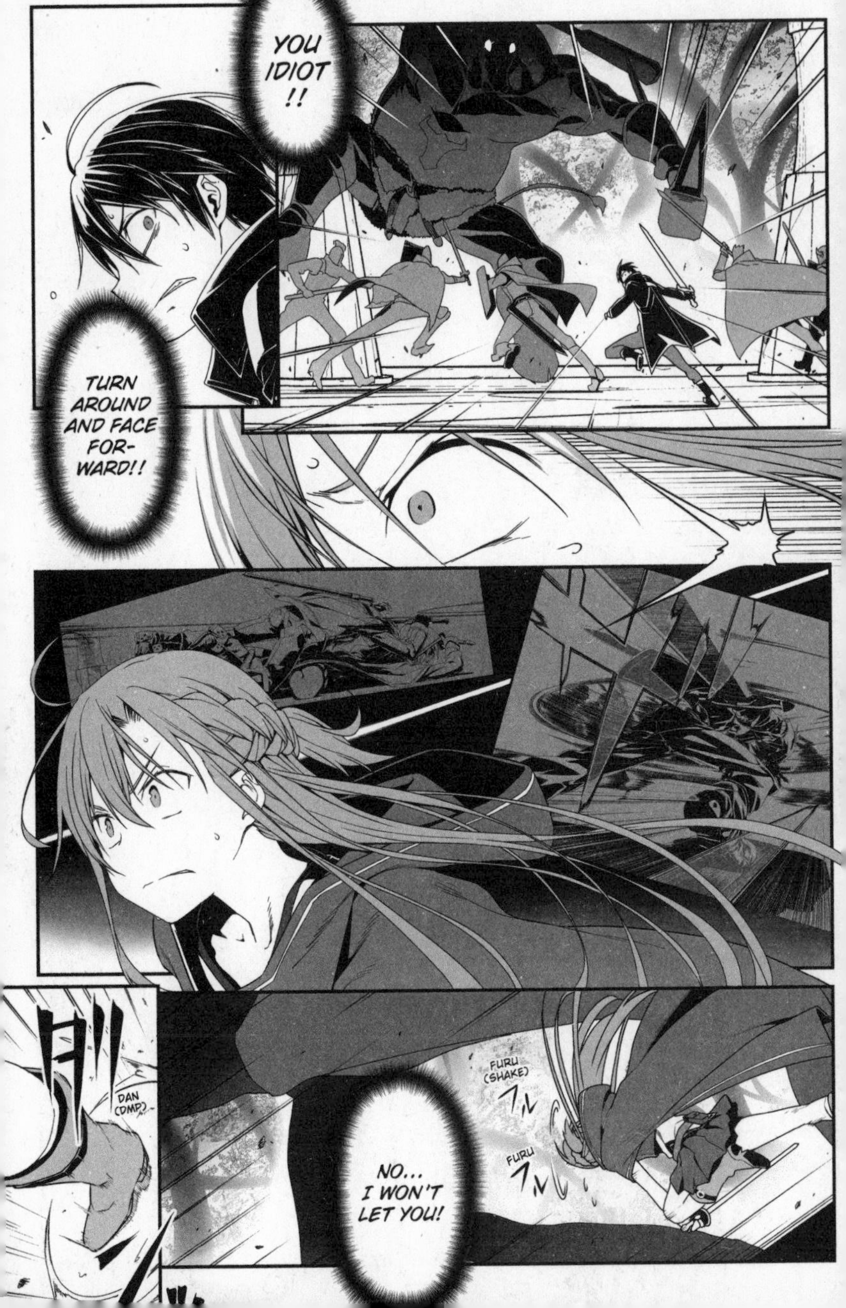
YOU IDIOT!!
TURN AROUND AND FACE FOR-WARD!!
FURU (SHAKE)
FURU
NO... I WON'T LET YOU!
DAN (DMP)

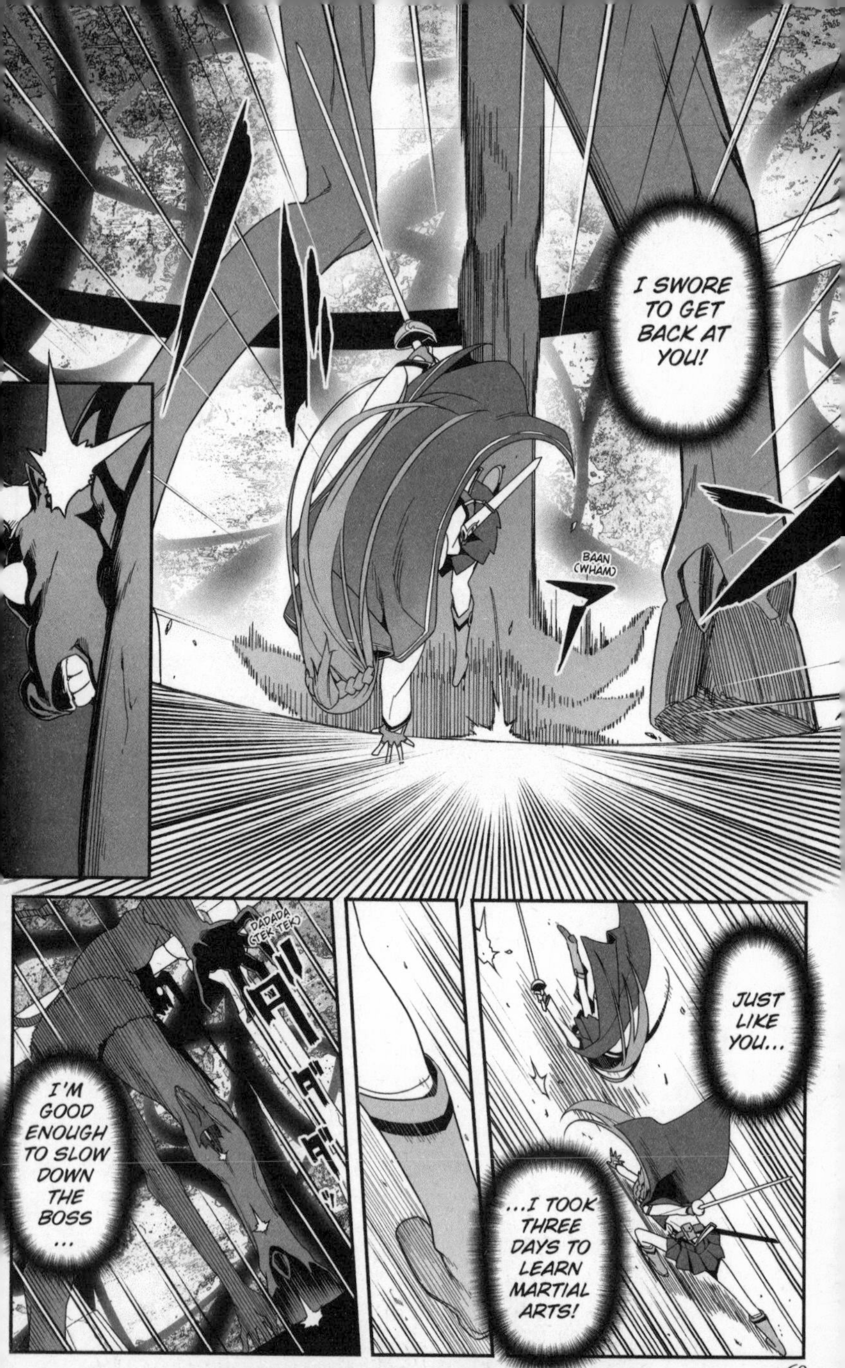
I SWORE TO GET BACK AT YOU!
BAAN (WHAM)
JUST LIKE YOU...
...I TOOK THREE DAYS TO LEARN MARTIAL ARTS!
DADADA (TEK TEK)
I'M GOOD ENOUGH TO SLOW DOWN THE BOSS...

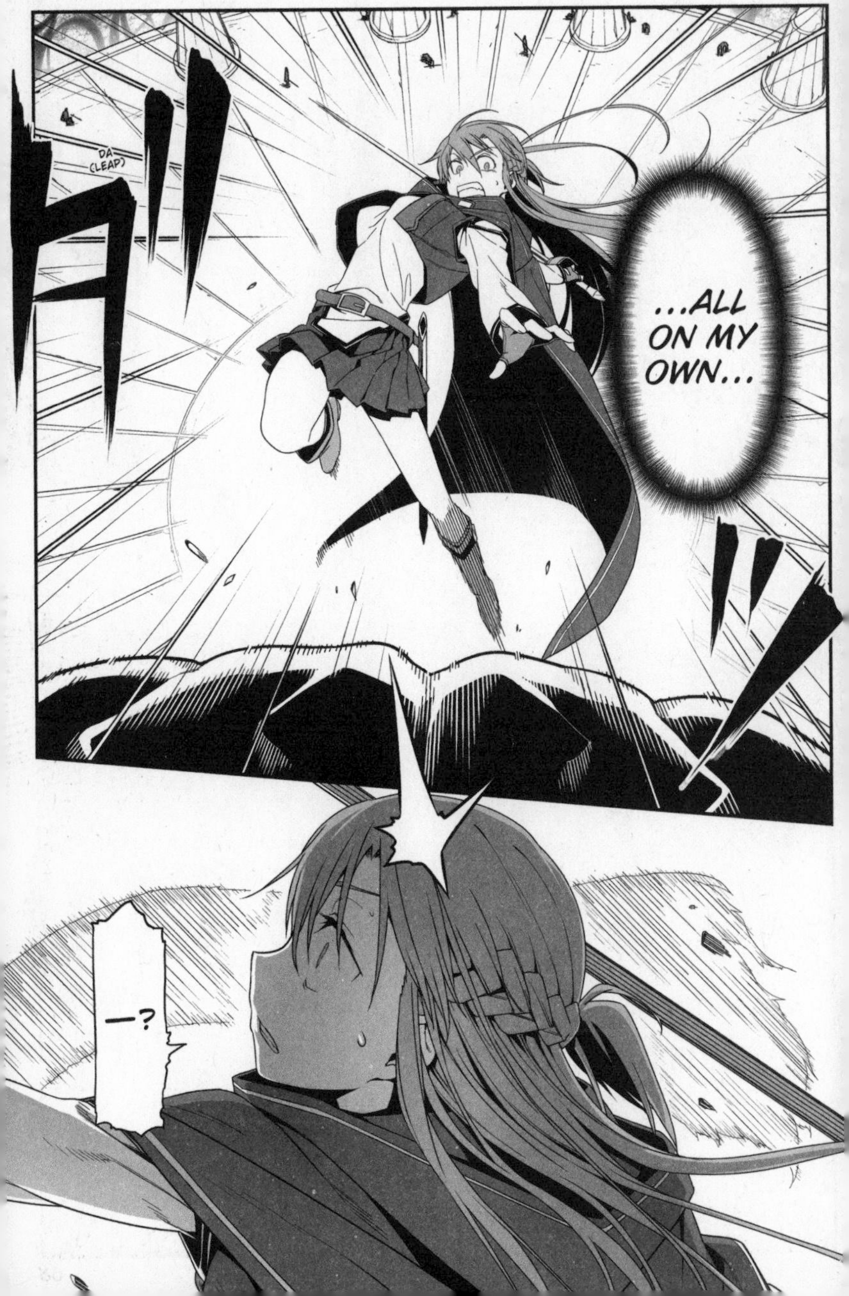
ダッ
DA (LEAP)
...ALL ON MY OWN...
—?

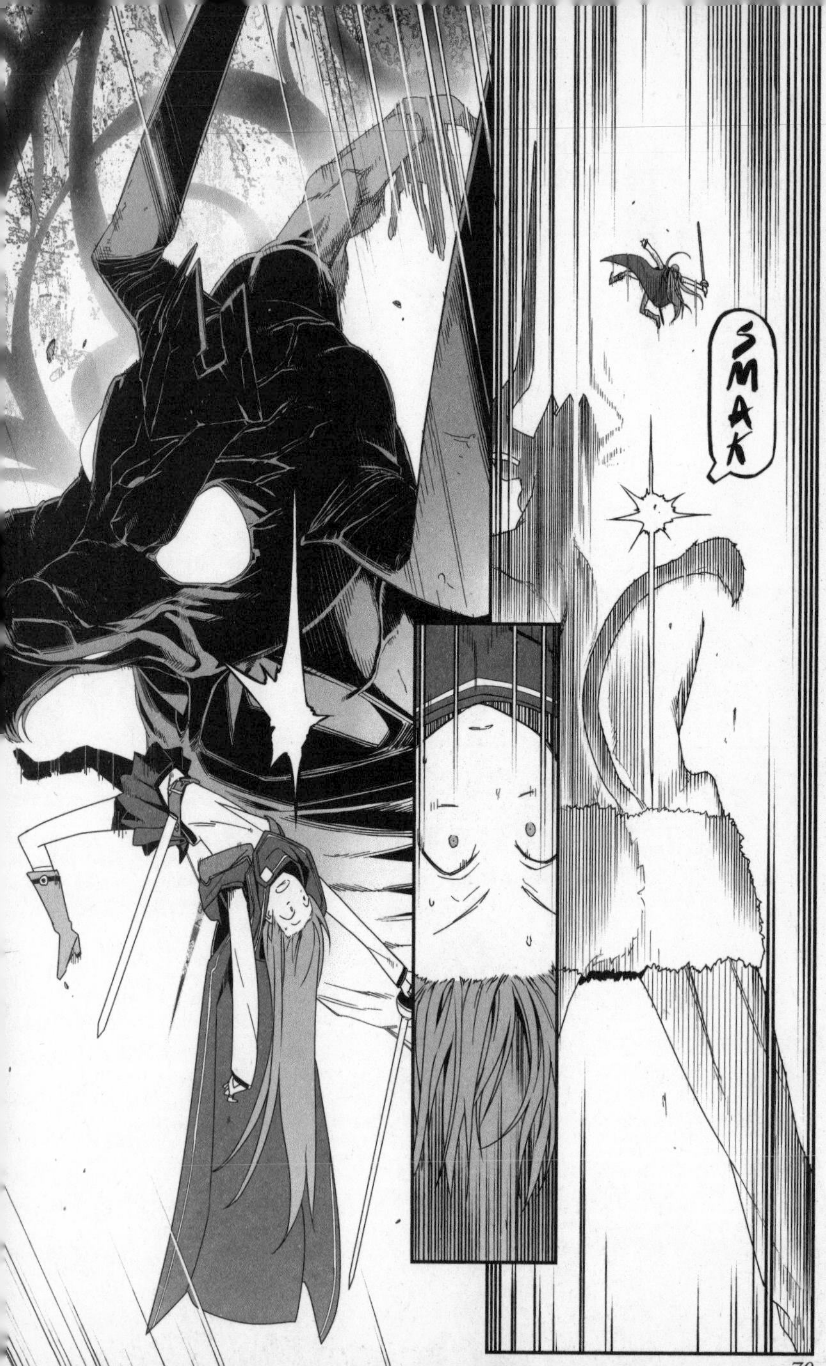
SMAK

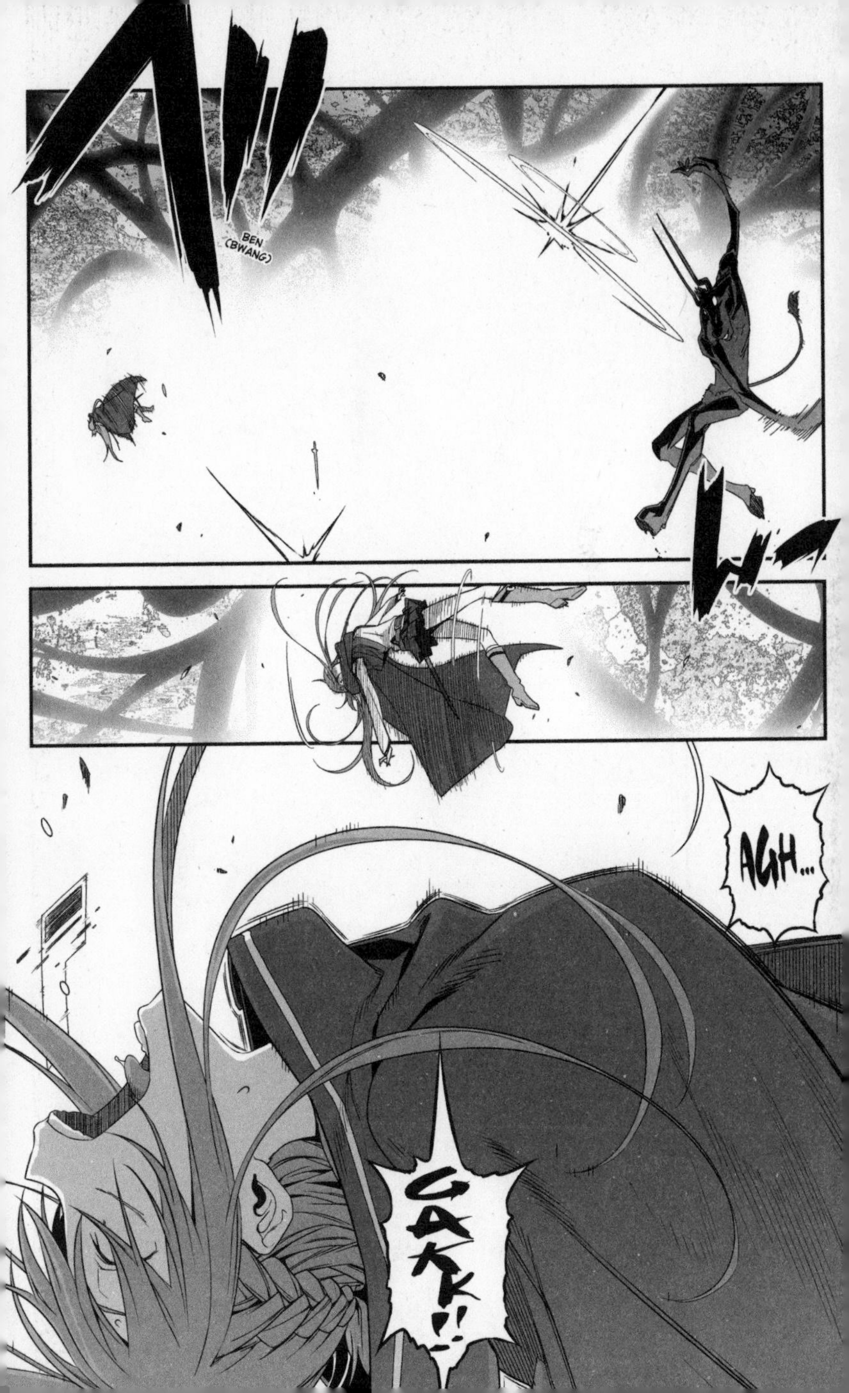
BEN
(BWANG)
AGH...
GAKK!!

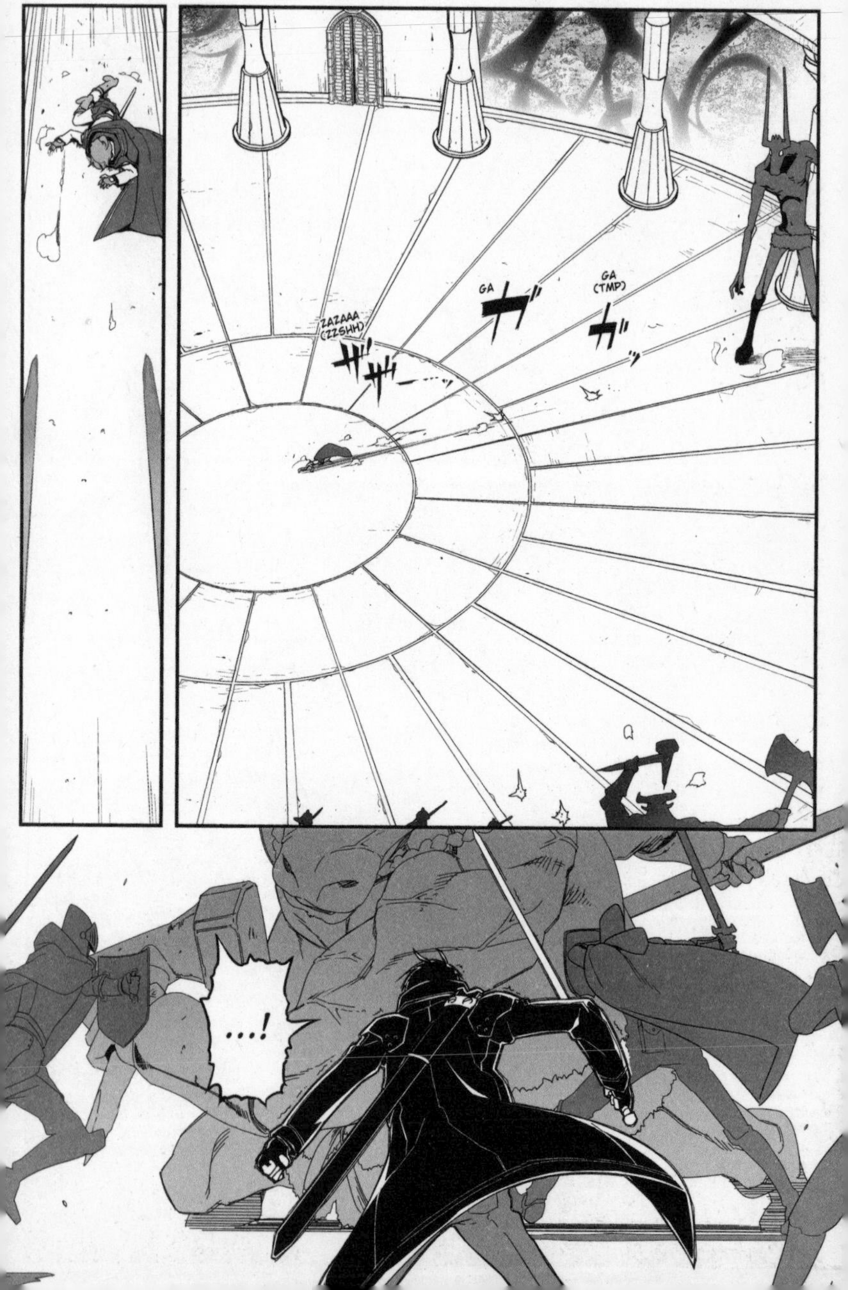
GA (TMP)
GA
ZAZAAA (ZZSHH)
...!

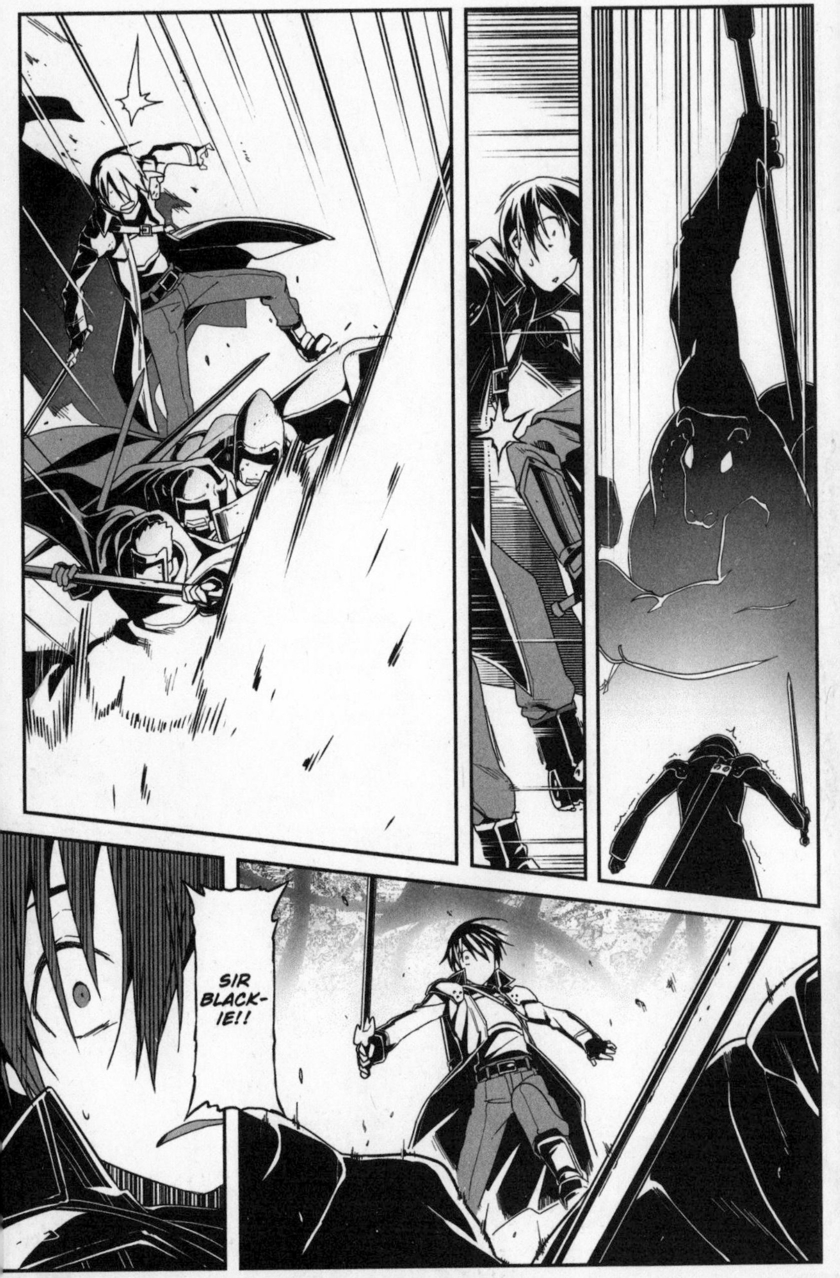
SIR BLACK-IE!!

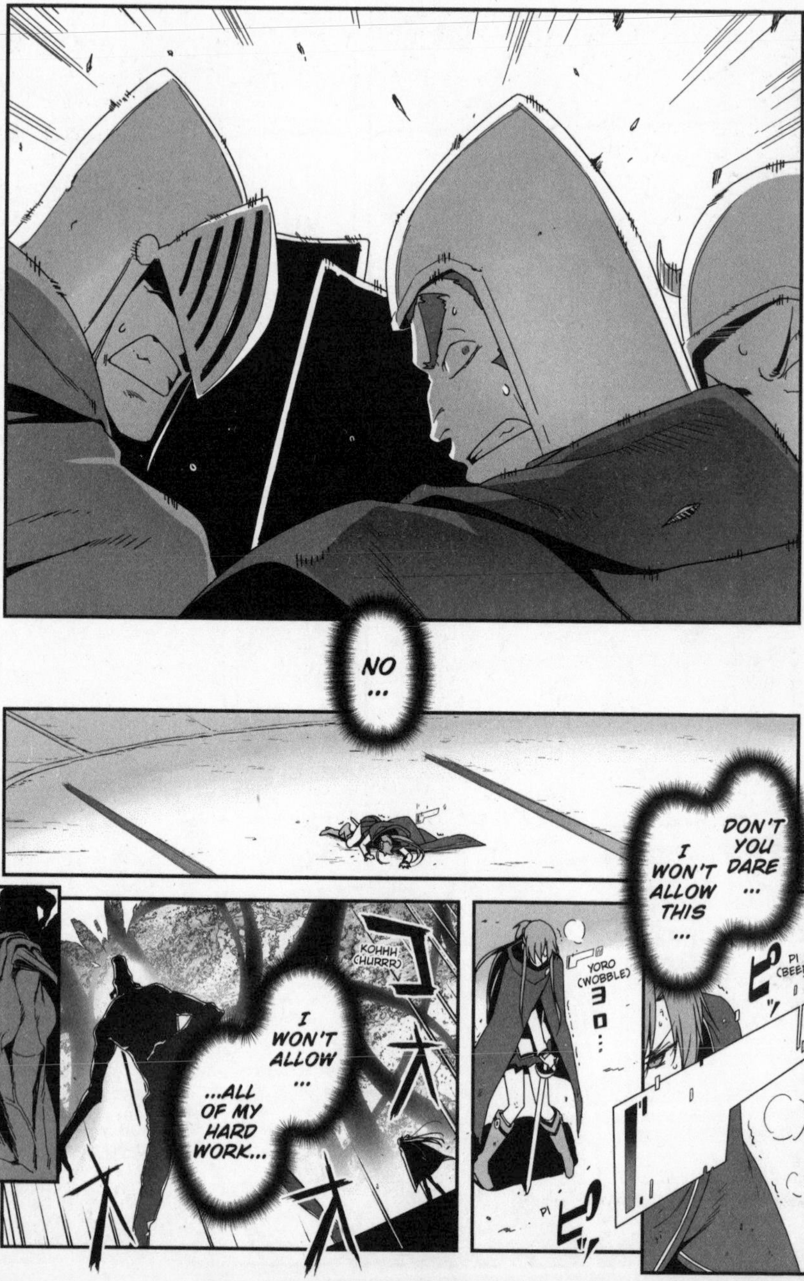
NO ...
DON'T YOU DARE ...
I WON'T ALLOW THIS ...
PI (BEEP)
YORO (WOBBLE)
PI
KOHHH (HURRR)
I WON'T ALLOW ...
...ALL OF MY HARD WORK...

...TO
GO...

...TO
WASTE
!!

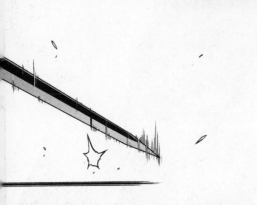

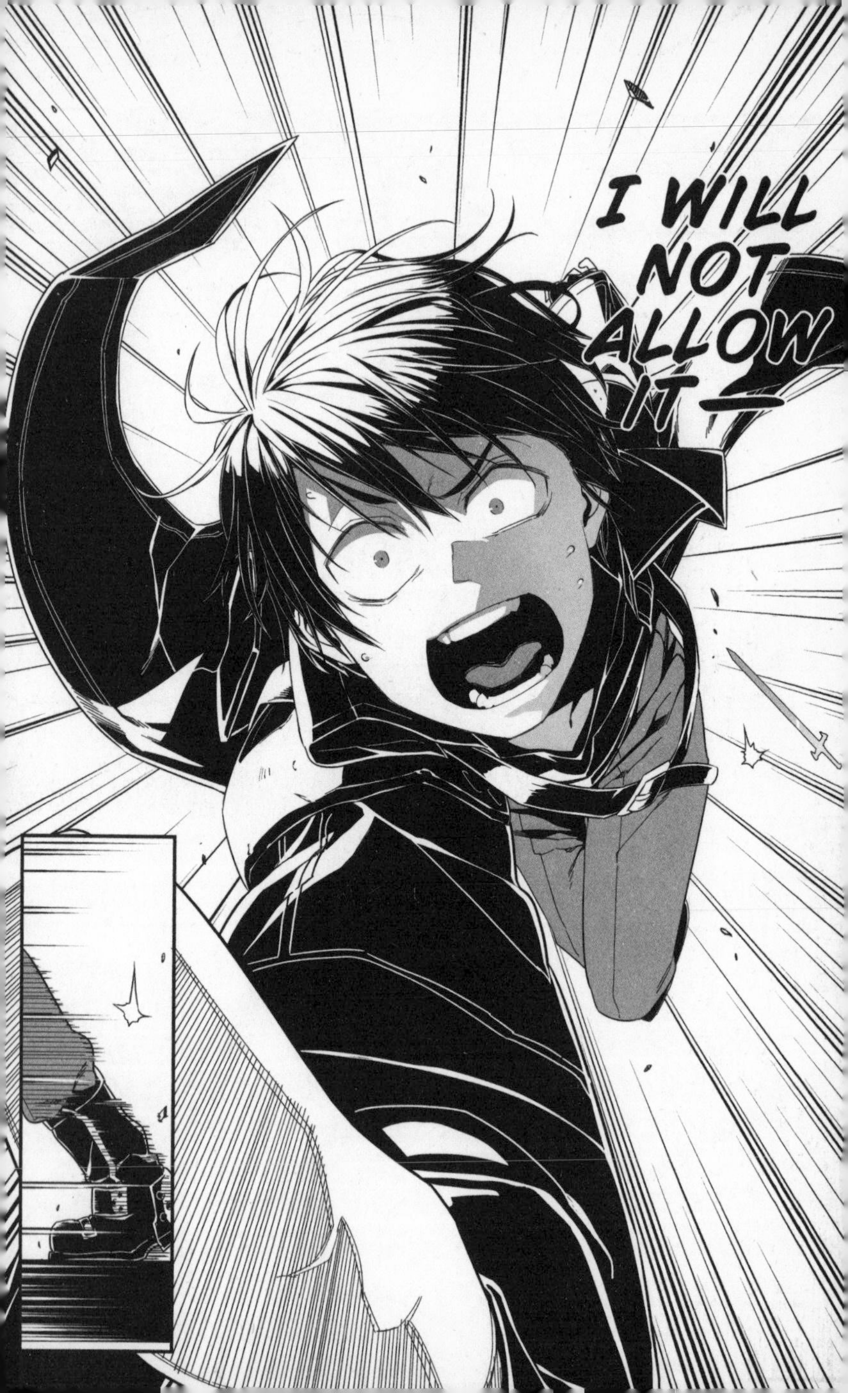
I WILL NOT ALLOW IT—

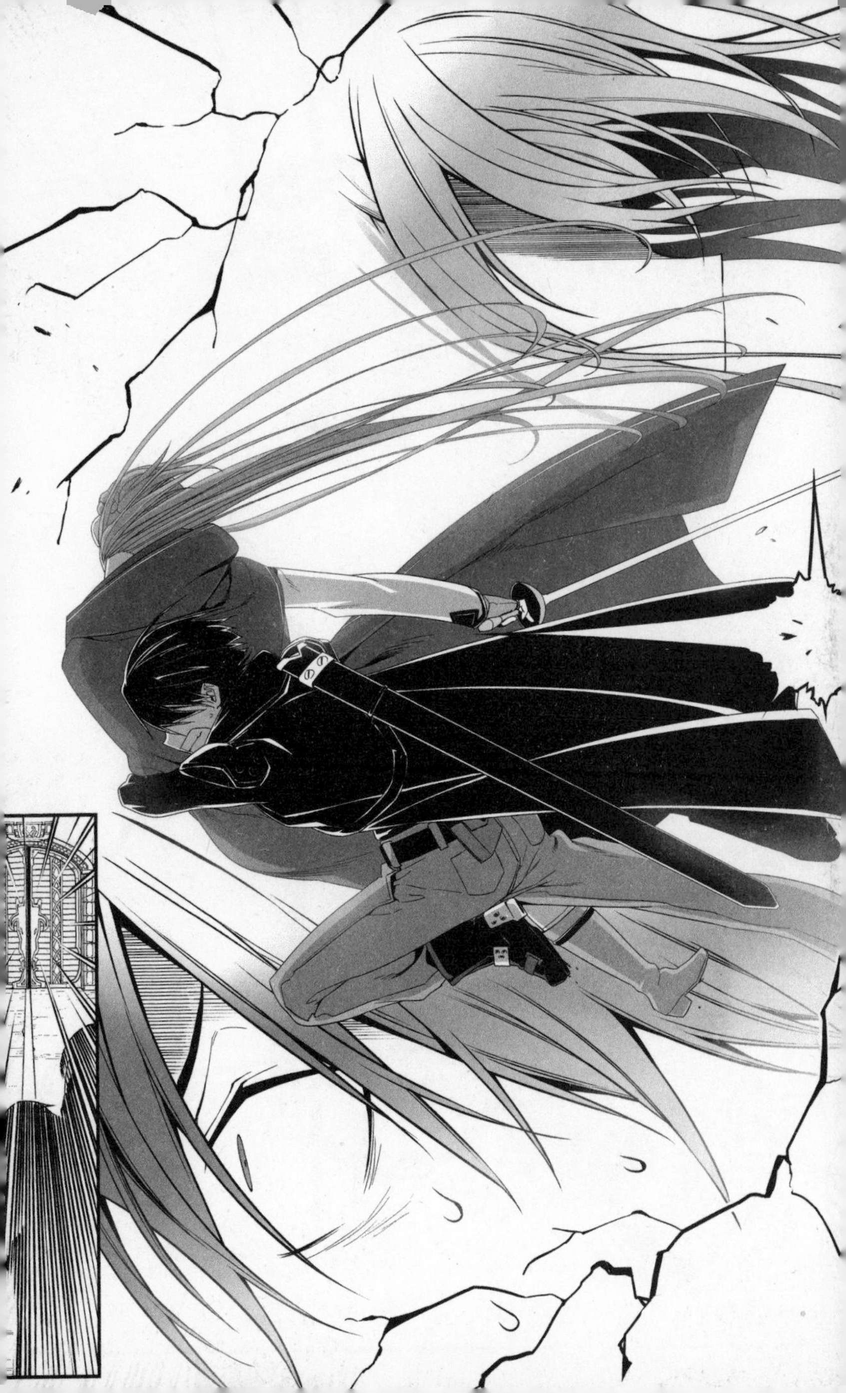

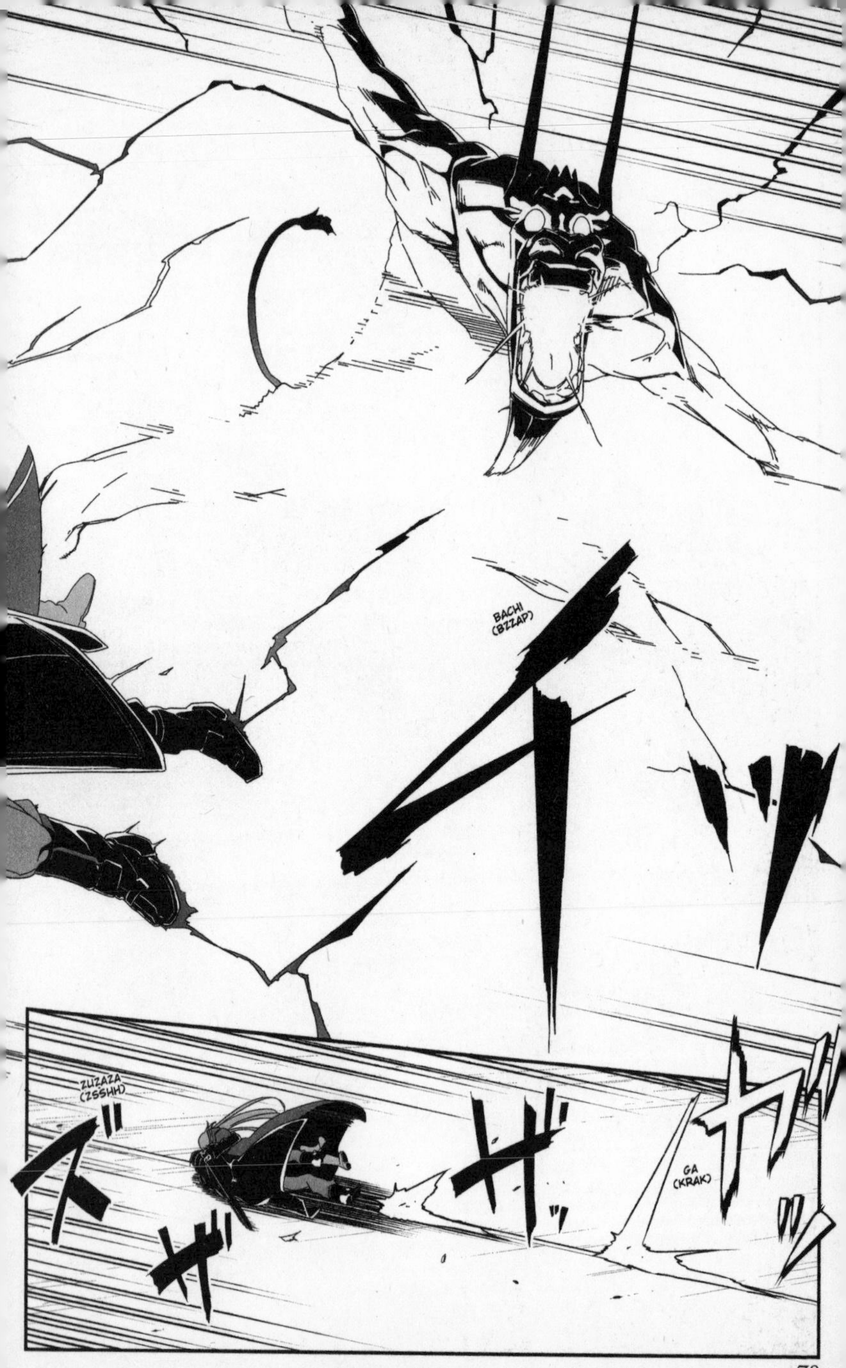
BACHI (BZZAP)
GA (KRAK)
ZUZAZA (ZSSHH)

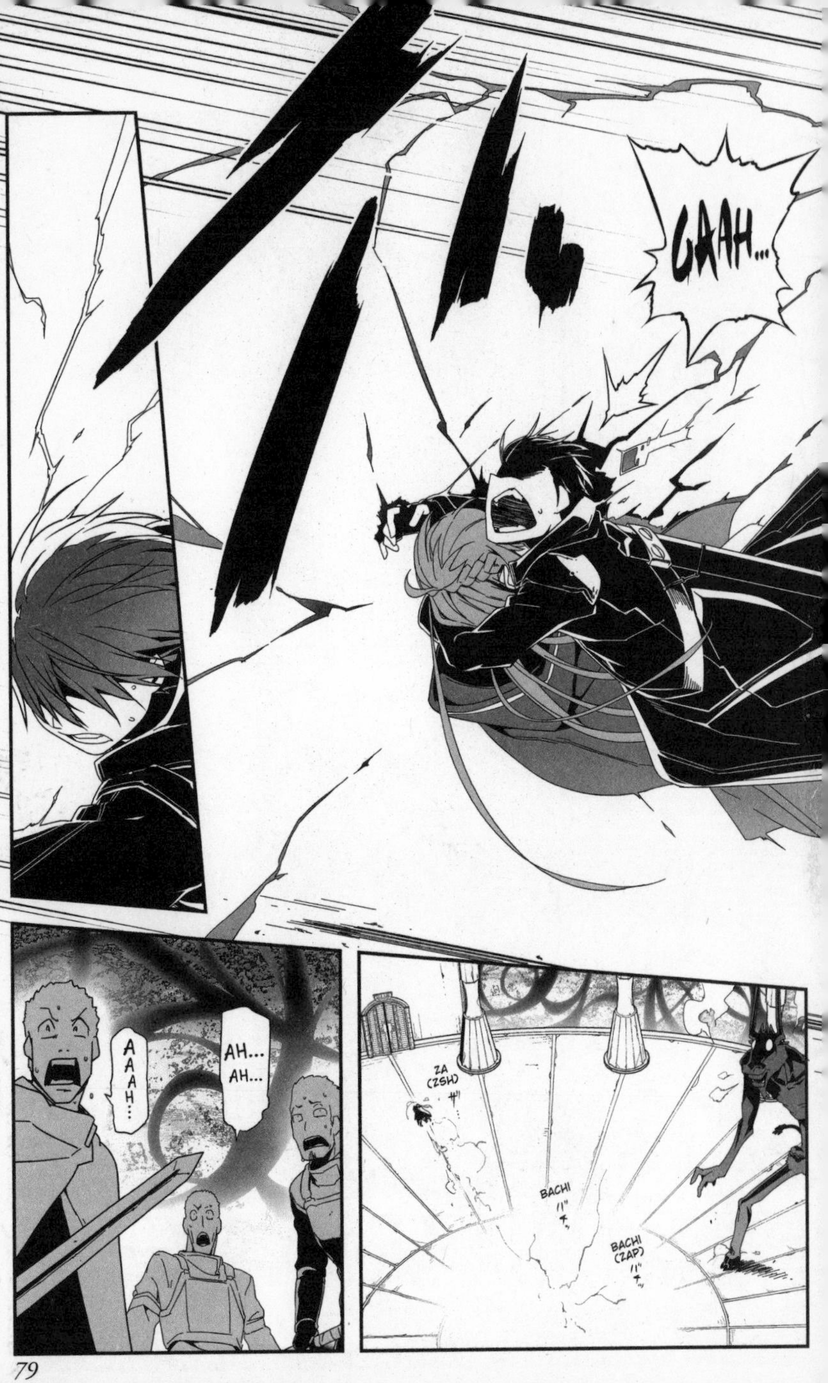
GAAH...
ZA (ZSH)
BACHI
BACHI (ZAP)
AH... AH...
AAAH...

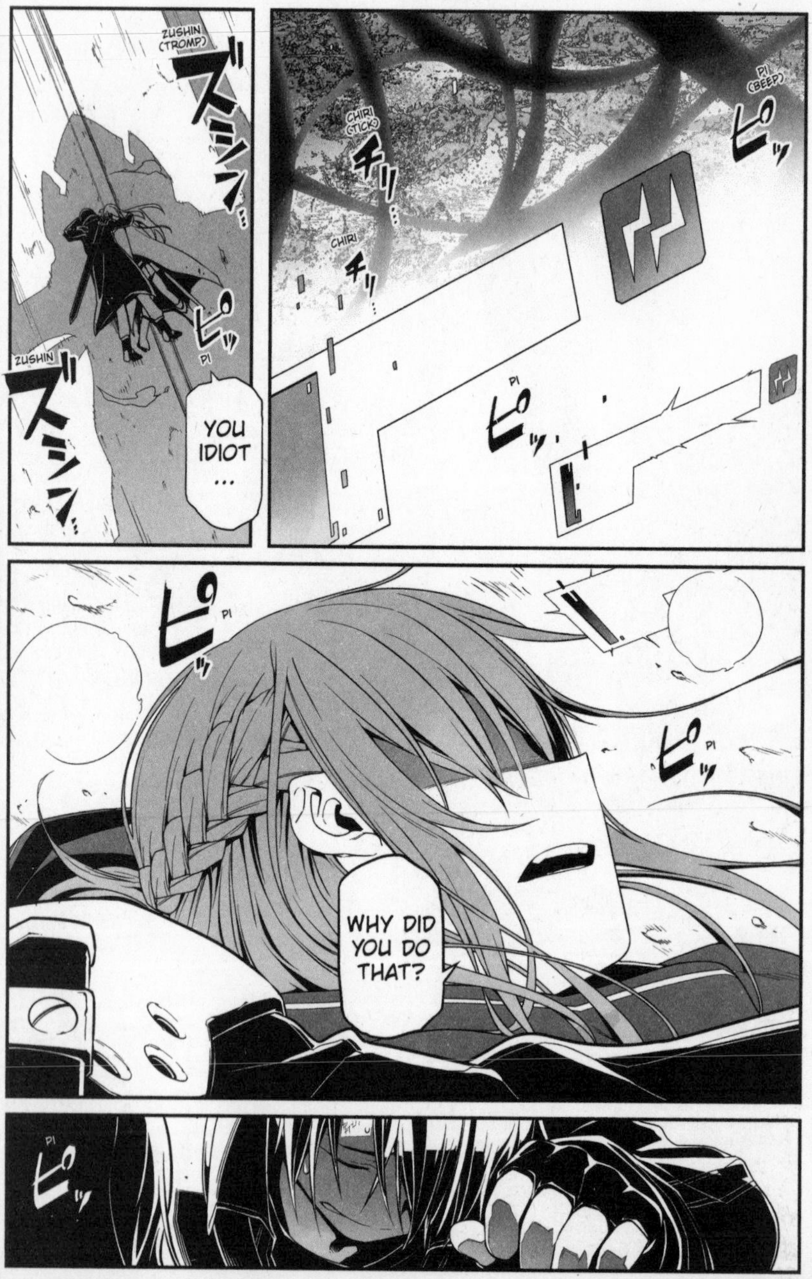
PI (BEEP)
CHIRI (TICK)
CHIRI
PI
ZUSHIN (TROMP)
PI
YOU IDIOT ...
ZUSHIN
PI
PI
WHY DID YOU DO THAT?
PI

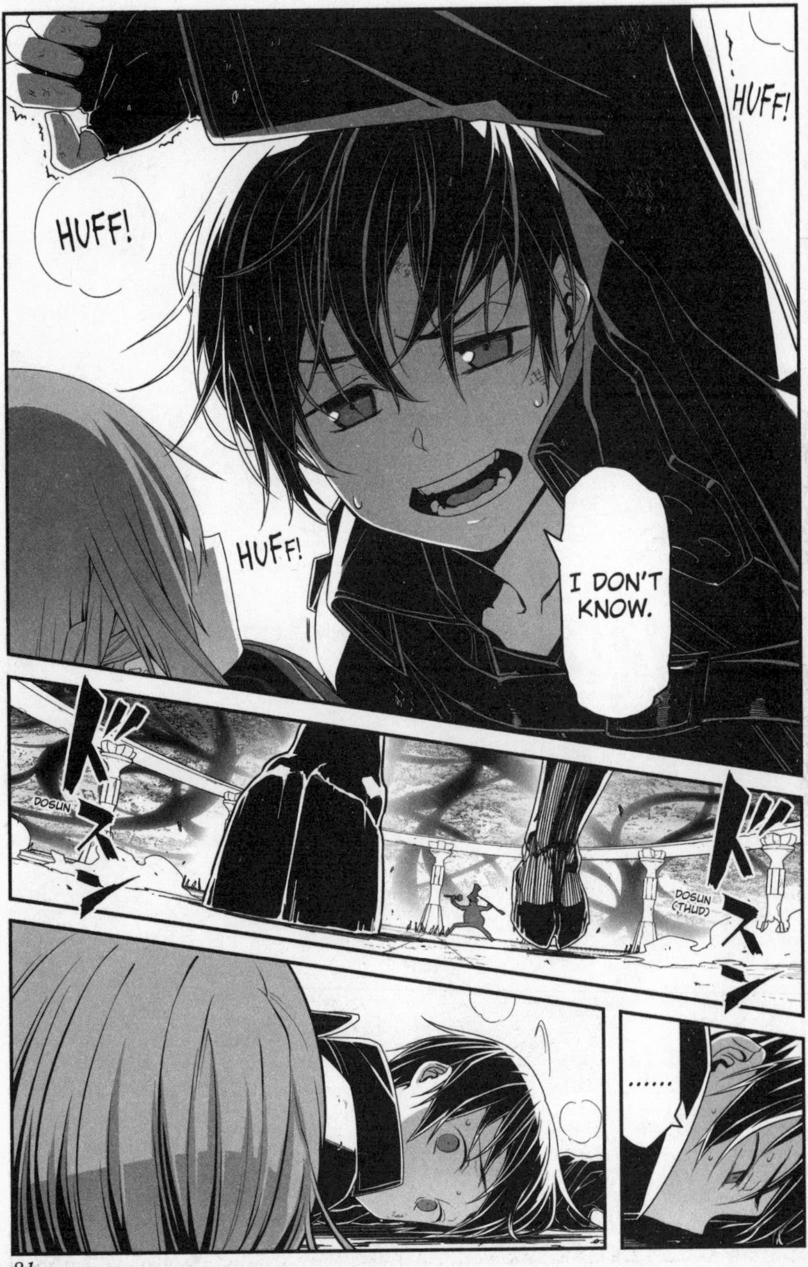
HUFF!
HUFF!
I DON'T KNOW.
HUFF!
ドスン
DOSUN (THUD)
ドスン
DOSUN
......

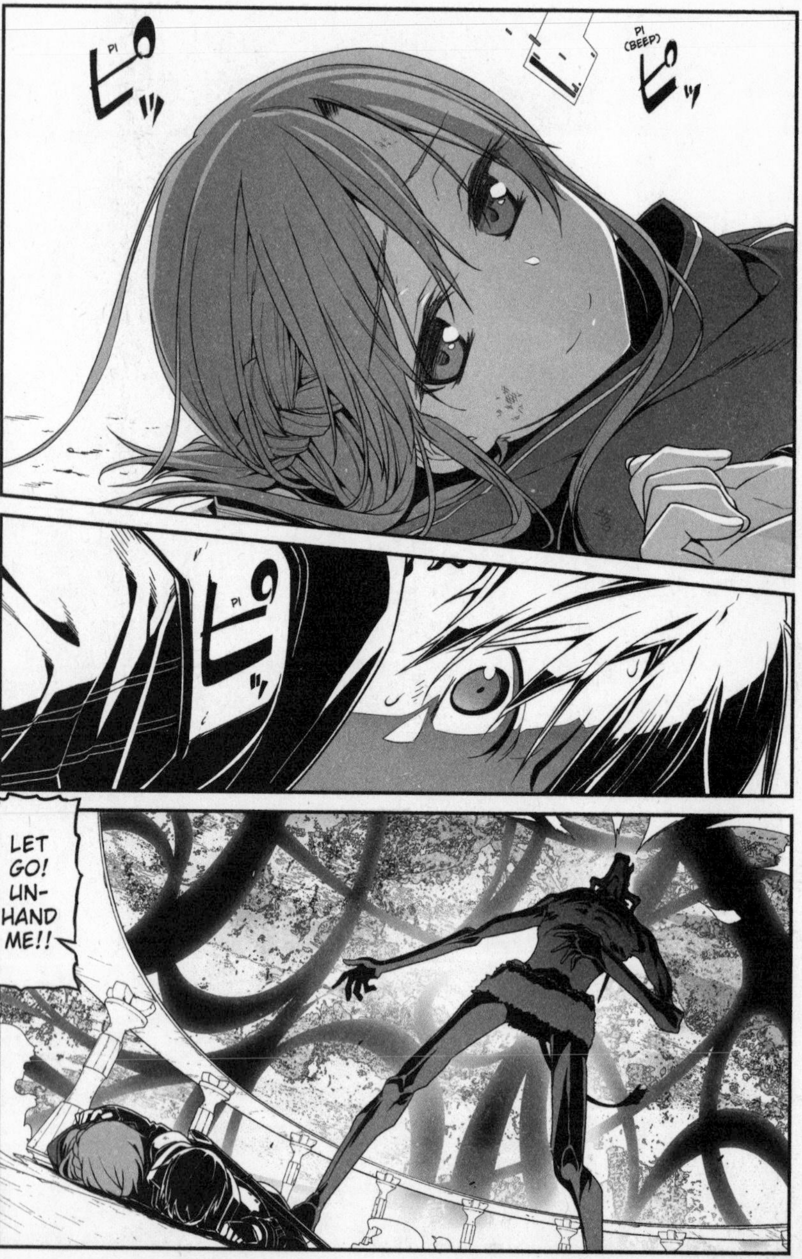
PI (BEEP)
ピッ
PI
ピッ
PI
ピッ
LET GO! UN-HAND ME!!

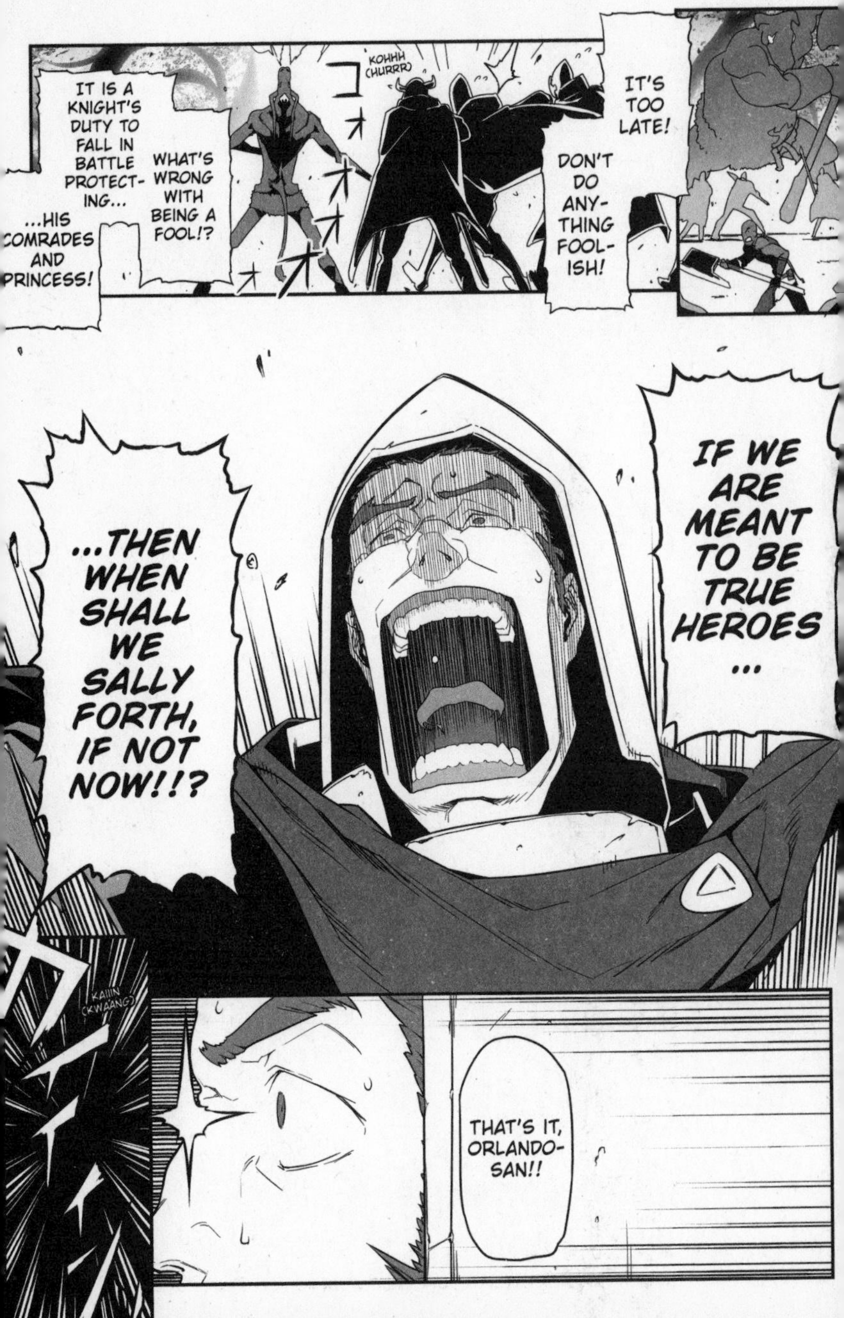
IT'S TOO LATE!
DON'T DO ANYTHING FOOLISH!
KOHHH (CHURRR)
WHAT'S WRONG WITH BEING A FOOL!?
IT IS A KNIGHT'S DUTY TO FALL IN BATTLE PROTECTING...
...HIS COMRADES AND PRINCESS!
IF WE ARE MEANT TO BE TRUE HEROES...
...THEN WHEN SHALL WE SALLY FORTH, IF NOT NOW!!?
THAT'S IT, ORLANDO-SAN!!
KAIIIN (KWAANG)

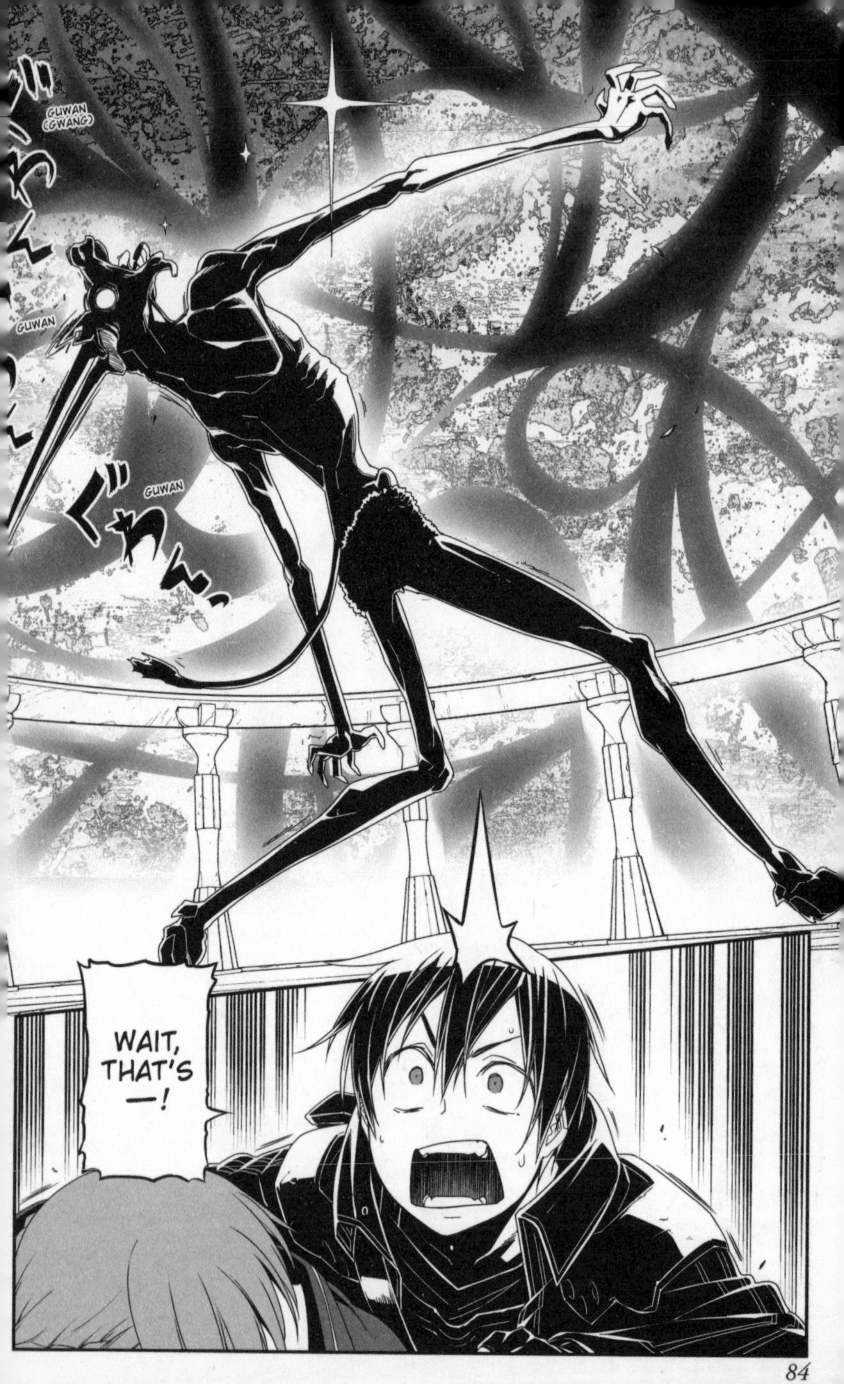
GUWAN (GWANG)
GUWAN
ぐわん
GUWAN
WAIT, THAT'S —!

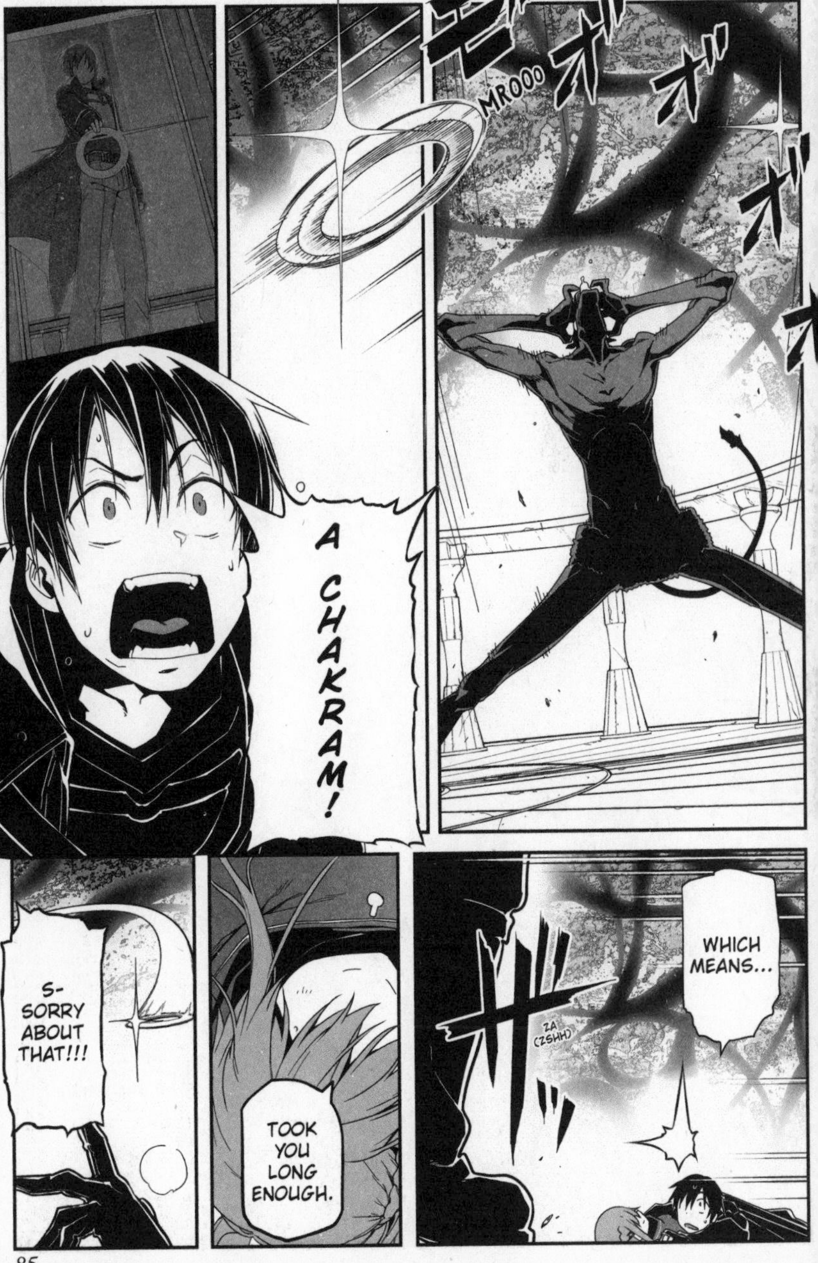
MROOO
A CHAKRAM!
WHICH MEANS...
ZA (ZSHH)
TOOK YOU LONG ENOUGH.
S-SORRY ABOUT THAT!!!

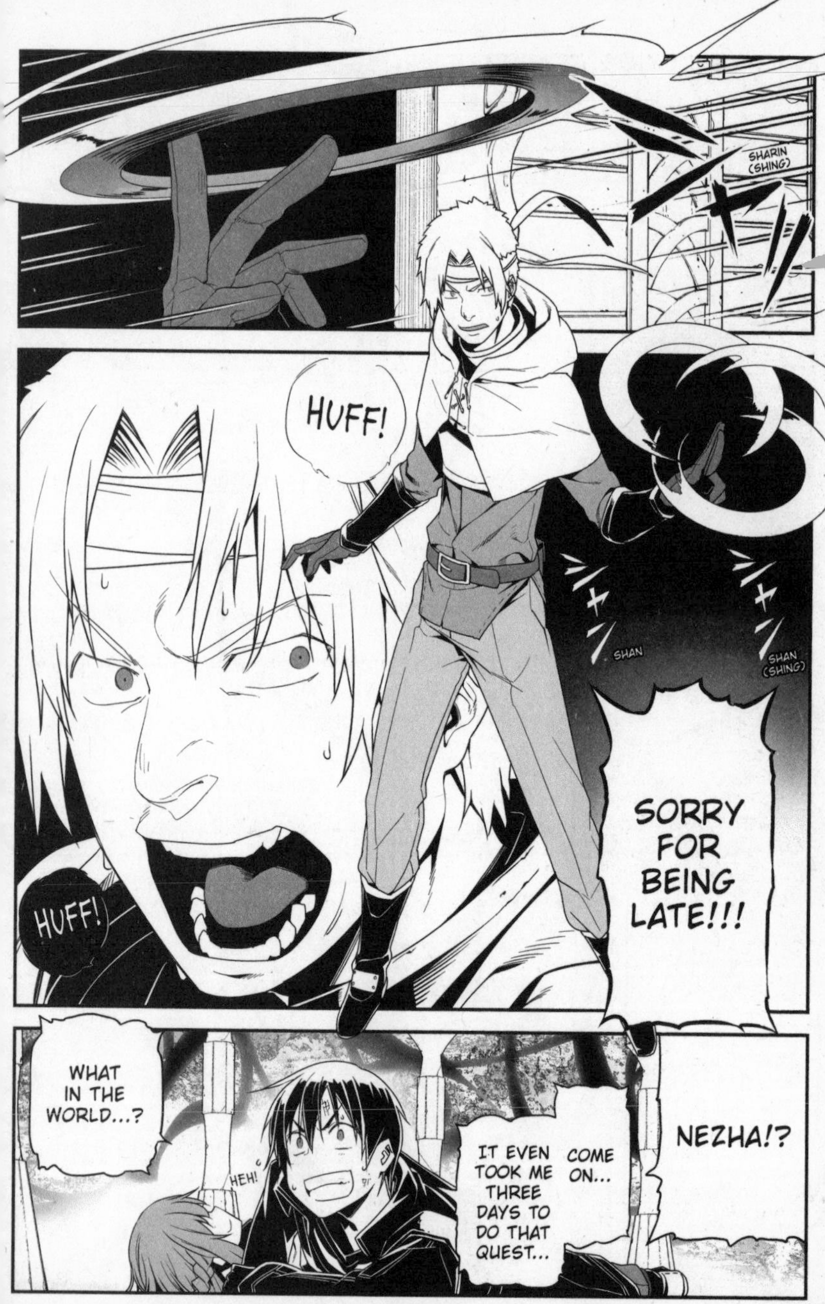
SHARIN (SHING)
SHAN (SHING)
SHAN
HUFF!
SORRY FOR BEING LATE!!!
HUFF!
NEZHA!?
COME ON...
IT EVEN TOOK ME THREE DAYS TO DO THAT QUEST...
HEH!
WHAT IN THE WORLD...?

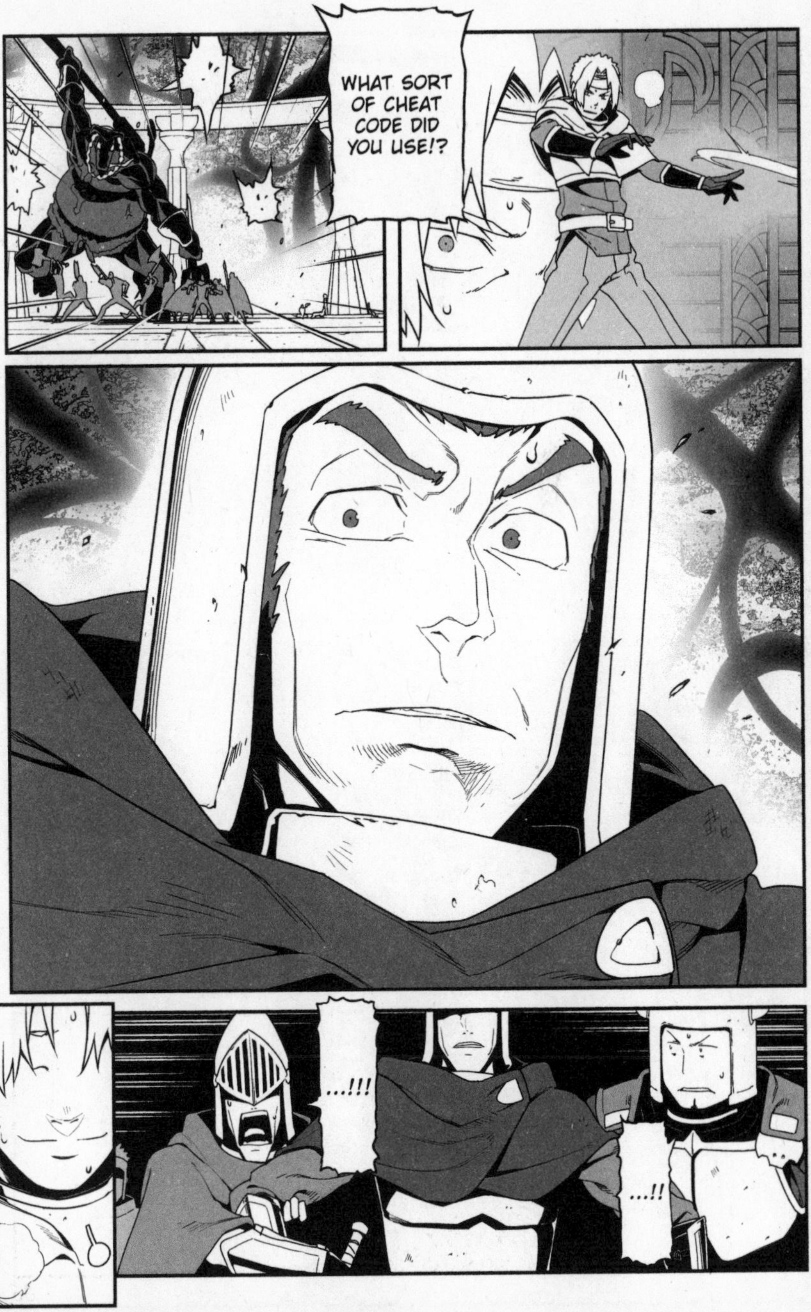
WHAT SORT OF CHEAT CODE DID YOU USE!?
...!!!
...!!

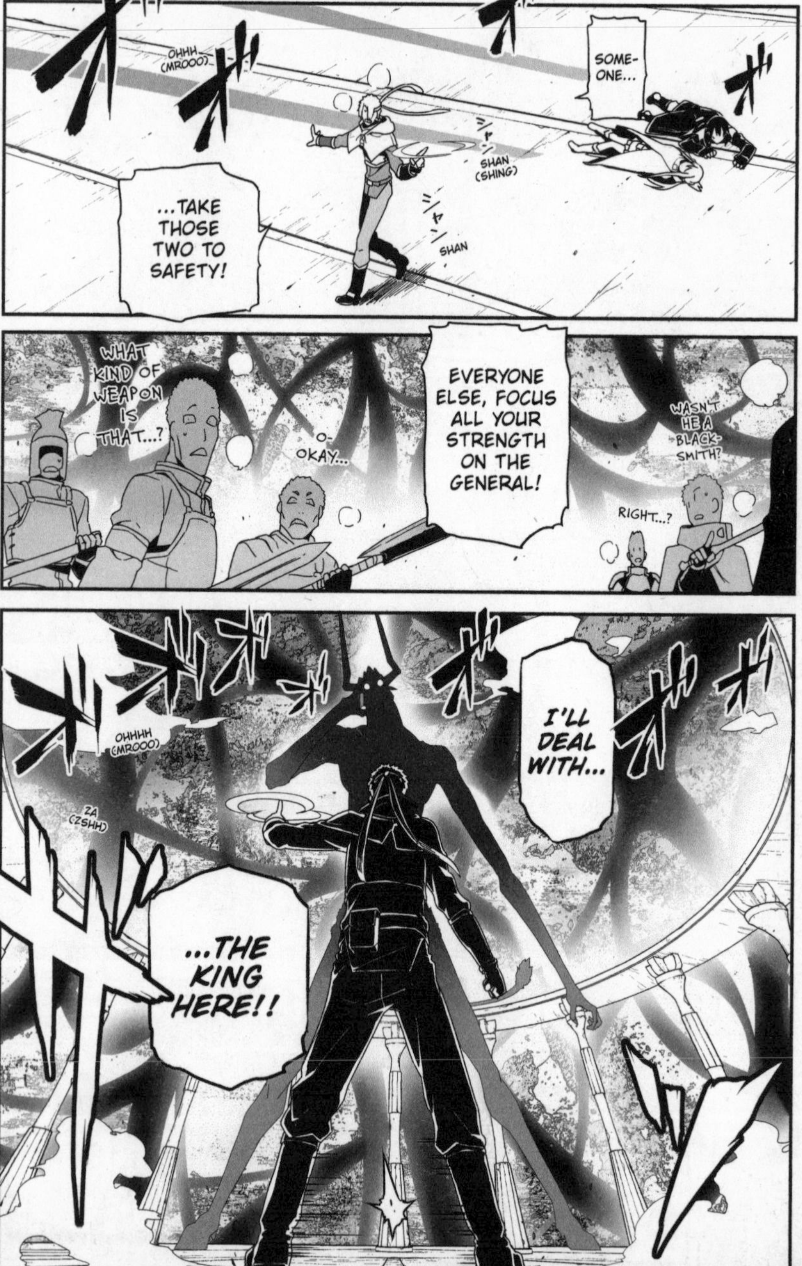
SOME-ONE...
OHHH (MROOO)
シャン
SHAN (SHING)
シャン
SHAN
...TAKE THOSE TWO TO SAFETY!
EVERYONE ELSE, FOCUS ALL YOUR STRENGTH ON THE GENERAL!
WASN'T HE A BLACK-SMITH?
RIGHT...?
O-OKAY...
WHAT KIND OF WEAPON IS THAT...?
I'LL DEAL WITH...
OHHHH (MROOO)
ZA (ZSHH)
...THE KING HERE!!

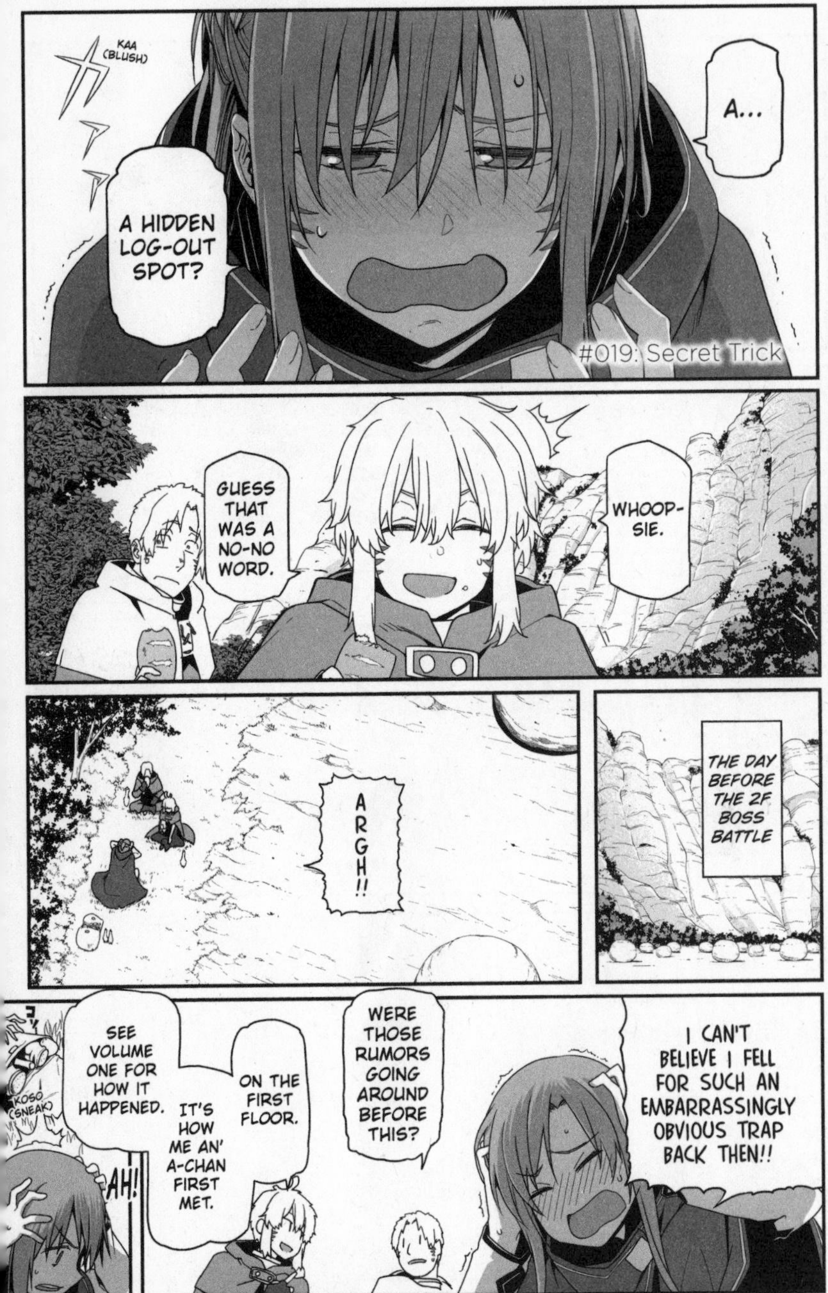
#019: Secret Trick
A...
KAA (BLUSH)
A HIDDEN LOG-OUT SPOT?
WHOOP-SIE.
GUESS THAT WAS A NO-NO WORD.
THE DAY BEFORE THE 2F BOSS BATTLE
ARGH!!
I CAN'T BELIEVE I FELL FOR SUCH AN EMBARRASSINGLY OBVIOUS TRAP BACK THEN!!
WERE THOSE RUMORS GOING AROUND BEFORE THIS?
ON THE FIRST FLOOR.
IT'S HOW ME AN' A-CHAN FIRST MET.
SEE VOLUME ONE FOR HOW IT HAPPENED.
AH!
KOSO (SNEAK)

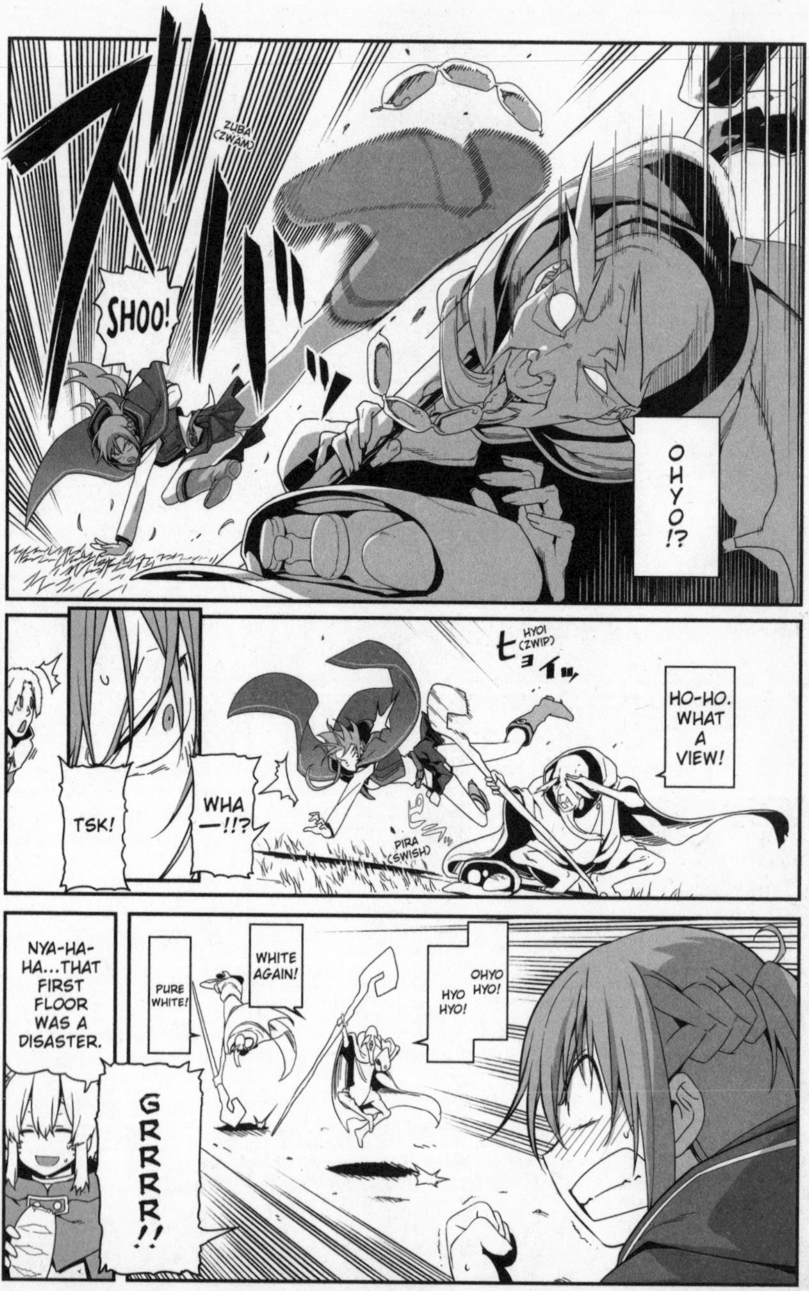
OHYO!?
ZUBA (ZWAM)
SHOO!
HYOI (ZWIP)
HO-HO. WHAT A VIEW!
PIRA (SWISH)
WHA—!!?
TSK!
OHYO HYO!
HYO HYO!
WHITE AGAIN!
PURE WHITE!
GRRRR!!
NYA-HA-HA...THAT FIRST FLOOR WAS A DISASTER.

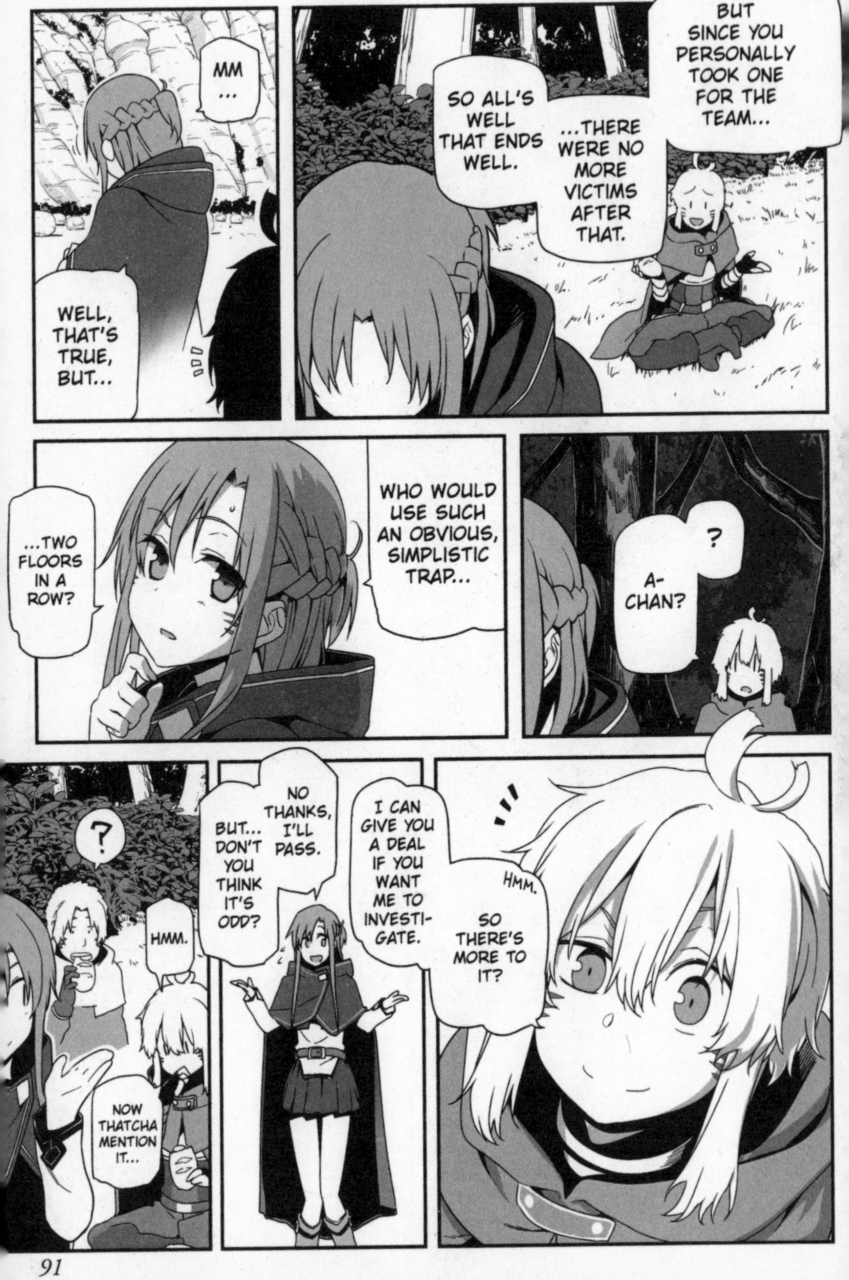
BUT SINCE YOU PERSONALLY TOOK ONE FOR THE TEAM...
...THERE WERE NO MORE VICTIMS AFTER THAT.
SO ALL'S WELL THAT ENDS WELL.
MM ...
WELL, THAT'S TRUE, BUT...
?
A-CHAN?
WHO WOULD USE SUCH AN OBVIOUS, SIMPLISTIC TRAP...
...TWO FLOORS IN A ROW?
HMM.
SO THERE'S MORE TO IT?
I CAN GIVE YOU A DEAL IF YOU WANT ME TO INVESTI-GATE.
NO THANKS, I'LL PASS.
BUT... DON'T YOU THINK IT'S ODD?
?
HMM.
NOW THATCHA MENTION IT...

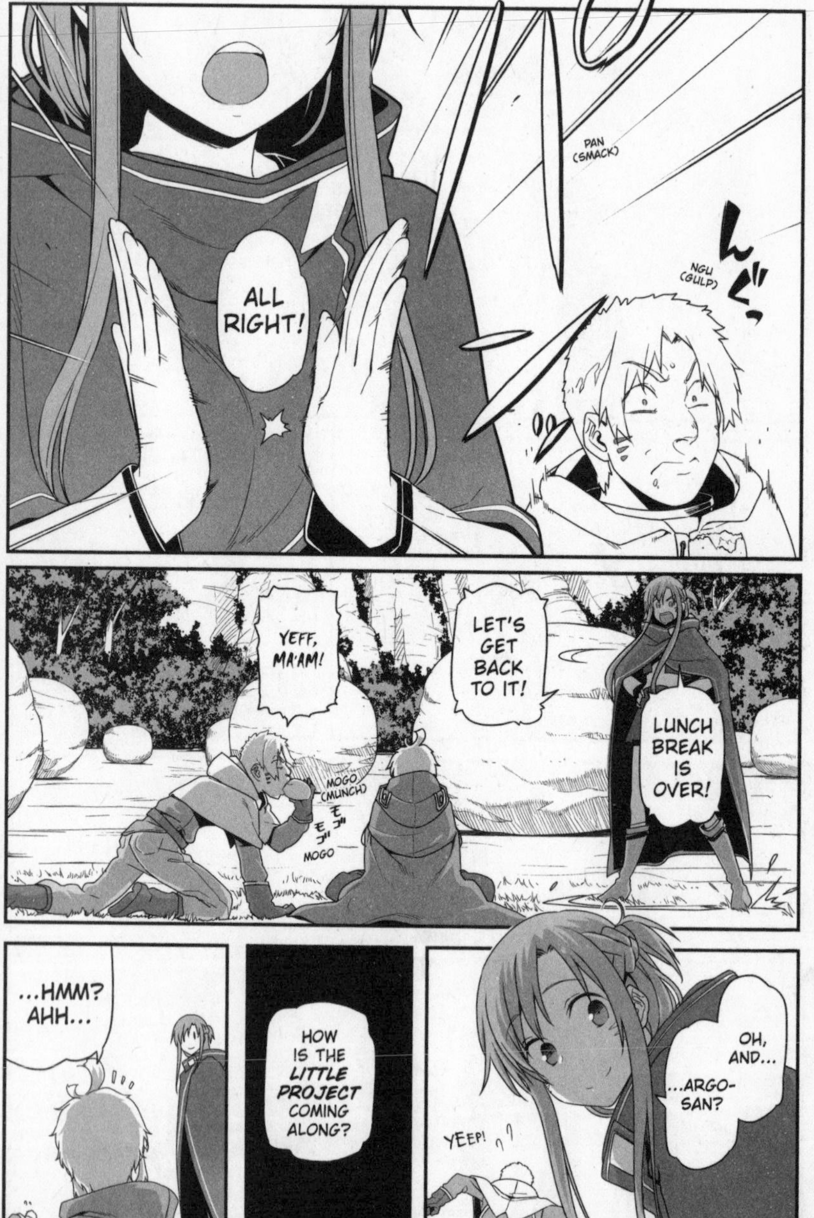
PAN (SMACK)
NGU (GULP)
ALL RIGHT!
LUNCH BREAK IS OVER!
LET'S GET BACK TO IT!
YEFF, MA'AM!
MOGO (MUNCH)
MOGO
OH, AND...
...ARGO-SAN?
YEEP!
HOW IS THE *LITTLE PROJECT* COMING ALONG?
...HMM? AHH...

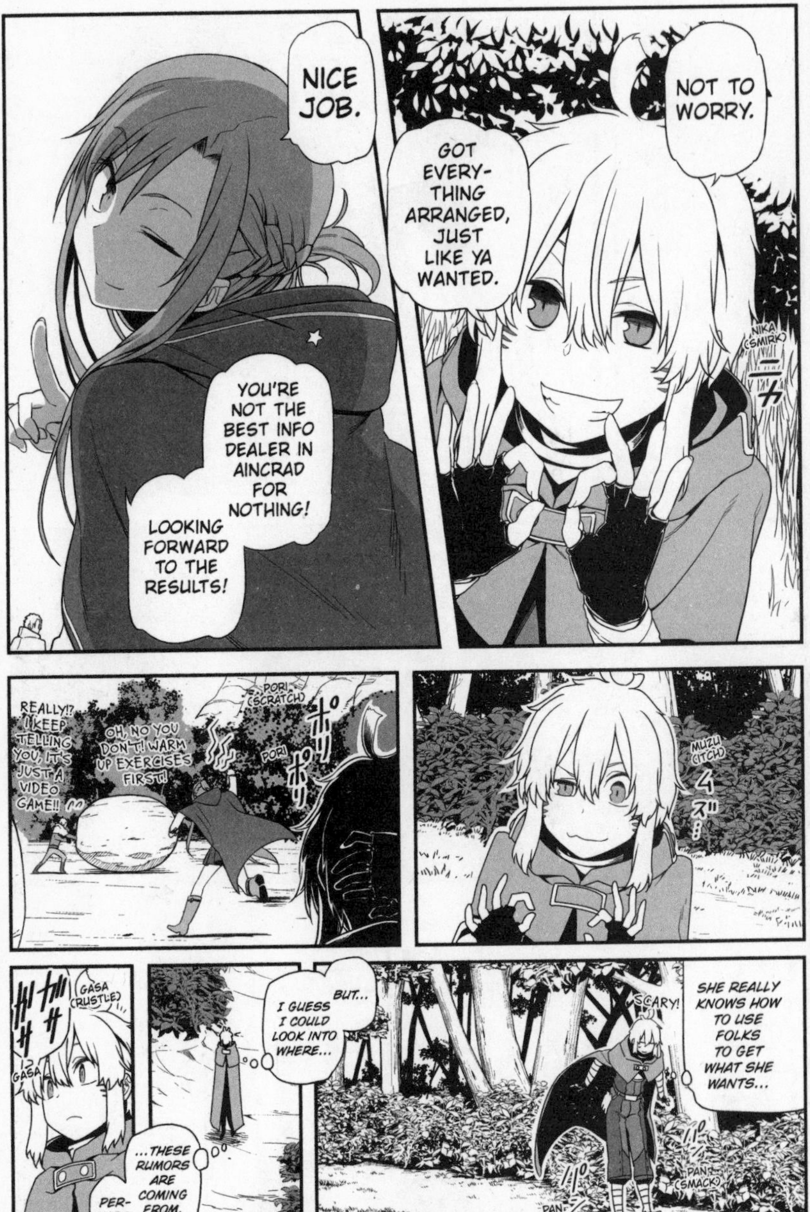
NOT TO WORRY.
GOT EVERY-THING ARRANGED, JUST LIKE YA WANTED.
NIKA (SMIRK)
ニカ
NICE JOB.
YOU'RE NOT THE BEST INFO DEALER IN AINCRAD FOR NOTHING!
LOOKING FORWARD TO THE RESULTS!
MUZU (ITCH)
ムズ…
PORI (SCRATCH)
ポリ
PORI!
ポリ
OH, NO YOU DON'T! WARM UP EXERCISES FIRST!
REALLY!? I KEEP TELLING YOU, IT'S JUST A VIDEO GAME!!
SCARY!
SHE REALLY KNOWS HOW TO USE FOLKS TO GET WHAT SHE WANTS...
PAN (SMACK)
PAN
BUT... I GUESS I COULD LOOK INTO WHERE...
...THESE RUMORS ARE COMING FROM.
PER-HAPS.
GASA (RUSTLE)
ガサ ガサ
GASA

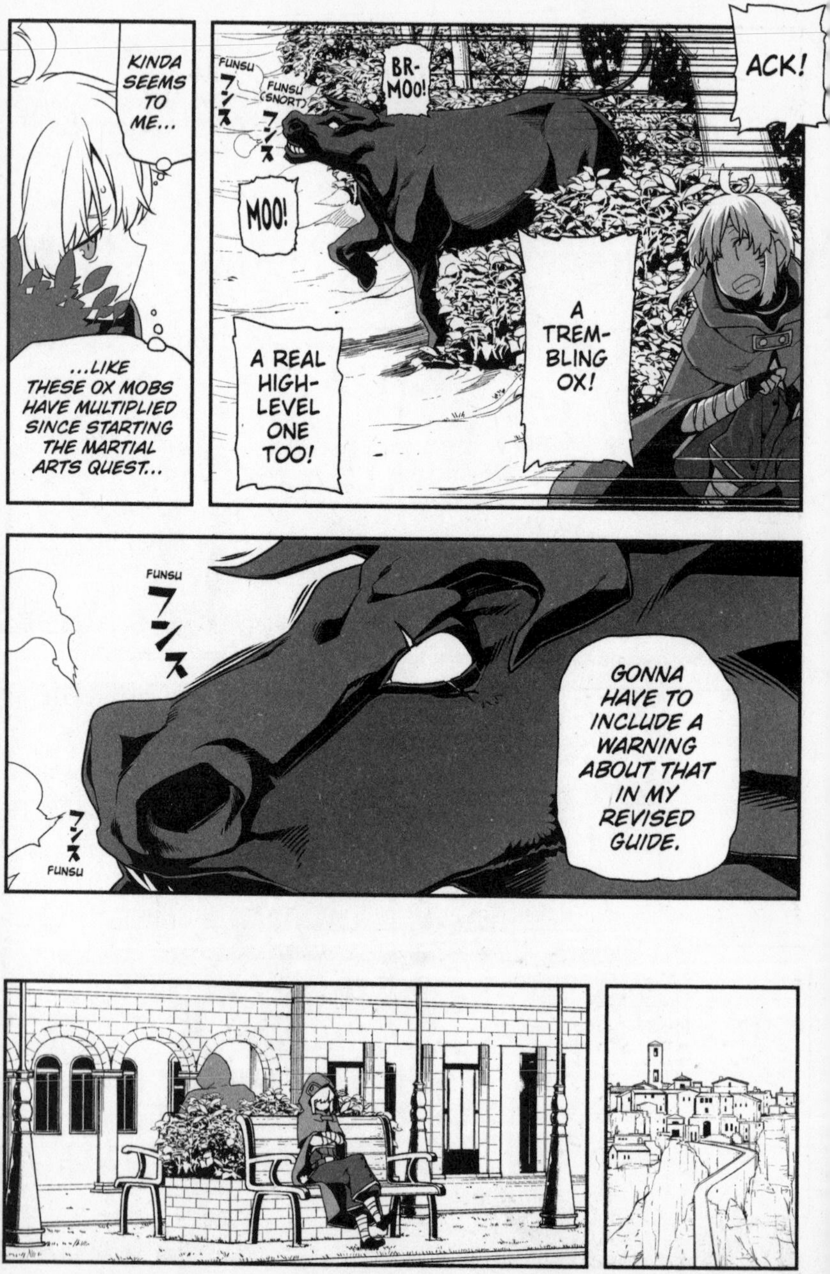

ACK!
BR-MOO!
FUNSU (SNORT)
FUNSU
MOO!
A TREMBLING OX!
A REAL HIGH-LEVEL ONE TOO!
KINDA SEEMS TO ME...
...LIKE THESE OX MOBS HAVE MULTIPLIED SINCE STARTING THE MARTIAL ARTS QUEST...
GONNA HAVE TO INCLUDE A WARNING ABOUT THAT IN MY REVISED GUIDE.
FUNSU
FUNSU

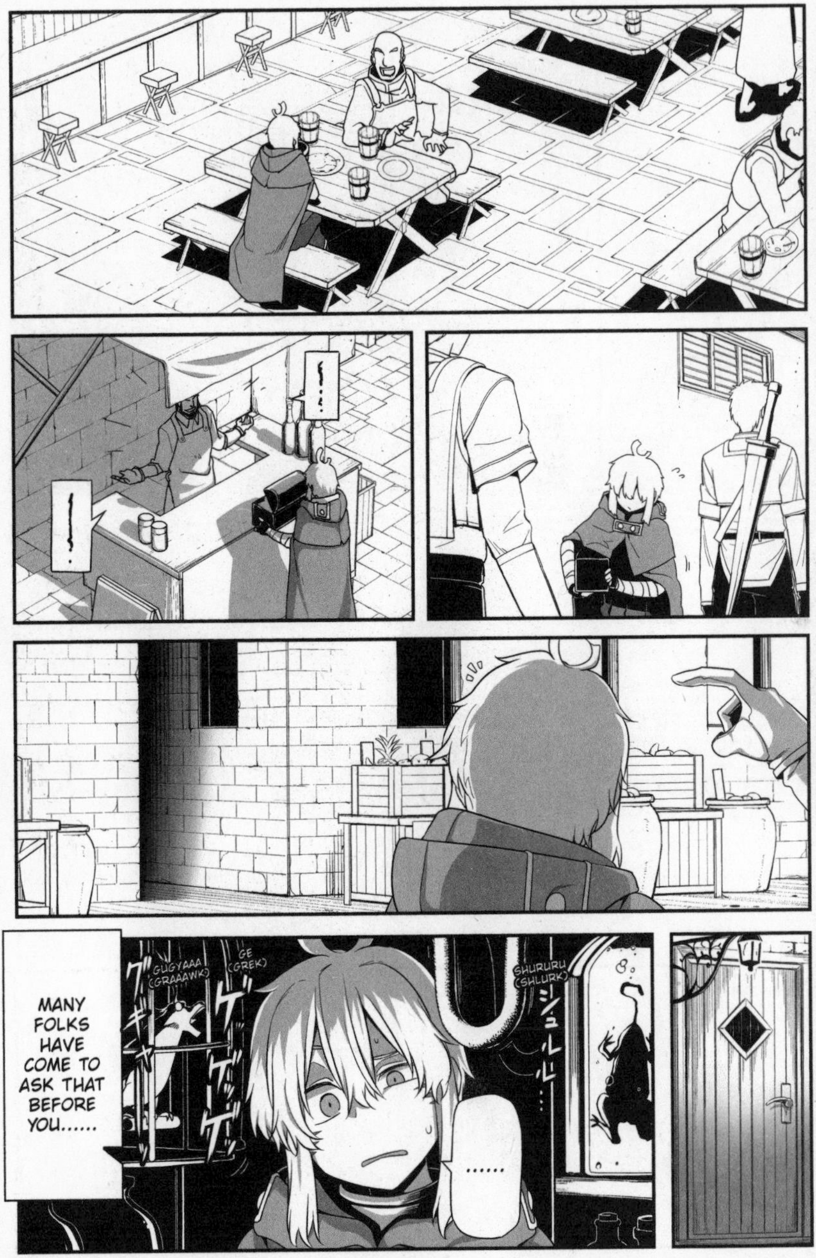
SHURURU (SHLURK)
GE (GREK)
GUGYAAA (GRAAAWK)
MANY FOLKS HAVE COME TO ASK THAT BEFORE YOU......
......

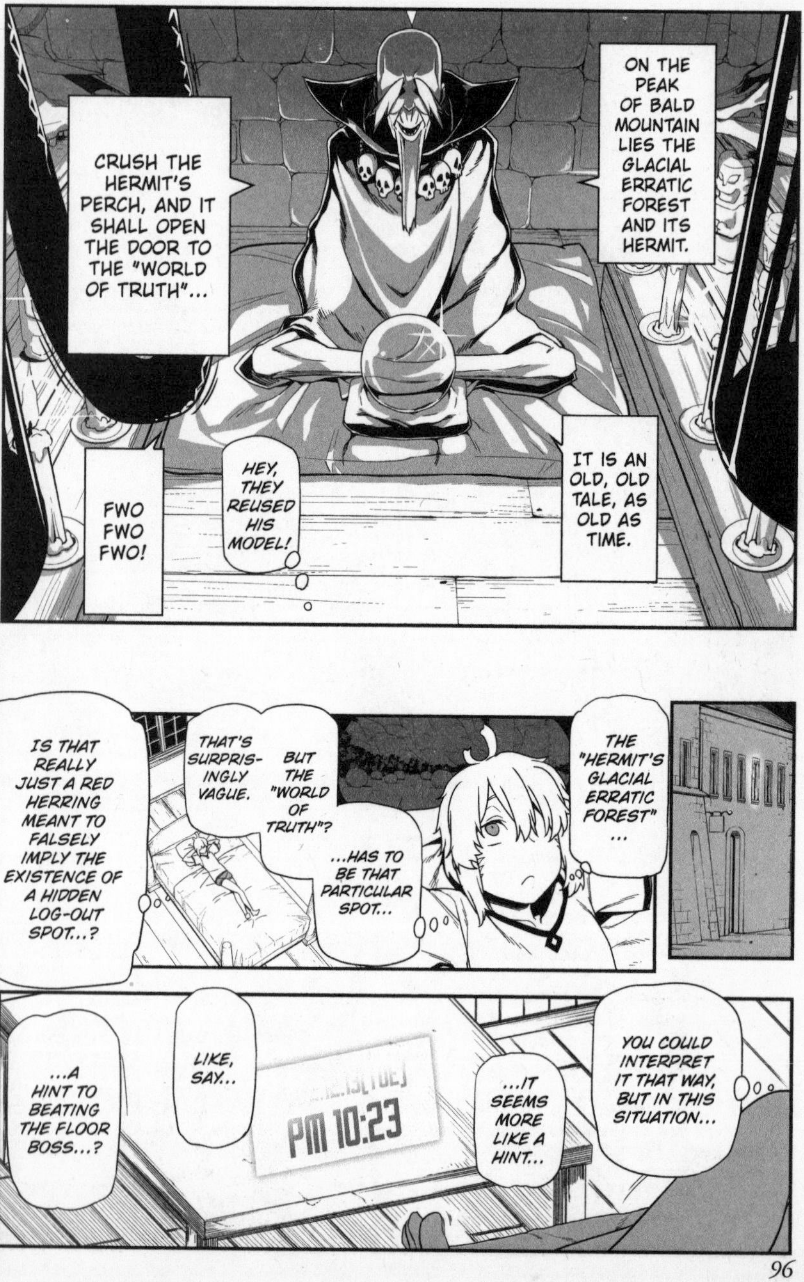
ON THE PEAK OF BALD MOUNTAIN LIES THE GLACIAL ERRATIC FOREST AND ITS HERMIT.
CRUSH THE HERMIT'S PERCH, AND IT SHALL OPEN THE DOOR TO THE "WORLD OF TRUTH"...
IT IS AN OLD, OLD TALE, AS OLD AS TIME.
HEY, THEY REUSED HIS MODEL!
FWO FWO FWO!
THE "HERMIT'S GLACIAL ERRATIC FOREST"...
BUT THE "WORLD OF TRUTH"?
THAT'S SURPRISINGLY VAGUE.
...HAS TO BE THAT PARTICULAR SPOT...
IS THAT REALLY JUST A RED HERRING MEANT TO FALSELY IMPLY THE EXISTENCE OF A HIDDEN LOG-OUT SPOT...?
YOU COULD INTERPRET IT THAT WAY, BUT IN THIS SITUATION...
...IT SEEMS MORE LIKE A HINT...
PM 10:23
LIKE, SAY...
...A HINT TO BEATING THE FLOOR BOSS...?

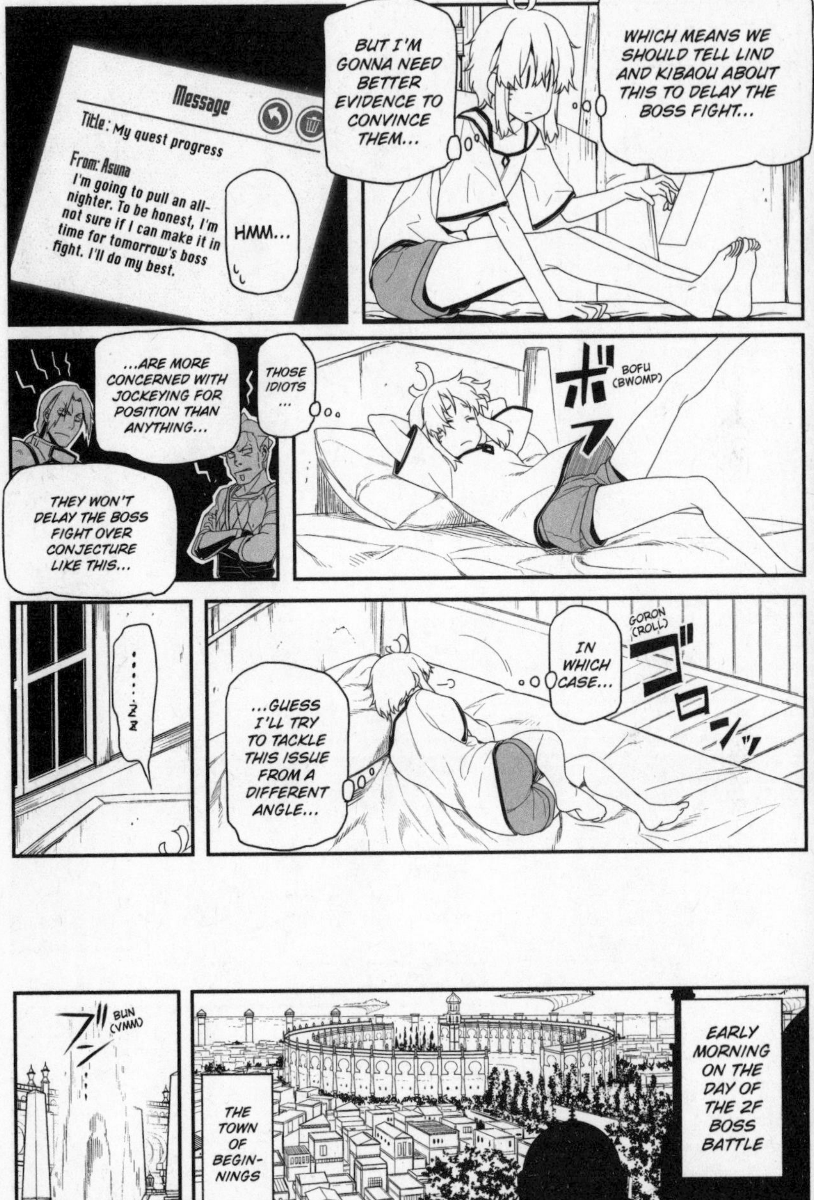
WHICH MEANS WE SHOULD TELL LIND AND KIBAOU ABOUT THIS TO DELAY THE BOSS FIGHT...
BUT I'M GONNA NEED BETTER EVIDENCE TO CONVINCE THEM...
Message
Title: My quest progress
From: Asuna
I'm going to pull an all-nighter. To be honest, I'm not sure if I can make it in time for tomorrow's boss fight. I'll do my best.
HMM...
BOFU (BWOMP)
THOSE IDIOTS...
...ARE MORE CONCERNED WITH JOCKEYING FOR POSITION THAN ANYTHING...
THEY WON'T DELAY THE BOSS FIGHT OVER CONJECTURE LIKE THIS...
GORON (ROLL)
IN WHICH CASE...
...GUESS I'LL TRY TO TACKLE THIS ISSUE FROM A DIFFERENT ANGLE...
......zz
EARLY MORNING ON THE DAY OF THE 2F BOSS BATTLE
THE TOWN OF BEGINNINGS
BUN (VMM)

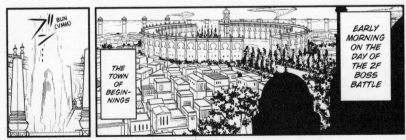

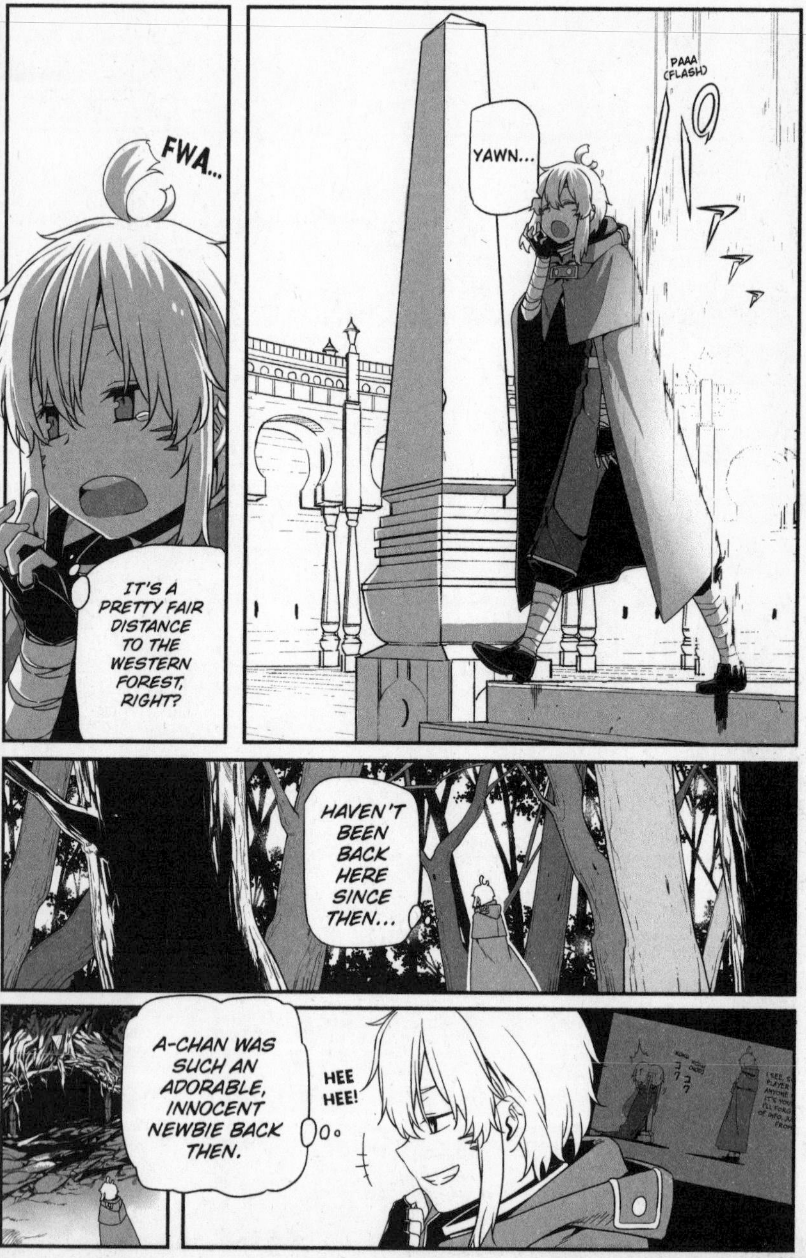
PAAA (FLASH)
YAWN...
FWA...
IT'S A PRETTY FAIR DISTANCE TO THE WESTERN FOREST, RIGHT?
HAVEN'T BEEN BACK HERE SINCE THEN...
HEE HEE!
A-CHAN WAS SUCH AN ADORABLE, INNOCENT NEWBIE BACK THEN.

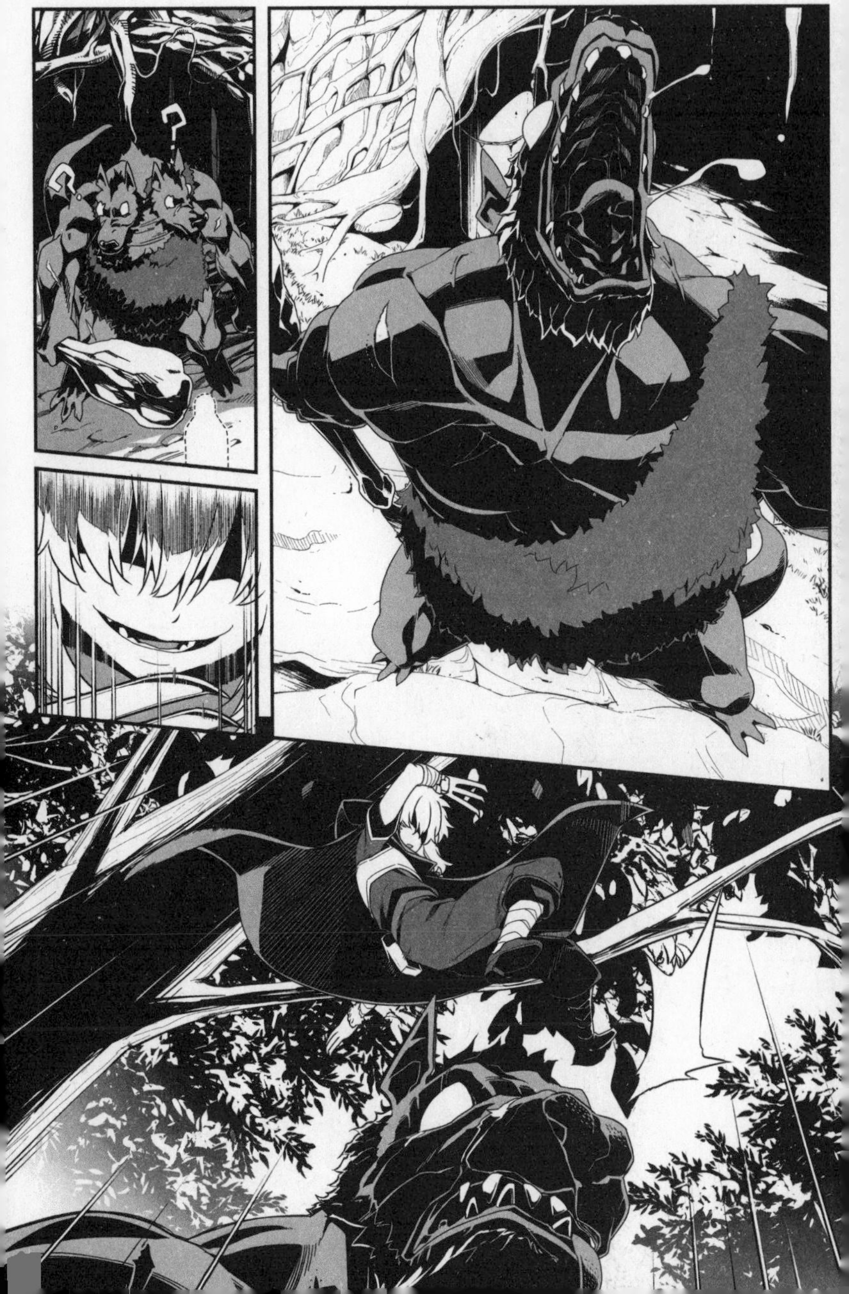
?
?

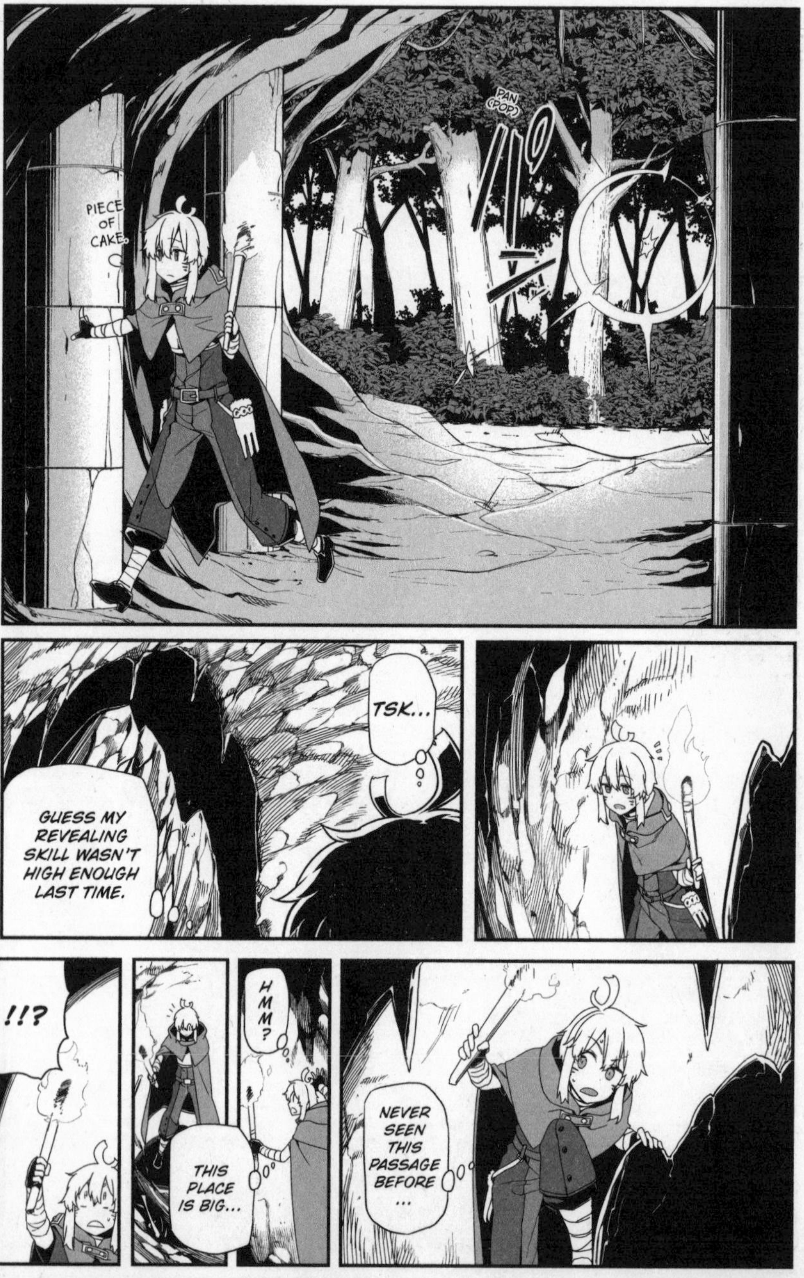
PAN (POP)
PIECE OF CAKE.
TSK...
GUESS MY REVEALING SKILL WASN'T HIGH ENOUGH LAST TIME.
NEVER SEEN THIS PASSAGE BEFORE ...
HMM?
THIS PLACE IS BIG...
!!?

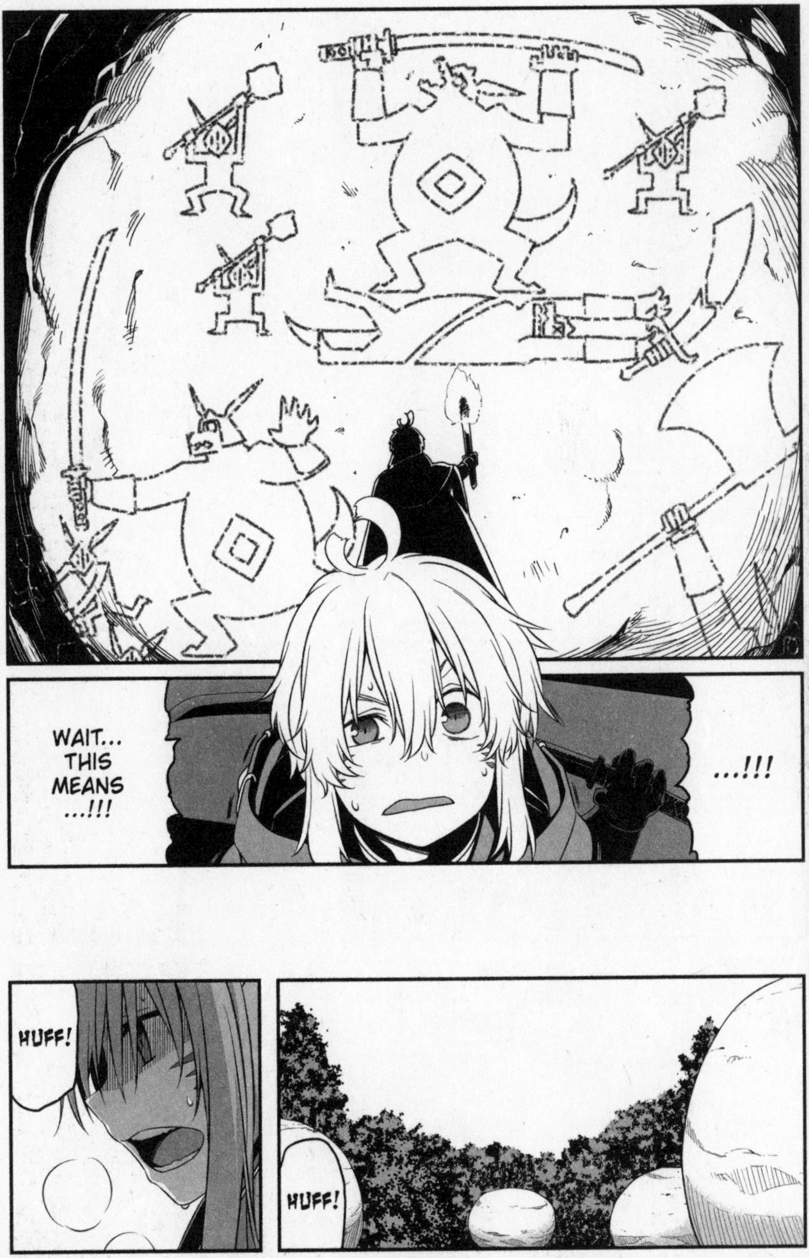
...!!!
WAIT... THIS MEANS ...!!!
HUFF!
HUFF!

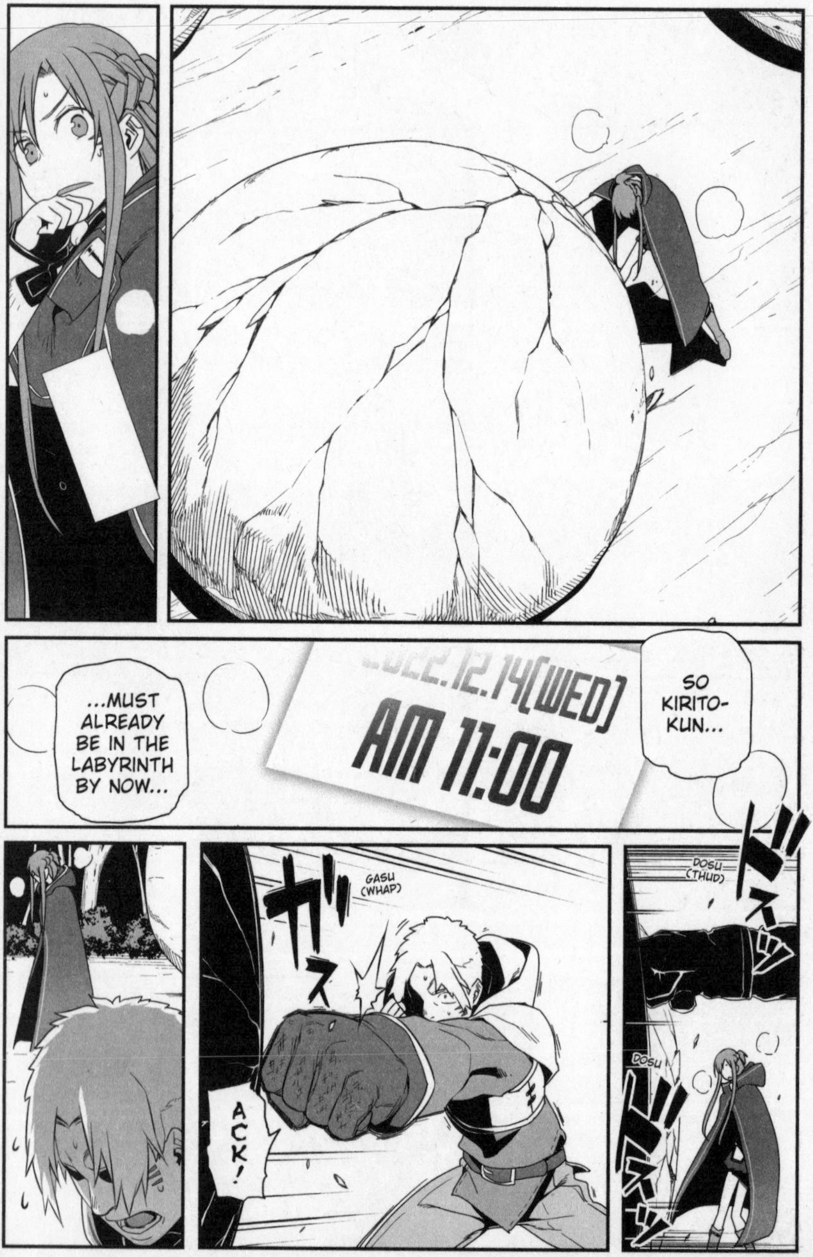
SO KIRITO-KUN...
022.12.14[WED]
AM 11:00
...MUST ALREADY BE IN THE LABYRINTH BY NOW...
DOSU (THUD)
DOSU
GASU (WHAP)
ACK!

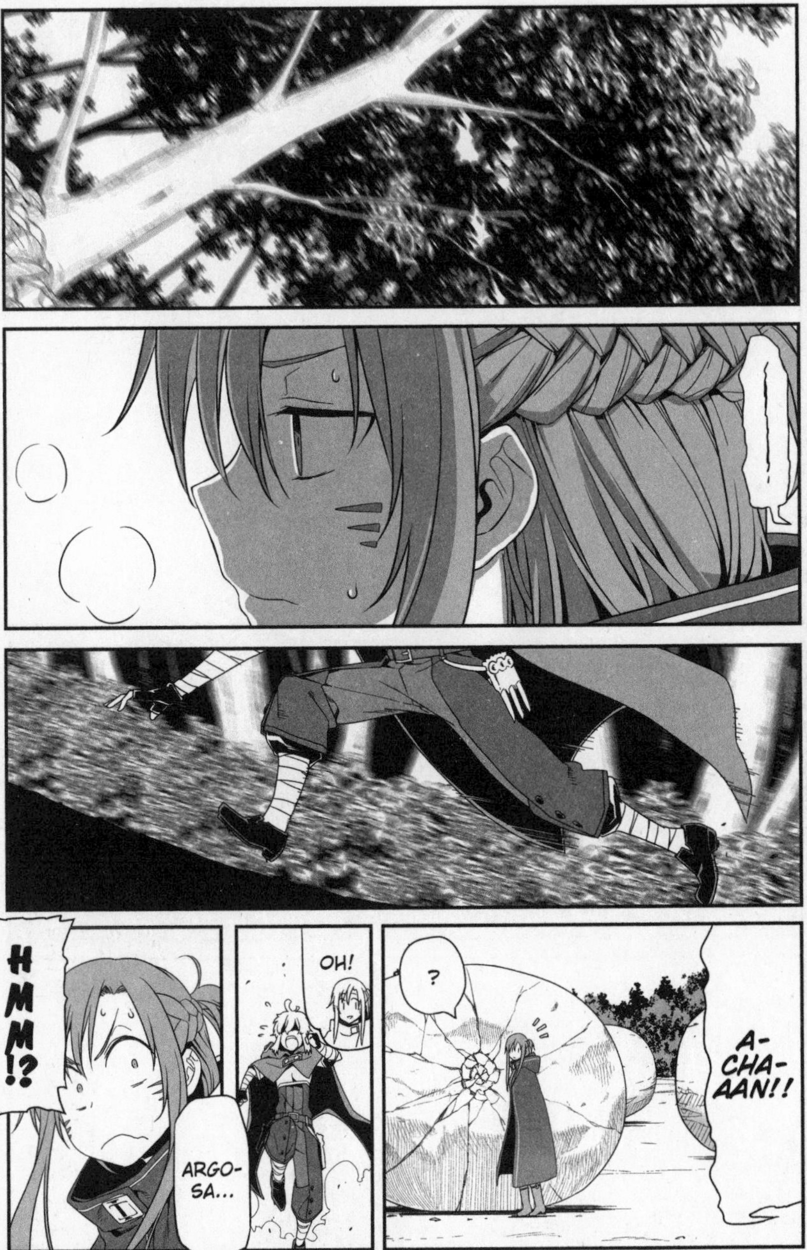
!
A-CHA-AAN!!
?
OH!
ARGO-SA...
HMM!?

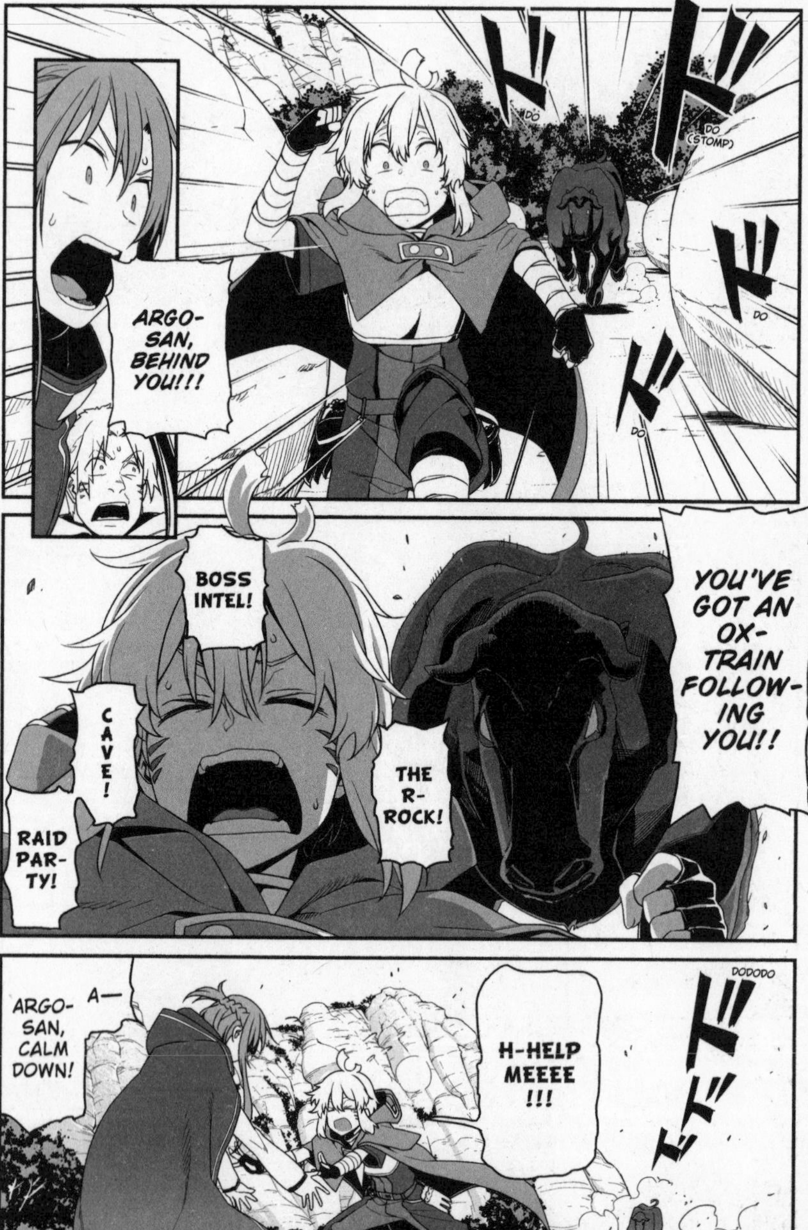
DO
(STOMP)
DO
DO
DO
ARGO-SAN, BEHIND YOU!!!
YOU'VE GOT AN OX-TRAIN FOLLOWING YOU!!
BOSS INTEL!
THE R-ROCK!
CAVE!
RAID PARTY!
DODODO
H-HELP MEEEE!!!
A—
ARGO-SAN, CALM DOWN!

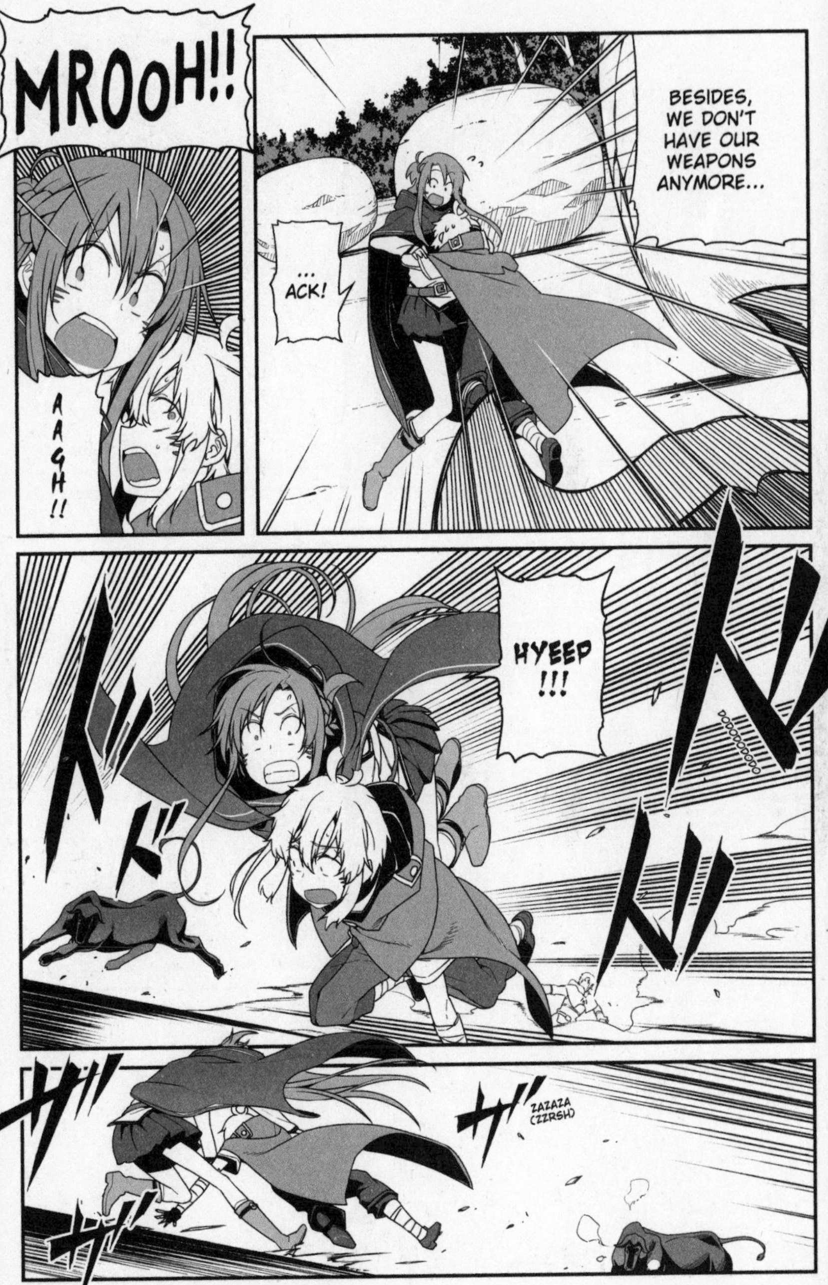

BESIDES, WE DON'T HAVE OUR WEAPONS ANYMORE...
... ACK!
MROOH!!
AAGH!!
DODODODODO
HYEEP!!!
ZAZAZA (ZZRSH)

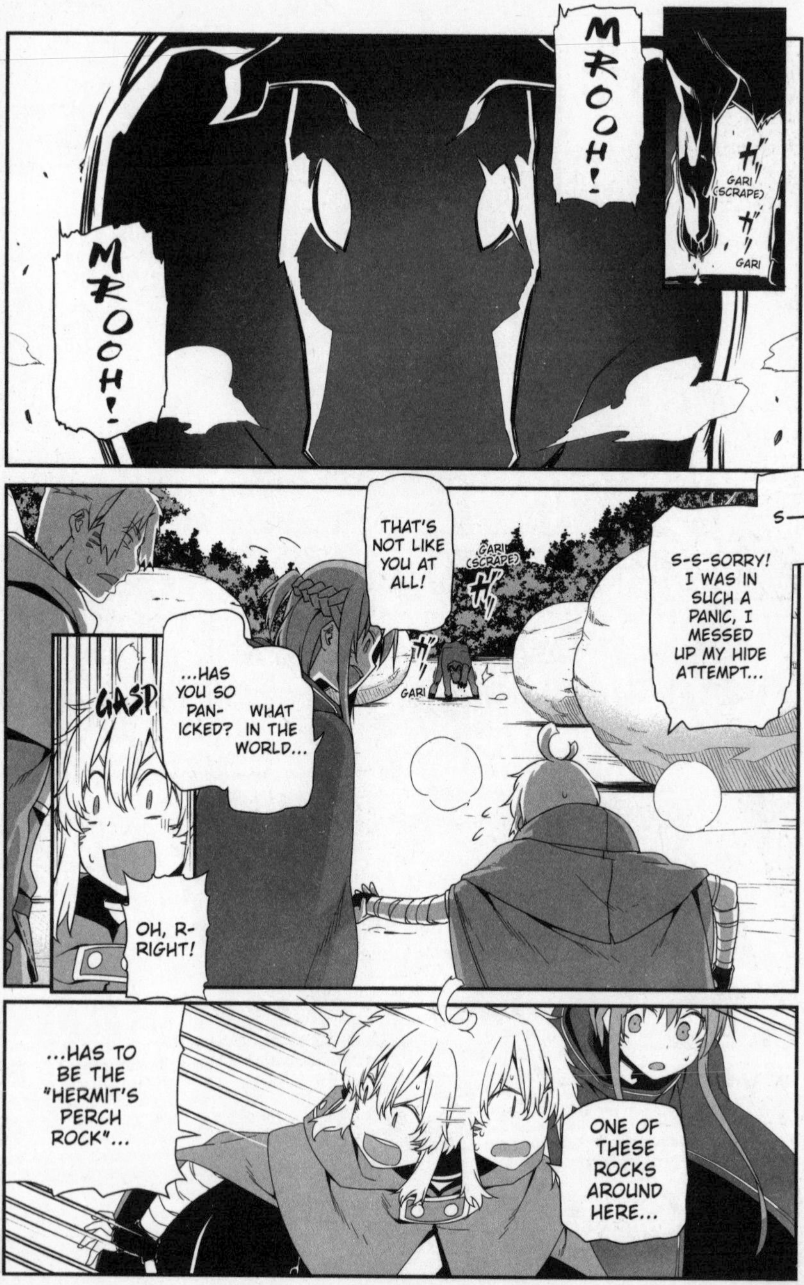
GARI (SCRAPE)
GARI
MROOH!
MROOH!
S—
S-S-SORRY! I WAS IN SUCH A PANIC, I MESSED UP MY HIDE ATTEMPT...
THAT'S NOT LIKE YOU AT ALL!
GARI (SCRAPE)
GARI
WHAT IN THE WORLD...
...HAS YOU SO PAN-ICKED?
GASP
OH, R-RIGHT!
ONE OF THESE ROCKS AROUND HERE...
...HAS TO BE THE "HERMIT'S PERCH ROCK"...

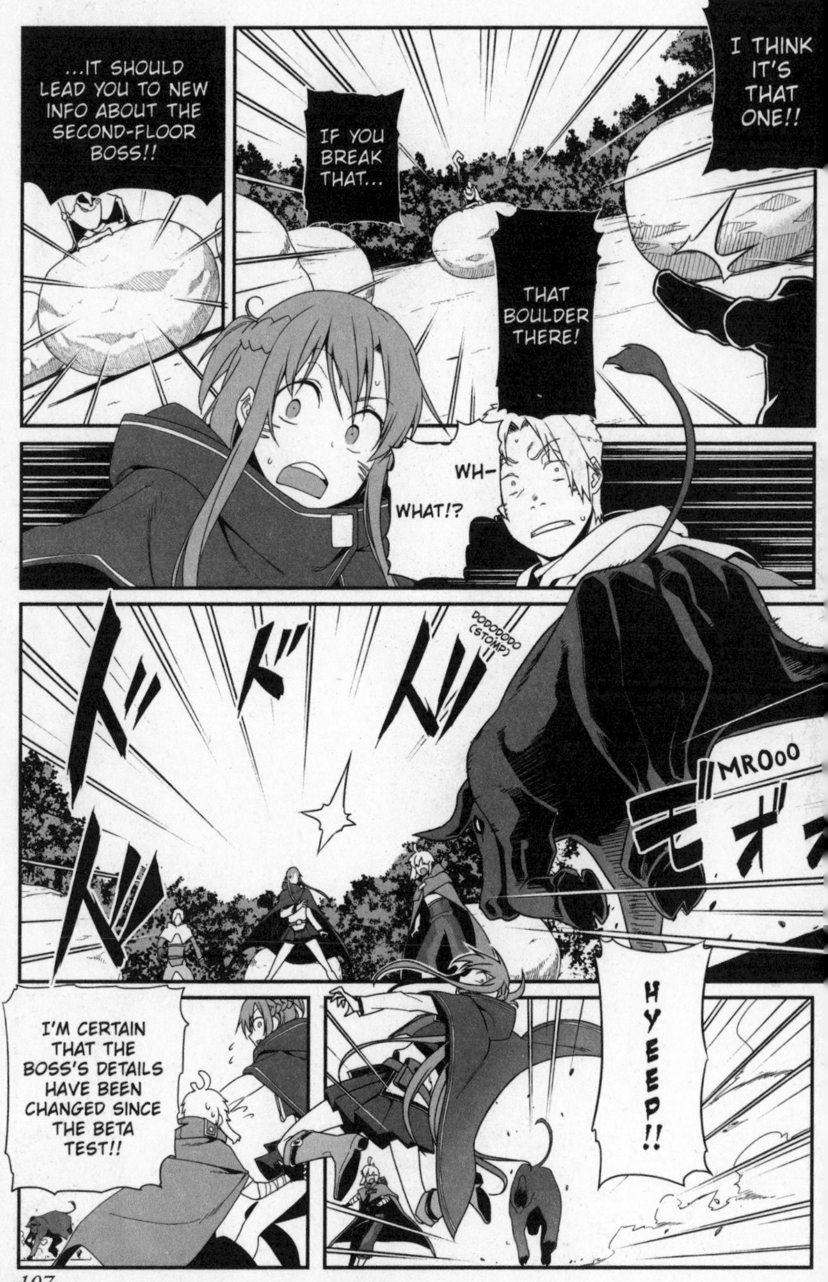
I THINK IT'S THAT ONE!!
THAT BOULDER THERE!
IF YOU BREAK THAT...
...IT SHOULD LEAD YOU TO NEW INFO ABOUT THE SECOND-FLOOR BOSS!!
WH-
WHAT!?
DODODODO (STOMP)
ドドドド
MROoo
HYEEP!!
I'M CERTAIN THAT THE BOSS'S DETAILS HAVE BEEN CHANGED SINCE THE BETA TEST!!

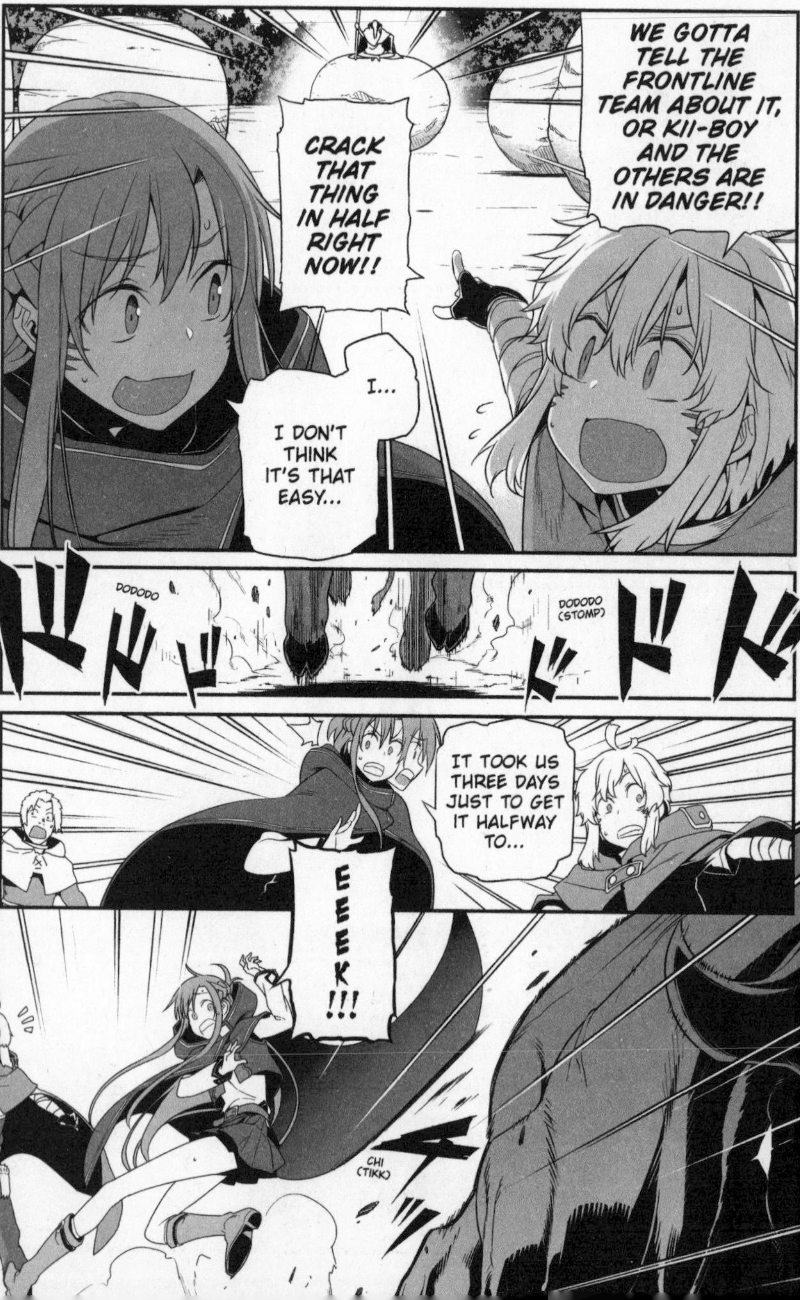
WE GOTTA TELL THE FRONTLINE TEAM ABOUT IT, OR KII-BOY AND THE OTHERS ARE IN DANGER!!
CRACK THAT THING IN HALF RIGHT NOW!!
I...
I DON'T THINK IT'S THAT EASY...
DODODO (STOMP)
DODODO
IT TOOK US THREE DAYS JUST TO GET IT HALFWAY TO...
EEEEK!!!
CHI (TIKK)

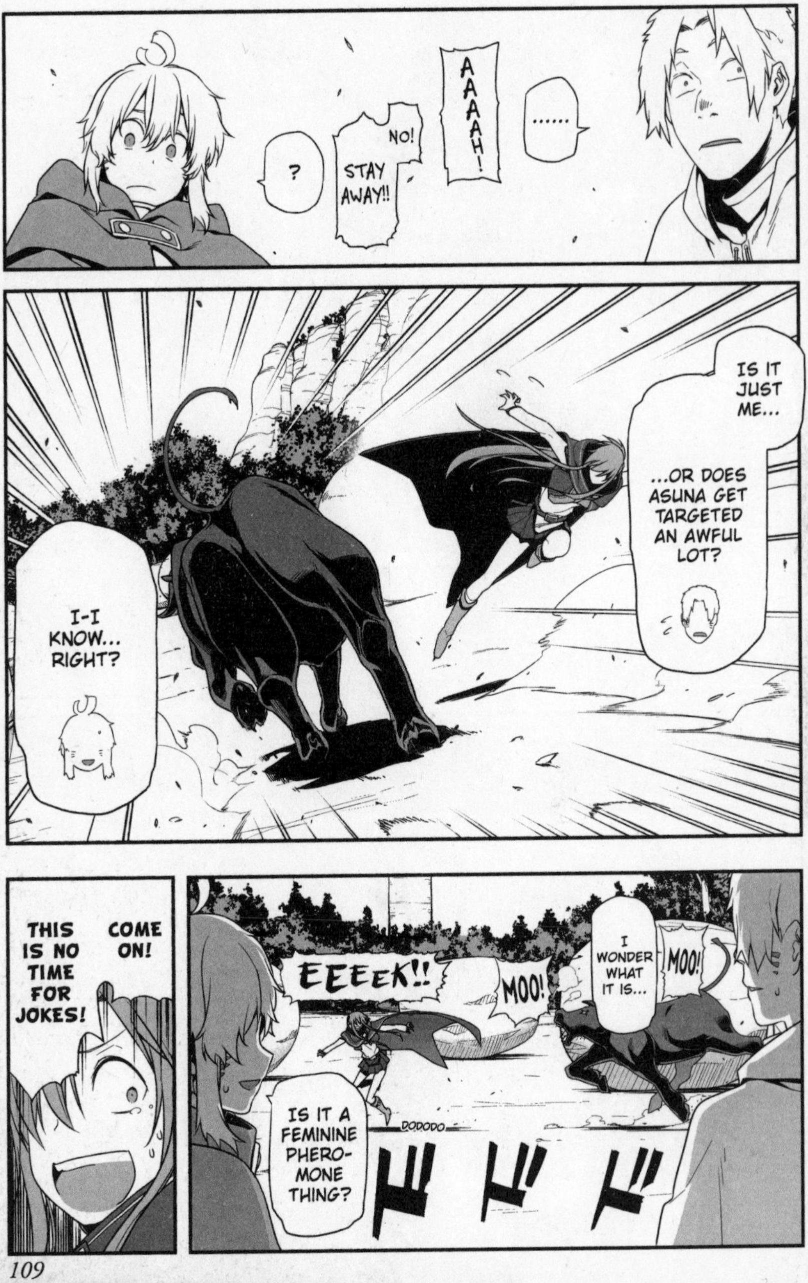
......
AAAAAH!
NO! STAY AWAY!!
?
IS IT JUST ME...
...OR DOES ASUNA GET TARGETED AN AWFUL LOT?
I-I KNOW... RIGHT?
I WONDER WHAT IT IS...
MOO!
MOO!
EEEEK!!
IS IT A FEMININE PHERO-MONE THING?
DODODO
ドドド
COME ON!
THIS IS NO TIME FOR JOKES!

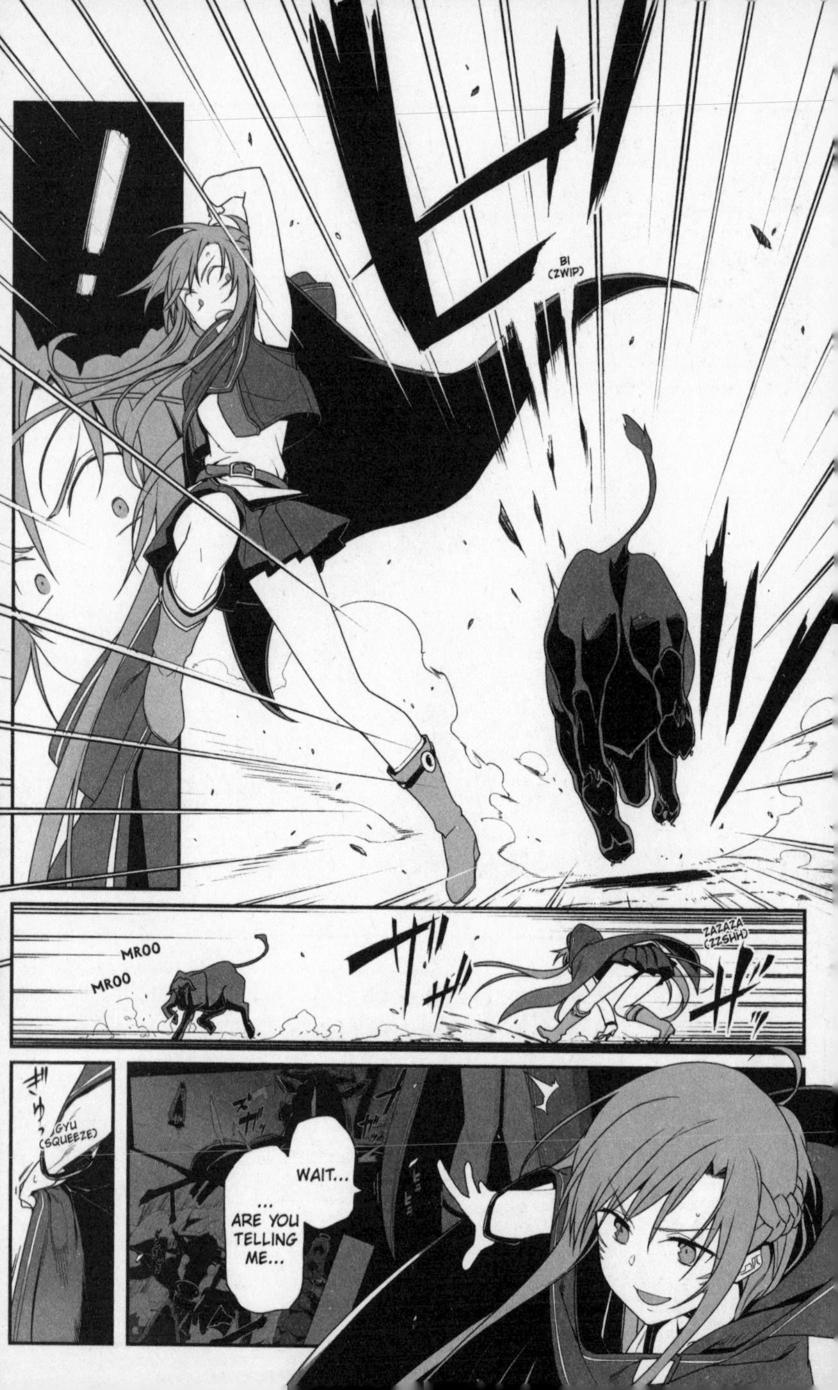
!
BI (ZWIP)
ZAZAZA (ZZSHH)
MROO
MROO
WAIT...
... ARE YOU TELLING ME...
GYU (SQUEEZE)

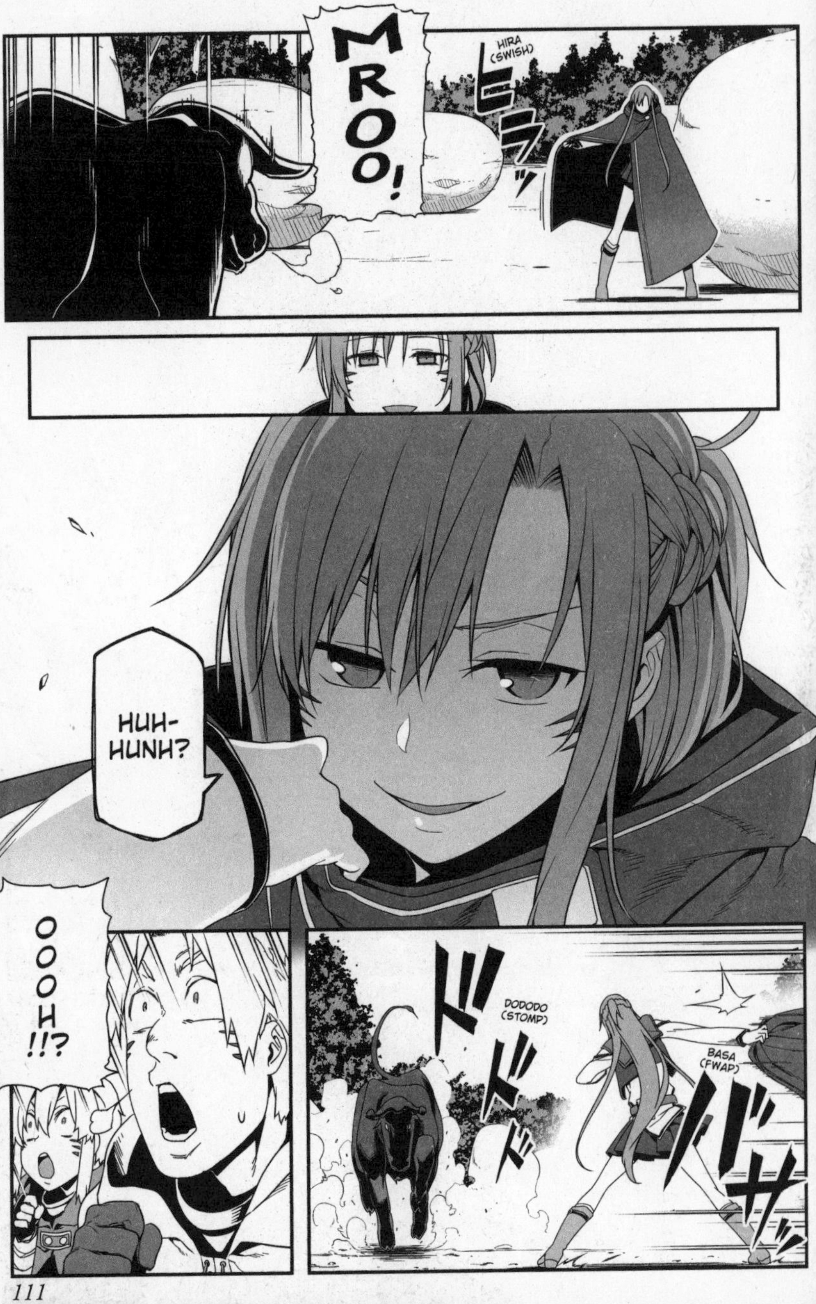
HIRA (SWISH)
MROO!
HUH-HUNH?
BASA (FWAP)
DODODO (STOMP)
OOOOH!!?

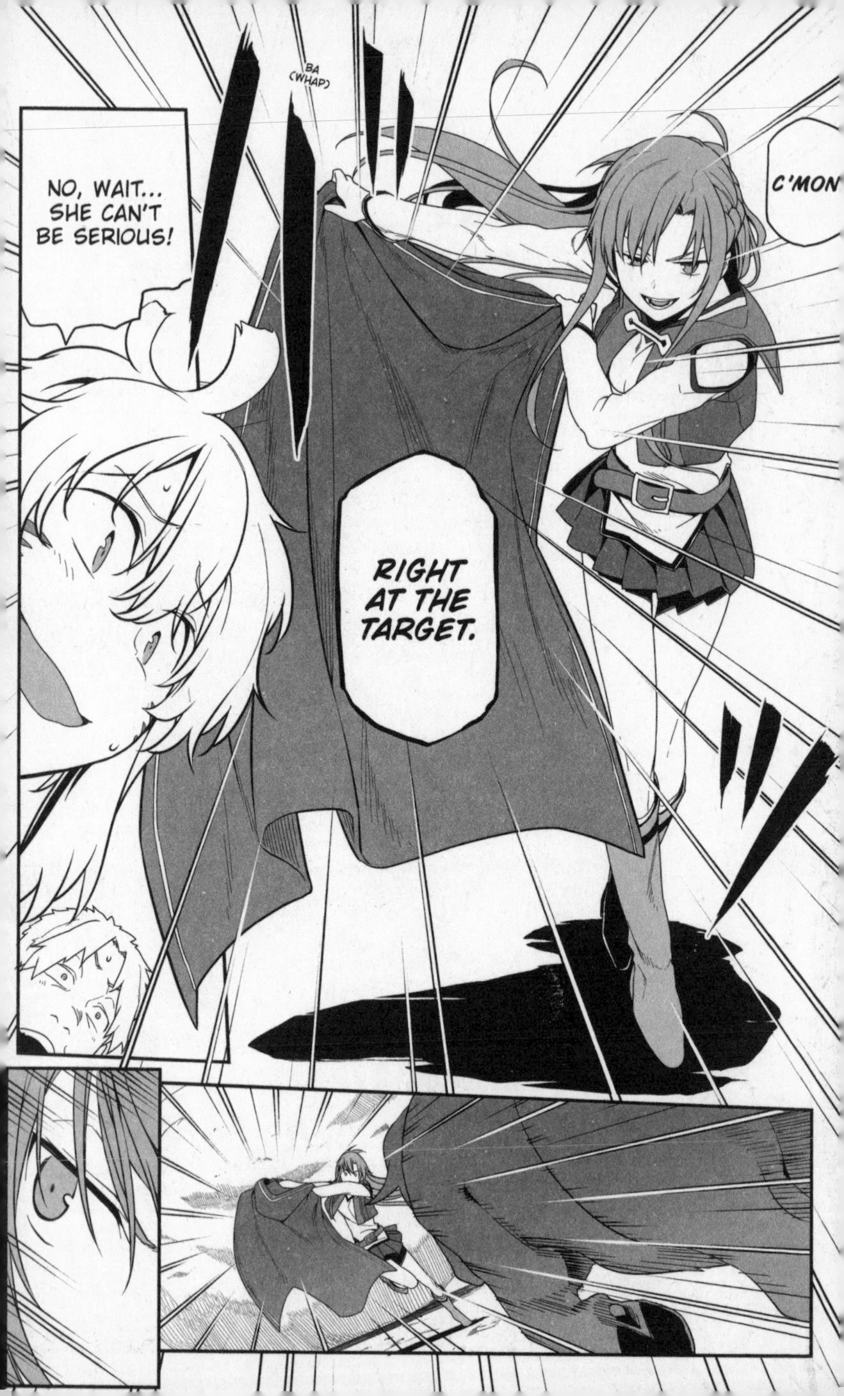
C'MON
BA (WHAP)
NO, WAIT... SHE CAN'T BE SERIOUS!
RIGHT AT THE TARGET.

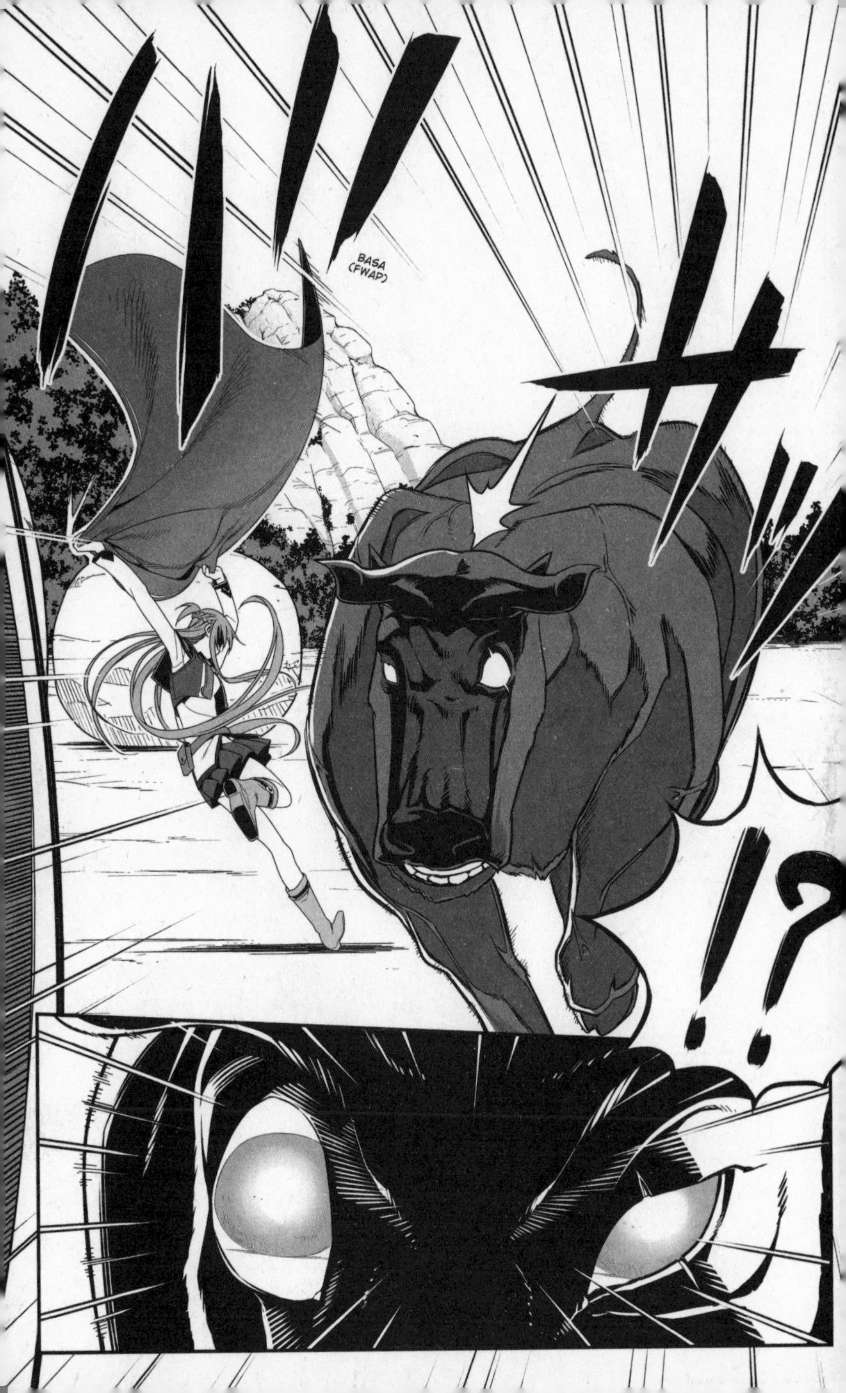
BASA
(FWAP)
!?

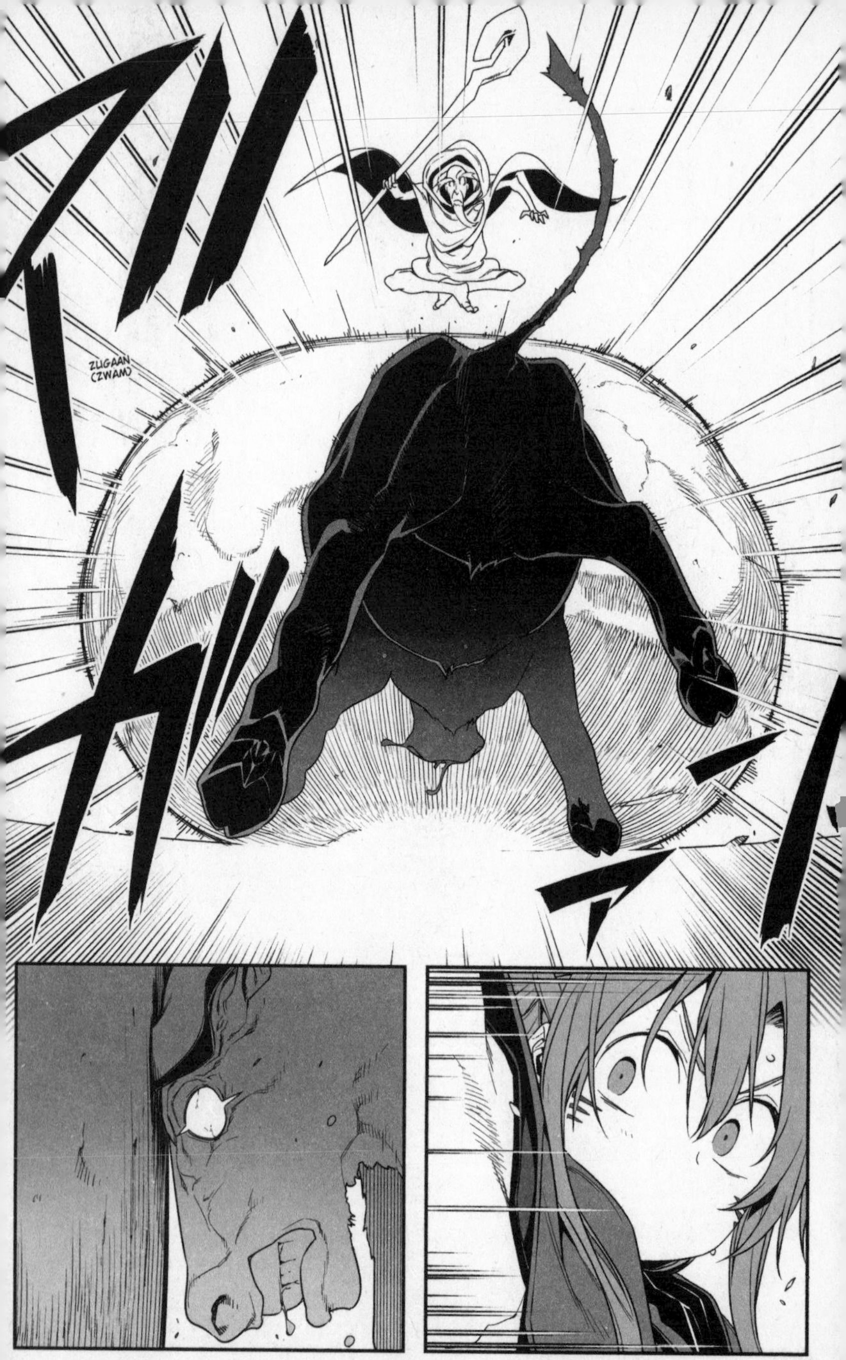
ZUGAAN
(ZWAM)

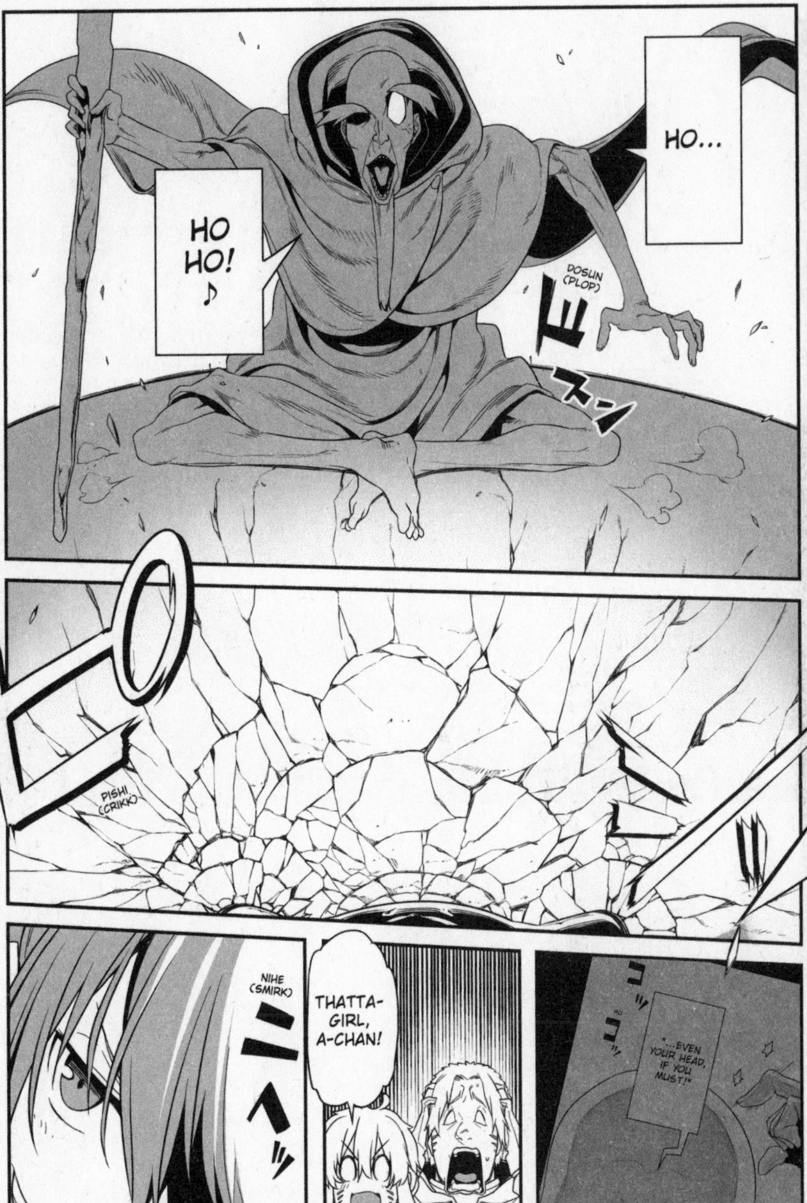

HO...
DOSUN (PLOP)
HO HO! ♪
PISHI (CRIKK)
"...EVEN YOUR HEAD, IF YOU MUST!"
THATTA-GIRL, A-CHAN!
NIHE (SMIRK)

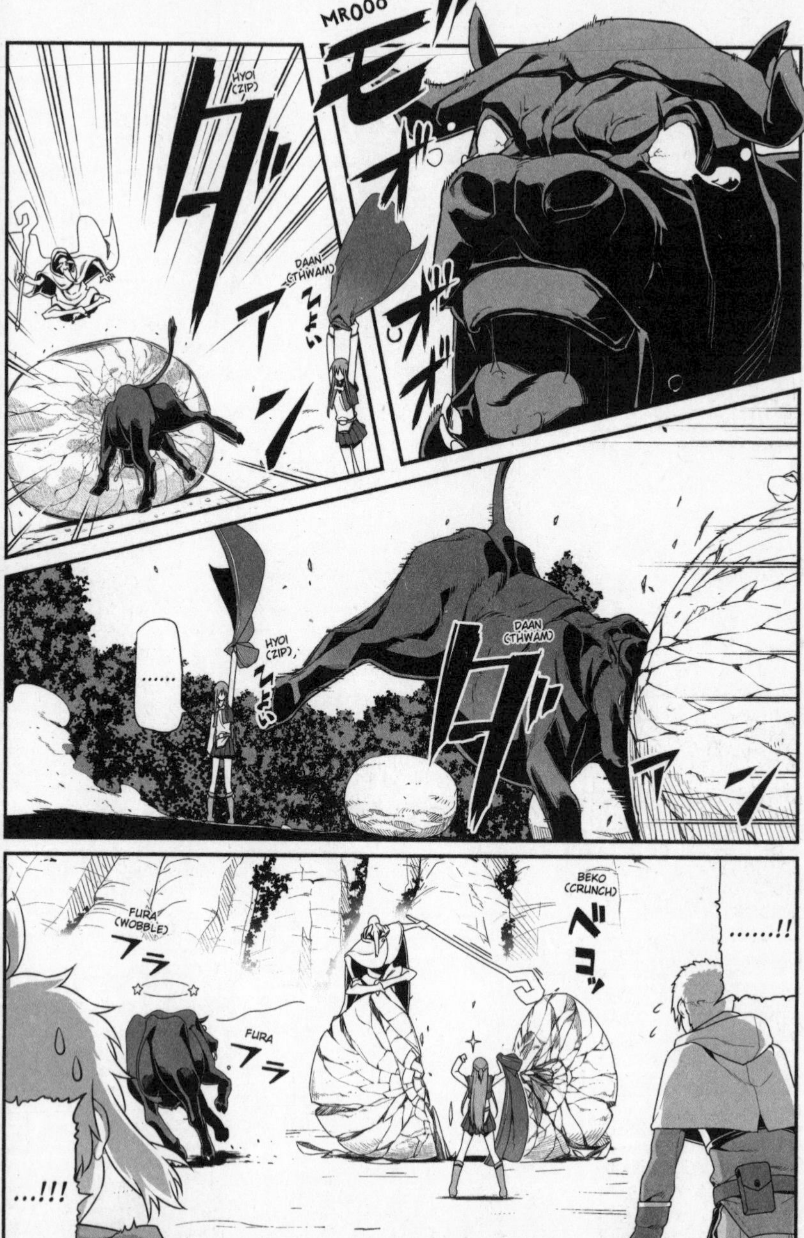
MROOO
モ"オオオ
HYOI (ZIP)
ひょい
DAAN (THWAM)
ドッアン
HYOI (ZIP)
ひょい
DAAN (THWAM)
ドッアン
......
BEKO (CRUNCH)
ベコッ
......!!
FURA (WOBBLE)
フラ
FURA
フラ
...!!!

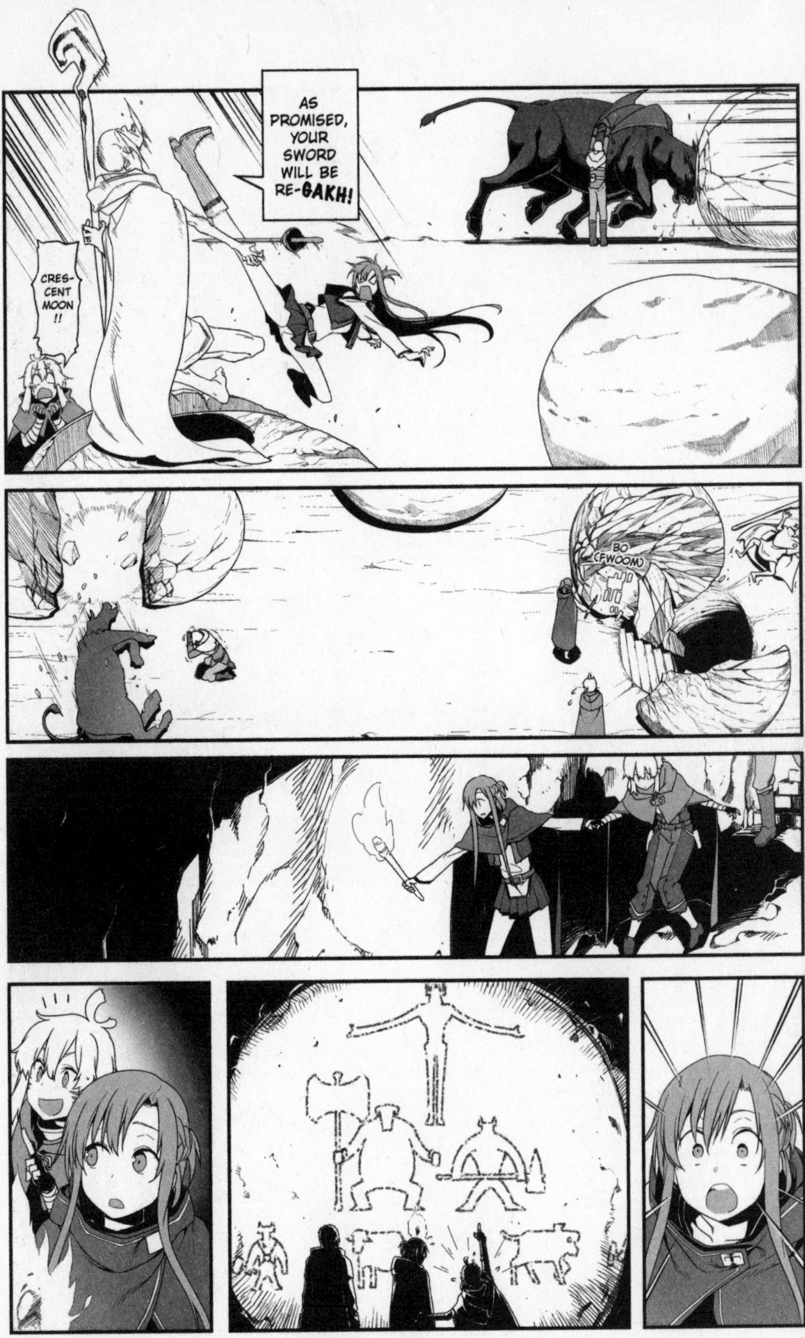
AS PROMISED, YOUR SWORD WILL BE RE-GAKH!
CRES-CENT MOON !!
BO (FWOOM)

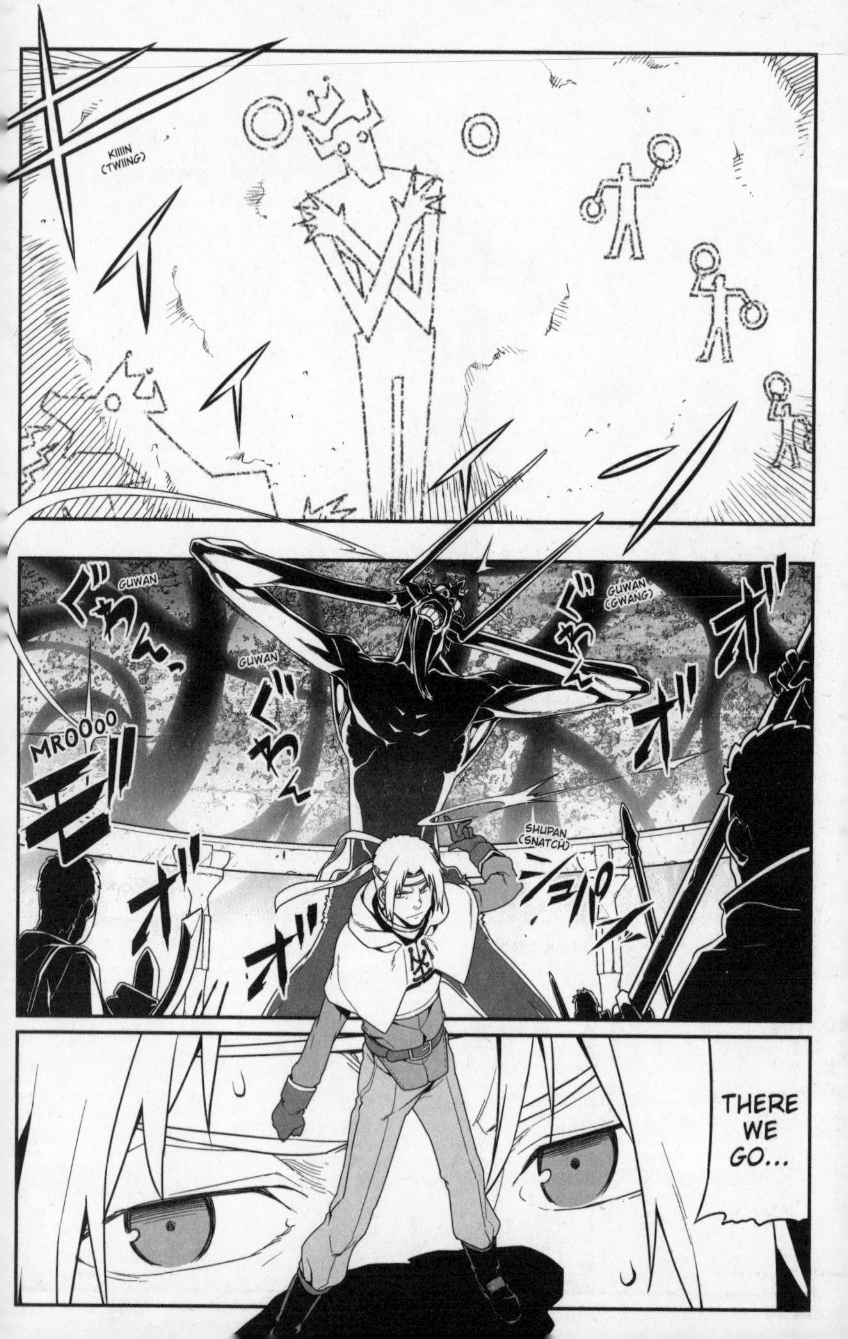
KIIIIN (TWIING)
GUWAN (GWANG)
GUWAN
GUWAN
MROOOO
SHUPAN (SNATCH)
THERE WE GO...

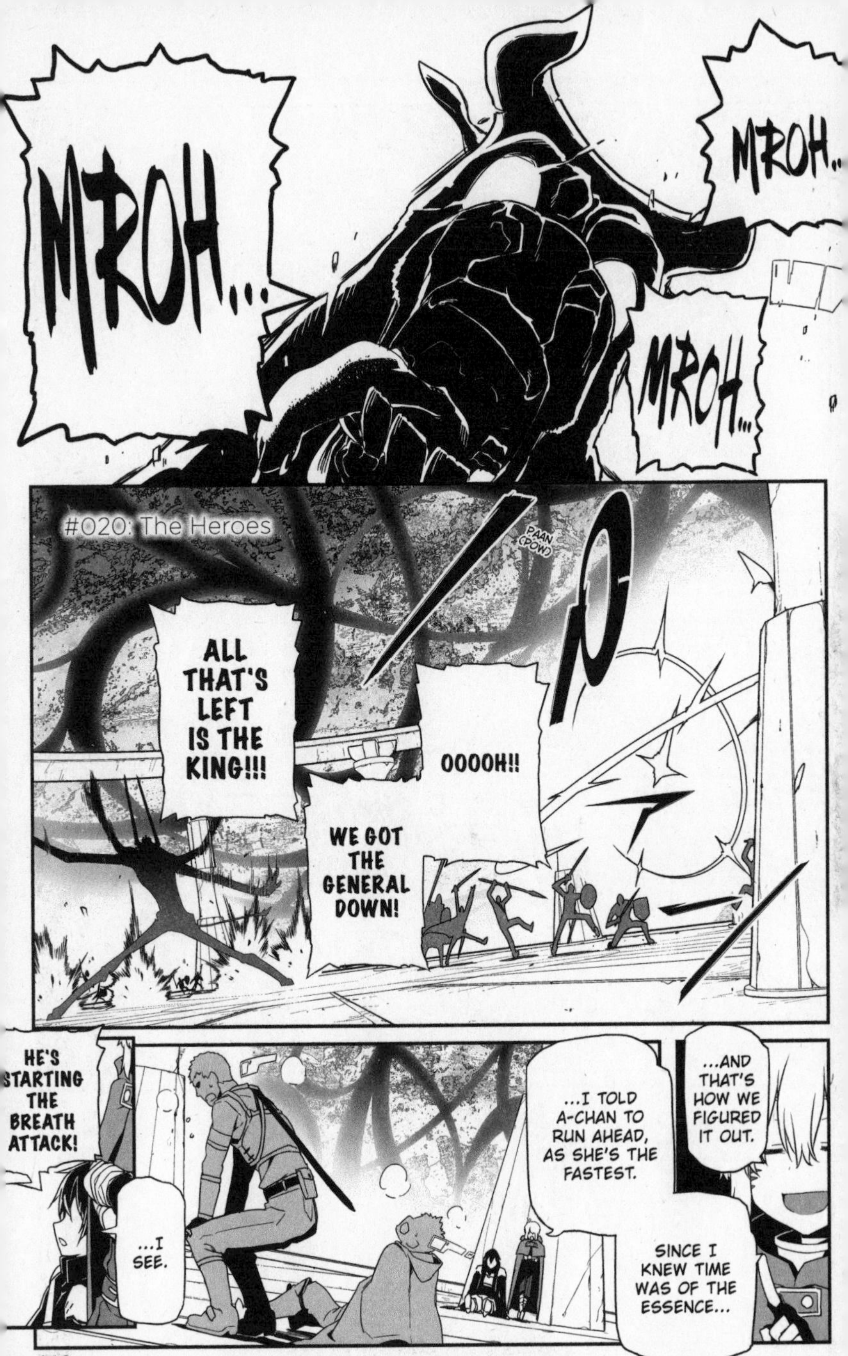
MROH..
MROH...
MROH...
#020: The Heroes
PAAN (POW)
OOOOH!!
WE GOT THE GENERAL DOWN!
ALL THAT'S LEFT IS THE KING!!!
...AND THAT'S HOW WE FIGURED IT OUT.
...I TOLD A-CHAN TO RUN AHEAD, AS SHE'S THE FASTEST.
SINCE I KNEW TIME WAS OF THE ESSENCE...
HE'S STARTING THE BREATH ATTACK!
...I SEE.

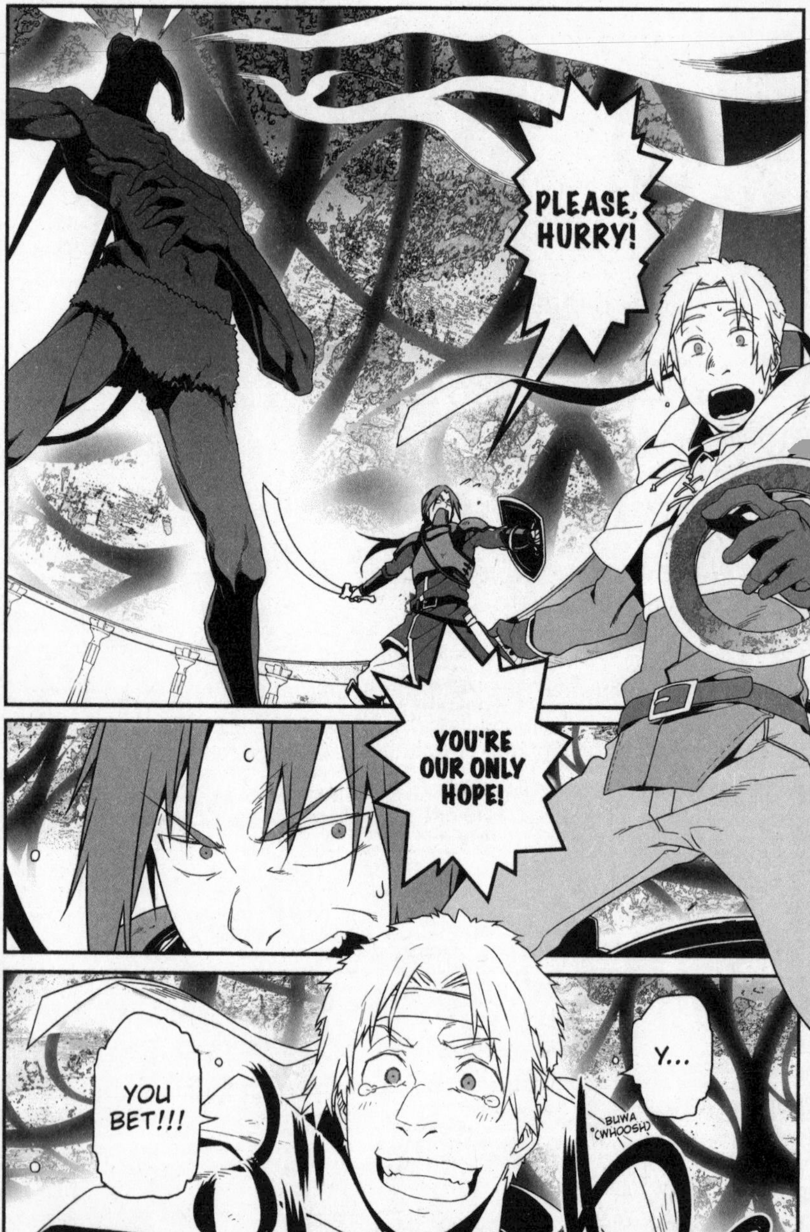
PLEASE, HURRY!
YOU'RE OUR ONLY HOPE!
Y...
BUWA (WHOOSH)
YOU BET!!!

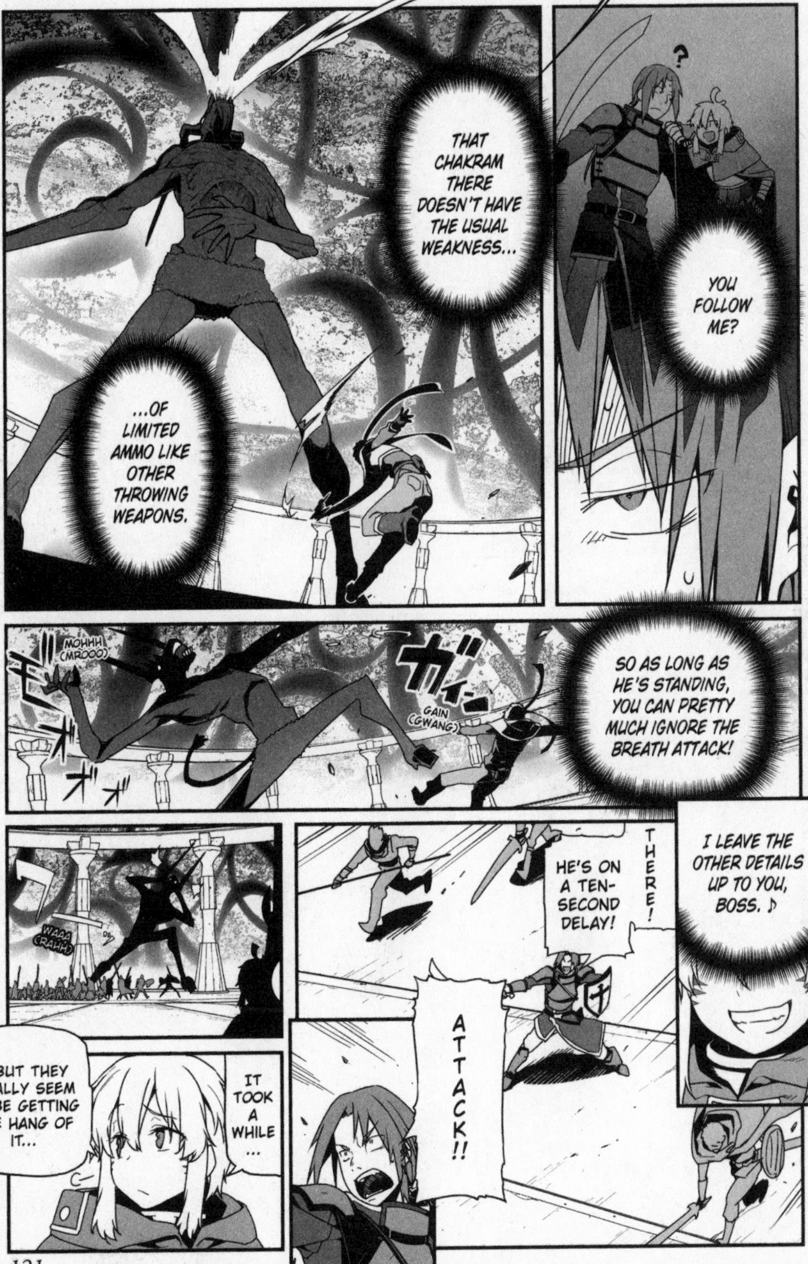
?
YOU FOLLOW ME?
THAT CHAKRAM THERE DOESN'T HAVE THE USUAL WEAKNESS...
...OF LIMITED AMMO LIKE OTHER THROWING WEAPONS.
SO AS LONG AS HE'S STANDING, YOU CAN PRETTY MUCH IGNORE THE BREATH ATTACK!
ガィー
GAIN (GWANG)
MOHHH (MROOO)
I LEAVE THE OTHER DETAILS UP TO YOU, BOSS. ♪
THERE!
HE'S ON A TEN-SECOND DELAY!
ATTACK!!
WAAA (RAHH)
IT TOOK A WHILE ...
..BUT THEY NALLY SEEM BE GETTING HE HANG OF IT...

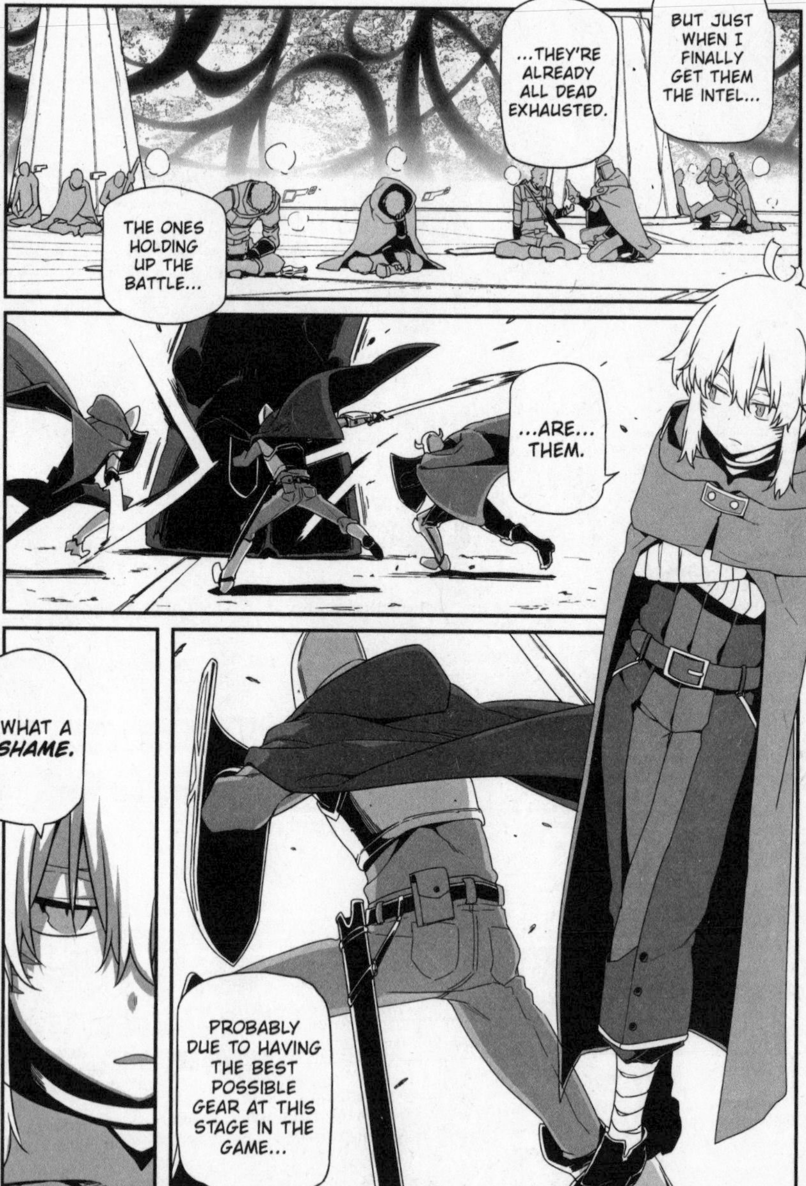
BUT JUST WHEN I FINALLY GET THEM THE INTEL...
...THEY'RE ALREADY ALL DEAD EXHAUSTED.
THE ONES HOLDING UP THE BATTLE...
...ARE... THEM.
PROBABLY DUE TO HAVING THE BEST POSSIBLE GEAR AT THIS STAGE IN THE GAME...
WHAT A SHAME.

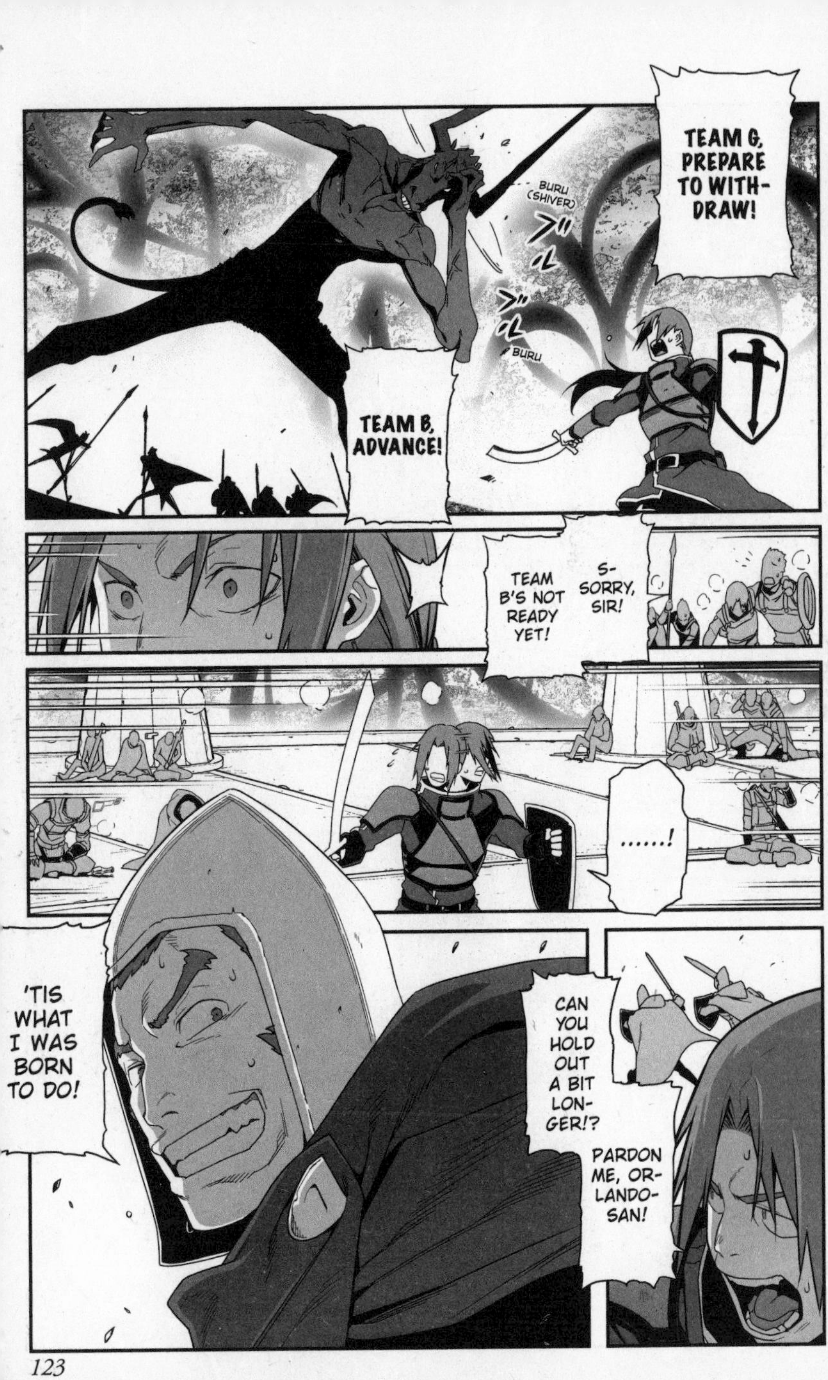
TEAM G, PREPARE TO WITH-DRAW!
BURU (SHIVER)
BURU
TEAM B, ADVANCE!
S-SORRY, SIR!
TEAM B'S NOT READY YET!
......!
CAN YOU HOLD OUT A BIT LON-GER!?
PARDON ME, OR-LANDO-SAN!
'TIS WHAT I WAS BORN TO DO!

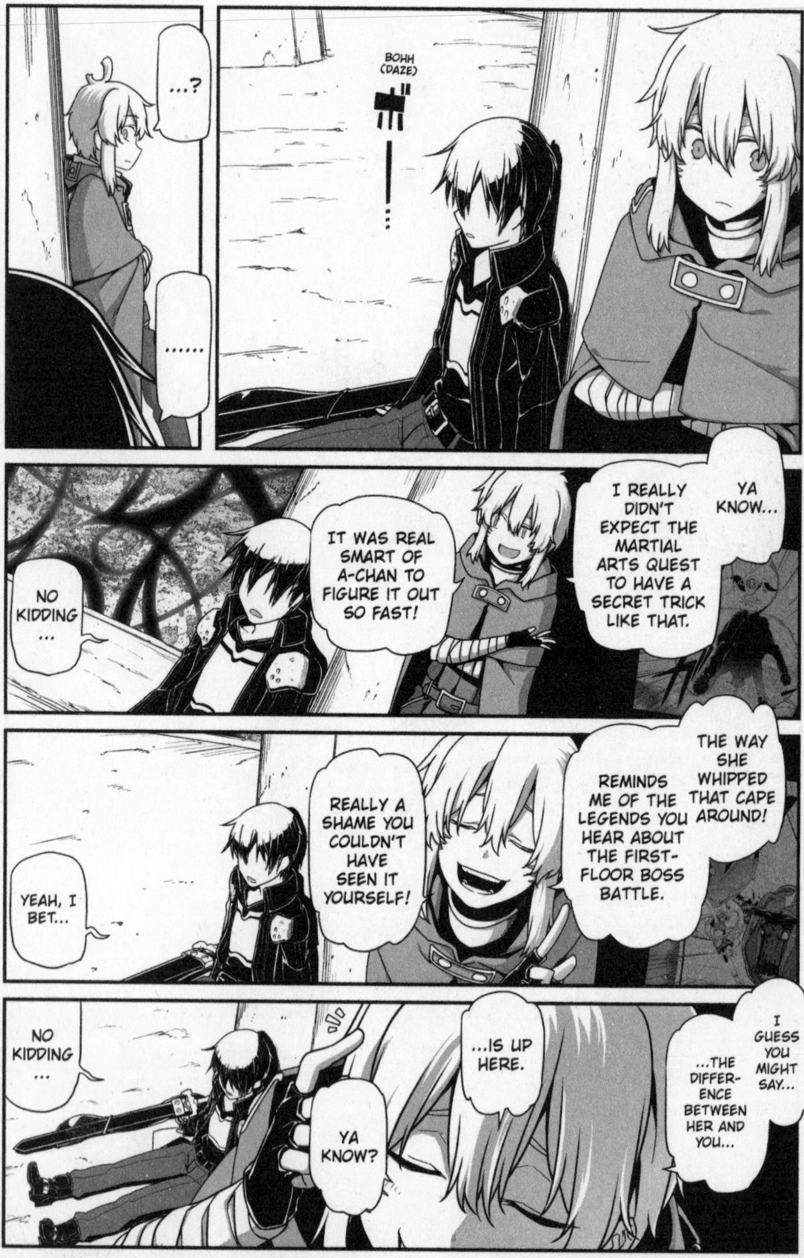
BOHH (DAZE)
...?
......
YA KNOW...
I REALLY DIDN'T EXPECT THE MARTIAL ARTS QUEST TO HAVE A SECRET TRICK LIKE THAT.
IT WAS REAL SMART OF A-CHAN TO FIGURE IT OUT SO FAST!
NO KIDDING...
THE WAY SHE WHIPPED THAT CAPE AROUND!
REMINDS ME OF THE LEGENDS YOU HEAR ABOUT THE FIRST-FLOOR BOSS BATTLE.
REALLY A SHAME YOU COULDN'T HAVE SEEN IT YOURSELF!
YEAH, I BET...
I GUESS YOU MIGHT SAY...
...THE DIFFERENCE BETWEEN HER AND YOU...
...IS UP HERE.
YA KNOW?
NO KIDDING...

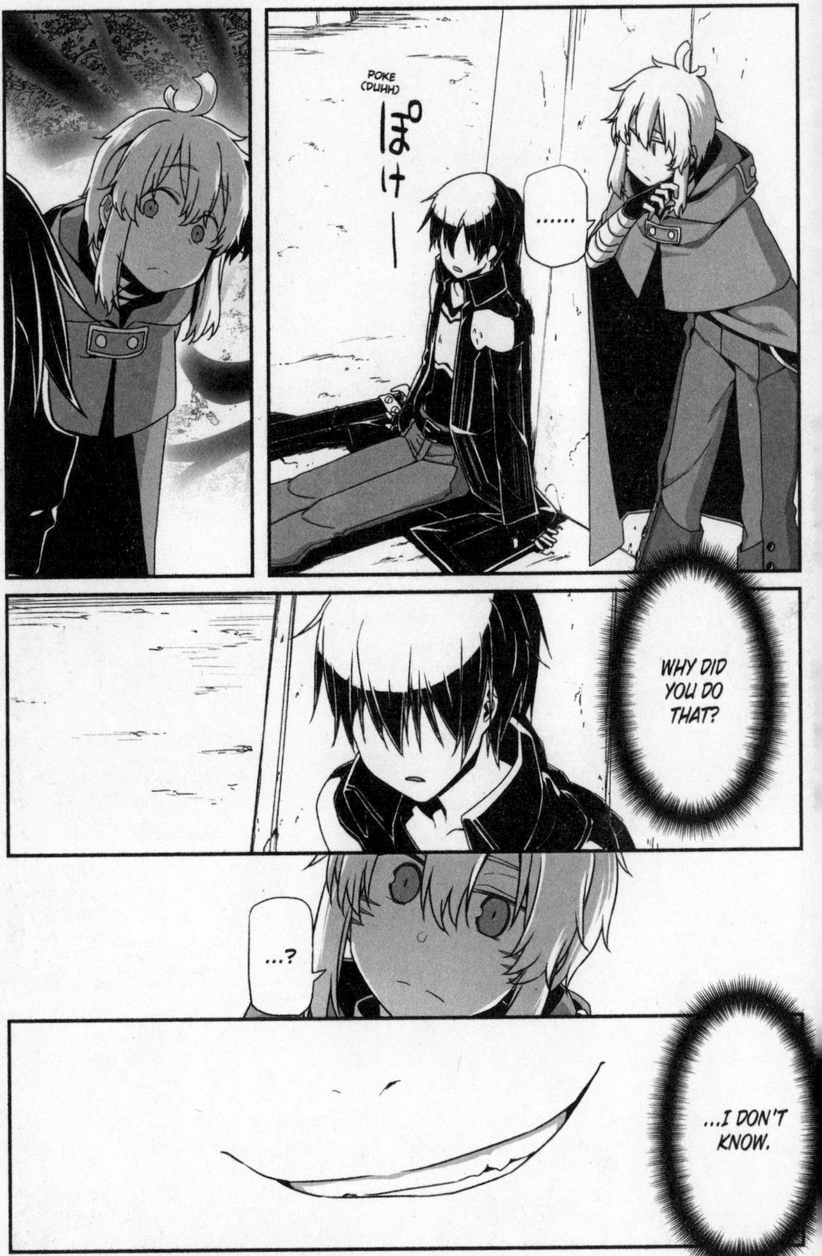
POKE (DUHH)
ぽけー
......
WHY DID YOU DO THAT?
...?
...I DON'T KNOW.

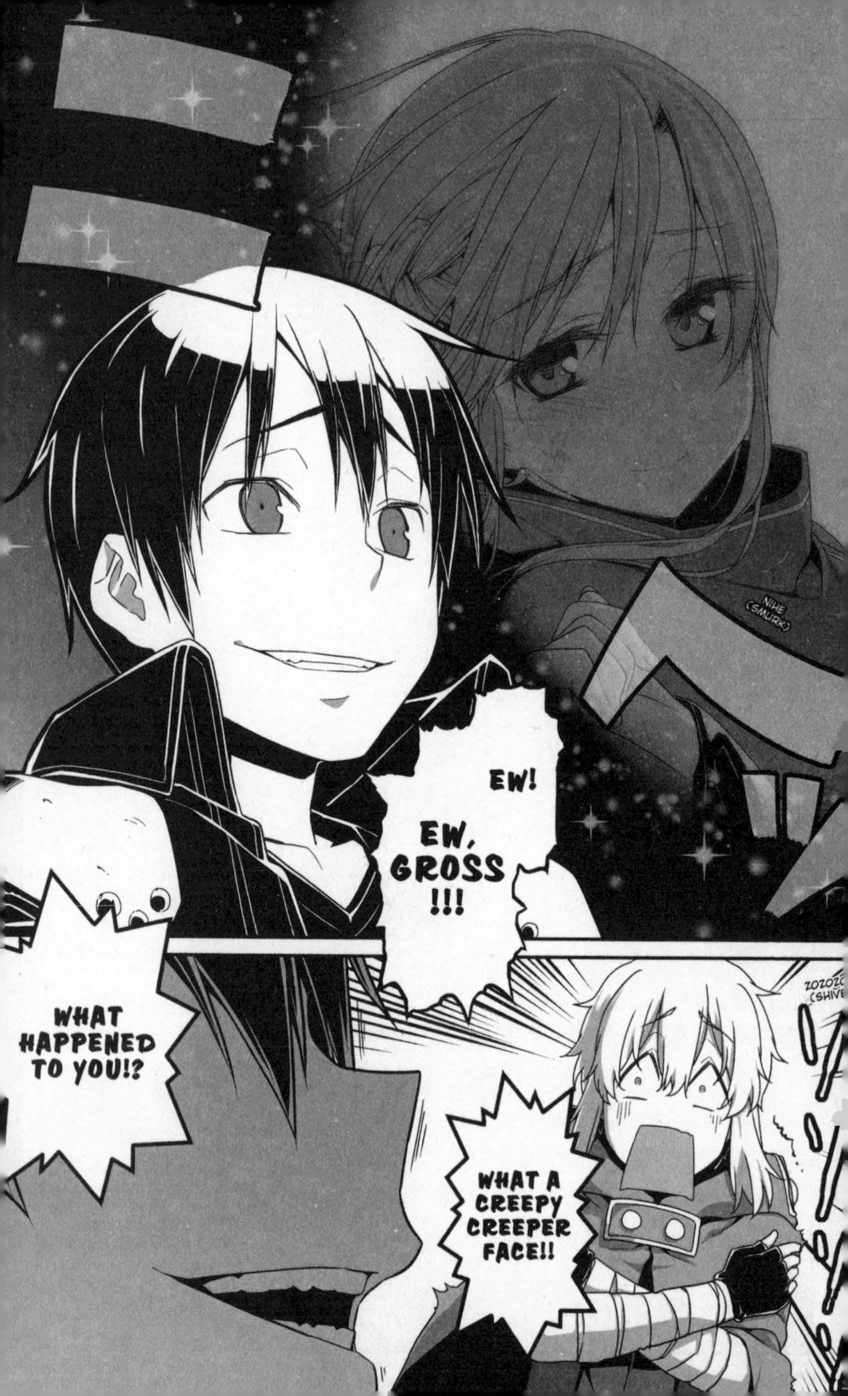
NIHE (SMURK)
EW!
EW, GROSS!!!
WHAT A CREEPY CREEPER FACE!!
WHAT HAPPENED TO YOU!?

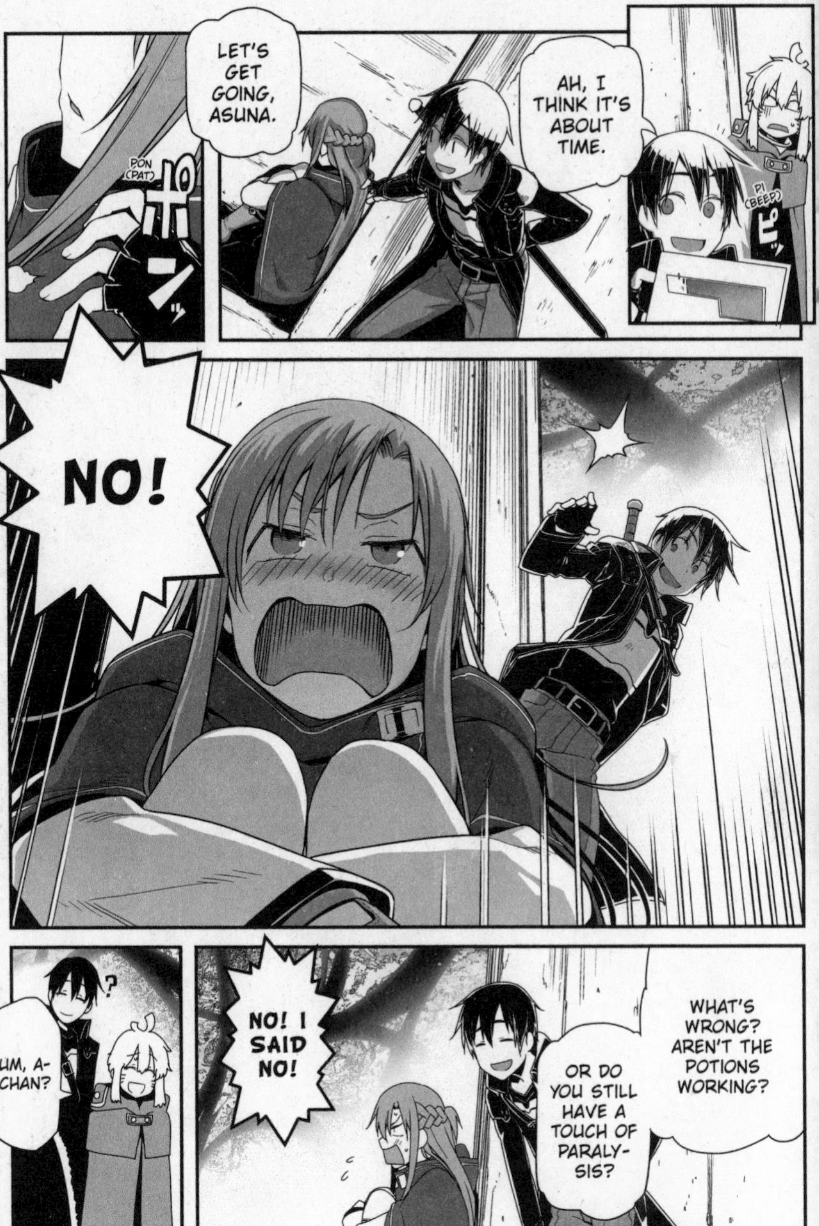
PI (BEEP)
AH, I THINK IT'S ABOUT TIME.
LET'S GET GOING, ASUNA.
PON (PAT)
NO!
WHAT'S WRONG? AREN'T THE POTIONS WORKING?
OR DO YOU STILL HAVE A TOUCH OF PARALY-SIS?
NO! I SAID NO!
?
UM, A-CHAN?

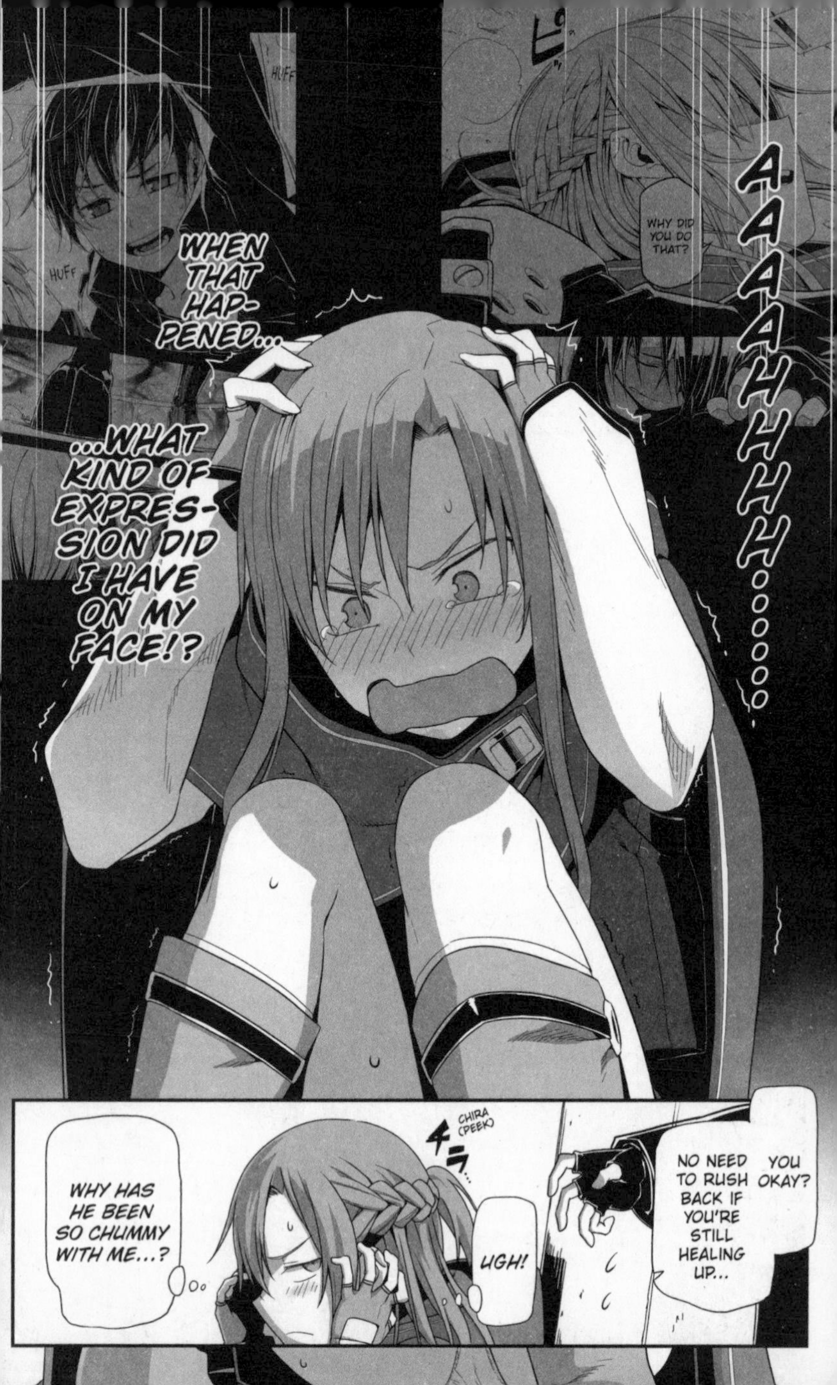

WHY DID YOU DO THAT?
HUFF
HUFF
AAAAHHHHH.......
WHEN THAT HAP-PENED...
...WHAT KIND OF EXPRES-SION DID I HAVE ON MY FACE!?
YOU OKAY?
NO NEED TO RUSH BACK IF YOU'RE STILL HEALING UP...
CHIRA (PEEK)
UGH!
WHY HAS HE BEEN SO CHUMMY WITH ME...?

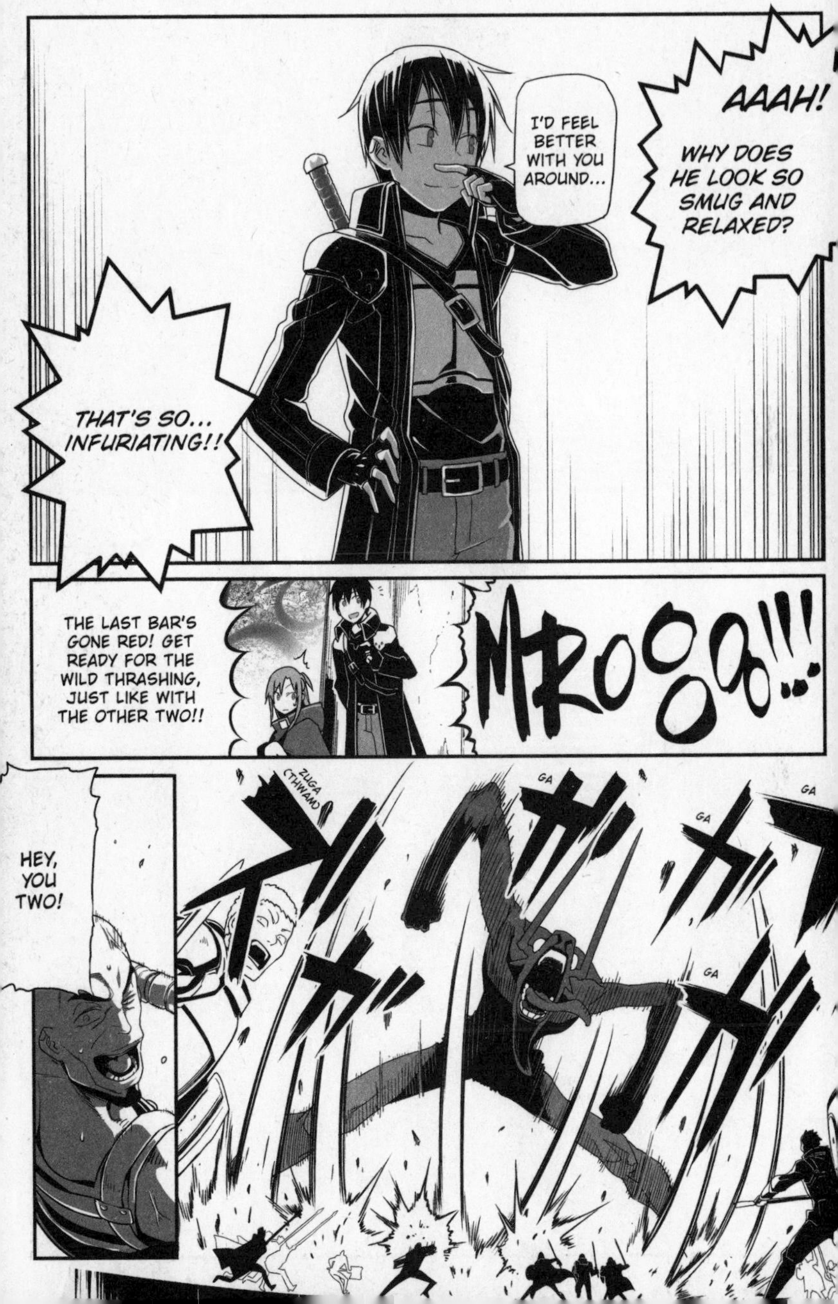
AAAH!
WHY DOES HE LOOK SO SMUG AND RELAXED?
I'D FEEL BETTER WITH YOU AROUND...
THAT'S SO... INFURIATING!!
MROOOO!!!
THE LAST BAR'S GONE RED! GET READY FOR THE WILD THRASHING, JUST LIKE WITH THE OTHER TWO!!
GA
GA
GA
GA
ZUGA (THWAM)
HEY, YOU TWO!

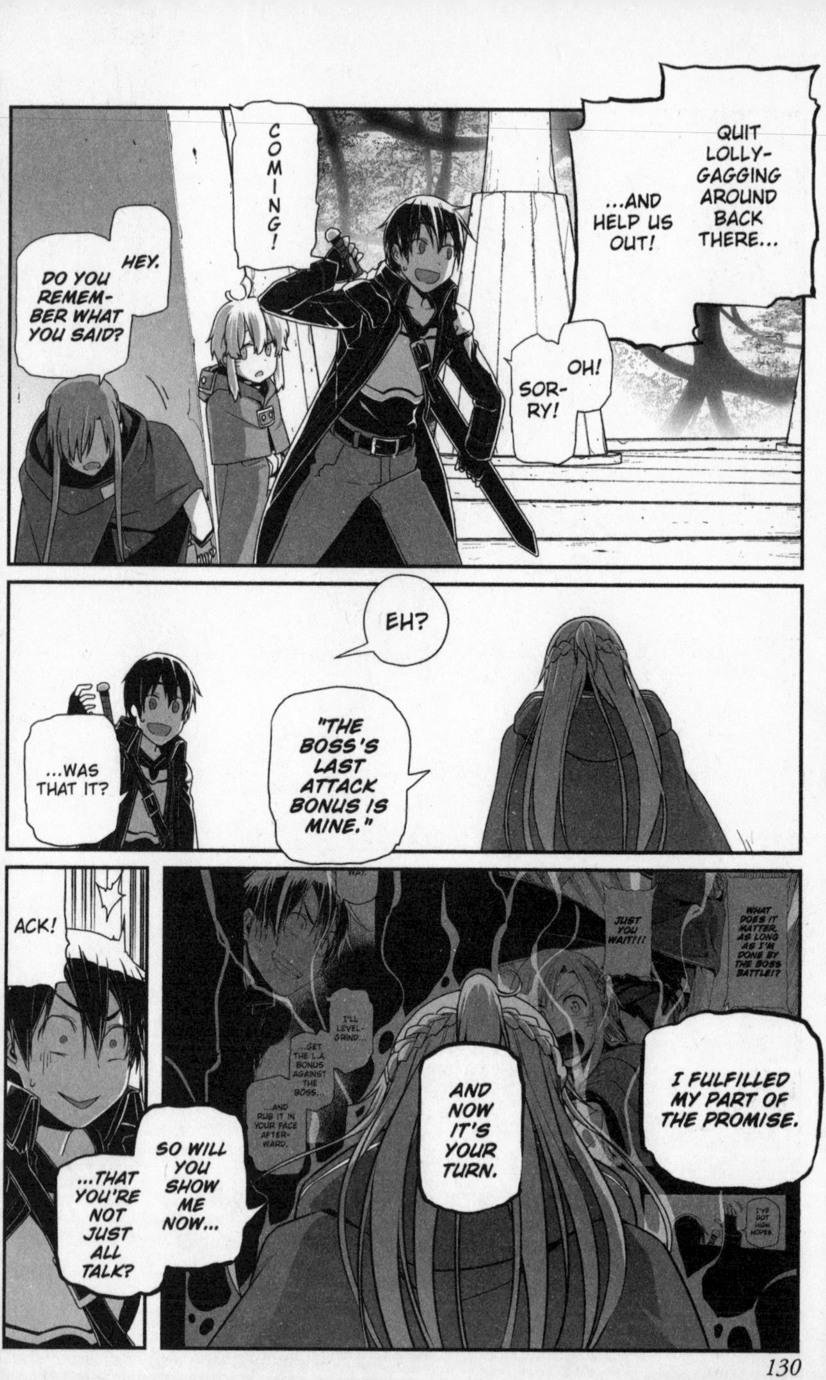
QUIT LOLLY-GAGGING AROUND BACK THERE...
...AND HELP US OUT!
OH! SORRY!
COMING!
HEY. DO YOU REMEMBER WHAT YOU SAID?
EH?
"THE BOSS'S LAST ATTACK BONUS IS MINE."
...WAS THAT IT?
WHAT DOES IT MATTER AS LONG AS I'M DONE BY THE BOSS BATTLE!?
JUST YOU WAIT!!!
I'LL LEVEL-GRIND...
...GET THE L.A. BONUS AGAINST THE BOSS...
...AND RUB IT IN YOUR FACE AFTERWARD.
I FULFILLED MY PART OF THE PROMISE.
AND NOW IT'S YOUR TURN.
I'VE GOT HIGH HOPES.
ACK!
SO WILL YOU SHOW ME NOW...
...THAT YOU'RE NOT JUST ALL TALK?

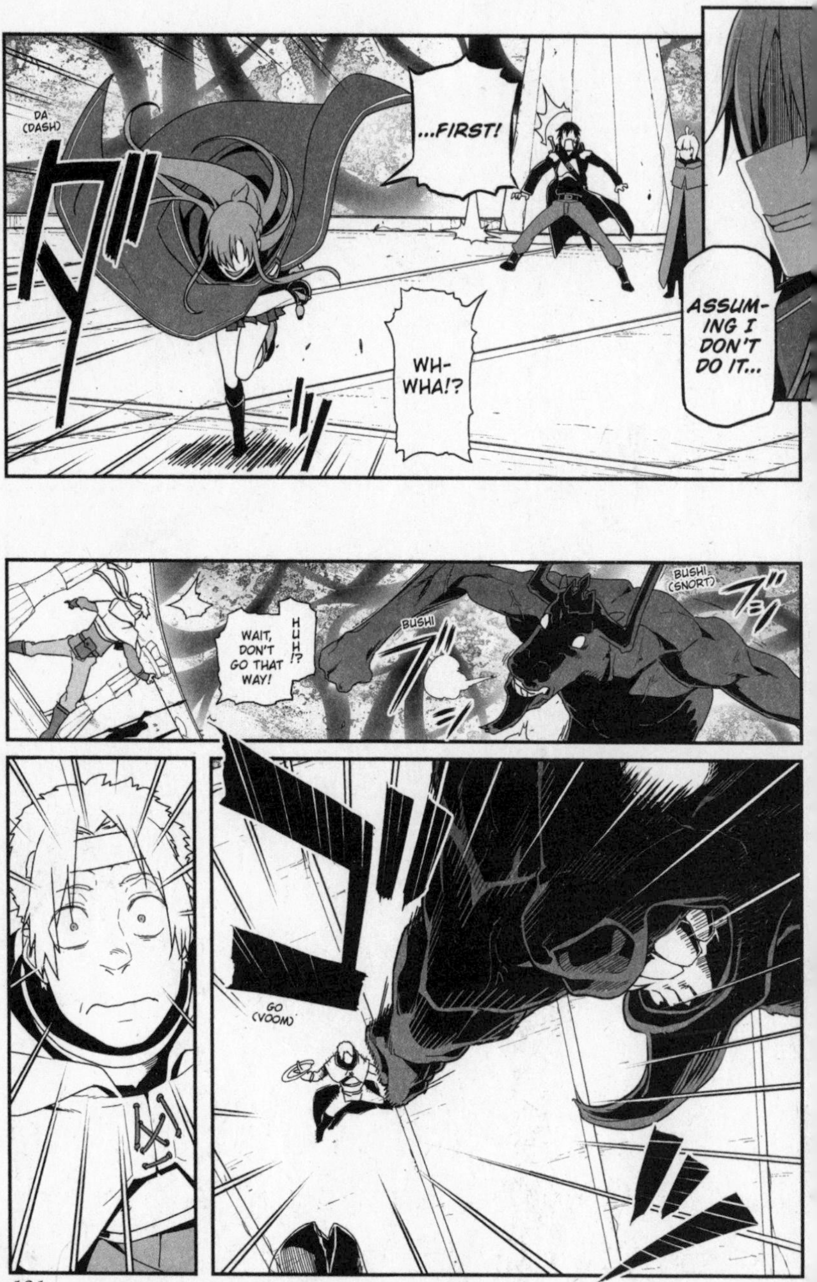
ASSUMING I DON'T DO IT...
...FIRST!
DA (DASH)
WH-WHA!?
BUSHI (SNORT)
BUSHI
HUH!?
WAIT, DON'T GO THAT WAY!
GO (VOOM)

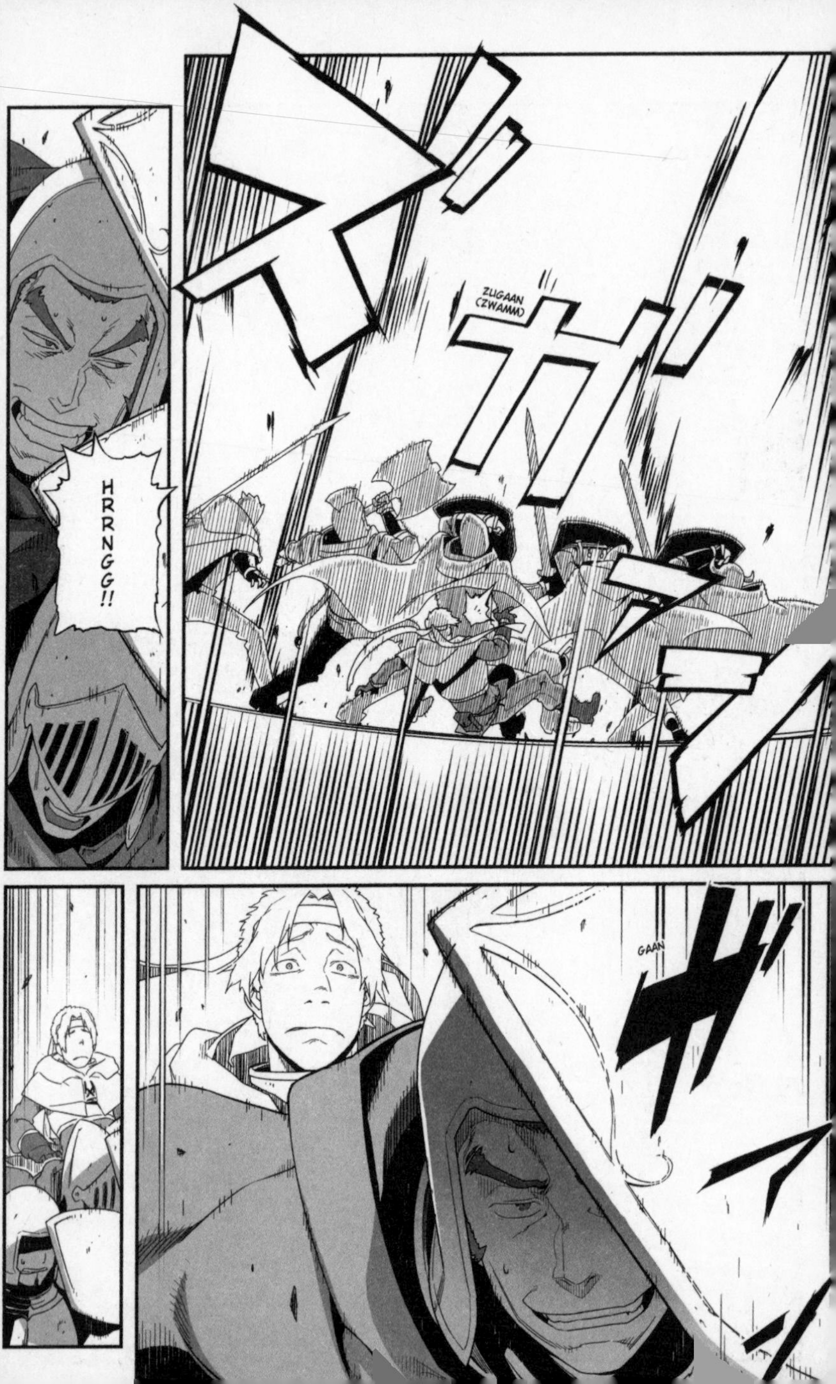
ZUGAAN (ZWAMM)
HRRNGG!!
GAAN

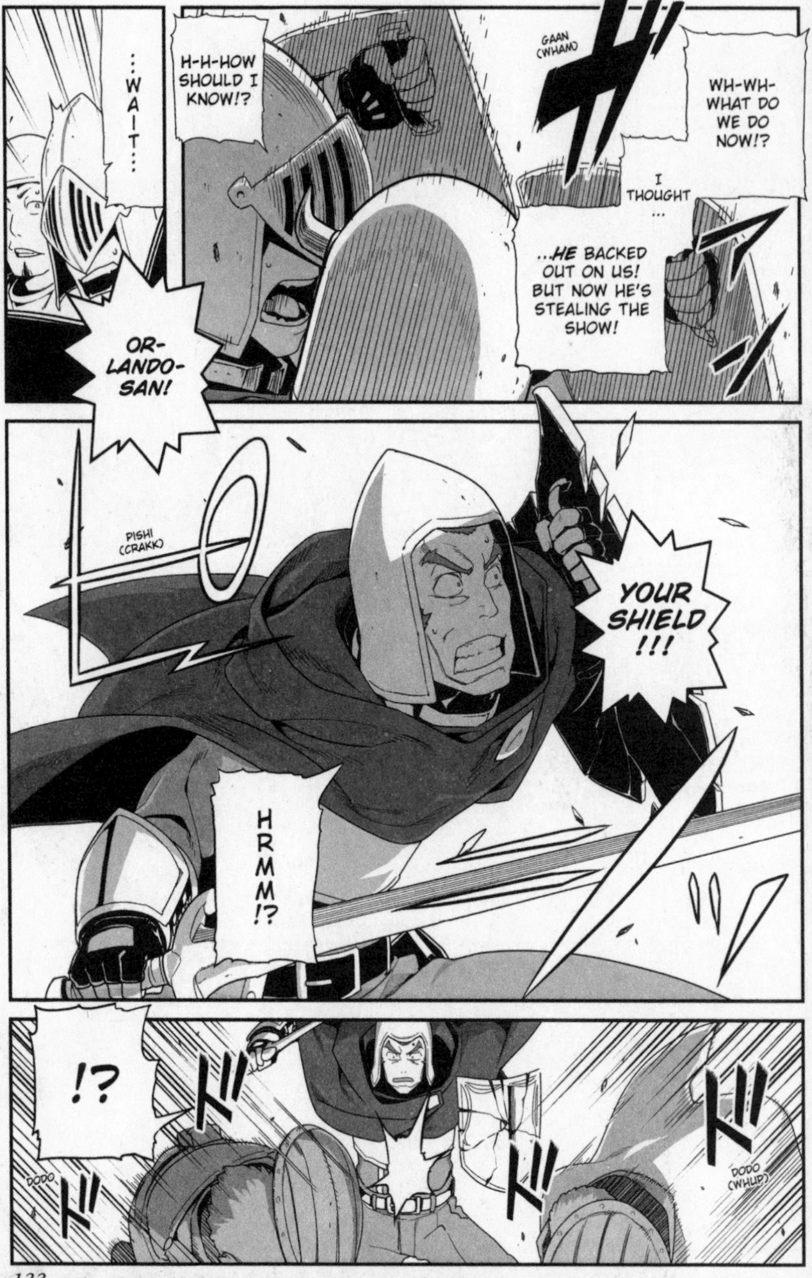
GAAN (WHAM)
WH-WH-WHAT DO WE DO NOW!?
I THOUGHT ...
...HE BACKED OUT ON US! BUT NOW HE'S STEALING THE SHOW!
H-H-HOW SHOULD I KNOW!?
OR-LANDO-SAN!
...WAIT...
YOUR SHIELD!!!
PISHI (CRAKK)
HRMM!?
DODO (WHUP)
!?
DODO

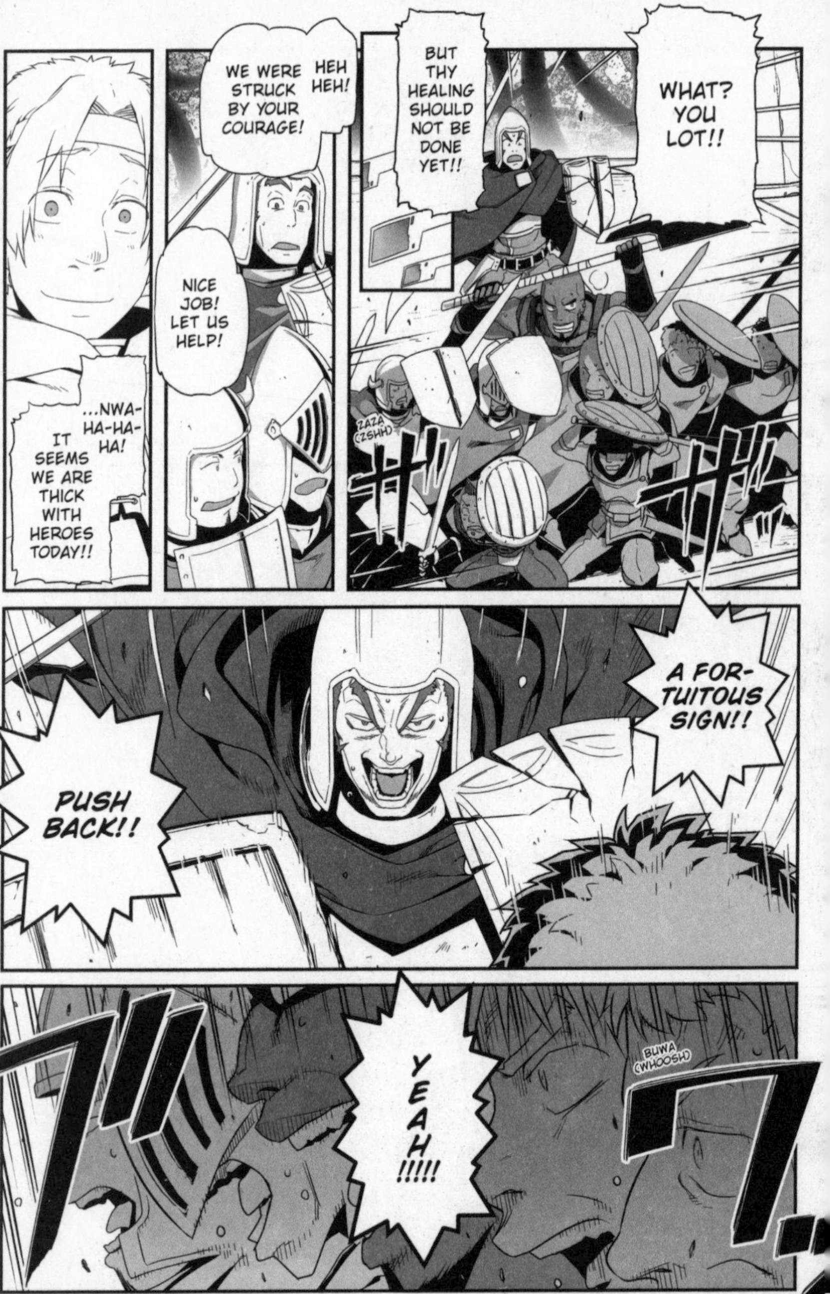
WHAT? YOU LOT!!
BUT THY HEALING SHOULD NOT BE DONE YET!!
ZAZA (ZSHH)
HEH HEH!
WE WERE STRUCK BY YOUR COURAGE!
NICE JOB! LET US HELP!
...NWA-HA-HA-HA!
IT SEEMS WE ARE THICK WITH HEROES TODAY!!
A FOR-TUITOUS SIGN!!
PUSH BACK!!
BUWA (WHOOSH)
YEAH!!!!!

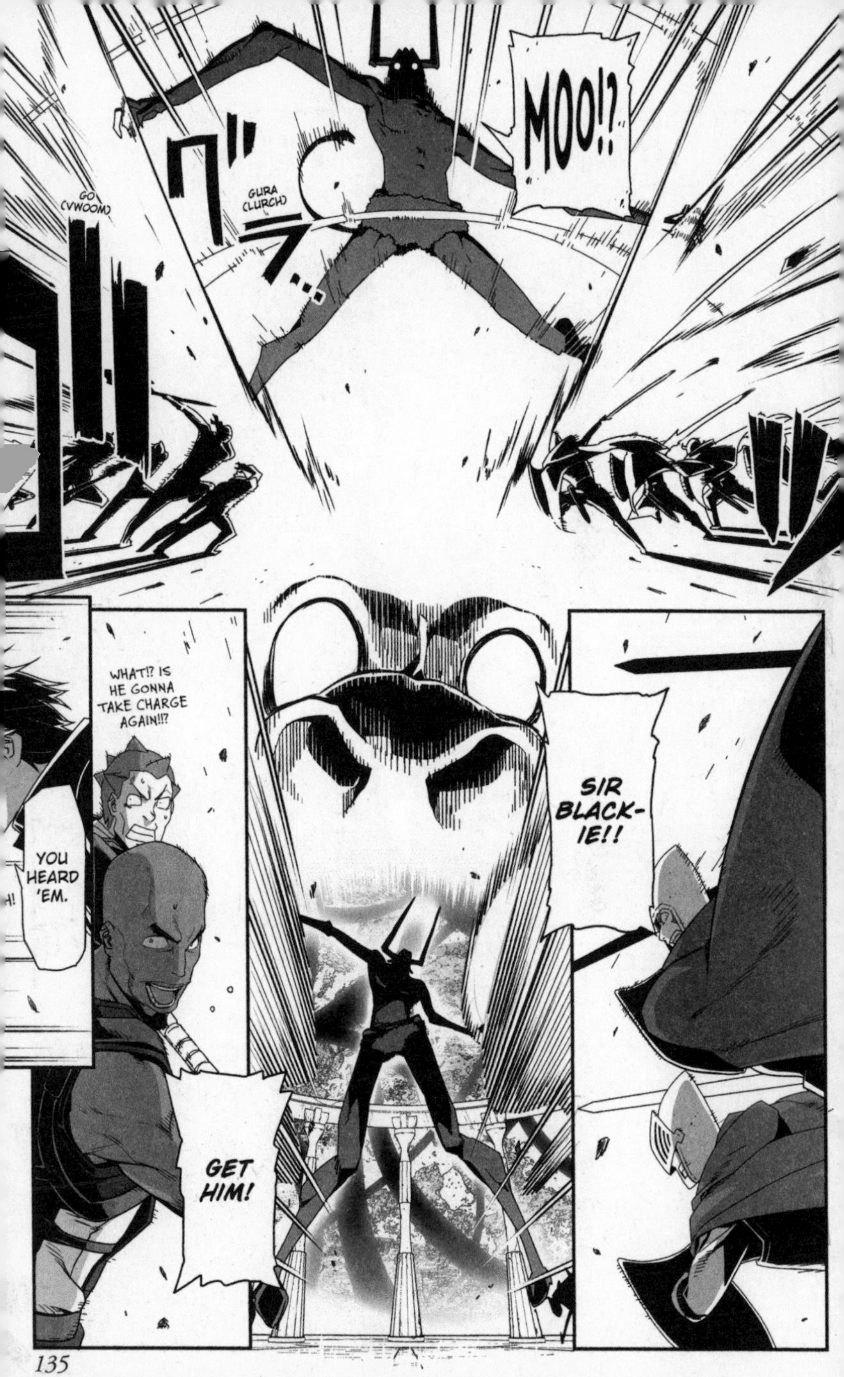
MOO!?
GURA (LURCH)
GO (VWOOM)
SIR BLACK-IE!!
WHAT!? IS HE GONNA TAKE CHARGE AGAIN!!?
YOU HEARD 'EM.
GET HIM!

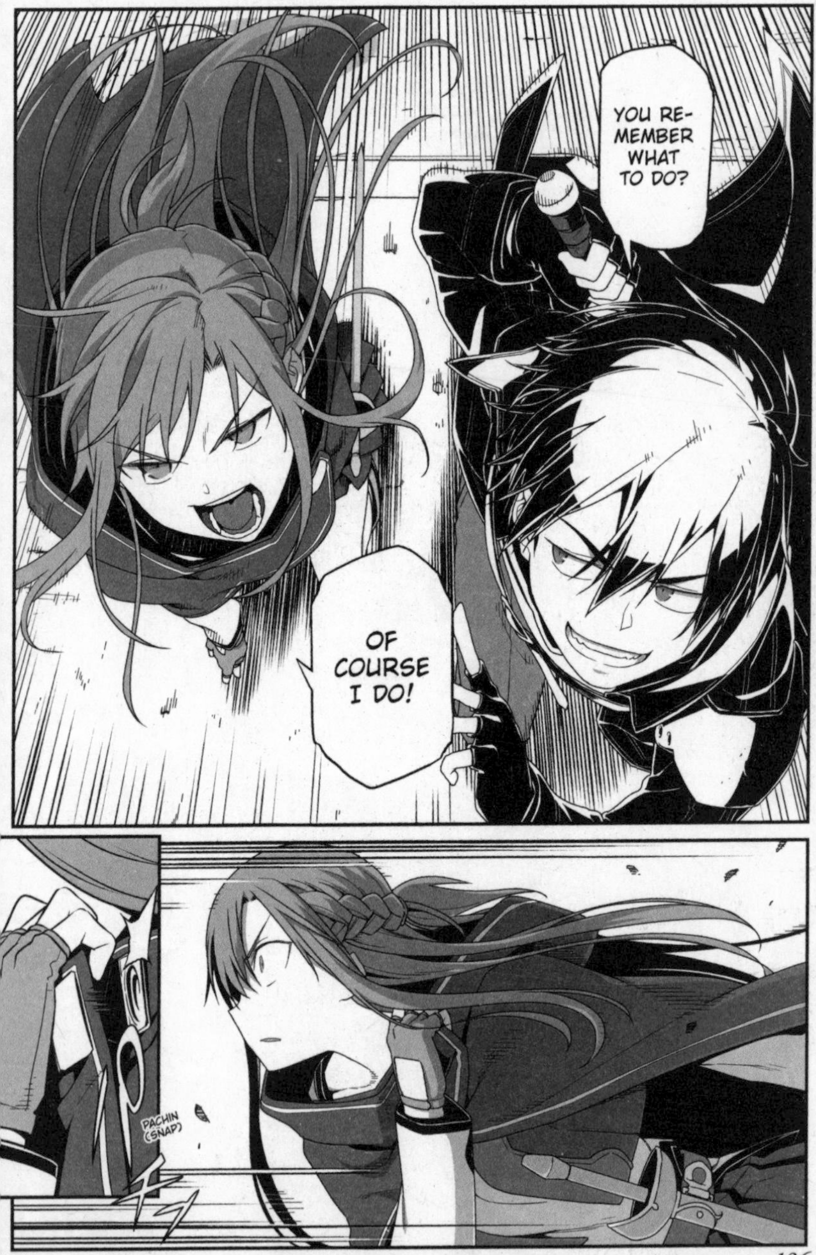
YOU RE-MEMBER WHAT TO DO?
OF COURSE I DO!
PACHIN (SNAP)

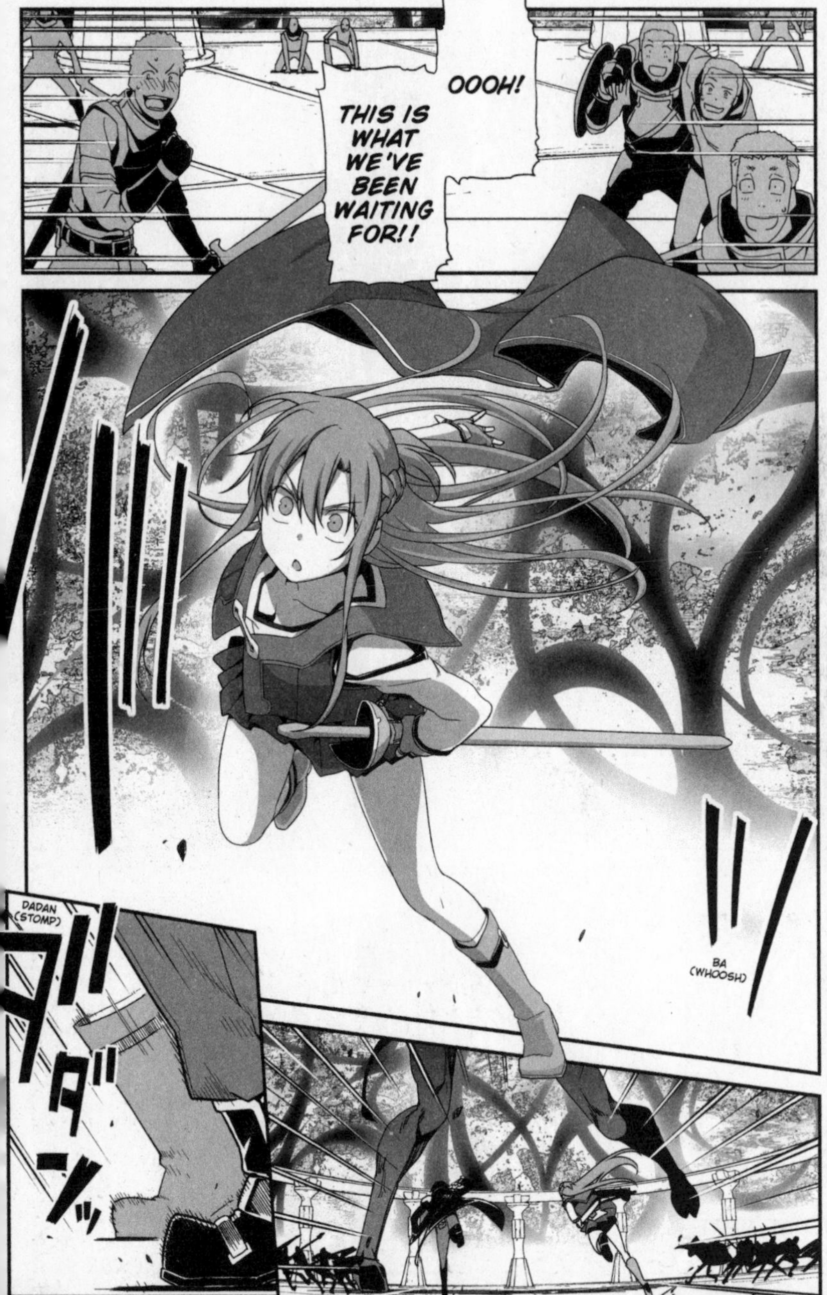
OOOH!
THIS IS WHAT WE'VE BEEN WAITING FOR!!
BA (WHOOSH)
DADAN (STOMP)

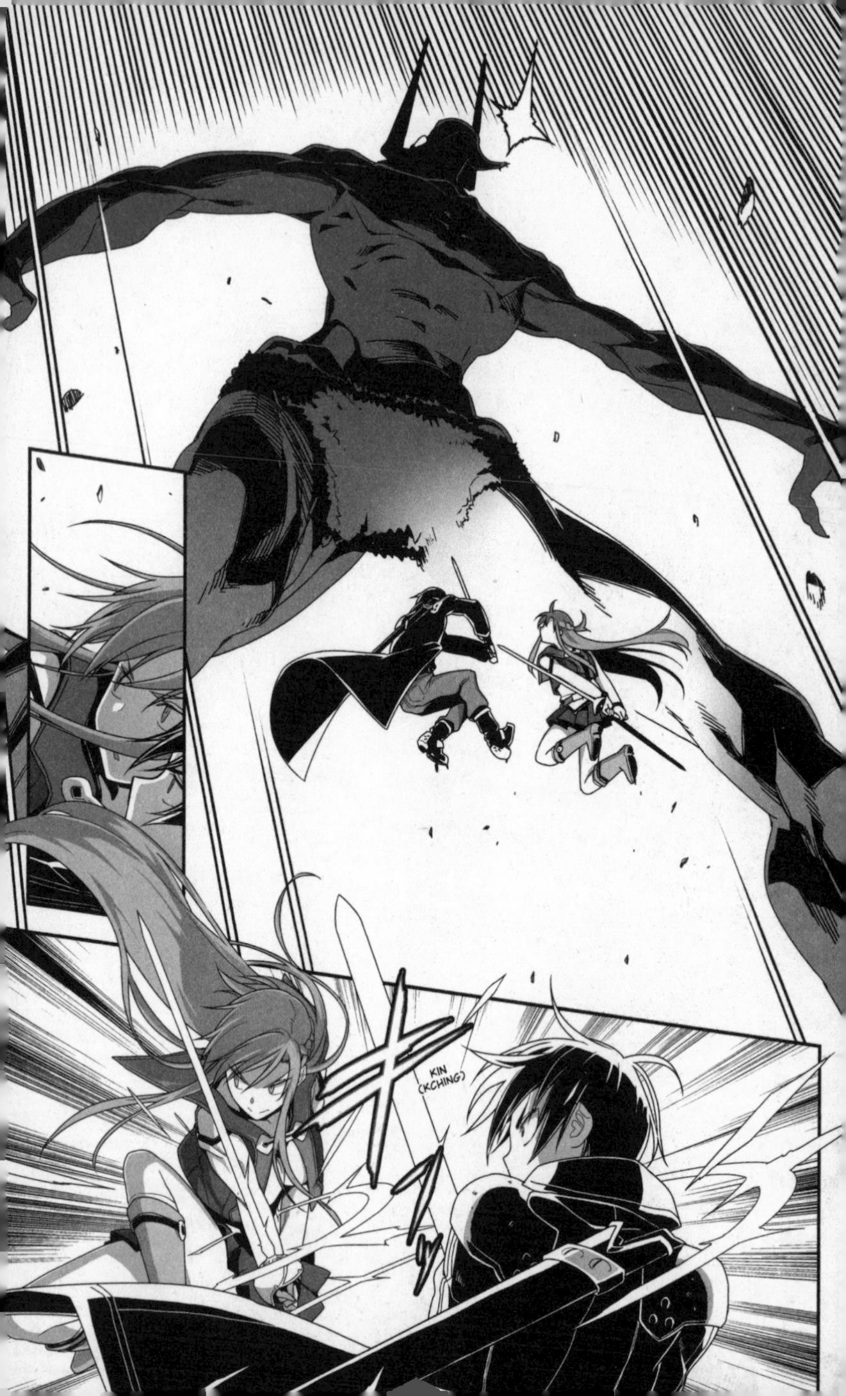
KIN
(KCHING)

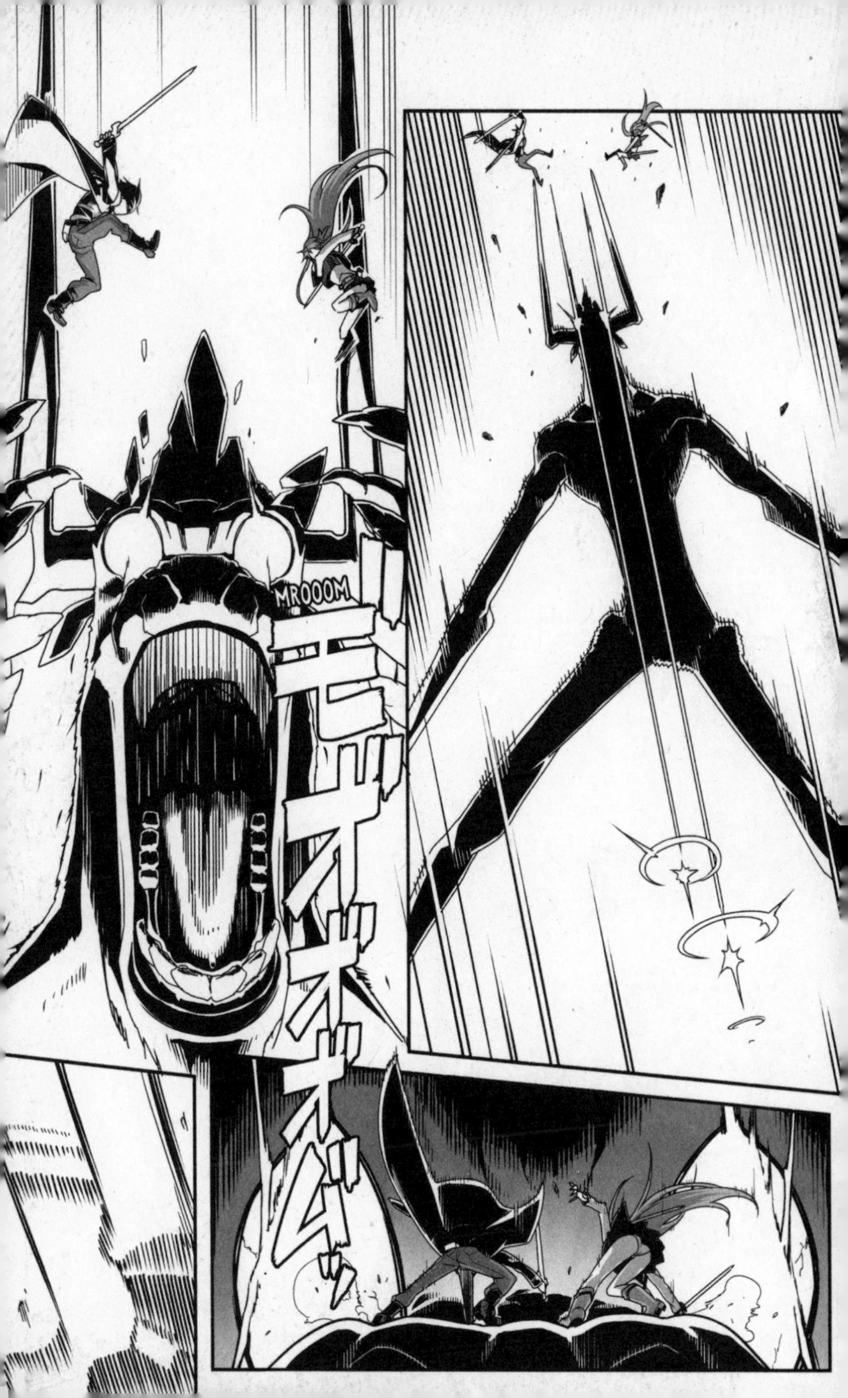
MROOOM

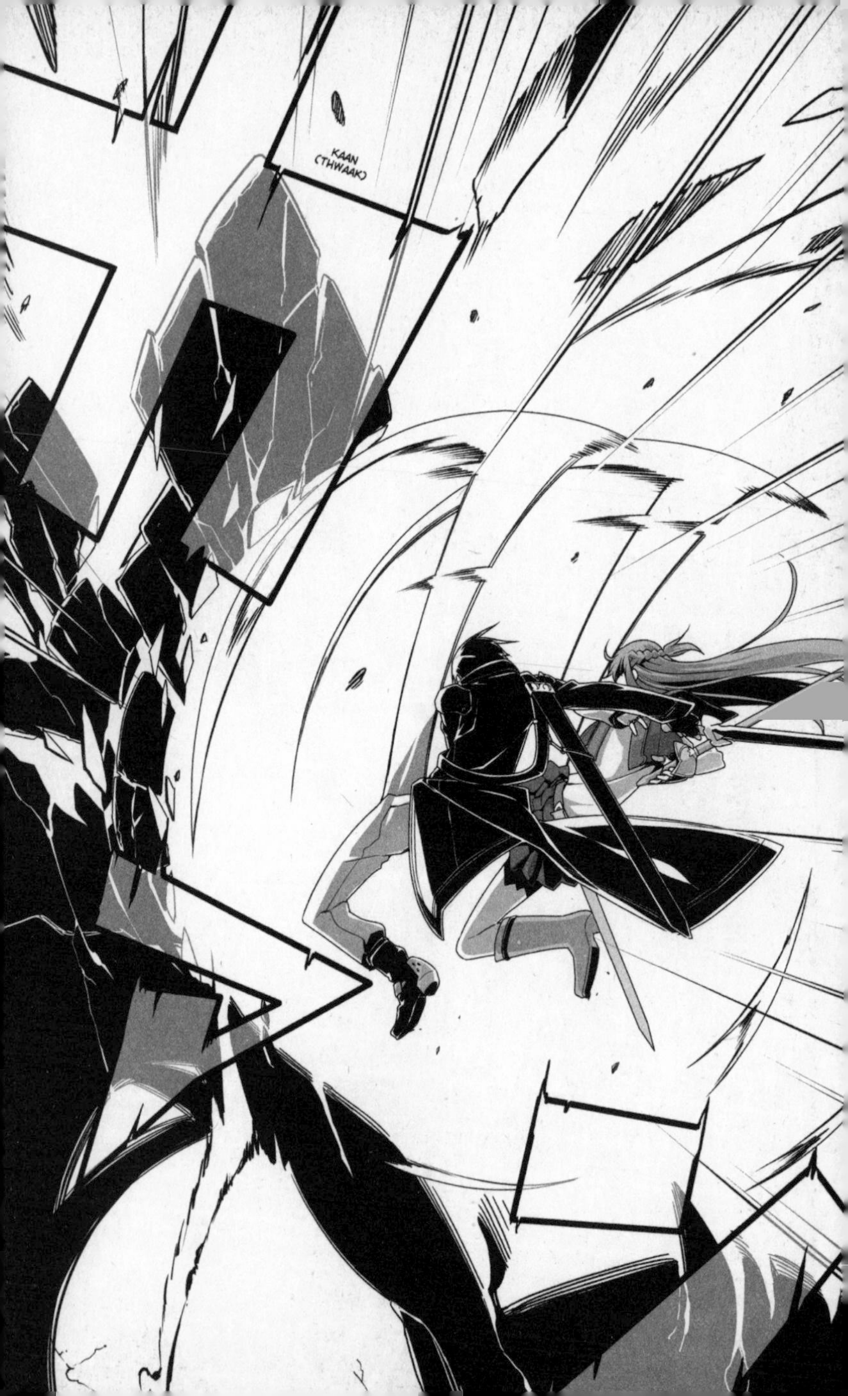
KAAN
(THWAAK)

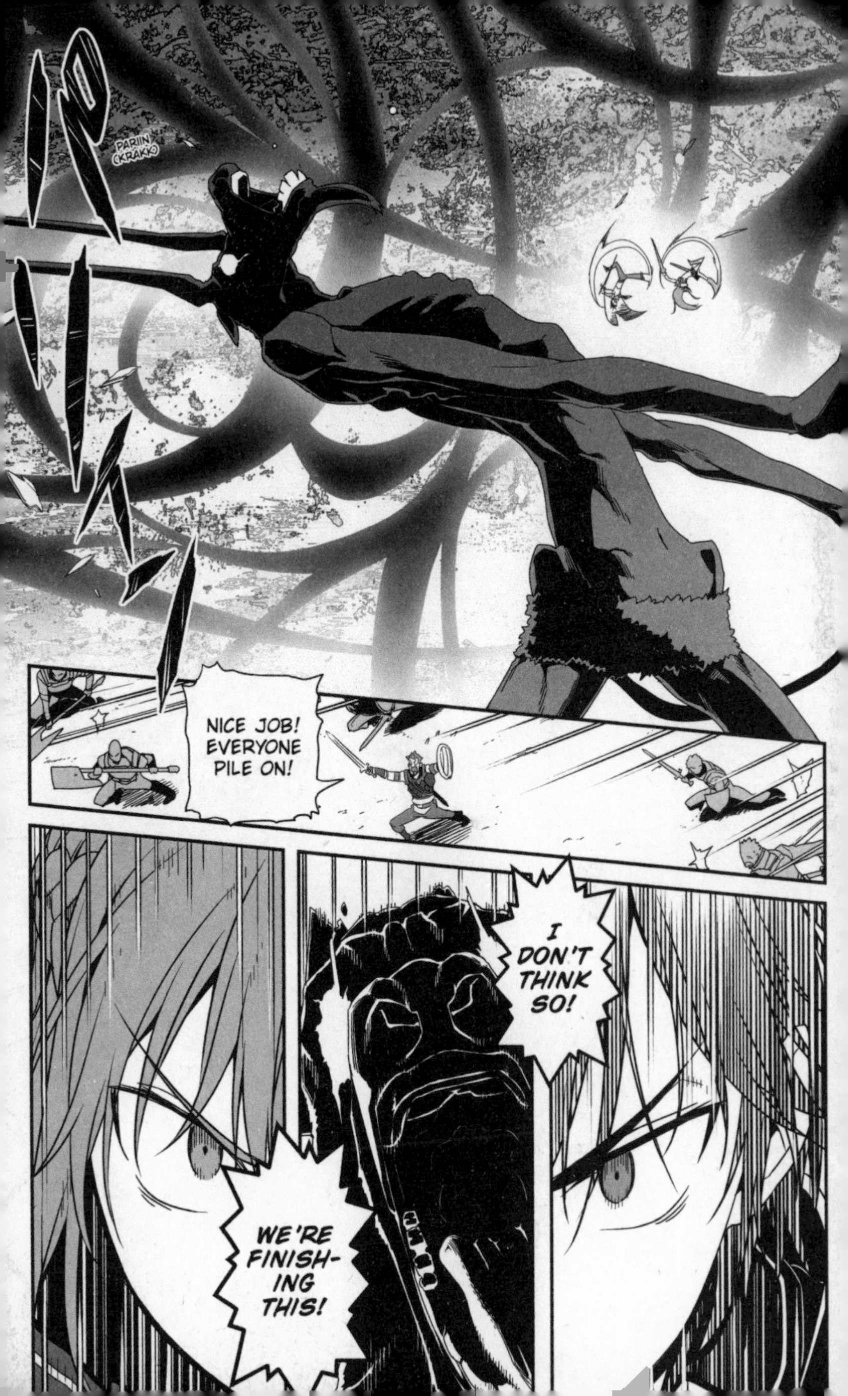
PARIIN
(KRAKK)
NICE JOB! EVERYONE PILE ON!
I DON'T THINK SO!
WE'RE FINISH-ING THIS!

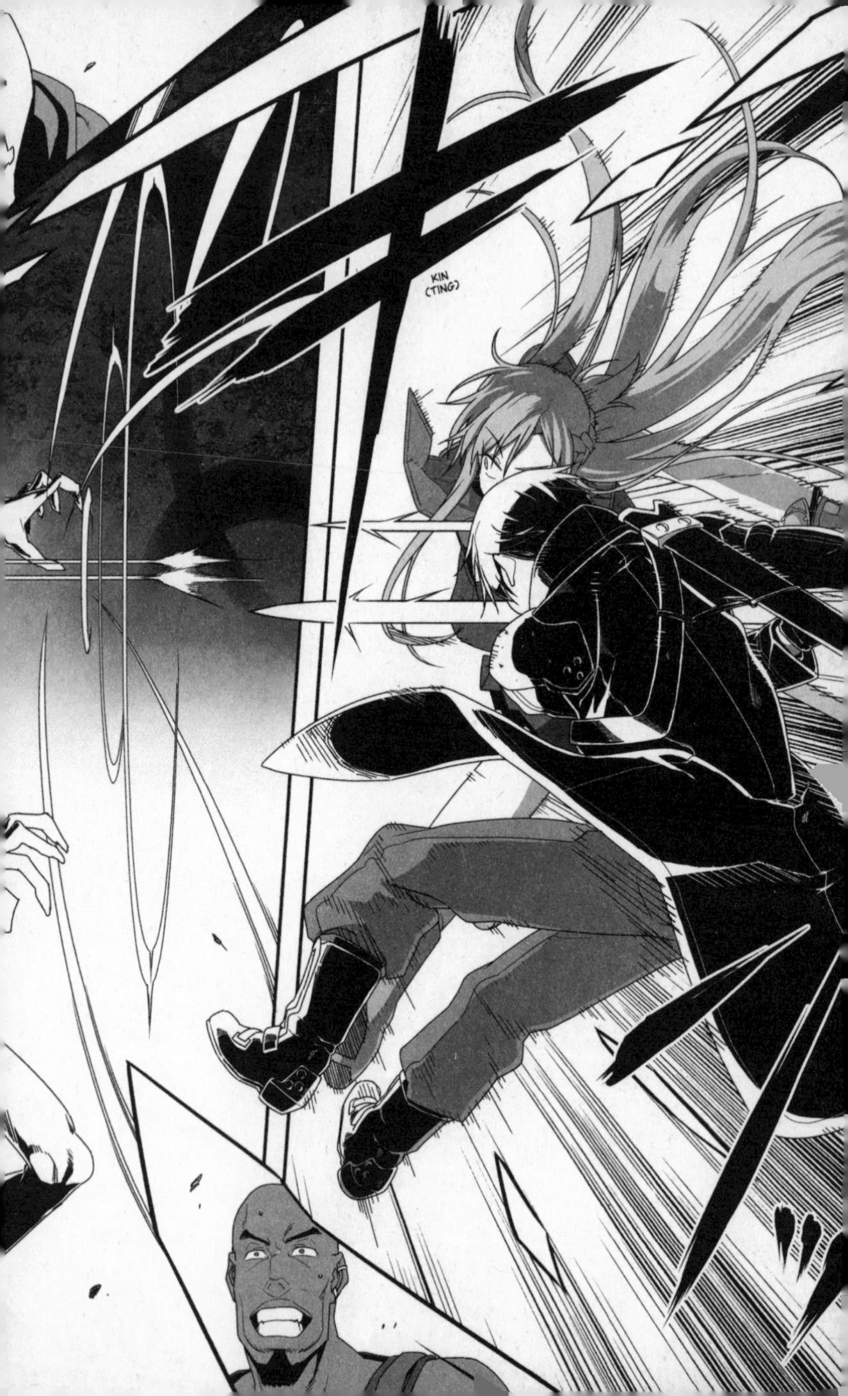
KIN
(TING)

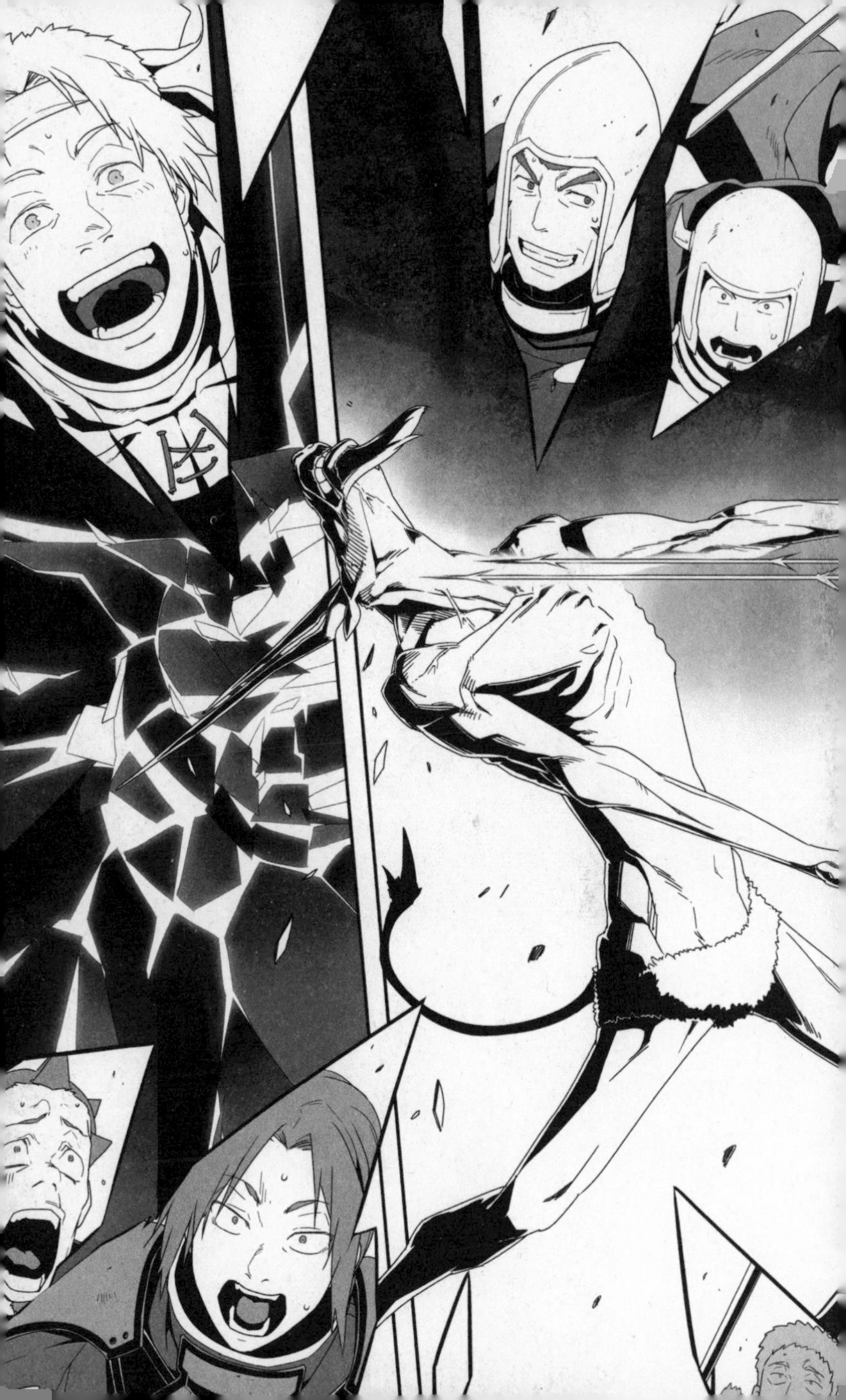

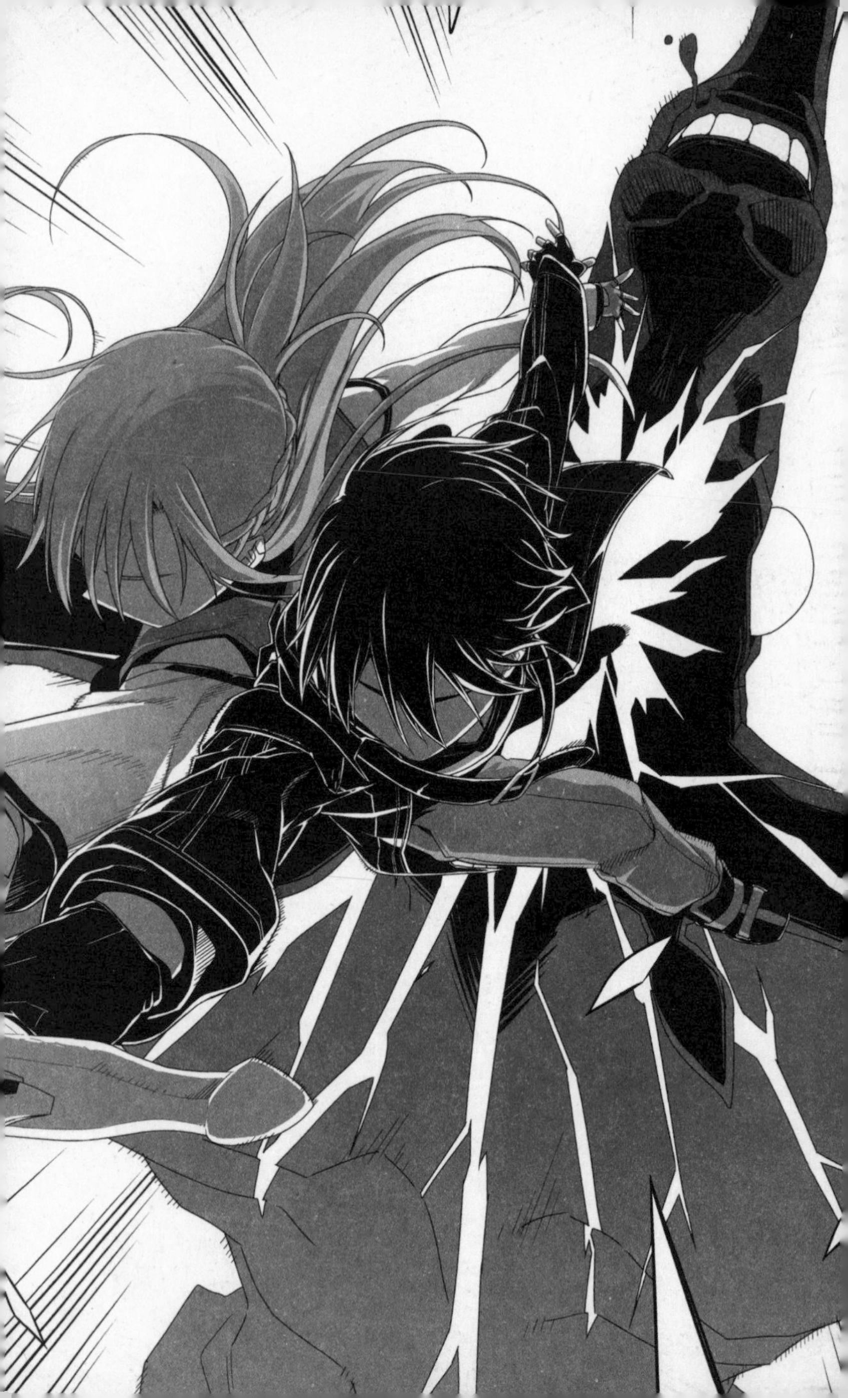

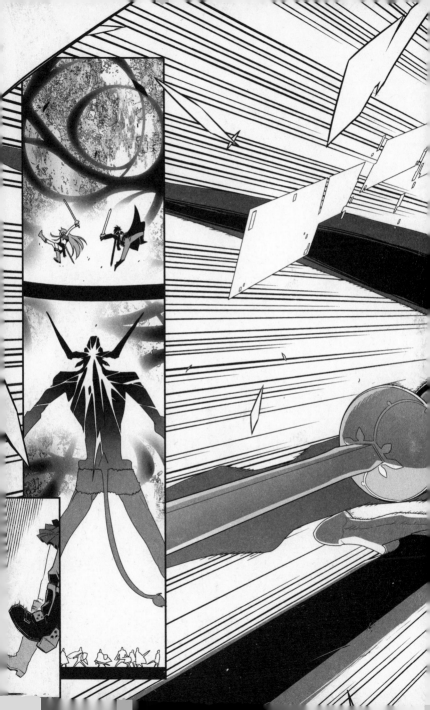

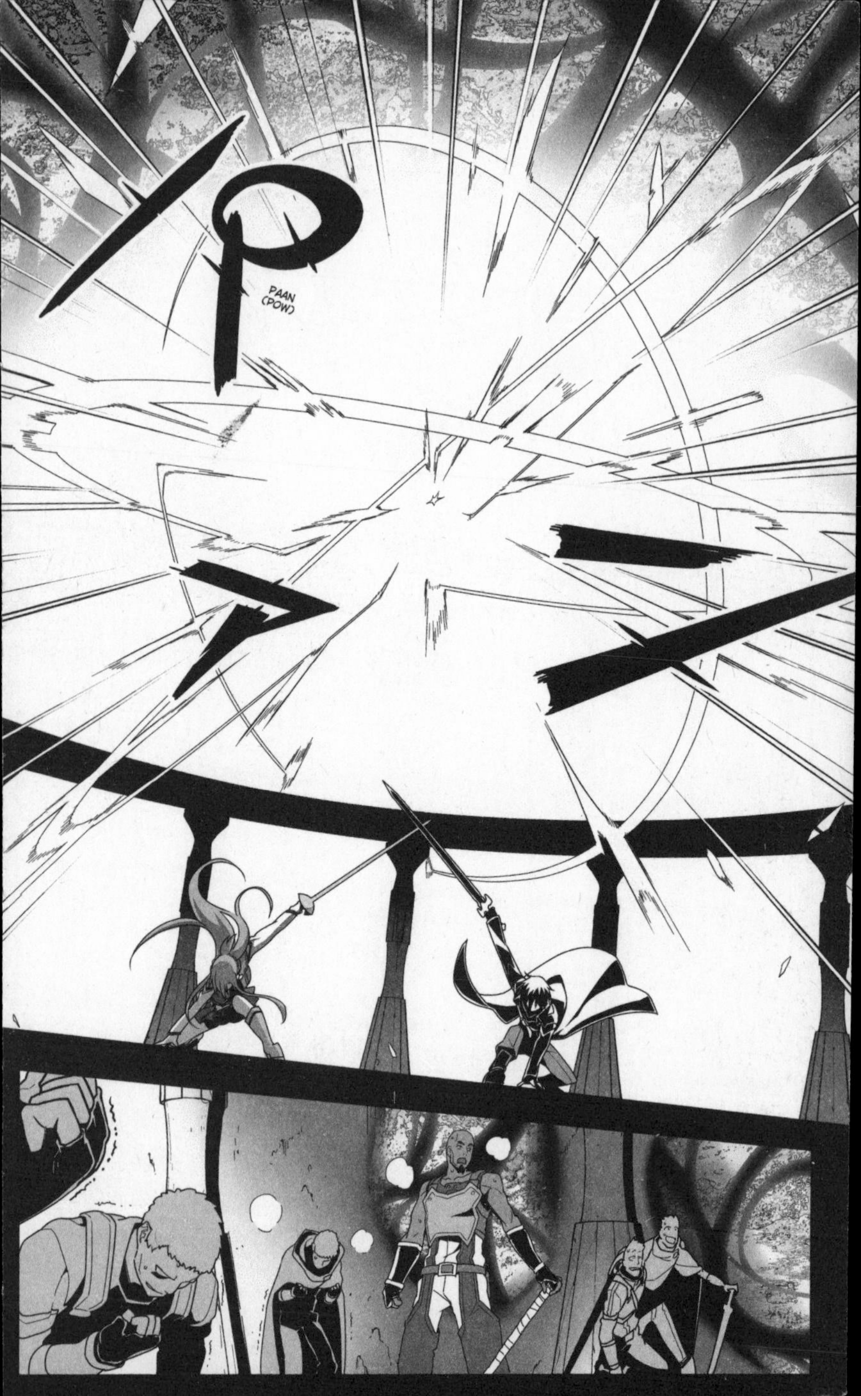
PAAN
(POW)

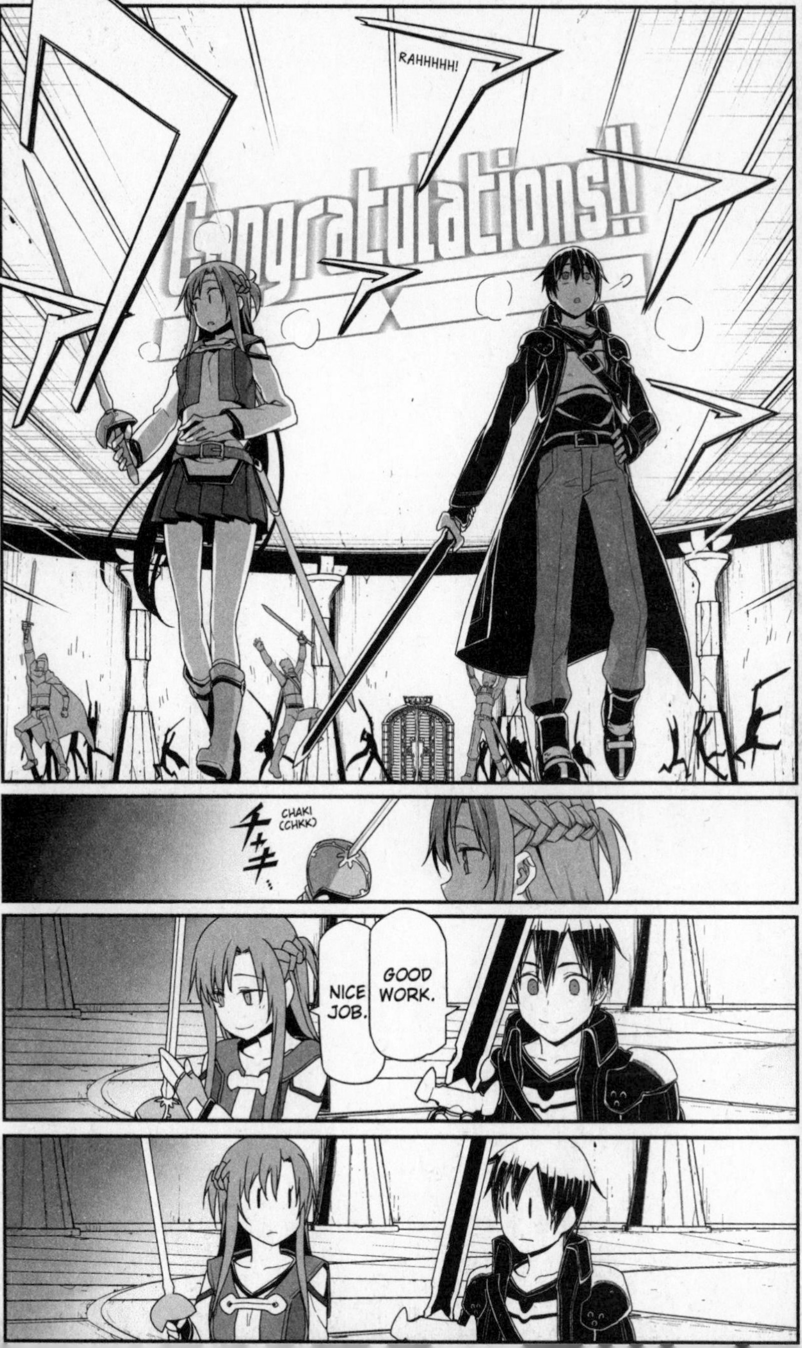
RAHHHHH!
Congratulations!!
CHAKI (CHKK)
チャキ…
GOOD WORK.
NICE JOB.

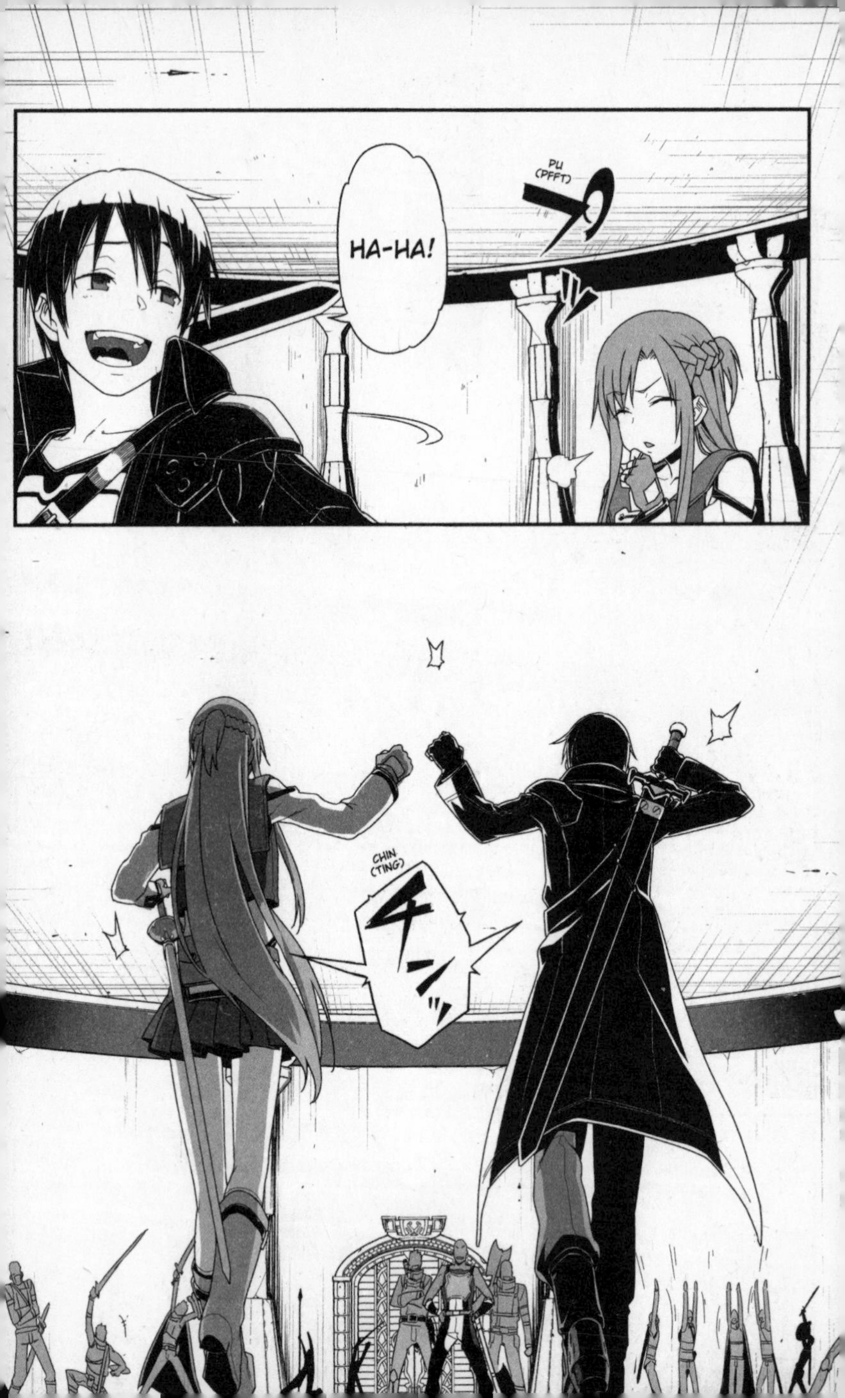
PU
(PFFT)
HA-HA!
CHIN
(TING)

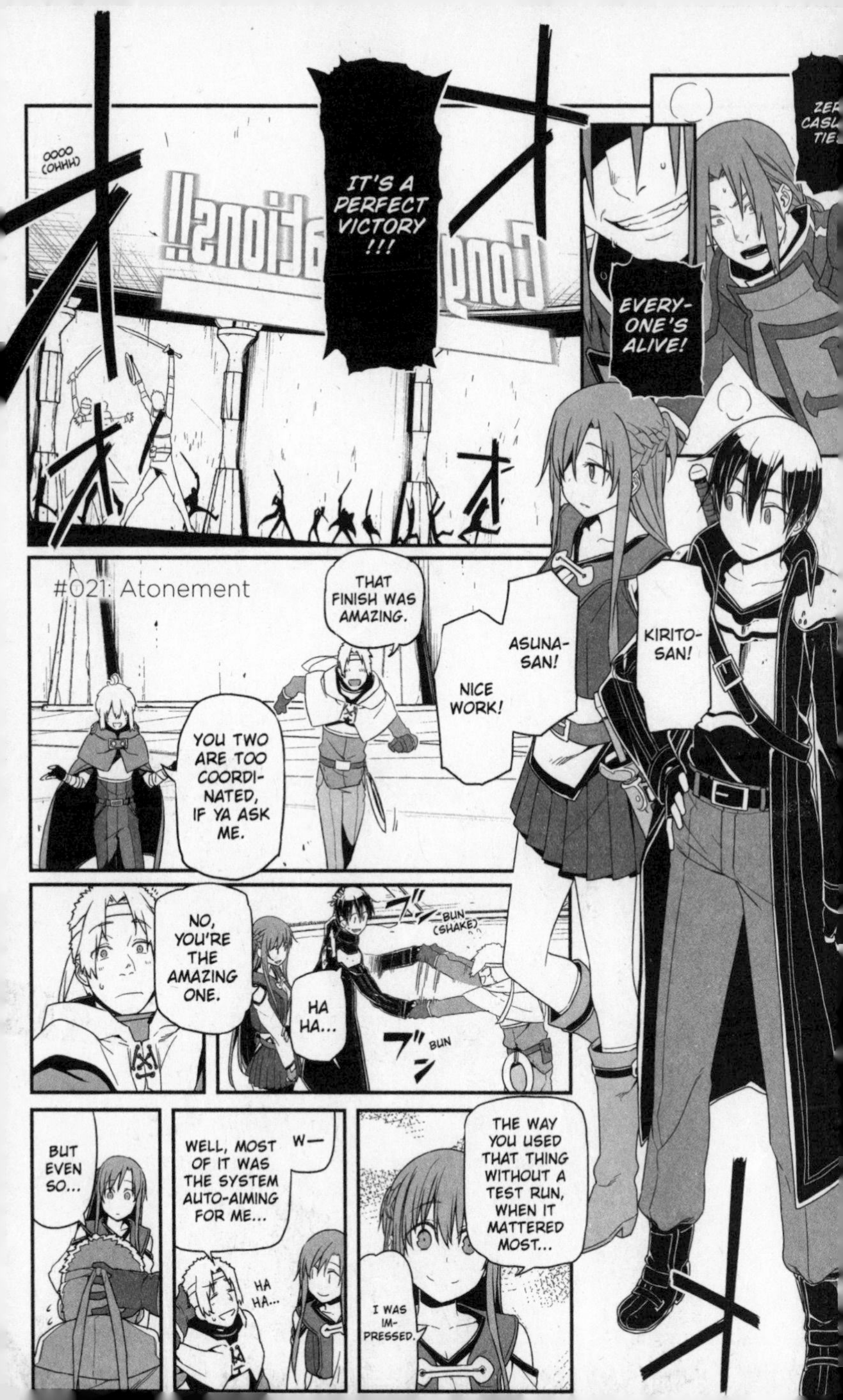
EVERY-ONE'S ALIVE!
IT'S A PERFECT VICTORY!!!
OOOO (OHHH)
#021: Atonement
KIRITO-SAN!
ASUNA-SAN!
NICE WORK!
THAT FINISH WAS AMAZING.
YOU TWO ARE TOO COORDINATED, IF YA ASK ME.
BUN (SHAKE)
HA HA...
BUN
NO, YOU'RE THE AMAZING ONE.
THE WAY YOU USED THAT THING WITHOUT A TEST RUN, WHEN IT MATTERED MOST...
I WAS IMPRESSED.
W—
WELL, MOST OF IT WAS THE SYSTEM AUTO-AIMING FOR ME...
HA HA...
BUT EVEN SO...

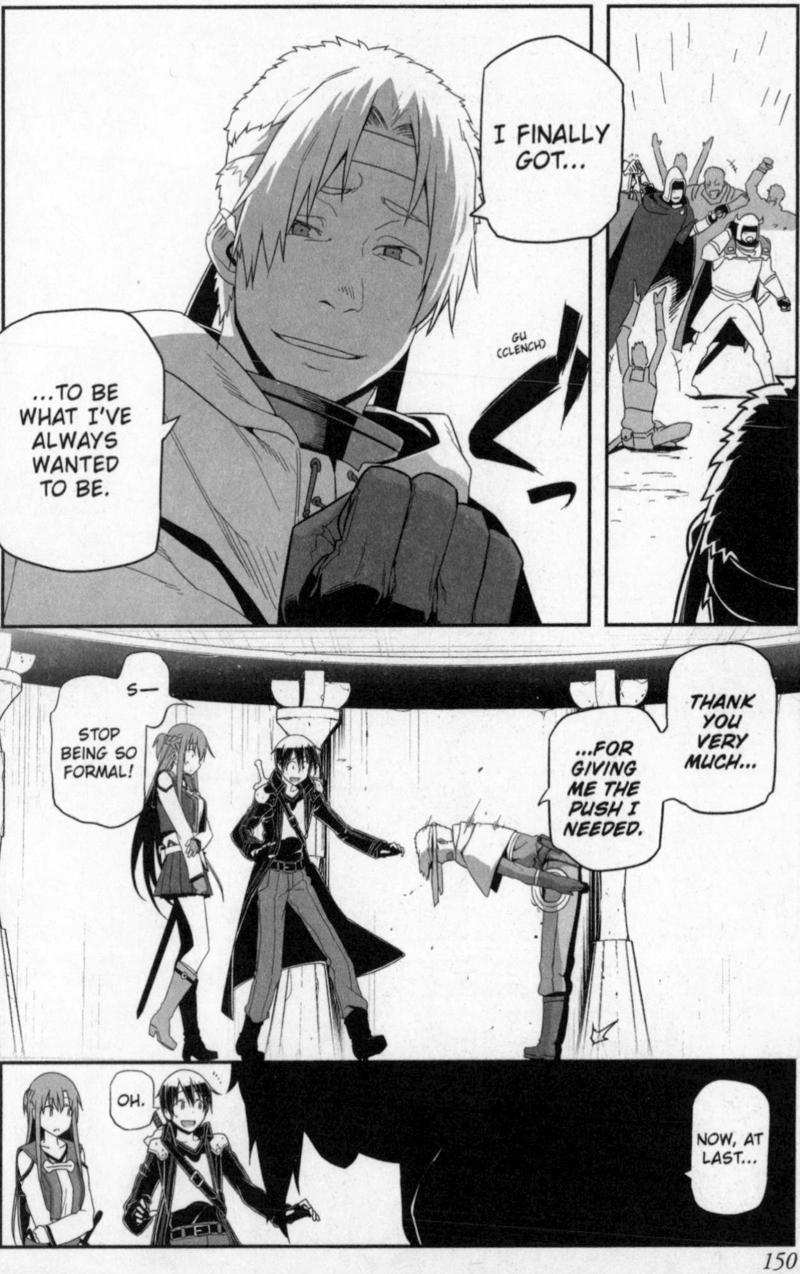
I FINALLY GOT...
GU (CLENCH)
...TO BE WHAT I'VE ALWAYS WANTED TO BE.
THANK YOU VERY MUCH...
...FOR GIVING ME THE PUSH I NEEDED.
S—
STOP BEING SO FORMAL!
NOW, AT LAST...
OH.

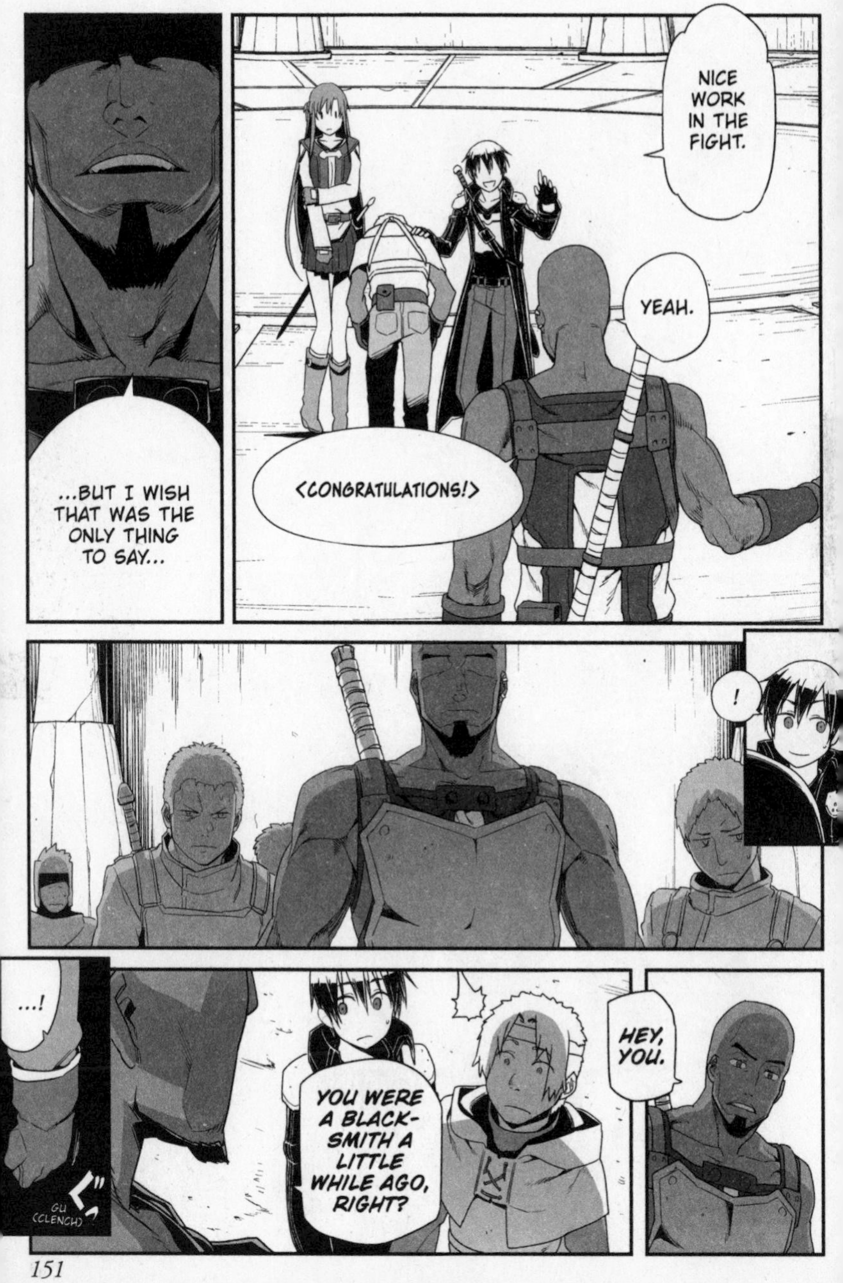
NICE WORK IN THE FIGHT.
YEAH.
<CONGRATULATIONS!>
...BUT I WISH THAT WAS THE ONLY THING TO SAY...
!
HEY, YOU.
YOU WERE A BLACK-SMITH A LITTLE WHILE AGO, RIGHT?
...!
GU (CLENCH)

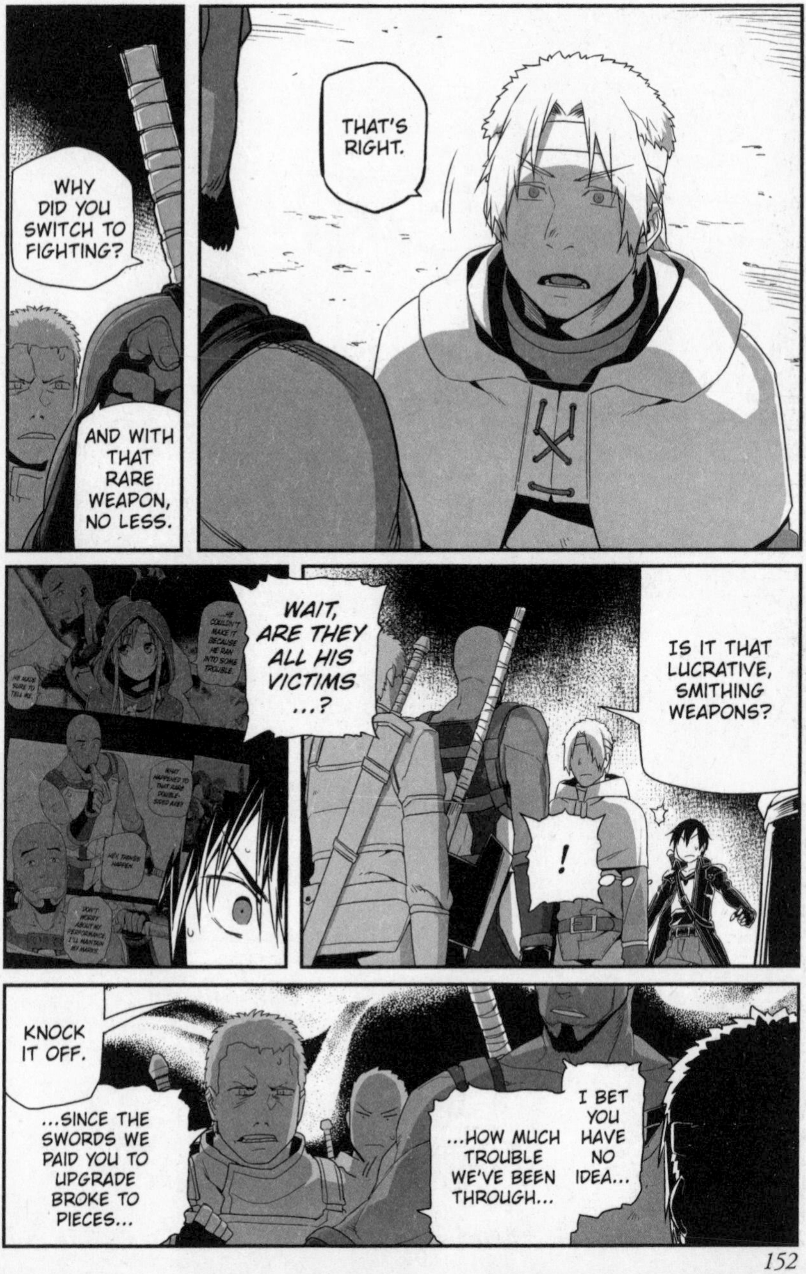
THAT'S RIGHT.
WHY DID YOU SWITCH TO FIGHTING?
AND WITH THAT RARE WEAPON, NO LESS.
IS IT THAT LUCRATIVE, SMITHING WEAPONS?
!
WAIT, ARE THEY ALL HIS VICTIMS ...?
...HE COULDN'T MAKE IT BECAUSE HE RAN INTO SOME TROUBLE.
HE MADE SURE TO TELL ME.
WHAT HAPPENED TO THAT RARE DOUBLE-SIDED AXE?
HEY, THINGS HAPPEN.
DON'T WORRY ABOUT MY PERFORMANCE. I'LL MAINTAIN MY MARKS.
KNOCK IT OFF.
I BET YOU HAVE NO IDEA...
...HOW MUCH TROUBLE WE'VE BEEN THROUGH...
...SINCE THE SWORDS WE PAID YOU TO UPGRADE BROKE TO PIECES...

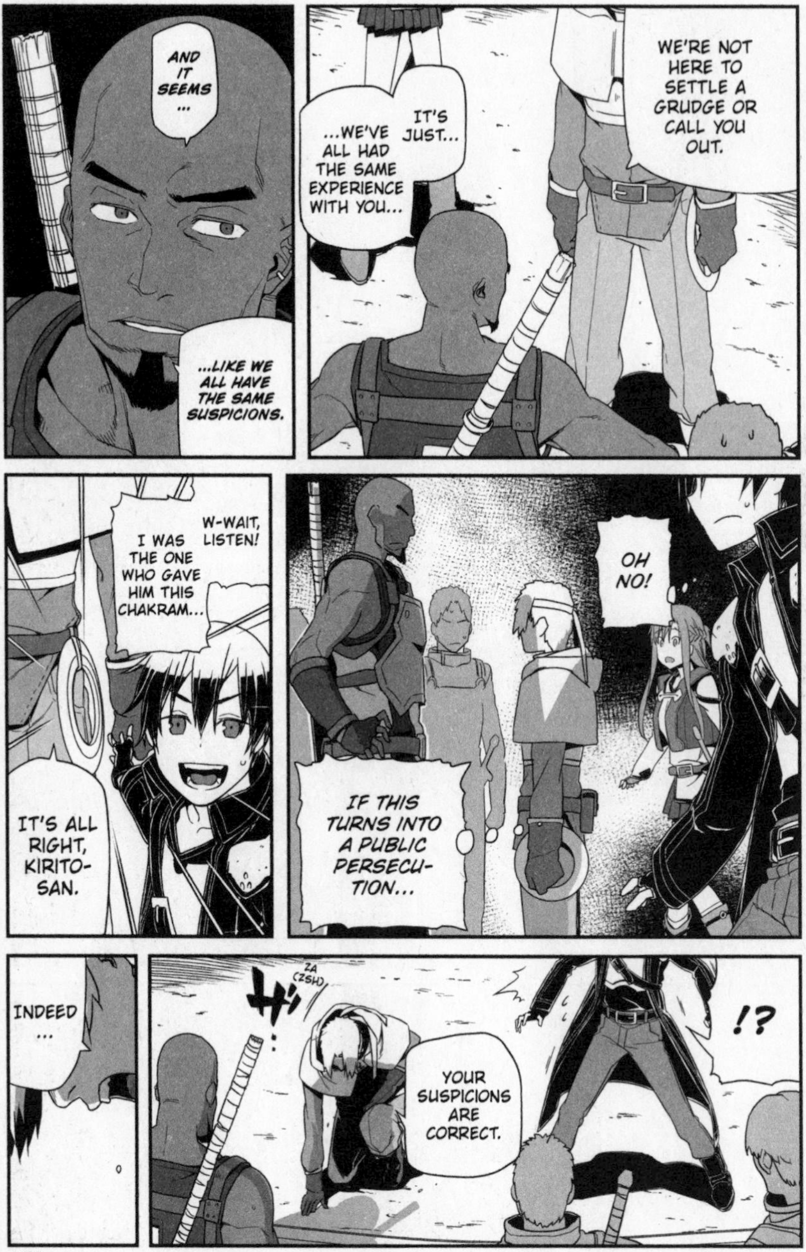
WE'RE NOT HERE TO SETTLE A GRUDGE OR CALL YOU OUT.
IT'S JUST...
...WE'VE ALL HAD THE SAME EXPERIENCE WITH YOU...
AND IT SEEMS...
...LIKE WE ALL HAVE THE SAME SUSPICIONS.
OH NO!
IF THIS TURNS INTO A PUBLIC PERSECUTION...
W-WAIT, LISTEN!
I WAS THE ONE WHO GAVE HIM THIS CHAKRAM...
IT'S ALL RIGHT, KIRITO-SAN.
!?
ZA (ZSH)
YOUR SUSPICIONS ARE CORRECT.
INDEED...

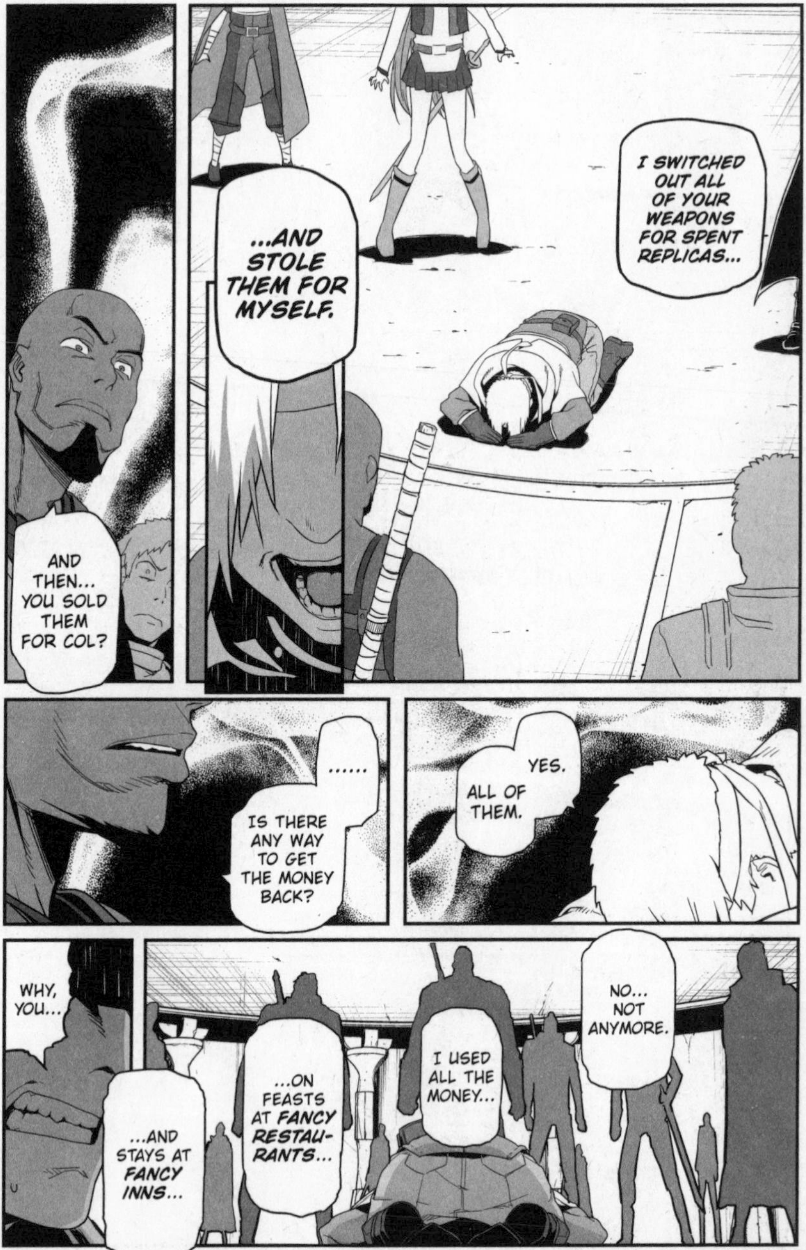
I SWITCHED OUT ALL OF YOUR WEAPONS FOR SPENT REPLICAS...
...AND STOLE THEM FOR MYSELF.
AND THEN... YOU SOLD THEM FOR COL?
YES. ALL OF THEM.
......
IS THERE ANY WAY TO GET THE MONEY BACK?
NO... NOT ANYMORE.
I USED ALL THE MONEY...
...ON FEASTS AT FANCY RESTAURANTS...
...AND STAYS AT FANCY INNS...
WHY, YOU...

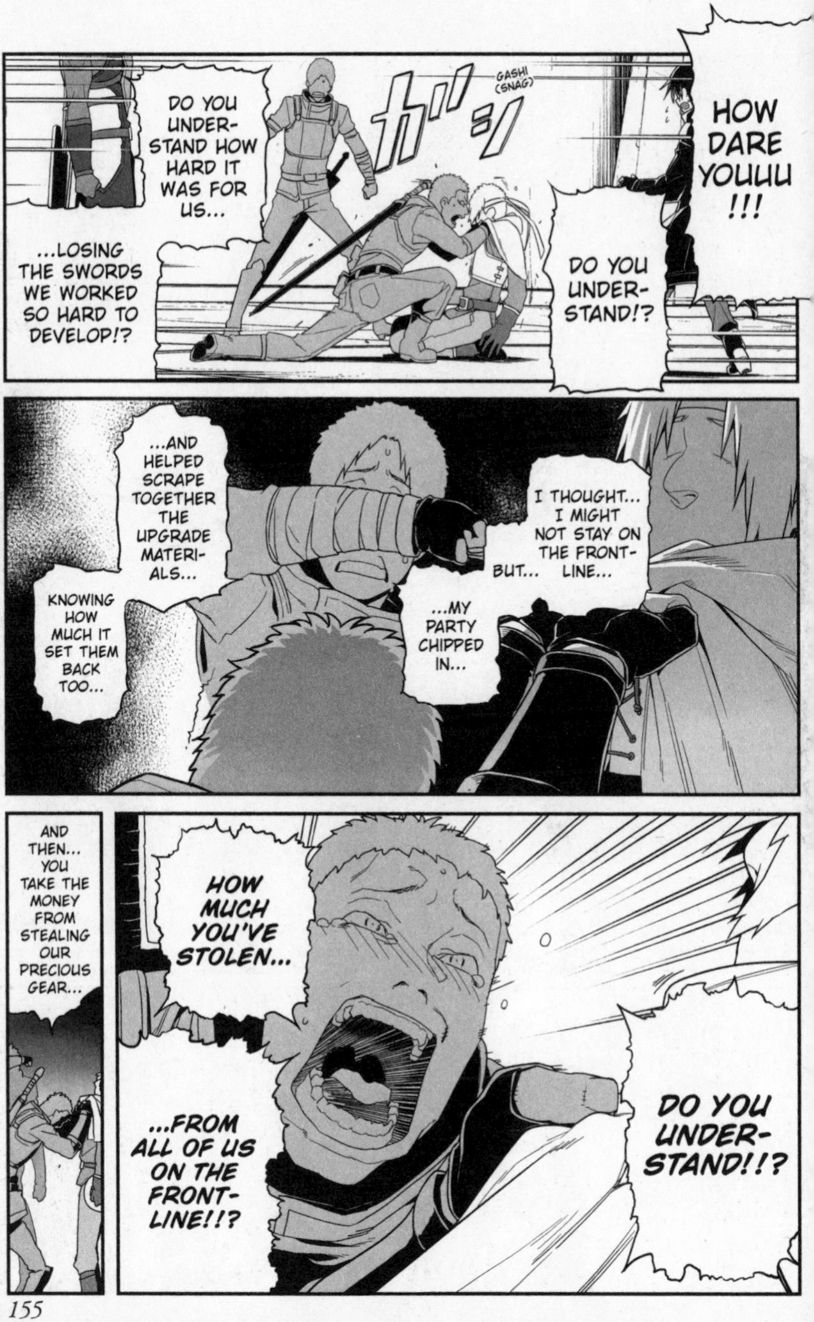
HOW DARE YOUUU !!!
DO YOU UNDERSTAND!?
GASHI (SNAG)
DO YOU UNDERSTAND HOW HARD IT WAS FOR US...
...LOSING THE SWORDS WE WORKED SO HARD TO DEVELOP!?
I THOUGHT... I MIGHT NOT STAY ON THE FRONT-LINE...
BUT...
...MY PARTY CHIPPED IN...
...AND HELPED SCRAPE TOGETHER THE UPGRADE MATERIALS...
KNOWING HOW MUCH IT SET THEM BACK TOO...
HOW MUCH YOU'VE STOLEN...
DO YOU UNDERSTAND!!?
...FROM ALL OF US ON THE FRONT-LINE!!?
AND THEN... YOU TAKE THE MONEY FROM STEALING OUR PRECIOUS GEAR...

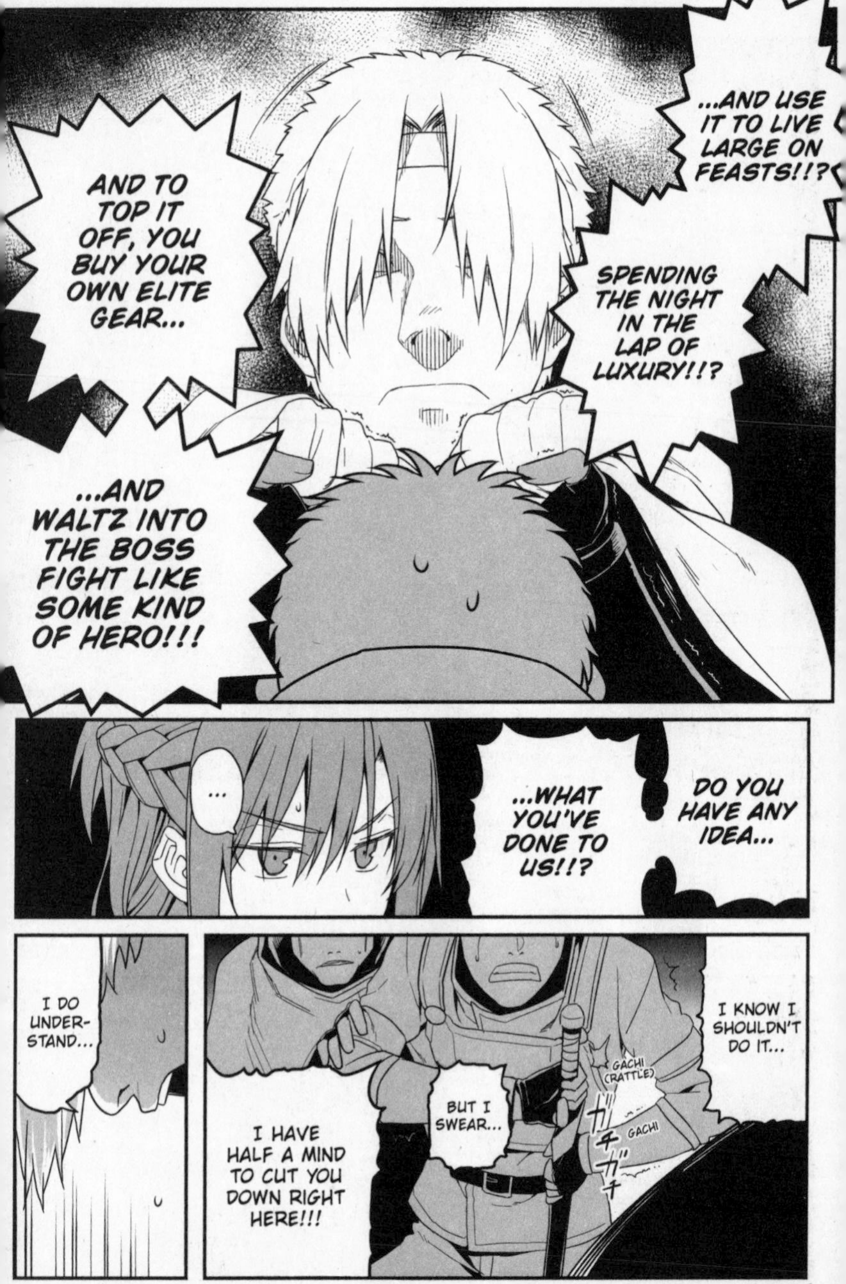
...AND USE IT TO LIVE LARGE ON FEASTS!!?
AND TO TOP IT OFF, YOU BUY YOUR OWN ELITE GEAR...
SPENDING THE NIGHT IN THE LAP OF LUXURY!!?
...AND WALTZ INTO THE BOSS FIGHT LIKE SOME KIND OF HERO!!!
DO YOU HAVE ANY IDEA...
...WHAT YOU'VE DONE TO US!!?
...
I KNOW I SHOULDN'T DO IT...
GACHI (RATTLE)
BUT I SWEAR...
GACHI
I HAVE HALF A MIND TO CUT YOU DOWN RIGHT HERE!!!
I DO UNDER-STAND...

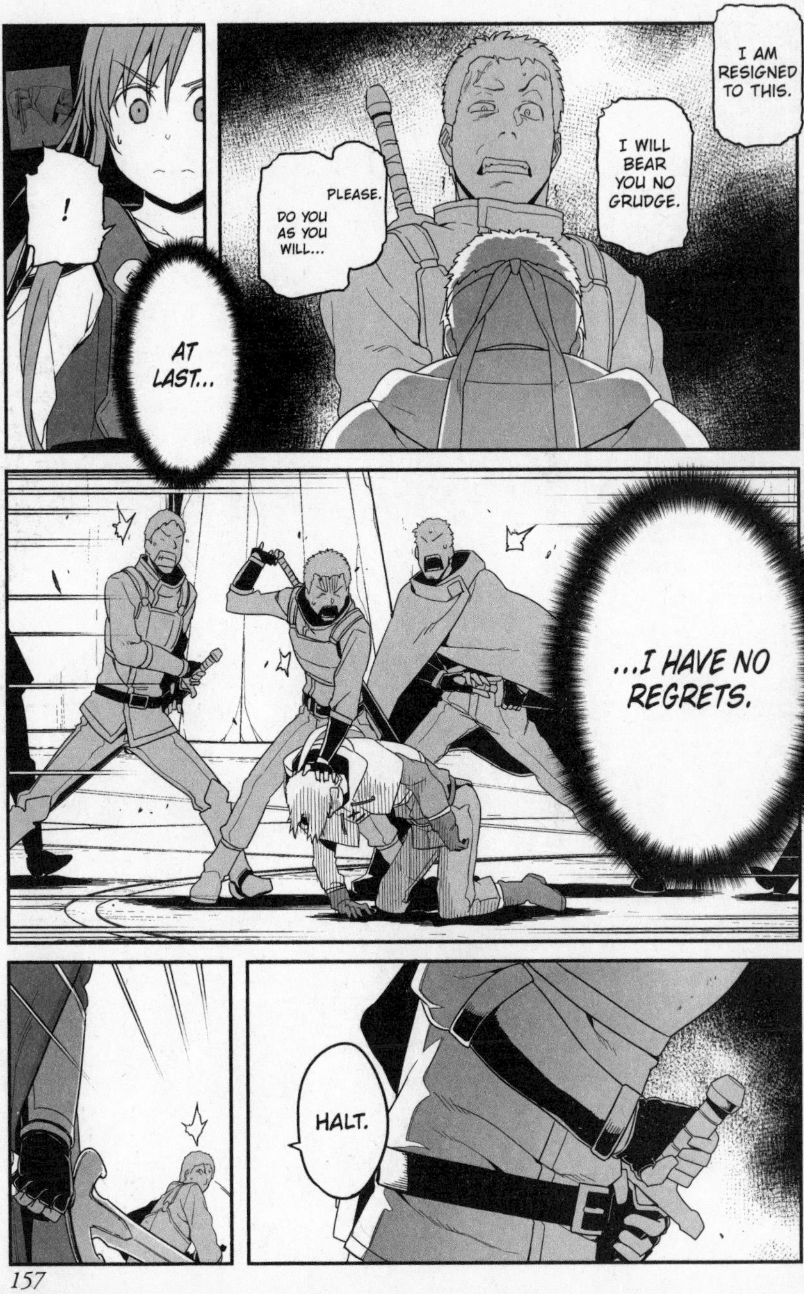
I AM RESIGNED TO THIS.
I WILL BEAR YOU NO GRUDGE.
PLEASE. DO YOU AS YOU WILL...
!
AT LAST...
...I HAVE NO REGRETS.
HALT.

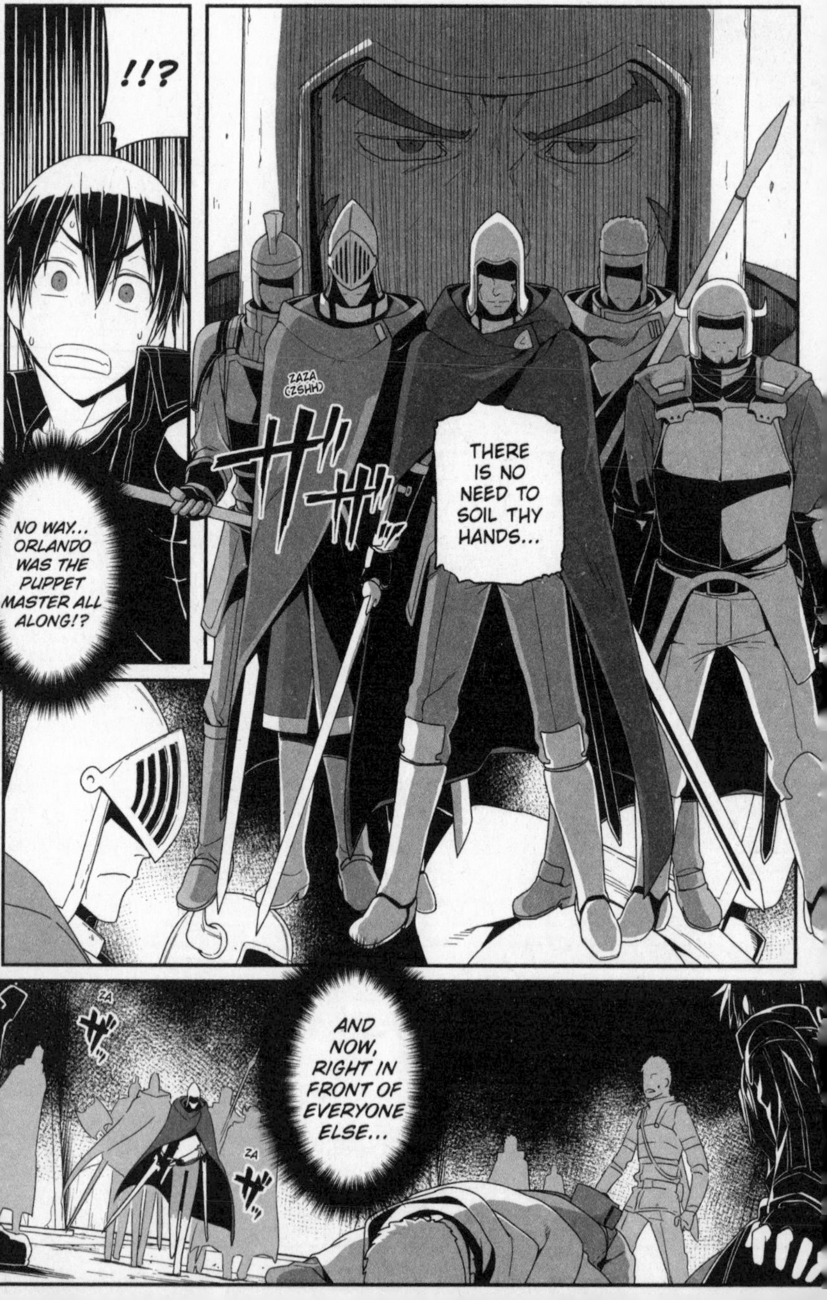
ZAZA (ZSHH)
THERE IS NO NEED TO SOIL THY HANDS...
!!?
NO WAY... ORLANDO WAS THE PUPPET MASTER ALL ALONG!?
AND NOW, RIGHT IN FRONT OF EVERYONE ELSE...
ZA
ZA

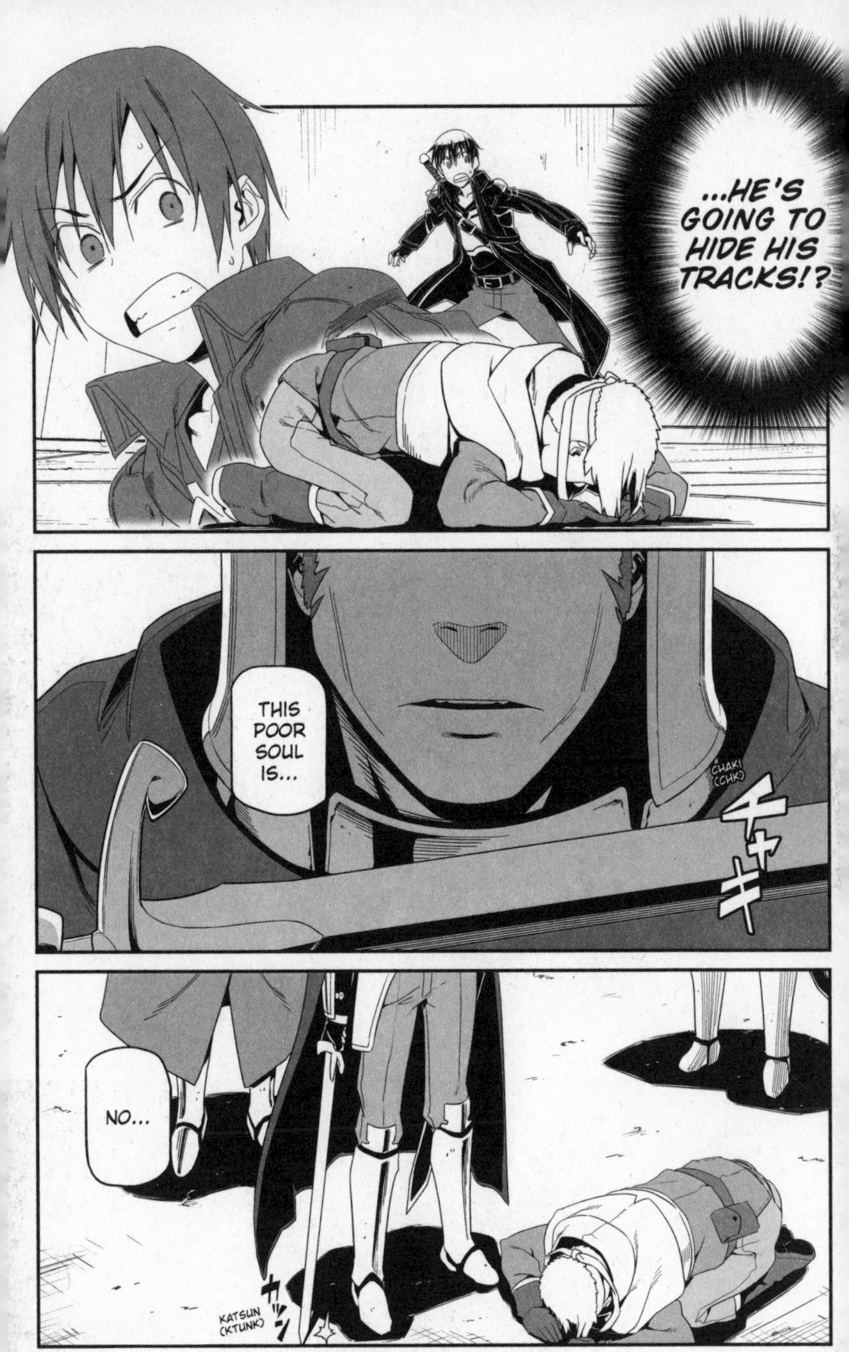
...HE'S GOING TO HIDE HIS TRACKS!?
THIS POOR SOUL IS...
CHAKI (CHK)
NO...
KATSUN (KTUNK)

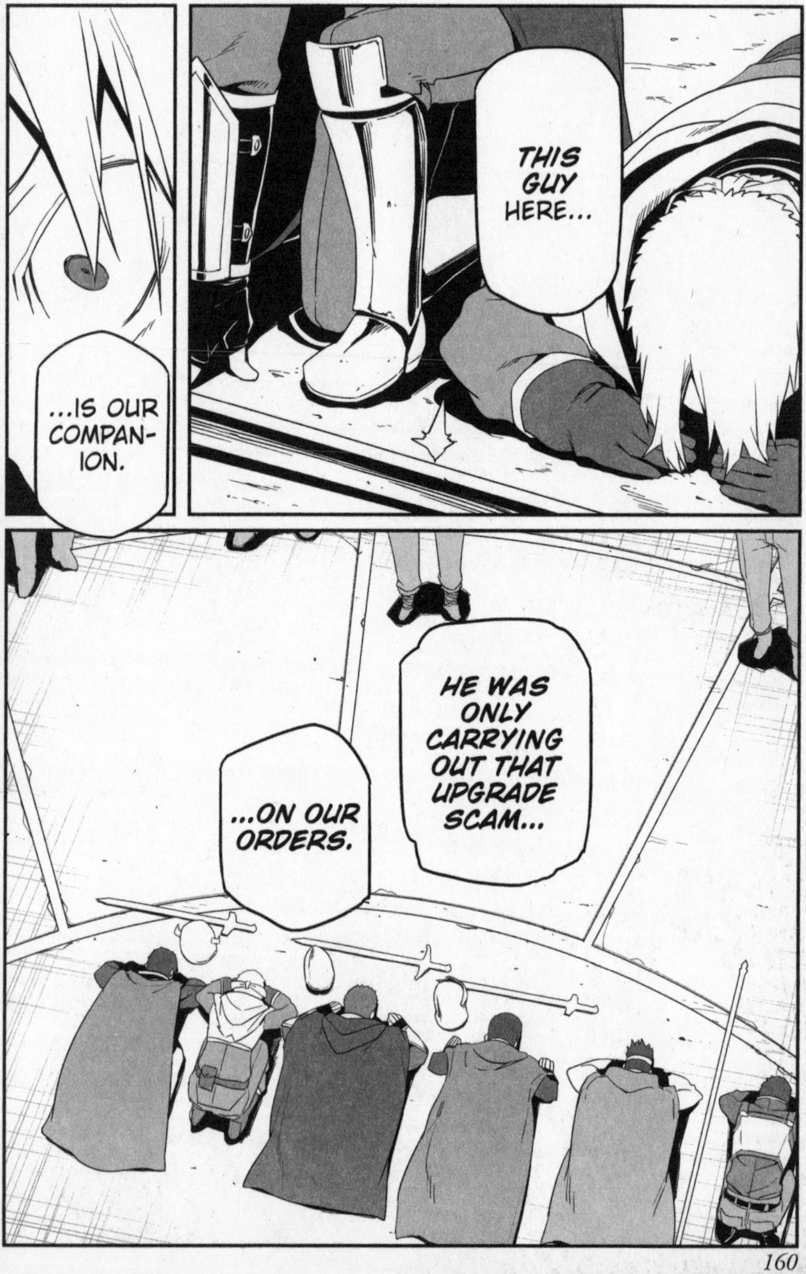
THIS GUY HERE...
...IS OUR COMPANION.
HE WAS ONLY CARRYING OUT THAT UPGRADE SCAM...
...ON OUR ORDERS.

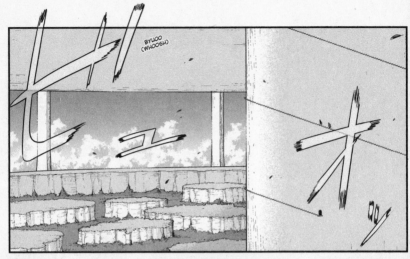

BYUOO
(WHOOSH)

STEP RIGHT UP!

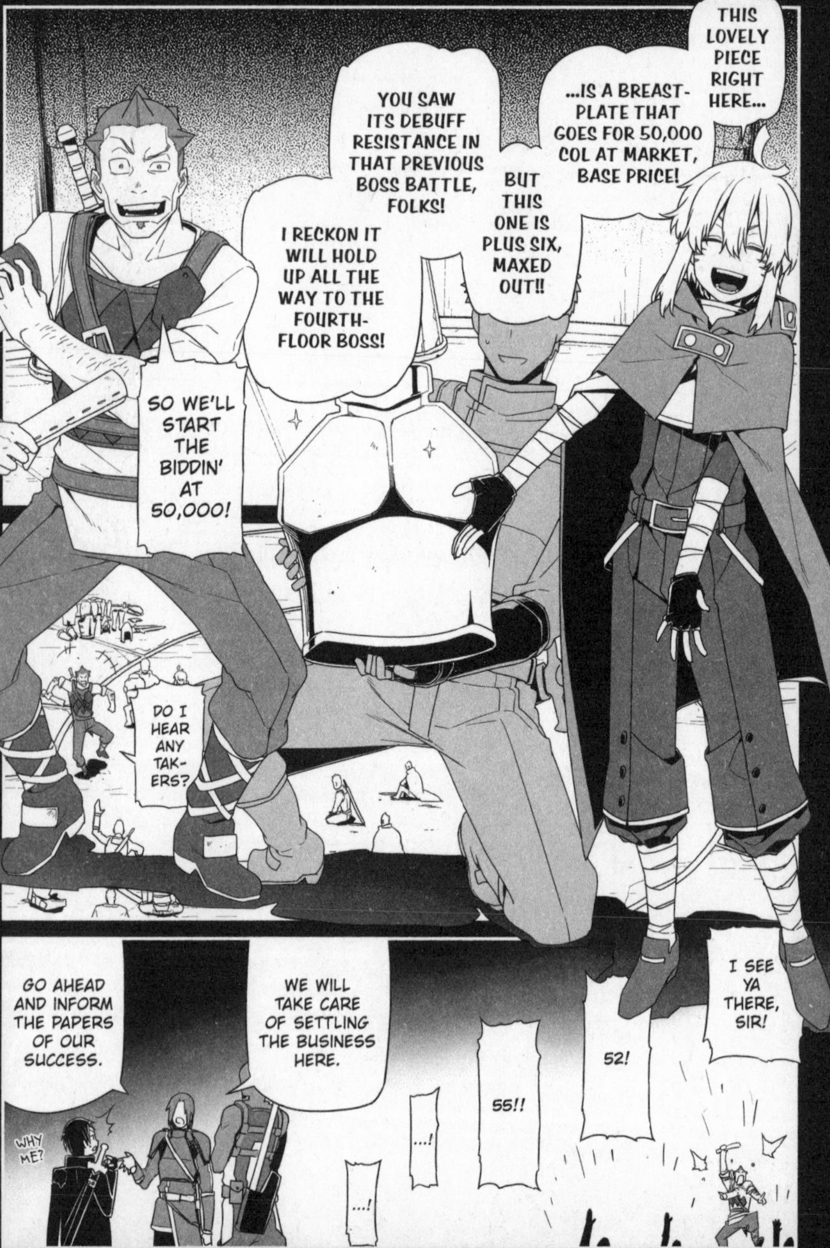
THIS LOVELY PIECE RIGHT HERE...
...IS A BREAST-PLATE THAT GOES FOR 50,000 COL AT MARKET, BASE PRICE!
BUT THIS ONE IS PLUS SIX, MAXED OUT!!
YOU SAW ITS DEBUFF RESISTANCE IN THAT PREVIOUS BOSS BATTLE, FOLKS!
I RECKON IT WILL HOLD UP ALL THE WAY TO THE FOURTH-FLOOR BOSS!
SO WE'LL START THE BIDDIN' AT 50,000!
DO I HEAR ANY TAKERS?
I SEE YA THERE, SIR!
52!
55!!
...!
...!
WE WILL TAKE CARE OF SETTLING THE BUSINESS HERE.
GO AHEAD AND INFORM THE PAPERS OF OUR SUCCESS.
WHY ME?

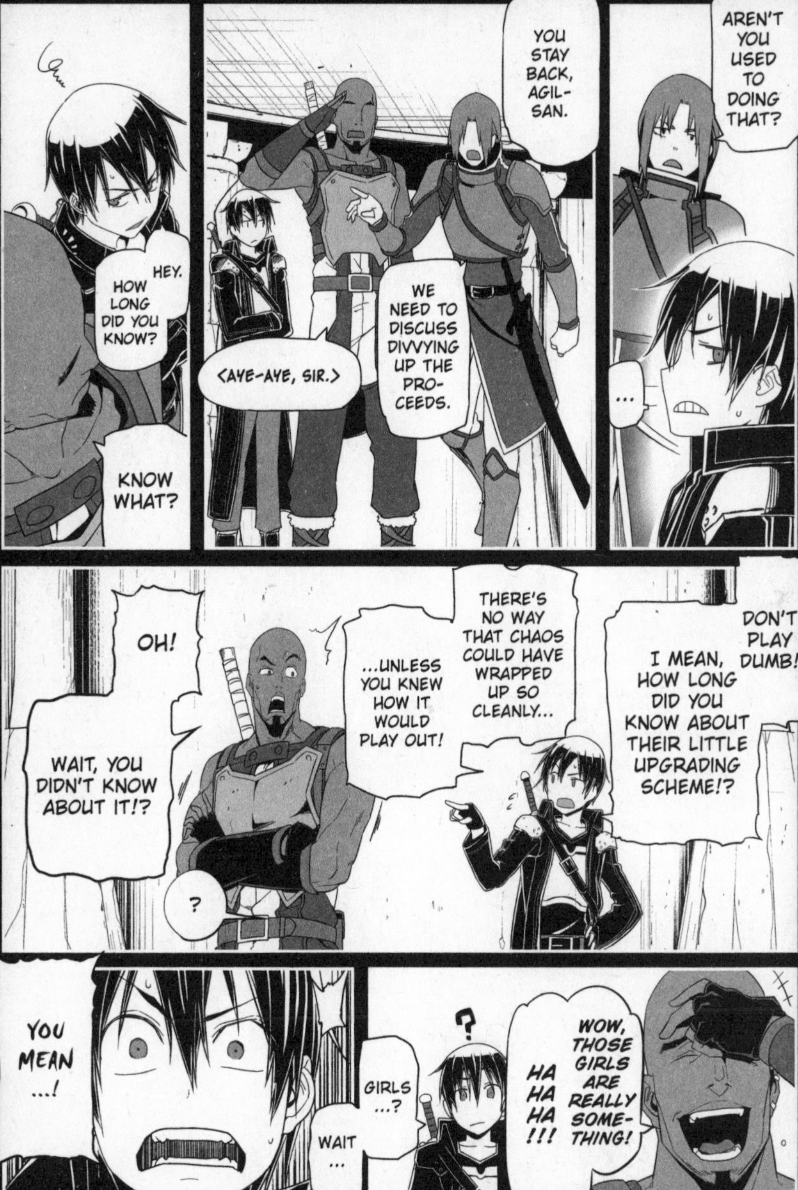
AREN'T YOU USED TO DOING THAT?
...
YOU STAY BACK, AGIL-SAN.
WE NEED TO DISCUSS DIVVYING UP THE PRO-CEEDS.
<AYE-AYE, SIR.>
HEY. HOW LONG DID YOU KNOW?
KNOW WHAT?
DON'T PLAY DUMB!
I MEAN, HOW LONG DID YOU KNOW ABOUT THEIR LITTLE UPGRADING SCHEME!?
THERE'S NO WAY THAT CHAOS COULD HAVE WRAPPED UP SO CLEANLY...
...UNLESS YOU KNEW HOW IT WOULD PLAY OUT!
?
OH!
WAIT, YOU DIDN'T KNOW ABOUT IT!?
WOW, THOSE GIRLS ARE REALLY SOME-THING!
HA HA HA !!!
?
GIRLS ...?
WAIT ...
YOU MEAN ...!

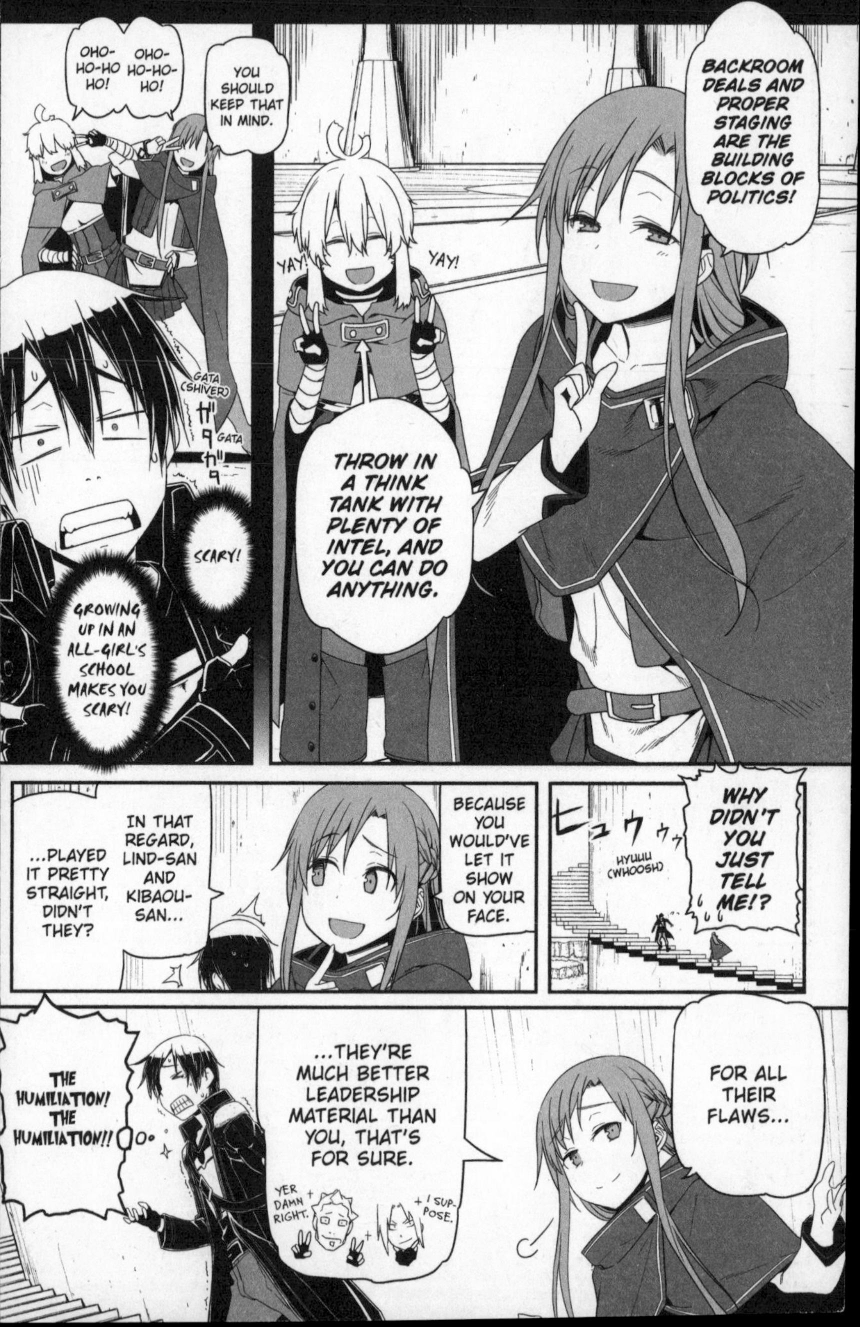
BACKROOM DEALS AND PROPER STAGING ARE THE BUILDING BLOCKS OF POLITICS!
YAY!
YAY!
THROW IN A THINK TANK WITH PLENTY OF INTEL, AND YOU CAN DO ANYTHING.
YOU SHOULD KEEP THAT IN MIND.
OHO-HO-HO-HO!
OHO-HO-HO-HO!
GATA (SHIVER)
ガタ
GATA
ガタ
SCARY!
GROWING UP IN AN ALL-GIRL'S SCHOOL MAKES YOU SCARY!
WHY DIDN'T YOU JUST TELL ME!?
ヒュウゥゥ
HYUUU (WHOOSH)
BECAUSE YOU WOULD'VE LET IT SHOW ON YOUR FACE.
IN THAT REGARD, LIND-SAN AND KIBAOU-SAN...
...PLAYED IT PRETTY STRAIGHT, DIDN'T THEY?
FOR ALL THEIR FLAWS...
...THEY'RE MUCH BETTER LEADERSHIP MATERIAL THAN YOU, THAT'S FOR SURE.
I SUP-POSE.
YER DAMN RIGHT.
THE HUMILIATION! THE HUMILIATION!!

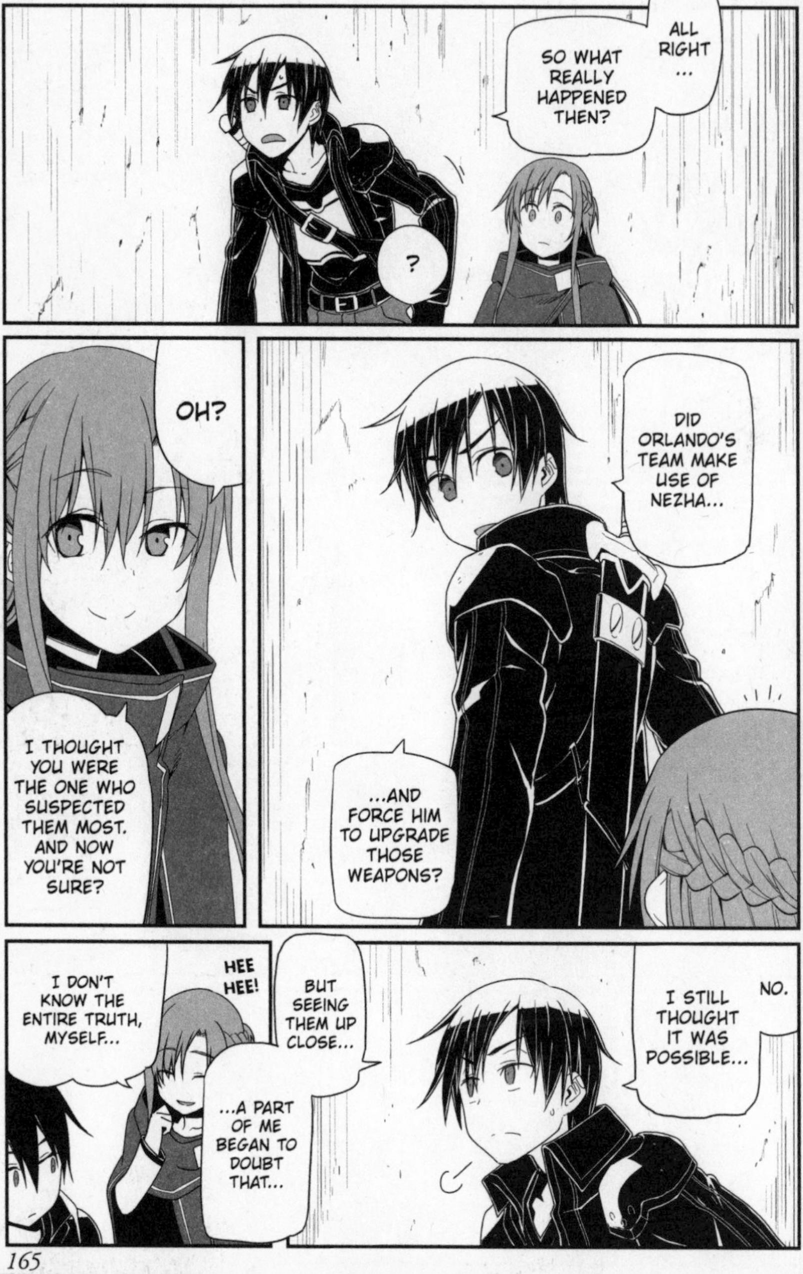
ALL RIGHT...
SO WHAT REALLY HAPPENED THEN?
?
DID ORLANDO'S TEAM MAKE USE OF NEZHA...
...AND FORCE HIM TO UPGRADE THOSE WEAPONS?
OH?
I THOUGHT YOU WERE THE ONE WHO SUSPECTED THEM MOST. AND NOW YOU'RE NOT SURE?
NO.
I STILL THOUGHT IT WAS POSSIBLE...
BUT SEEING THEM UP CLOSE...
...A PART OF ME BEGAN TO DOUBT THAT...
HEE HEE!
I DON'T KNOW THE ENTIRE TRUTH, MYSELF...

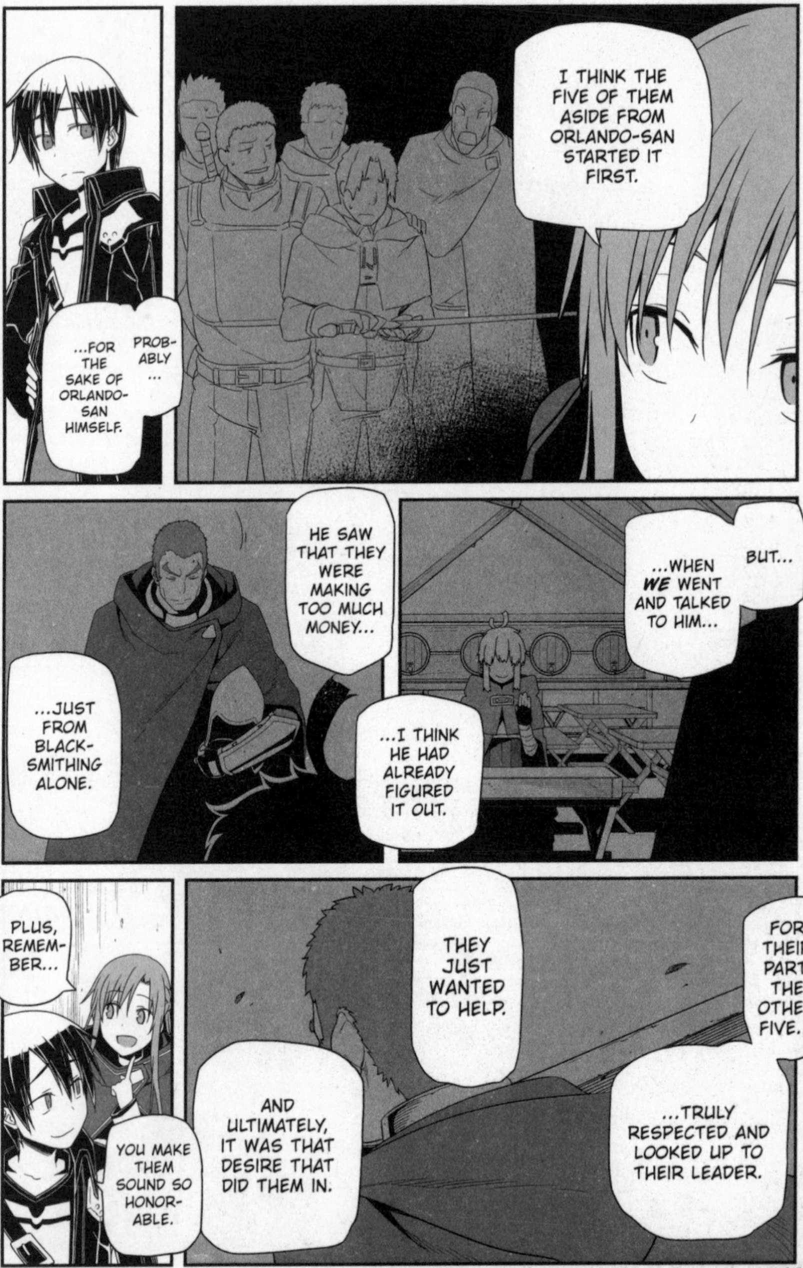
I THINK THE FIVE OF THEM ASIDE FROM ORLANDO-SAN STARTED IT FIRST.
PROBABLY...
...FOR THE SAKE OF ORLANDO-SAN HIMSELF.
BUT...
...WHEN **WE** WENT AND TALKED TO HIM...
...I THINK HE HAD ALREADY FIGURED IT OUT.
HE SAW THAT THEY WERE MAKING TOO MUCH MONEY...
...JUST FROM BLACKSMITHING ALONE.
FOR THEIR PART, THE OTHER FIVE...
...TRULY RESPECTED AND LOOKED UP TO THEIR LEADER.
THEY JUST WANTED TO HELP.
AND ULTIMATELY, IT WAS THAT DESIRE THAT DID THEM IN.
YOU MAKE THEM SOUND SO HONORABLE.
PLUS, REMEMBER...

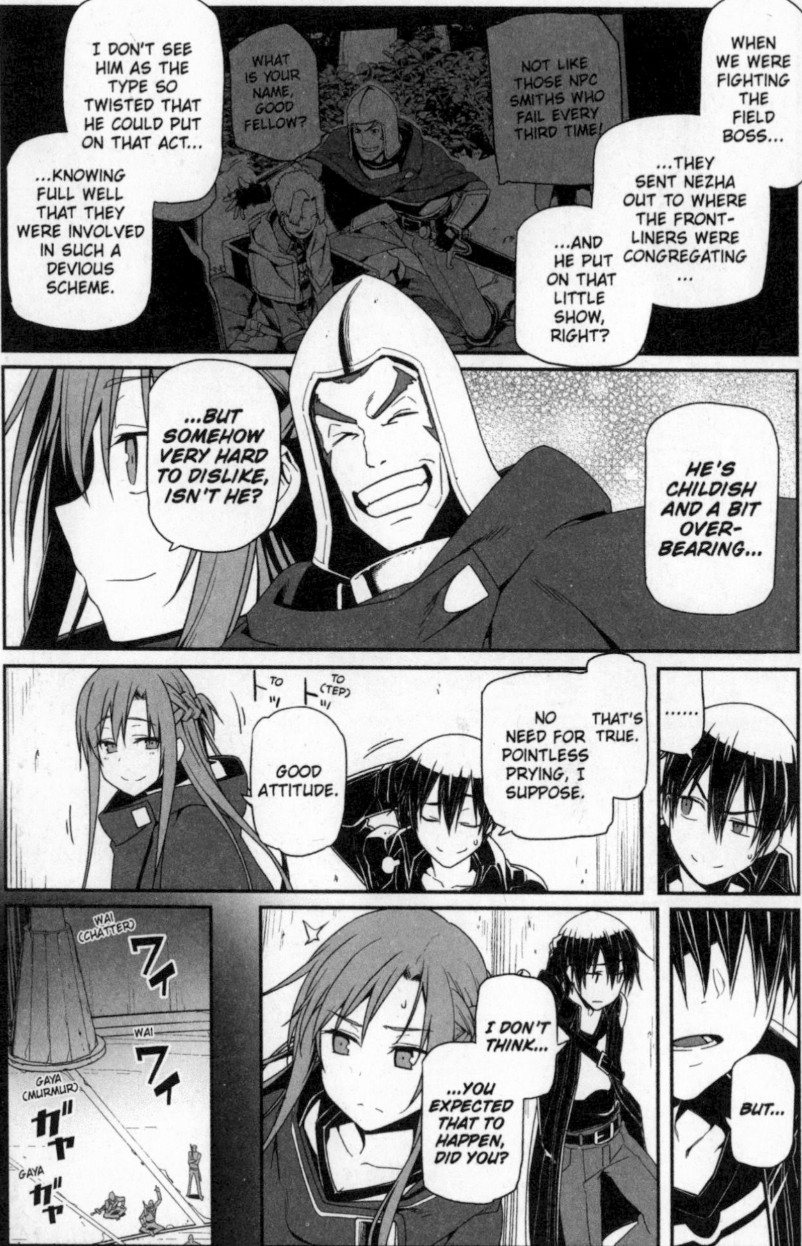
WHEN WE WERE FIGHTING THE FIELD BOSS...
...THEY SENT NEZHA OUT TO WHERE THE FRONT-LINERS WERE CONGREGATING...
...AND HE PUT ON THAT LITTLE SHOW, RIGHT?
NOT LIKE THOSE NPC SMITHS WHO FAIL EVERY THIRD TIME!
WHAT IS YOUR NAME, GOOD FELLOW?
I DON'T SEE HIM AS THE TYPE SO TWISTED THAT HE COULD PUT ON THAT ACT...
...KNOWING FULL WELL THAT THEY WERE INVOLVED IN SUCH A DEVIOUS SCHEME.
HE'S CHILDISH AND A BIT OVER-BEARING...
...BUT SOMEHOW VERY HARD TO DISLIKE, ISN'T HE?
......
THAT'S TRUE.
NO NEED FOR POINTLESS PRYING, I SUPPOSE.
TO (TEP)
TO
GOOD ATTITUDE.
BUT...
I DON'T THINK...
...YOU EXPECTED THAT TO HAPPEN, DID YOU?
WAI (CHATTER)
WAI
GAYA (MURMUR)
GAYA

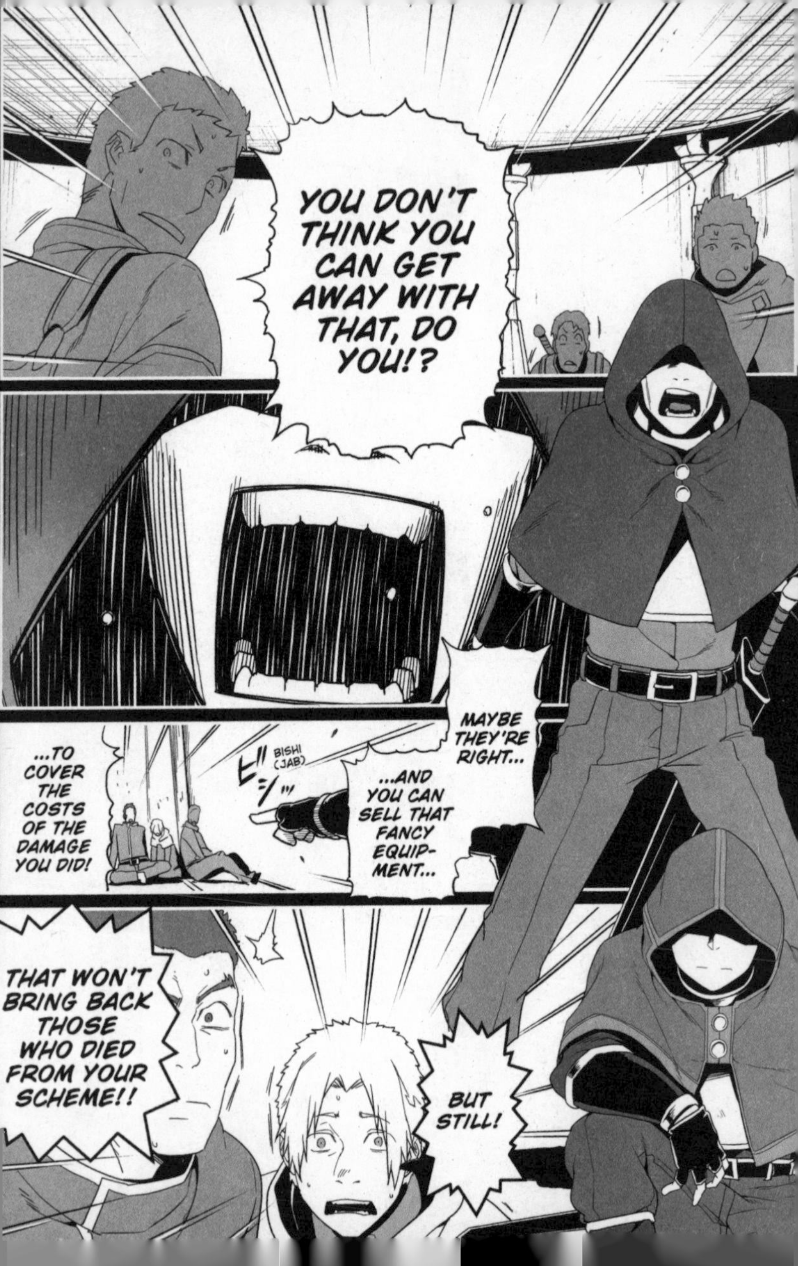
YOU DON'T THINK YOU CAN GET AWAY WITH THAT, DO YOU!?
MAYBE THEY'RE RIGHT...
...AND YOU CAN SELL THAT FANCY EQUIPMENT...
BISHI (JAB)
...TO COVER THE COSTS OF THE DAMAGE YOU DID!
BUT STILL!
THAT WON'T BRING BACK THOSE WHO DIED FROM YOUR SCHEME!!

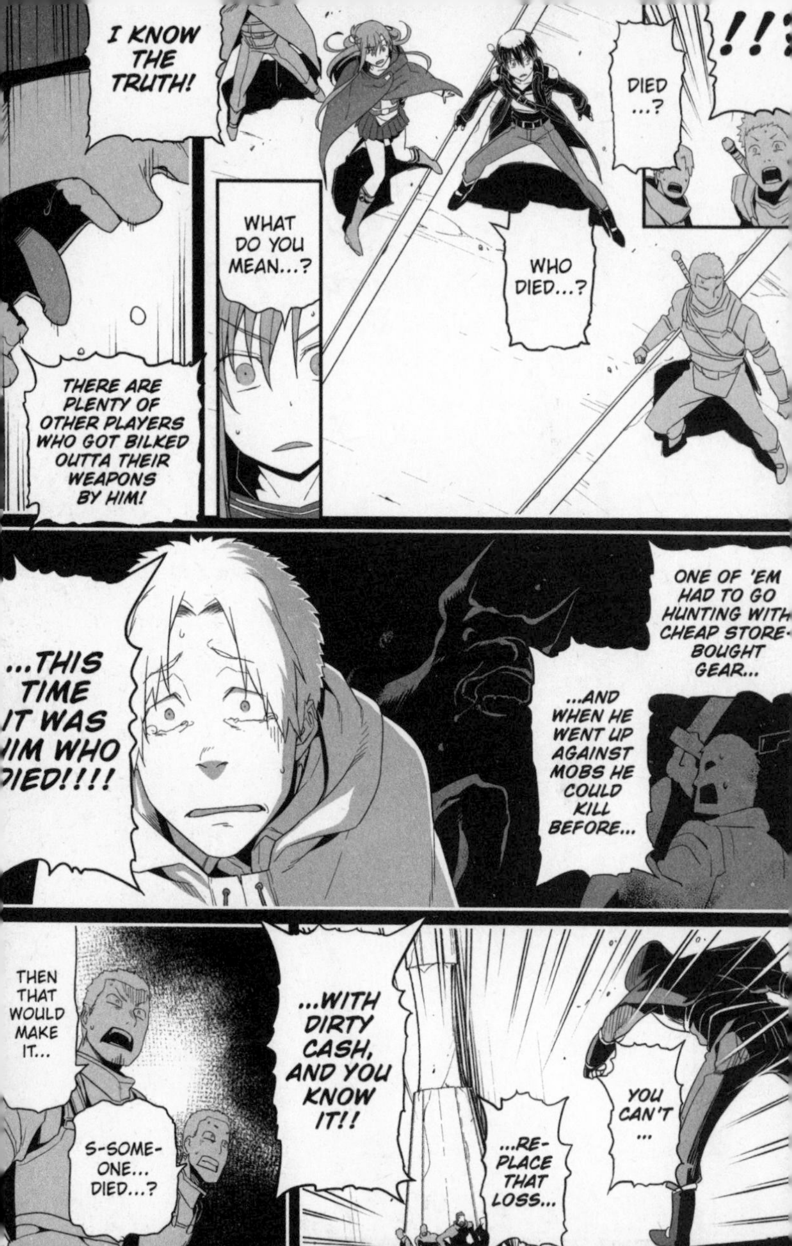
!!?
DIED...?
WHO DIED...?
WHAT DO YOU MEAN...?
I KNOW THE TRUTH!
THERE ARE PLENTY OF OTHER PLAYERS WHO GOT BILKED OUTTA THEIR WEAPONS BY HIM!
ONE OF 'EM HAD TO GO HUNTING WITH CHEAP STORE-BOUGHT GEAR...
...AND WHEN HE WENT UP AGAINST MOBS HE COULD KILL BEFORE...
...THIS TIME IT WAS HIM WHO DIED!!!!
YOU CAN'T...
...RE-PLACE THAT LOSS...
...WITH DIRTY CASH, AND YOU KNOW IT!!
THEN THAT WOULD MAKE IT...
S-SOME-ONE... DIED...?

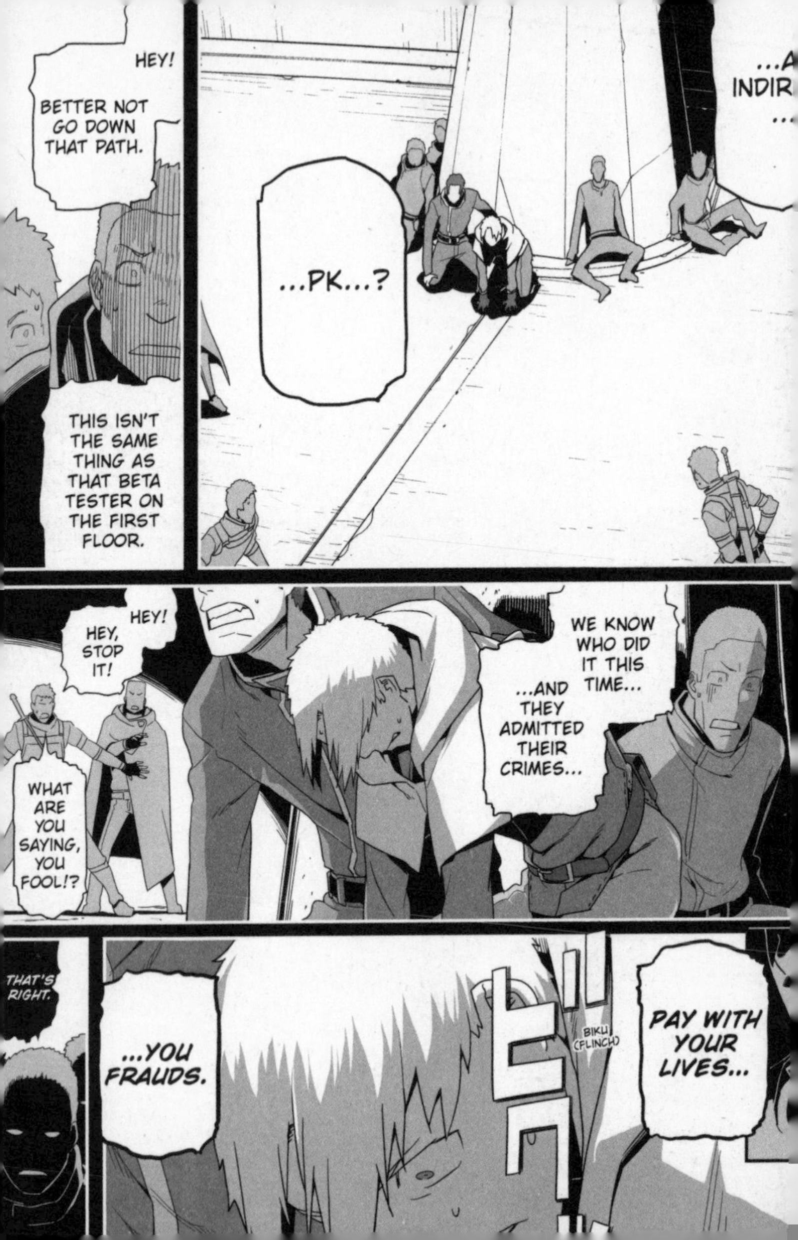
...PK...?
HEY!
BETTER NOT GO DOWN THAT PATH.
THIS ISN'T THE SAME THING AS THAT BETA TESTER ON THE FIRST FLOOR.
WE KNOW WHO DID IT THIS TIME...
...AND THEY ADMITTED THEIR CRIMES...
HEY! HEY, STOP IT!
WHAT ARE YOU SAYING, YOU FOOL!?
PAY WITH YOUR LIVES...
BIKU (FLINCH)
...YOU FRAUDS.
THAT'S RIGHT.

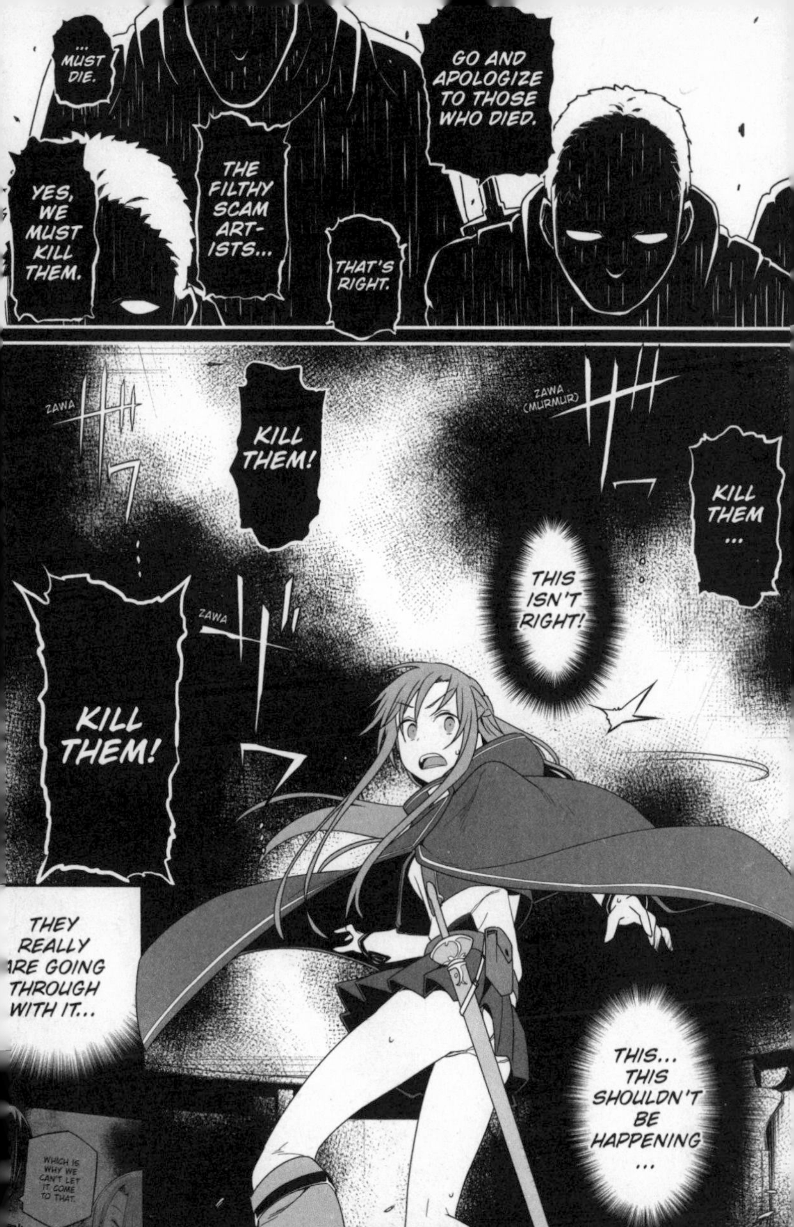
GO AND APOLOGIZE TO THOSE WHO DIED.
... MUST DIE.
THAT'S RIGHT.
THE FILTHY SCAM ART-ISTS...
YES, WE MUST KILL THEM.
ZAWA (MURMUR)
KILL THEM ...
KILL THEM!
ZAWA
THIS ISN'T RIGHT!
ZAWA
KILL THEM!
THIS... THIS SHOULDN'T BE HAPPENING ...
THEY REALLY ARE GOING THROUGH WITH IT...
WHICH IS WHY WE CAN'T LET IT COME TO THAT.

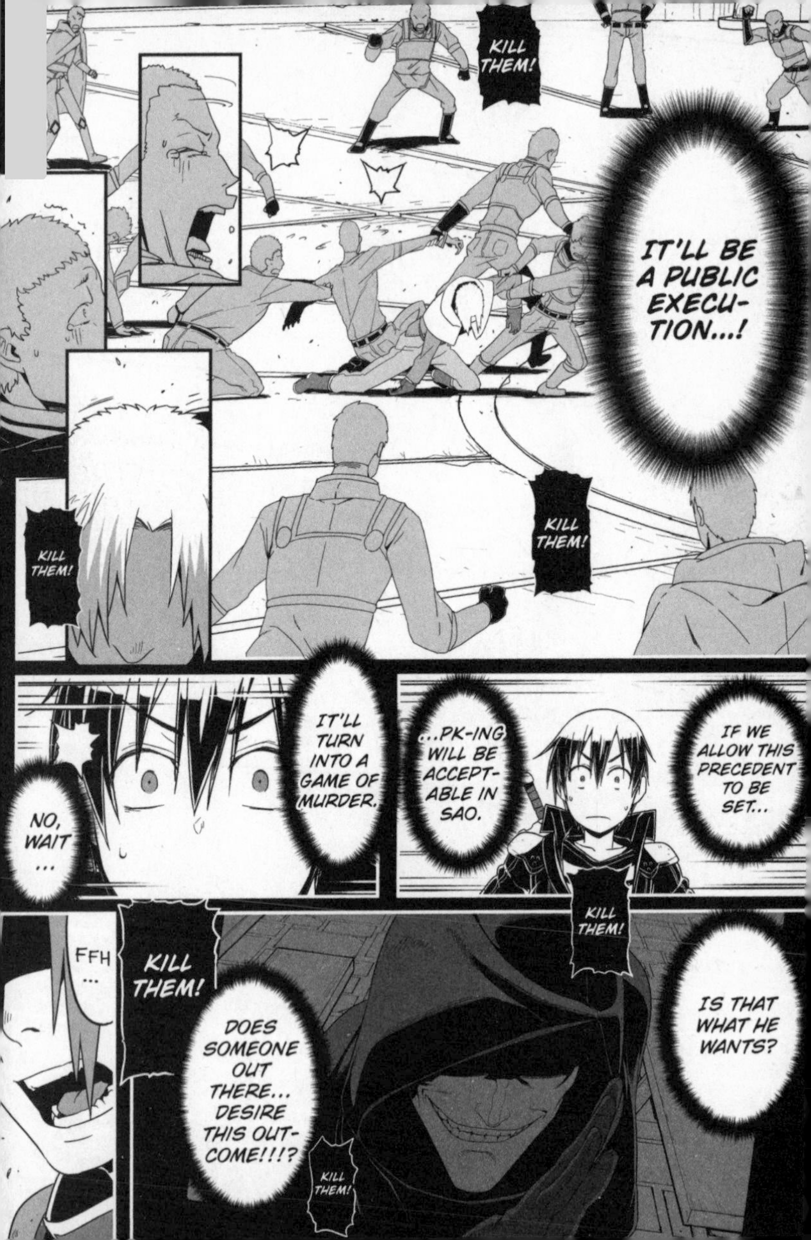
KILL THEM!
IT'LL BE A PUBLIC EXECUTION...!
KILL THEM!
KILL THEM!
IF WE ALLOW THIS PRECEDENT TO BE SET...
...PK-ING WILL BE ACCEPTABLE IN SAO.
IT'LL TURN INTO A GAME OF MURDER.
NO, WAIT ...
KILL THEM!
IS THAT WHAT HE WANTS?
DOES SOMEONE OUT THERE... DESIRE THIS OUTCOME!!!?
KILL THEM!
KILL THEM!
FFH ...

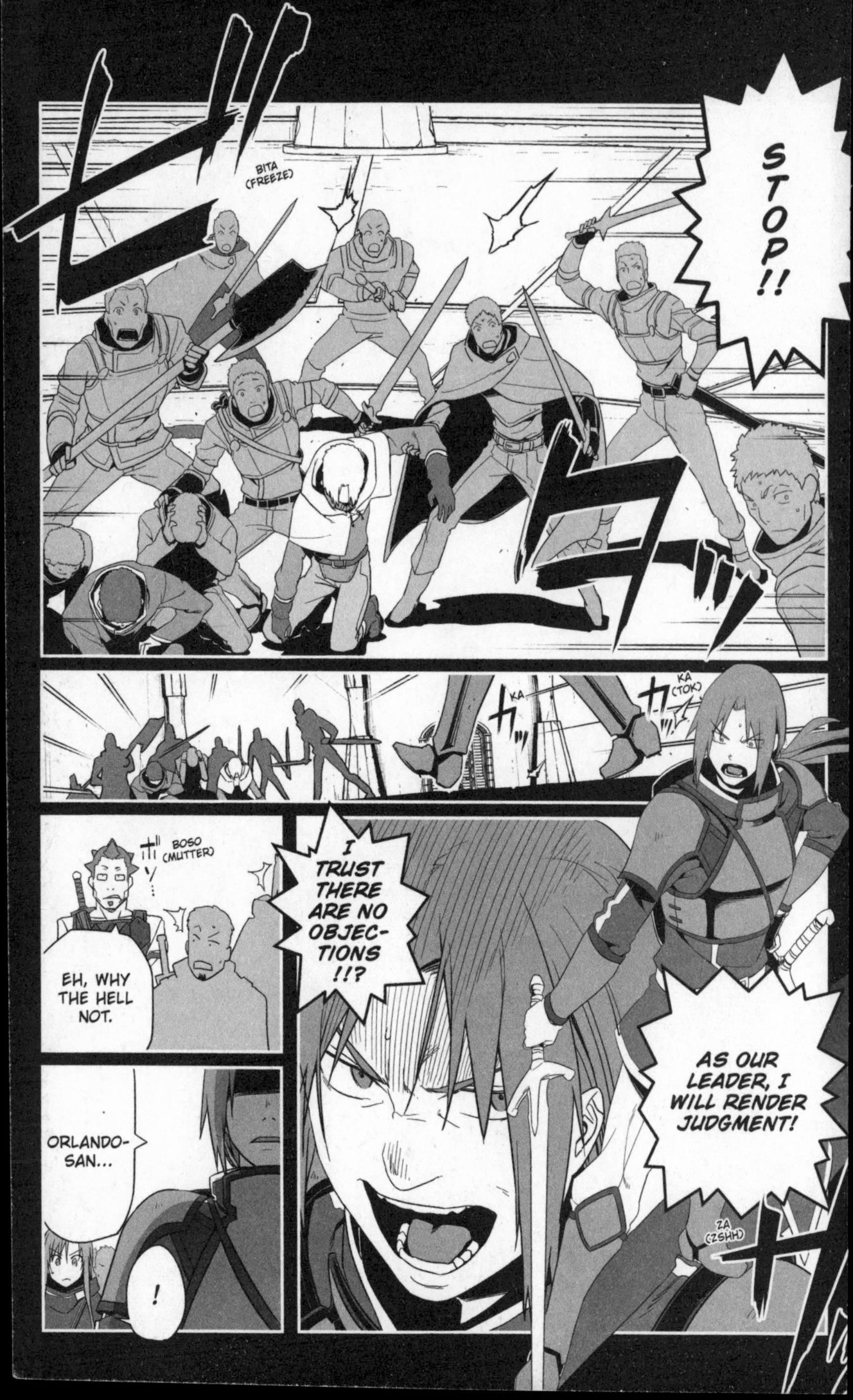
STOP!!
BITA (FREEZE)
KA (TOK)
KA
AS OUR LEADER, I WILL RENDER JUDGMENT!
ZA (ZSHH)
I TRUST THERE ARE NO OBJECTIONS!!?
BOSO (MUTTER)
EH, WHY THE HELL NOT.
ORLANDO-SAN...
!

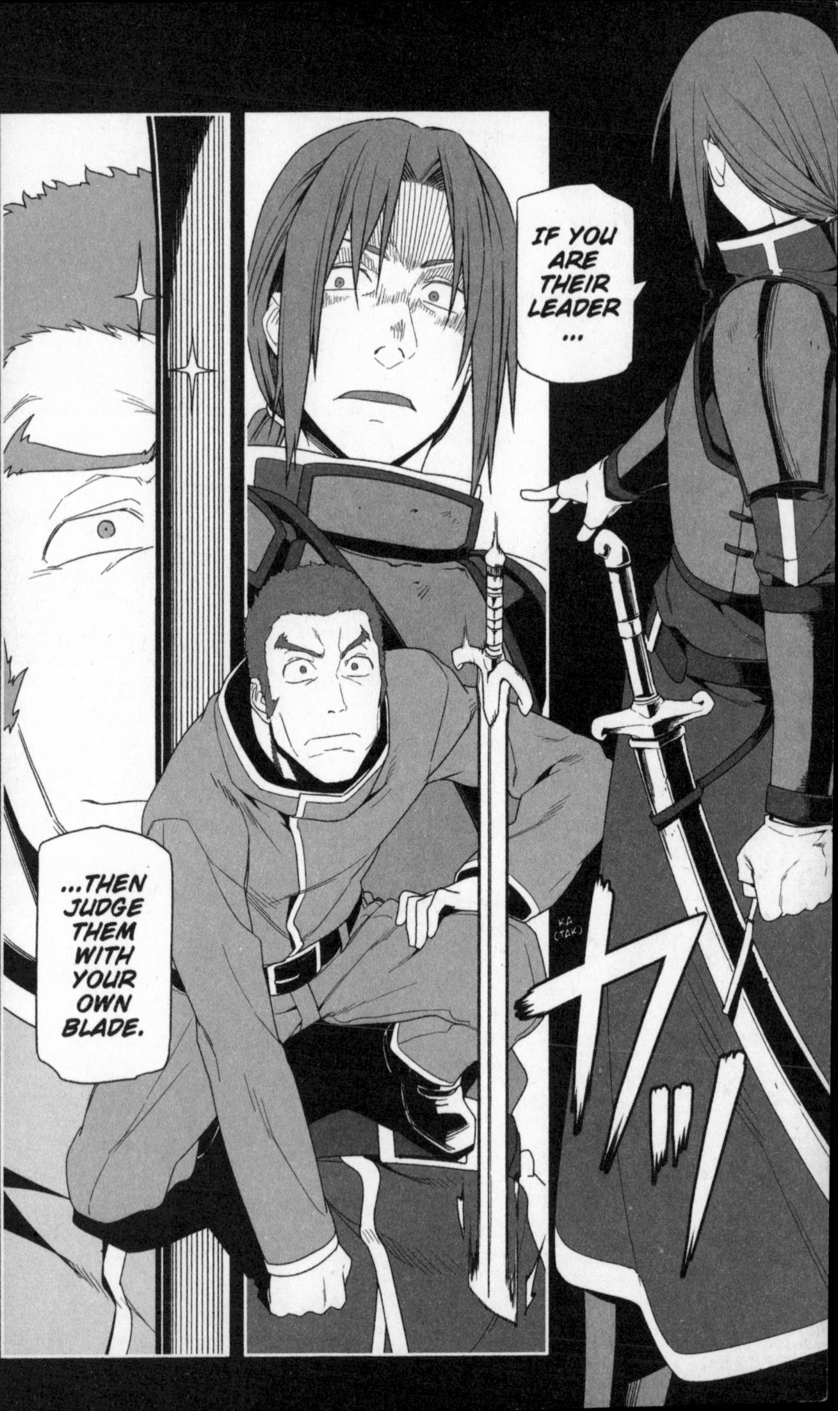
IF YOU ARE THEIR LEADER ...
KA (TAK)
...THEN JUDGE THEM WITH YOUR OWN BLADE.

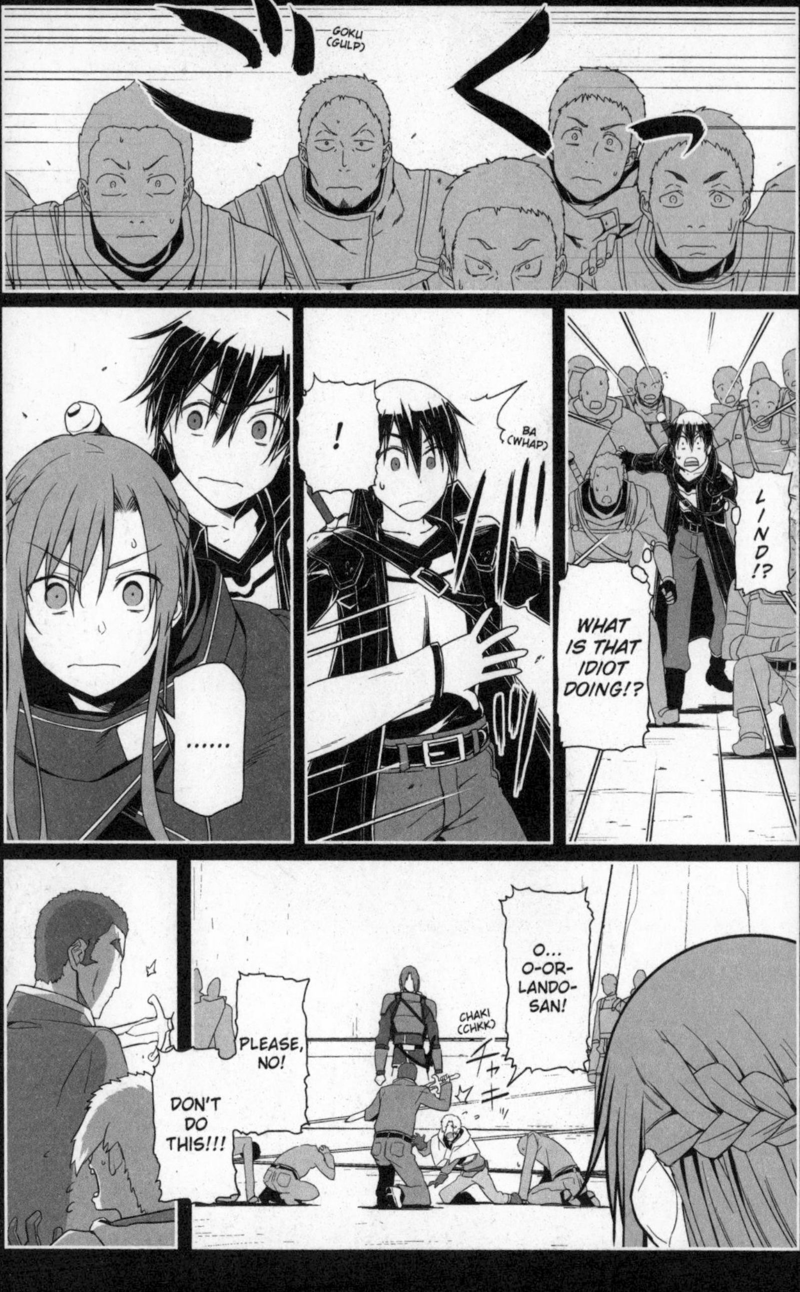
GOKU (GULP)
LIND!?
WHAT IS THAT IDIOT DOING!?
!
BA (WHAP)
......
O... O-OR-LANDO-SAN!
CHAKI (CHKK)
PLEASE, NO!
DON'T DO THIS!!!

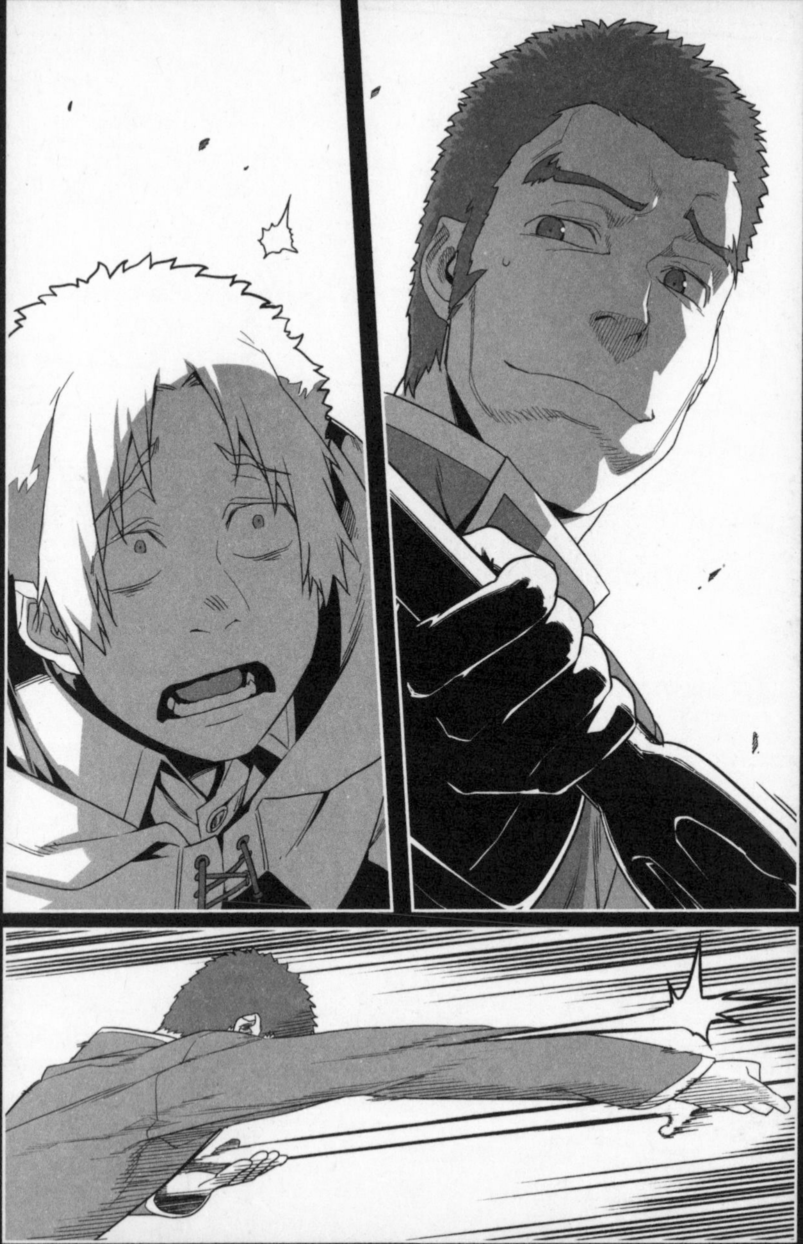

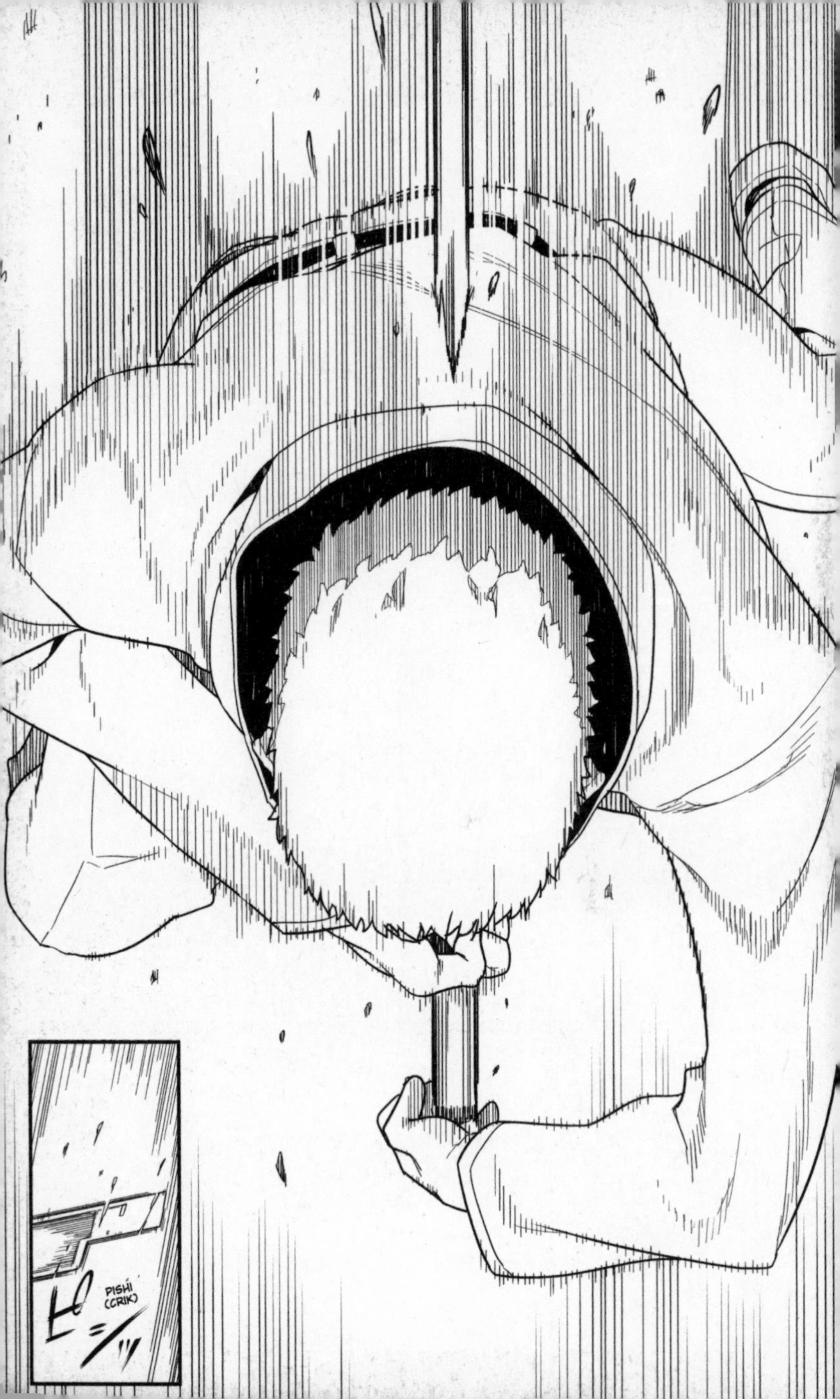
ピシ
PISHÍ
(CRIK)

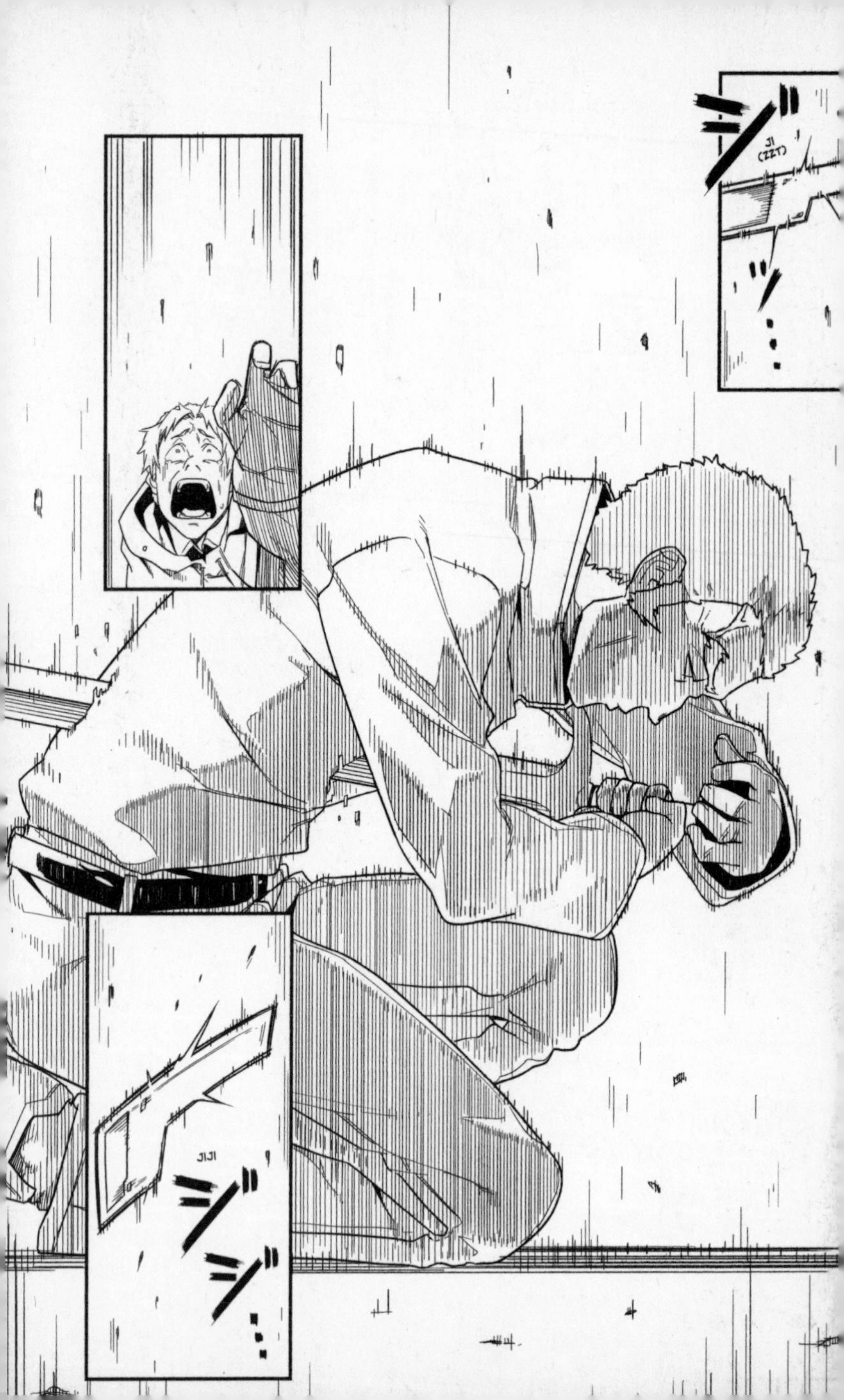
ジ ジ…
JI
(ZZT)
JIJI
ジ ジ…

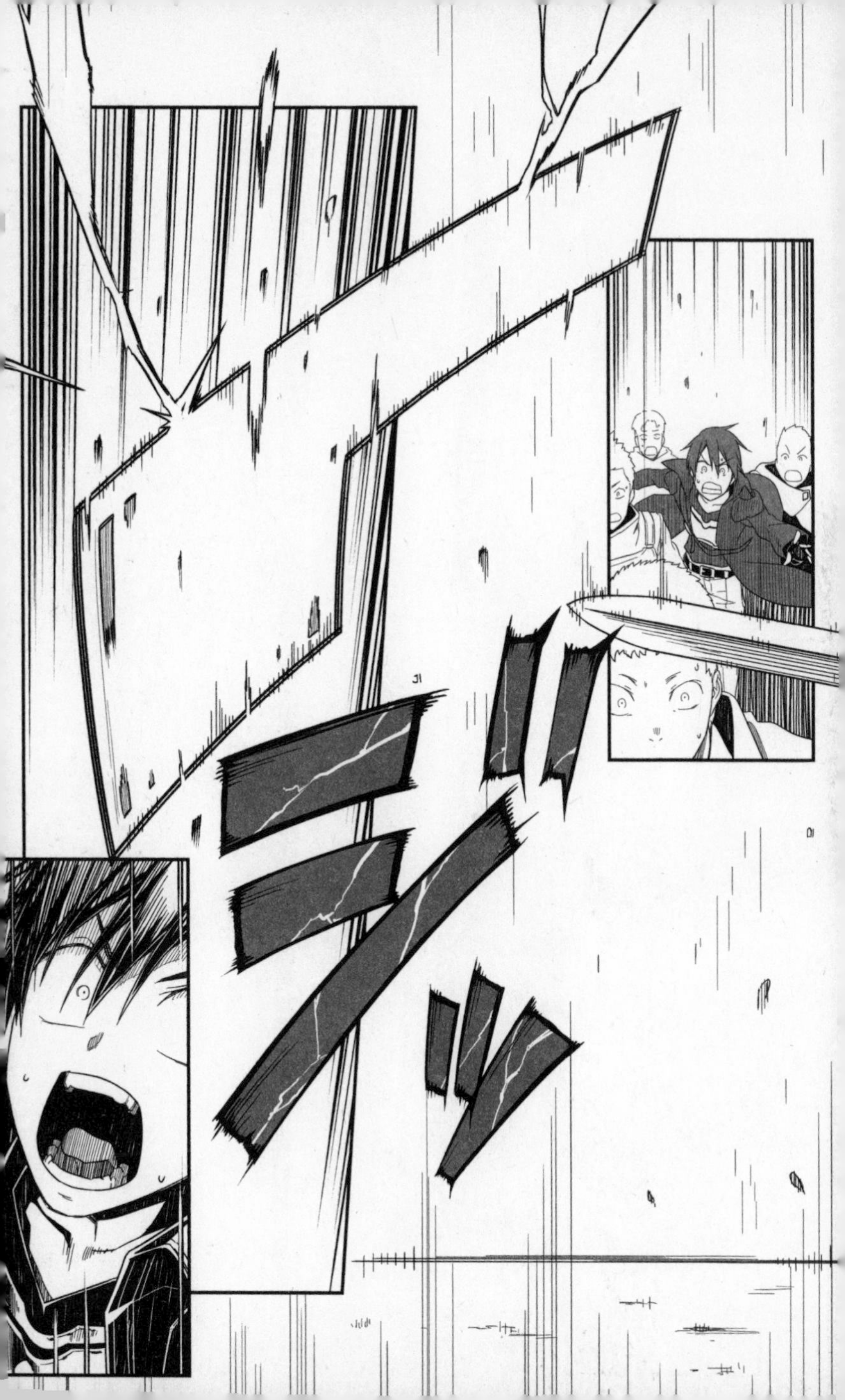
ジッ

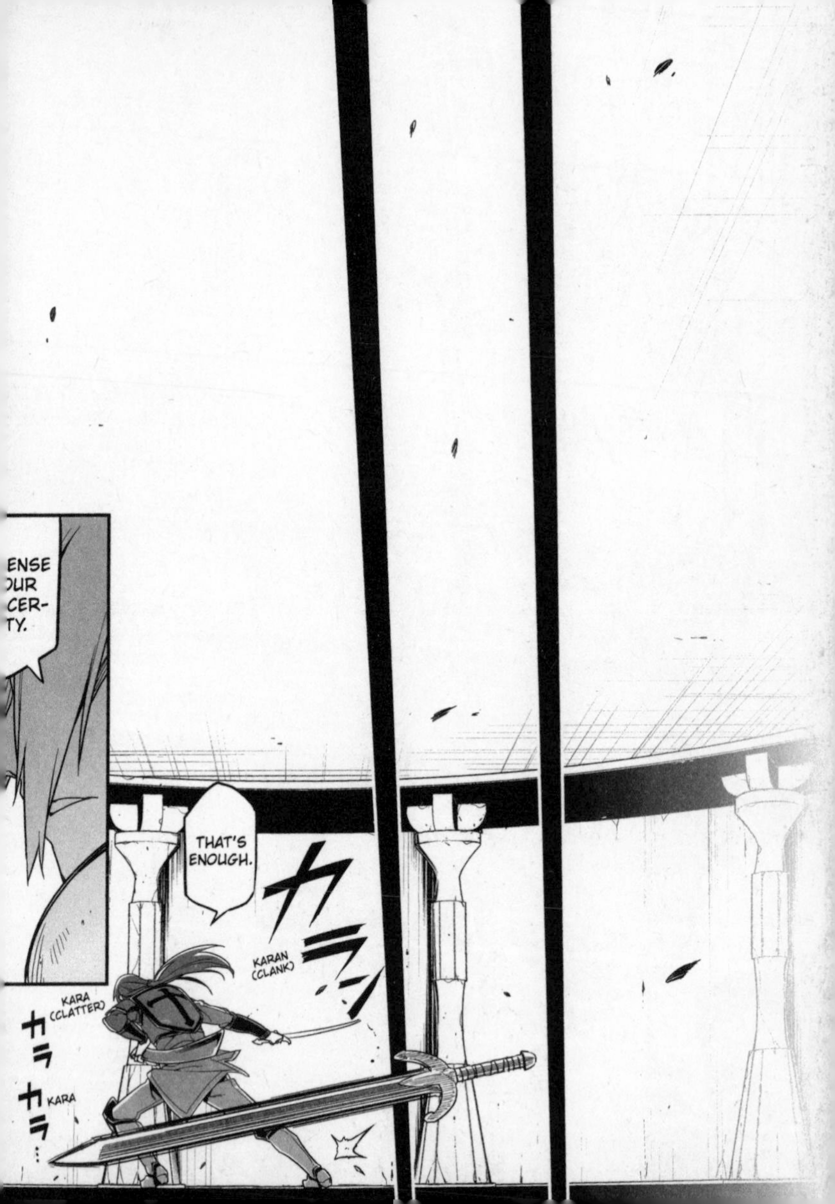
THAT'S ENOUGH.
カラン
KARAN (CLANK)
カラ
KARA (CLATTER)
カラ…
KARA
ENSE
OUR
CER-
TY.

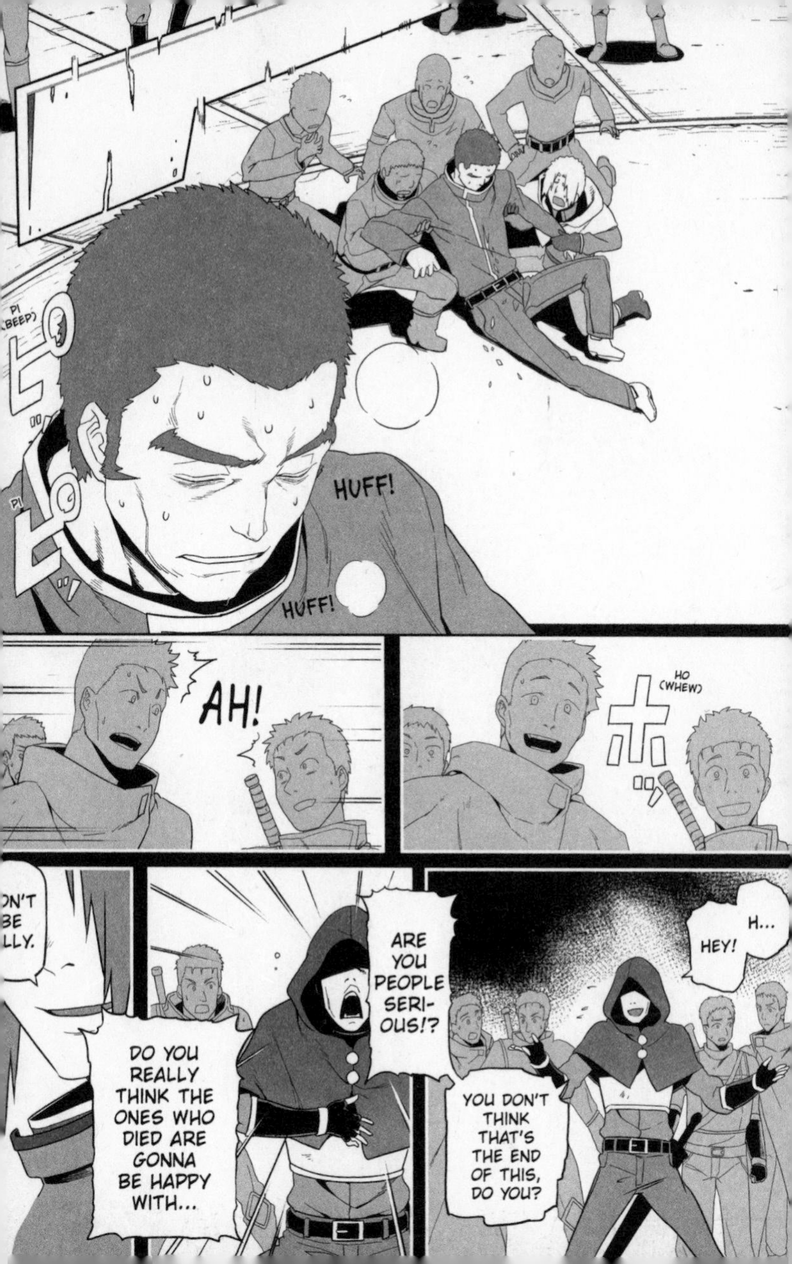
PI (BEEP)
PI
HUFF!
HUFF!
HO (WHEW)
AH!
H... HEY!
YOU DON'T THINK THAT'S THE END OF THIS, DO YOU?
ARE YOU PEOPLE SERI-OUS!?
DO YOU REALLY THINK THE ONES WHO DIED ARE GONNA BE HAPPY WITH...
ON'T BE LLY.

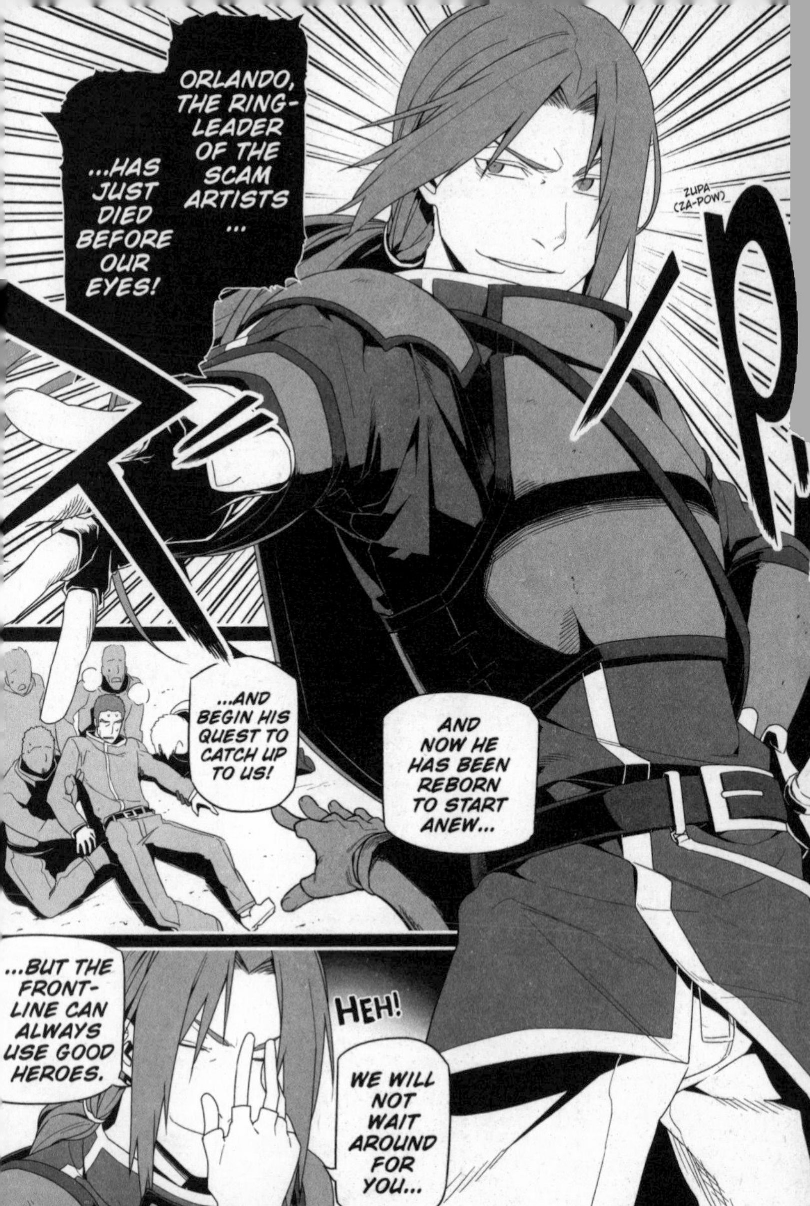
ORLANDO, THE RING-LEADER OF THE SCAM ARTISTS...
...HAS JUST DIED BEFORE OUR EYES!
ZUPA (ZA-POW)
AND NOW HE HAS BEEN REBORN TO START ANEW...
...AND BEGIN HIS QUEST TO CATCH UP TO US!
HEH!
WE WILL NOT WAIT AROUND FOR YOU...
...BUT THE FRONT-LINE CAN ALWAYS USE GOOD HEROES.

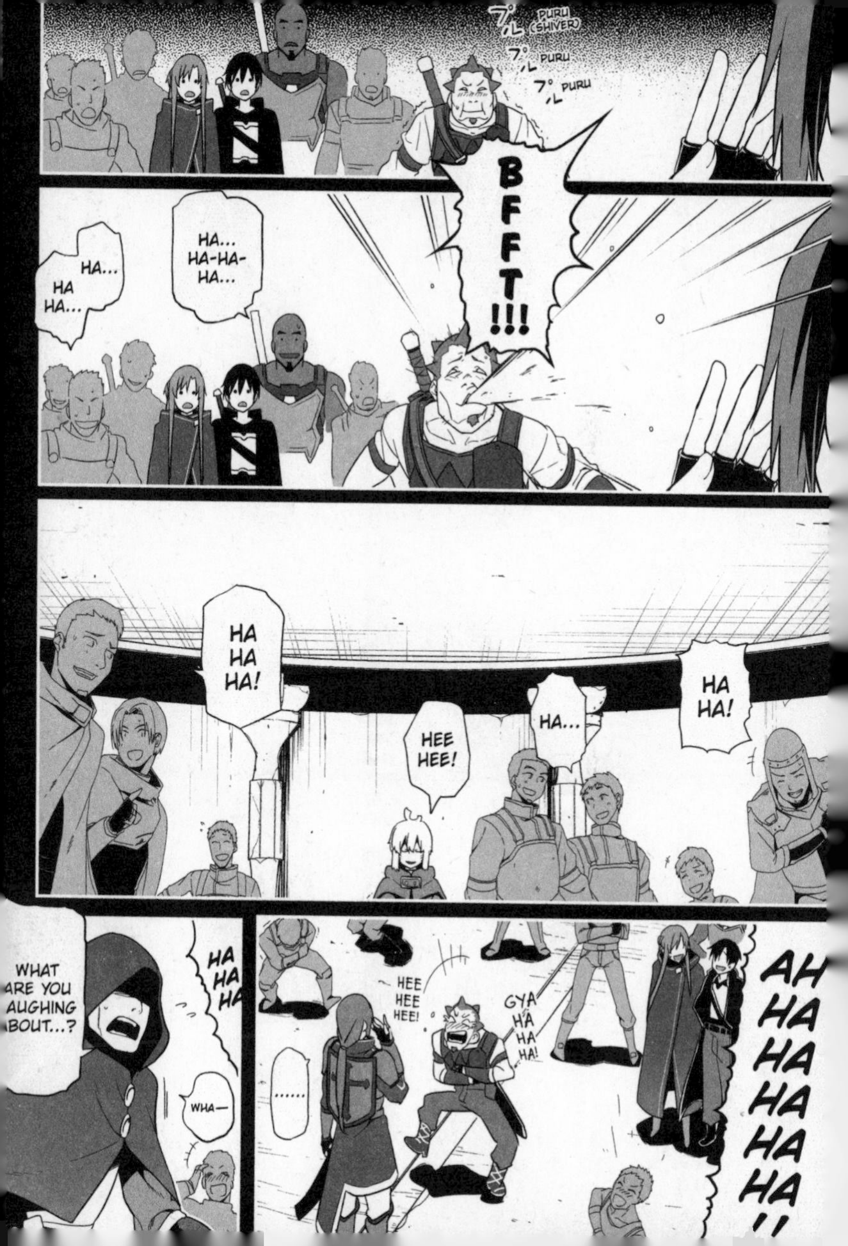

プル PURU (SHIVER)
プル PURU
プル PURU
BFFT!!!
HA... HA-HA-HA...
HA... HA HA...
HA HA!
HA...
HEE HEE!
HA HA HA!
AH HA HA HA HA HA HA HA!!
GYA HA HA HA!
HEE HEE HEE!
......
HA HA HA
WHA—
WHAT ARE YOU AUGHING BOUT...?

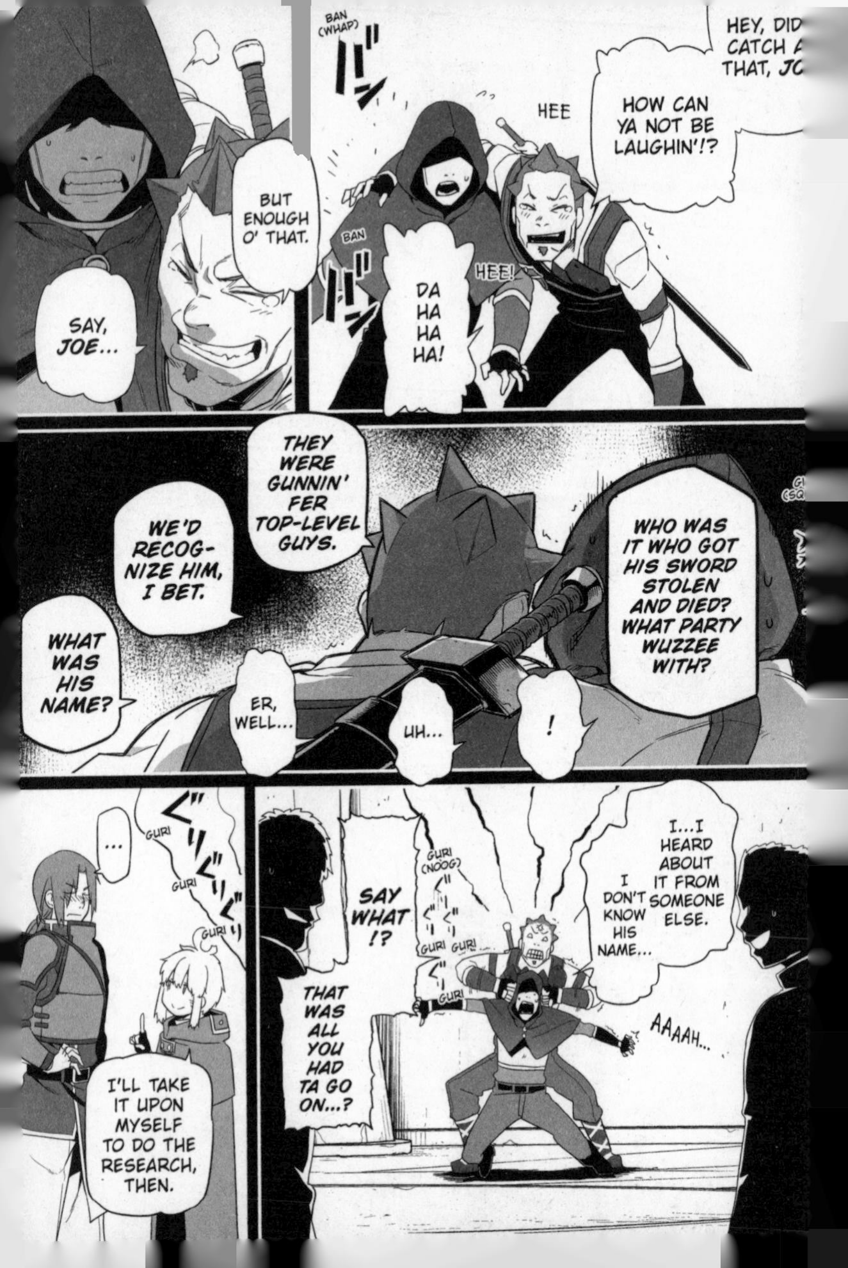
HEY, DID
CATCH A
THAT, JO
HOW CAN YA NOT BE LAUGHIN'!?
HEE
BAN (WHAP)
HEE!
BAN
DA HA HA HA!
BUT ENOUGH O' THAT.
SAY, JOE...
WHO WAS IT WHO GOT HIS SWORD STOLEN AND DIED? WHAT PARTY WUZZEE WITH?
!
UH...
THEY WERE GUNNIN' FER TOP-LEVEL GUYS.
WE'D RECOG-NIZE HIM, I BET.
ER, WELL...
WHAT WAS HIS NAME?
I...I HEARD ABOUT IT FROM SOMEONE ELSE.
I DON'T KNOW HIS NAME...
AAAAH...
GURI (NOOG)
GURI GURI
GURI
SAY WHAT!?
THAT WAS ALL YOU HAD TA GO ON...?
GURI
GURI
GURI
...
I'LL TAKE IT UPON MYSELF TO DO THE RESEARCH, THEN.

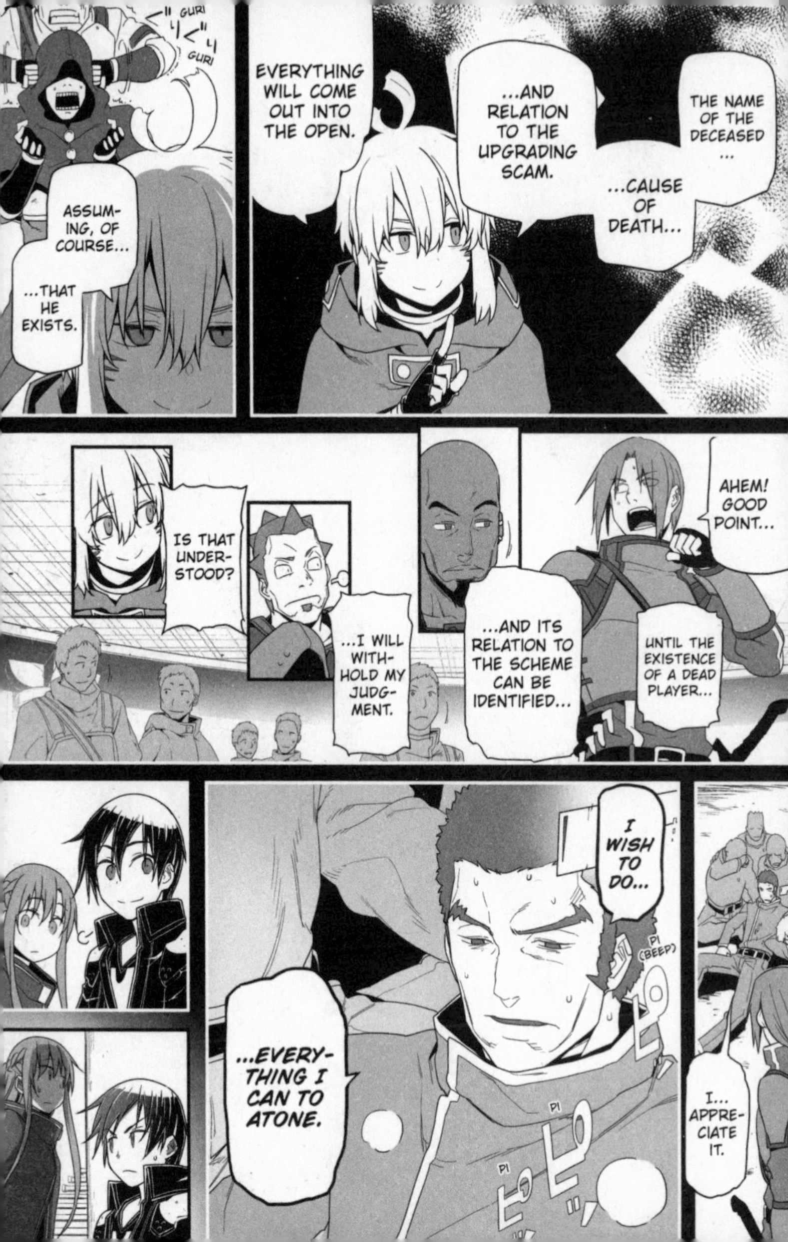
THE NAME OF THE DECEASED ...
...CAUSE OF DEATH...
...AND RELATION TO THE UPGRADING SCAM.
EVERYTHING WILL COME OUT INTO THE OPEN.
GURI GURI
ASSUM-ING, OF COURSE...
...THAT HE EXISTS.
AHEM! GOOD POINT...
UNTIL THE EXISTENCE OF A DEAD PLAYER...
...AND ITS RELATION TO THE SCHEME CAN BE IDENTIFIED...
...I WILL WITH-HOLD MY JUDG-MENT.
IS THAT UNDER-STOOD?
I... APPRE-CIATE IT.
I WISH TO DO...
PI (BEEP)
...EVERY-THING I CAN TO ATONE.
PI
PI

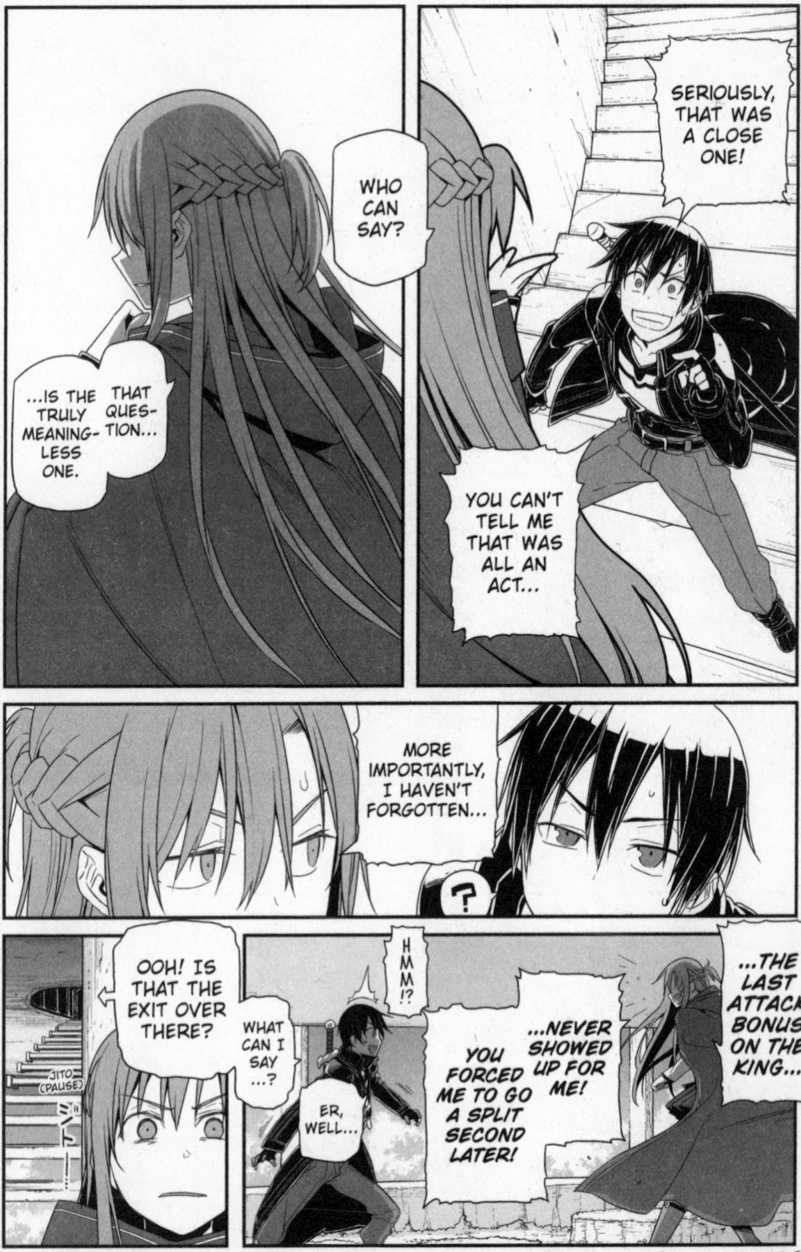
SERIOUSLY, THAT WAS A CLOSE ONE!
YOU CAN'T TELL ME THAT WAS ALL AN ACT...
WHO CAN SAY?
THAT QUES-TION...
...IS THE TRULY MEANING-LESS ONE.
MORE IMPORTANTLY, I HAVEN'T FORGOTTEN...
?
...THE LAST ATTACK BONUS ON THE KING...
...NEVER SHOWED UP FOR ME!
YOU FORCED ME TO GO A SPLIT SECOND LATER!
HMM!?
ER, WELL...
WHAT CAN I SAY ...?
OOH! IS THAT THE EXIT OVER THERE?
JITO (PAUSE)

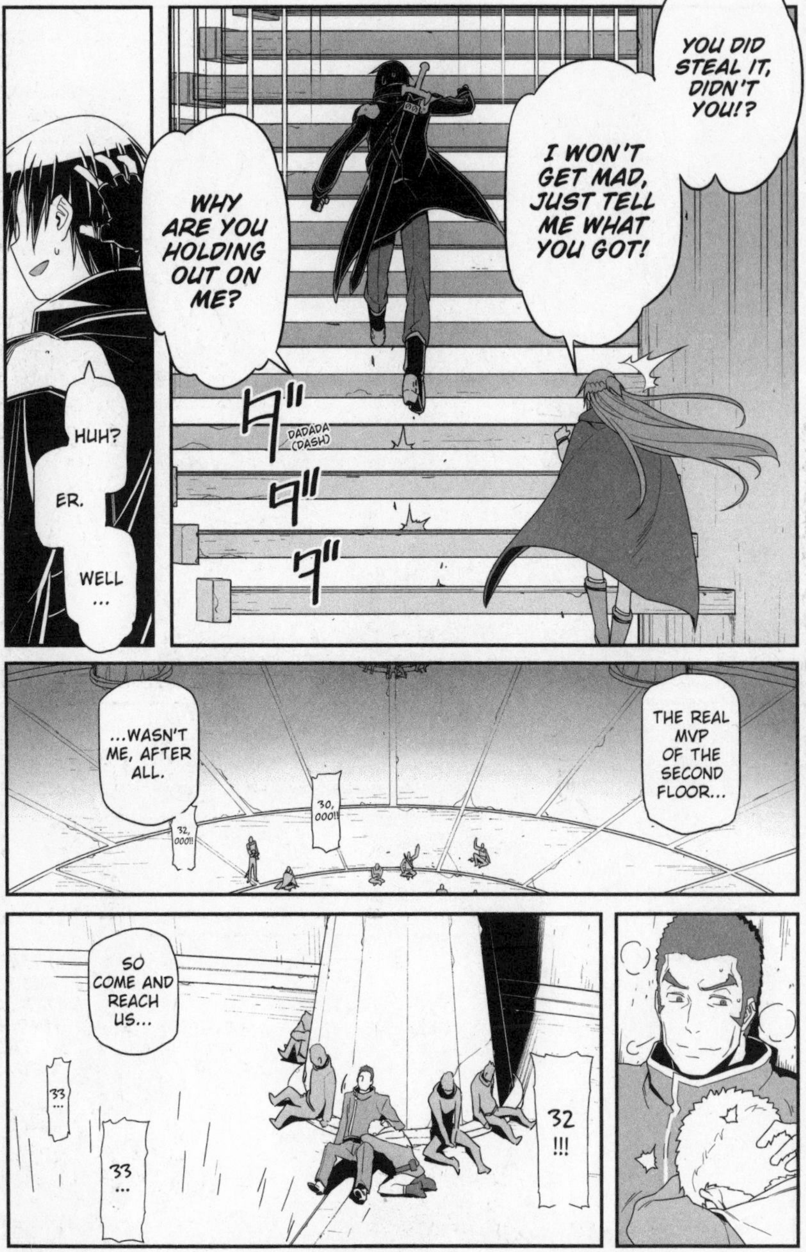
YOU DID STEAL IT, DIDN'T YOU!?
I WON'T GET MAD, JUST TELL ME WHAT YOU GOT!
WHY ARE YOU HOLDING OUT ON ME?
ダ ダ ダ
DADADA (DASH)
HUH?
ER.
WELL...
THE REAL MVP OF THE SECOND FLOOR...
30, 000!!
32, 000!!
...WASN'T ME, AFTER ALL.
32 !!!
SO COME AND REACH US...
33 ...
33 ...

THE REAL SAO STARTS FROM THE THIRD FLOOR...

IT DOES?

BE-SIDES...

WHY IS THAT?

TA (TEK)

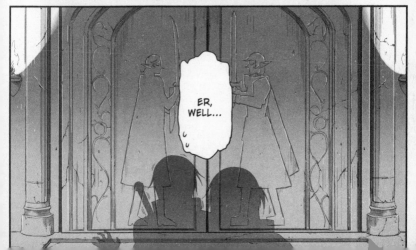

ER, WELL...

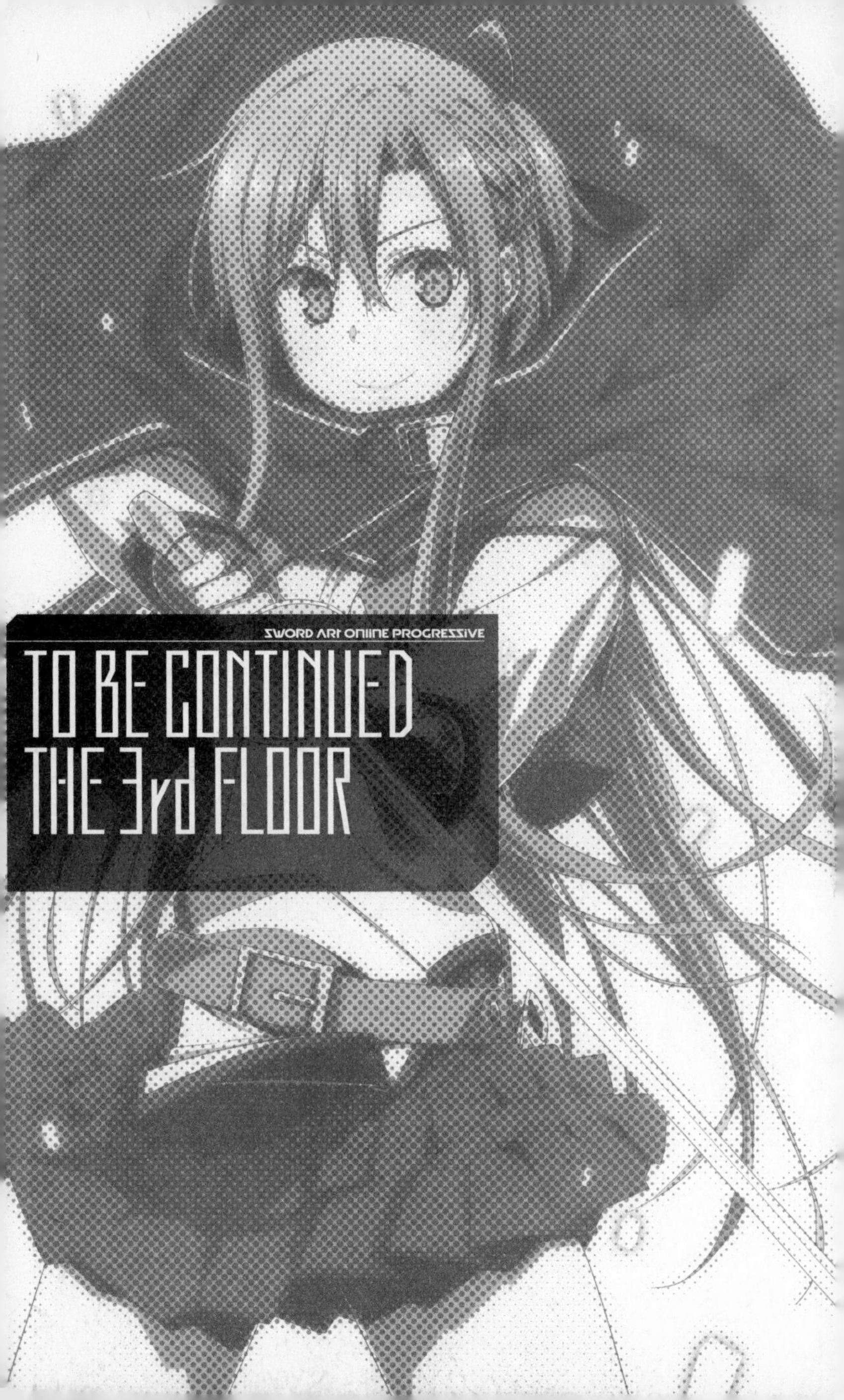
SWORD ART ONLINE PROGRESSIVE
TO BE CONTINUED
THE 3rd FLOOR

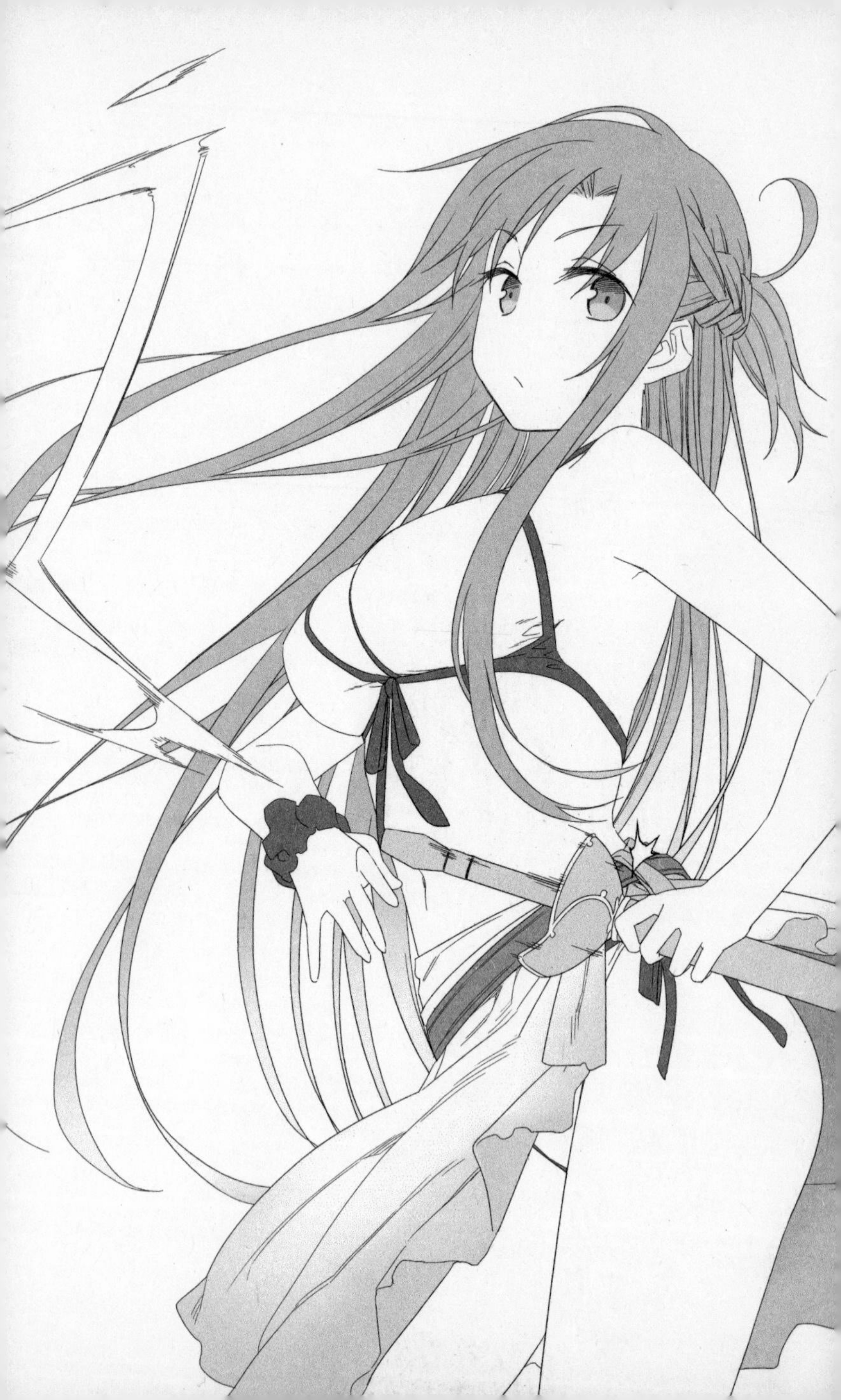

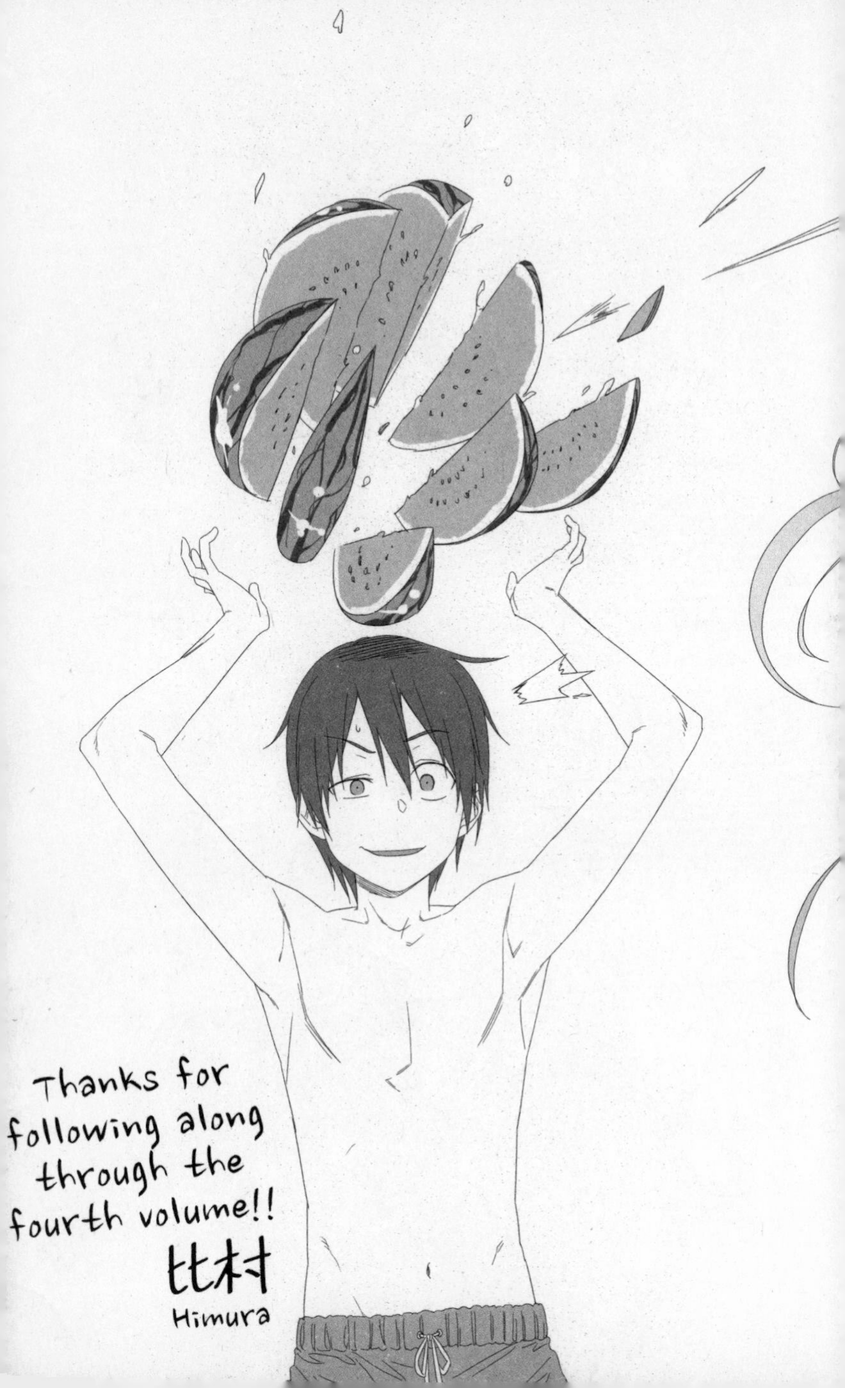
Thanks for following along through the fourth volume!!
比村
Himura

Special thanks to...

<CREATORS>

Reki Kawahara-sensei
abec-sensei

<GUEST>

Kichiroku-sensei

<ART STAFF>

Mura-san
Nazu Natsuki-san
Zerosu-san
Bambi Morino-san

<EDITOR>

Kentarou Ogino-san

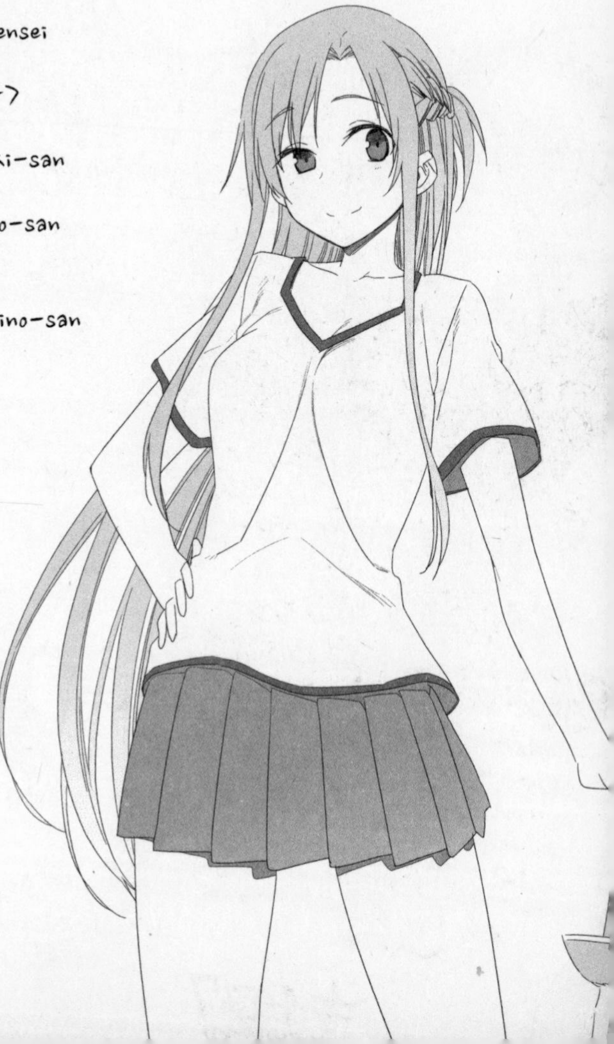

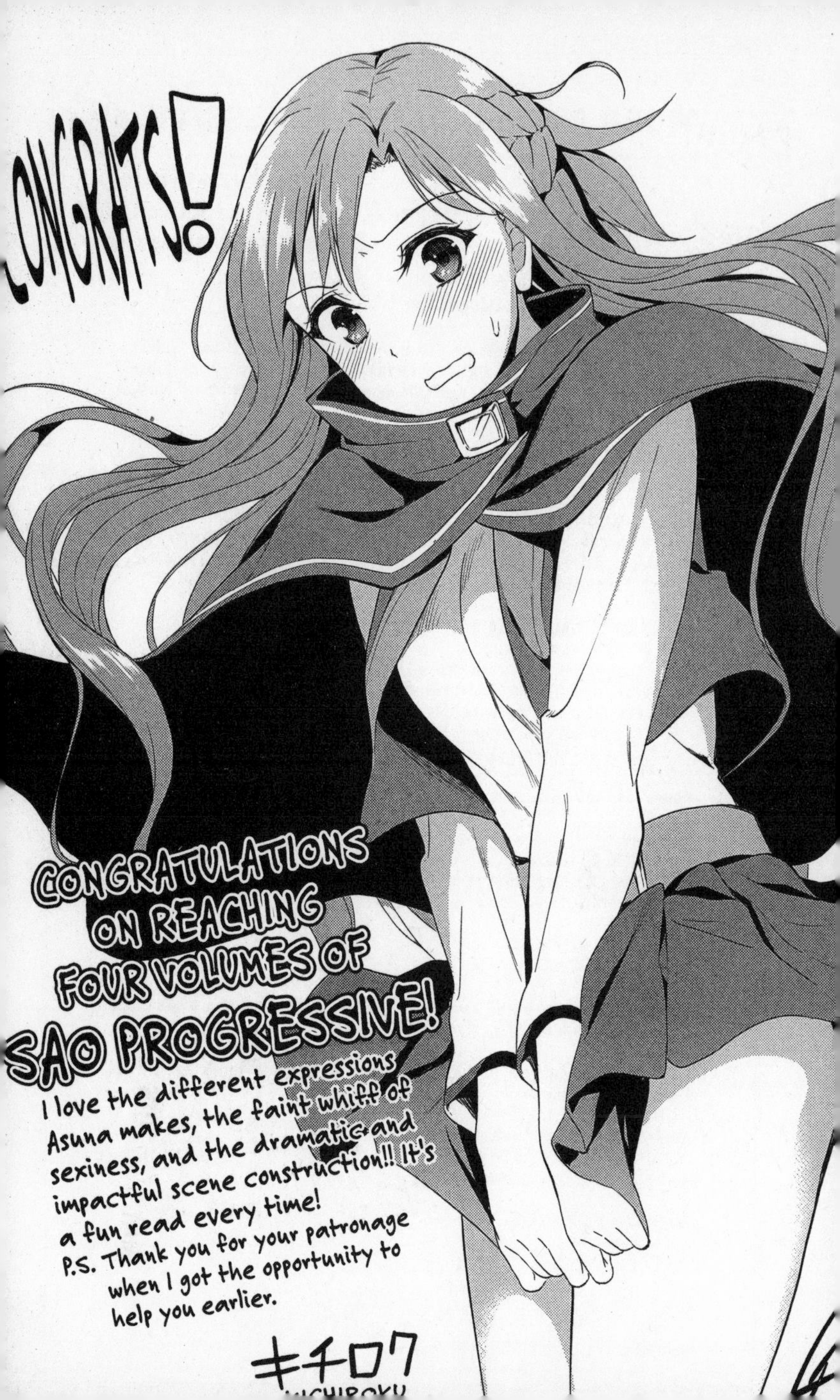
CONGRATS!
CONGRATULATIONS ON REACHING FOUR VOLUMES OF SAO PROGRESSIVE!
I love the different expressions Asuna makes, the faint whiff of sexiness, and the dramatic and impactful scene construction!! It's a fun read every time!
P.S. Thank you for your patronage when I got the opportunity to help you earlier.
キチロク

SWORD ART ONLINE: PROGRESSIVE ④

ART: KISEKI HIMURA
ORIGINAL STORY: REKI KAWAHARA
CHARACTER DESIGN: ABEC

Translation: Stephen Paul
Lettering: Brndn Blakeslee & Lys Blakeslee

This book is a work of fiction. Names, characters, places, and incidents are the product of the author's imagination or are used fictitiously. Any resemblance to actual events, locales, or persons, living or dead, is coincidental.

SWORD ART ONLINE: PROGRESSIVE
© REKI KAWAHARA/KISEKI HIMURA 2015
All rights reserved.
Edited by ASCII MEDIA WORKS
First published in Japan in 2015 by KADOKAWA CORPORATION, Tokyo.
English translation rights arranged with KADOKAWA CORPORATION, Tokyo, through Tuttle-Mori Agency, Inc., Tokyo.

English translation © 2016 by Hachette Book Group, Inc.

All rights reserved. In accordance with the U.S. Copyright Act of 1976, the scanning, uploading, and electronic sharing of any part of this book without the permission of the publisher is unlawful piracy and theft of the author's intellectual property. If you would like to use material from the book (other than for review purposes), prior written permission must be obtained by contacting the publisher at permissions@hbgusa.com. Thank you for your support of the author's rights.

Yen Press
Hachette Book Group
1290 Avenue of the Americas
New York, NY 10104

www.HachetteBookGroup.com
www.YenPress.com

Yen Press is an imprint of Hachette Book Group, Inc. The Yen Press name and logo are trademarks of Hachette Book Group, Inc.

The publisher is not responsible for websites (or their content) that are not owned by the publisher.

Library of Congress Control Number: 2015956857

First Yen Press Edition: March 2016

ISBN: 978-0-316-31465-7

10 9 8 7 6 5 4 3 2 1

BVG

Printed in the United States of America